Night Rising

VAMPIRE BABYLON

BOOK ONE

Night Rising

Vampire Babylon
Book One

Chris Marie Green

ACE BOOKS, NEW YORK

THE BERKLEY PUBLISHING GROUP
Published by the Penguin Group
Penguin Group (USA) Inc.
375 Hudson Street, New York, New York 10014, USA
Penguin Group (Canada), 90 Eglinton Avenue East, Suite 700, Toronto, Ontario M4P 2Y3, Canada (a division of Pearson Penguin Canada Inc.)
Penguin Books Ltd., 80 Strand, London WC2R 0RL, England
Penguin Group Ireland, 25 St. Stephen's Green, Dublin 2, Ireland (a division of Penguin Books Ltd.)
Penguin Group (Australia), 250 Camberwell Road, Camberwell, Victoria 3124, Australia (a division of Pearson Australia Group Pty. Ltd.)
Penguin Books India Pvt. Ltd., 11 Community Centre, Panchsheel Park, New Delhi—110 017, India
Penguin Group (NZ), 67 Apollo Drive, Mairangi Bay, Auckland 1310, New Zealand (a division of Pearson New Zealand Ltd.)
Penguin Books (South Africa) (Pty.) Ltd., 24 Sturdee Avenue, Rosebank, Johannesburg 2196, South Africa

Penguin Books Ltd., Registered Offices: 80 Strand, London WC2R 0RL, England

This is an original publication of The Berkley Publishing Group.

Cover art and design by Larry Rostant.
Text design by Kristin del Rosario.

First edition: February 2007

Library of Congress Cataloging-in-Publication Data

Green, Crystal.
Night rising / Chris Marie Green.—1st ed.
p. cm.—(Vampire Babylon; bk. 1)
ISBN-13: 978-0-441-01467-5 (trade pbk.) 1. Women stunt performers—Fiction. 2. Fathers and daughters—Fiction. 3. Hollywood (Los Angeles, Calif.)—Fiction. 4. Vampires—Fiction. I. Title.
PS3607.R4326N54 2007
813'.6—dc22 2006027964

PRINTED IN THE UNITED STATES OF AMERICA

10 9 8 7 6 5 4 3 2

To Mom and Dad,
who show me the light every day

I would like to acknowledge Sheree Whitefeather and Judy Duarte, two critique partners who keep their eyes wide open; Wally Lind and the crimescenewriter web loop for all their guidance (I'd like to add that all errors are my own.); Pamela Harty and Deidre Knight, who put such faith into me and my books; and Ginjer Buchanan, the one whose support allows the Underground to exist. Thank you, everyone, for everything you do.

ONE

Rising

A red mist hung over Los Angeles at midnight, a mist so thick that it blocked the moon's glow.

One so dense it almost hid what would become another shocking Tinseltown legend by the time morning rolled around.

The damp air had been tinted with the crimson neon of a dingy alley's bar sign: Lenny's, it read in cursive beneath the tilt of a cartoon martini. As the wiring flickered on and off, so did the atmosphere, an apathetic heartbeat on the fringes of Hollywood Boulevard.

A police radio from one of the many black-and-whites blocking the entrances to the alley broke the silence with a burst of static, then buzzed to nothing. A hushed crowd was gathering on the slick pavement nearby, people craning their necks to gape through the fog and into the slender passageway. And even though the cops were doing their damnedest to contain the scene, they couldn't cover up the accident.

At least, that's what they'd called it at first.

An "accident."

From the looks of the Aston Martin, it was a fair assessment. The sleek machine was nothing more than wheezing, twisted steel embracing an electrical pole, an abstract sculpture you might find in the victim's own Malibu mansion. But that's where the "accident" ended and the horror began.

Nothing made sense anymore after the cops looked past the car and toward the dead man.

The world's biggest action star had his back to the bar's door, his muscled arms spread wide, his hands pierced by shrapnel, pinning him down. His head, with that glorious fall of golden hair, hung to one side, a wedge of sparkling, jagged window glass embedded in his forehead. His million-dollar blue eyes were closed, his aging yet still bankable face bathed in red. He'd died just moments ago, unable to speak around the blood that was choking him.

Sure, freak accidents sometimes happened. Bodies flew from crashed cars, metal followed, people died.

But what the beat cops couldn't figure out was the rest of it: the way the victim's shirt had been torn open to reveal the bare chest so many women had swooned over.

The way shattered glass had cut into his skin, forming one word.

REPENT.

Soon, the detectives arrived. Overworked, underpaid, their clothing rumpled by long hours on the job and a lack of giving a shit about appearances. A detective, one who haunted the perimeter, took a long glance at Jesse Shane, Big-time Movie Star, and just nodded his head.

"You get what you ask for," he said to himself, then ambled into the darkness.

There was so much glass and metal gouging Shane's legs that blood had pooled and trickled over the ground, heading toward a nearby square of sewer grating. The police merely walked around it as the star's life flowed away from him, leaking past the grating and into the echoing darkness of the underground.

Drip, drip . . .

They worked until their eyes glazed over from cynical exhaustion. But what the average cop wouldn't discover was a mouth, yawning open, just beneath the sewer grating. It was catching every drop of cooled liquid on its tongue.

Drip, drip . . .

Hidden from view, the creature swallowed, blocking out the noise from above, closing its eyes and shuddering in pure delight, in agonizing need.

Digging its claws into the skin of its palms, the thing leaned its head back again, blood splashing onto its chin, then into its mouth. A slant of wan light caught the gleam of iron fangs as it gulped down the taste of beautiful memory.

More, thought the thing while the blood wet its throat.

More.

As keen yearning tore through the creature, it licked its lips and opened its mouth again, whimpering from the hunger, the sharp craving. Waiting for the next drop to fall.

More.

Meanwhile, back up above in the streets, the cops went about their business, trying to solve the mystery of Jesse Shane, a man whose life had ended in its prime.

A man whose bizarre death would, oddly enough, keep him alive for years to come.

TWO
ABOVE

Eleven Years Later

WHEN Dawn Madison got back to L.A., her dad had already been missing for four days.

That's right. Frank Madison, age forty-seven, a towering charmer with linebacker shoulders and hands strong enough to crack heads when his usual job as hired muscle called for it, was gone, just like that. A fading picture on a Wanted poster. Or maybe even an image on a milk carton or, more appropriately, a bottle of Ex-Lax or whatever geriatrics were gulping down these days. Because in La-La Land, you might as well be dead if you were over thirty. Harsh, but true.

Not that Dawn really believed at this point that he was in actual trouble. Every so often, the man went off her radar, hopping on his Harley to take a spin up the California coast so he could carouse with the finest elements of society in roadside greasy spoons and bars. Or sometimes he went on mysterious fishing trips near Mexico only to resurface a week later with crazy stories about mermaids or any variety of tall tales he could bullshit after drinking enough tequila to disable a small army.

It's just that, this time, someone else had contacted Dawn to tell her about his absence and, damn it all, if they thought his MIA act was worth calling her about, she was compelled to check into it. Pronto. No matter where he'd gone off to this month.

As dusk mingled with the smog, she pulled to the curb of his latest place of employment—some kind of investigation agency—then cut the engine of her battered Corolla. For a full minute, she couldn't move. Didn't really want to.

What if all she found was bad news? Or what if . . . ?

Thoughts of her mom crept along the edges of Dawn's memory, taunting her with the specter of death. The guarantee that nothing lasted forever, even if you spent long nights awake and alone, wishing you had the power to make things different.

But . . . Dawn blocked out a sadness that'd dogged her for years. She'd never known her mom except through beautiful images and painful comparisons. So why did the emptiness still feel like it'd been inflicted only a second ago?

Shaking it off, Dawn threw open the car door, slammed it shut. Eva Claremont had nothing to do with Frank. He'd be okay. No need to get rattled. Come midnight, Dawn would probably find herself back on a plane zooming across the country, cussing at Frank and letting him run free again.

So nix the worrywart act, she thought, walking toward the private investigation agency, a Spanish Revival house with the dubious title of Limpet and Associates hand-painted on a small sign hanging from its hinges over the porch. It reeked of golden-age glamour: iron grating covering the large circular, curtained windows; red-tiled roof basking under the watch of a worshipful sky; tan stucco patching the aging face of the exterior. The only thing that didn't seem to go with the whole Black-Dahlia-dollhouse feel was a gothic iron cross poised over the doorway.

How very medieval chic. How terribly L.A.

As she approached the door, lights flared on and washed over her. What was this, prison?

Ringing the doorbell, she fanned her face, chasing away the July humidity, then checked her clunky watch, exhaling in frustration because it was already quarter to eight and she was pretty sure that Mr. Limpet had closed down for the day.

The chimes echoed throughout the building. She jammed the bell again. When Kiko Daniels had called her last night, she'd come running, all the way from a job in Virginia, but maybe she hadn't gotten here fast enough . . . ?

Jeez, *chill*, she thought. If the guys at work could see you now, you'd never live it down. They don't call you "Mad Dog" on the set for nothing, baby.

Clean out of patience, Dawn fumbled with the cell phone in her jeans pocket. But then the heavy door whooshed open, and she stopped. Stared.

Darkness stretched in front of her.

"Hello?" The greeting bounced off the walls.

Just as she was wondering whether to go on in or to take a few prudent steps backward—yeah, like prudence came naturally to her—she heard a sigh gushing from somewhere near hip level.

A young "little person" stood there, hand on his hip, wearing such an astounding look of exasperation that she felt like apologizing without knowing what she was sorry for. He was blond, with round blue eyes, long sandy lashes, rosebud lips, and a dimple in his chin under a faint soul patch. Kinda pretty, if you asked Dawn.

"What?" he demanded in a familiar tinny, scratchy voice.

Kiko, the guy who'd called her?

He didn't seem to like her hesitation. "You think I'm a bug pinned to a piece of velvet for your amusement?"

"No," she said, otherwise speechless. His rudeness shocked her more than anything. God, over the course of four films and three

TV shows as a stuntwoman, she'd worked with dwarves, giants, and even a woman who could pull her lip over her head. Dawn, herself, frequently spent her days falling out windows, being thrown into walls by evil creatures, and fighting villains with roundhouse kicks and tae kwon do punches.

Out-of-the-ordinary was a regular part of Dawn's world.

"Well . . . ?" he added.

She tried not to revert to any trademark assertiveness, i.e., bitchery. Frank had always told her to be nice unless the person deserved a split lip. And she'd needed *a lot* of lessons about "nice" while growing up. So, even though she was irritated by this guy's mouth, Dawn supposed this was pretty much a situation that called for "nice."

Sticking out her hand, she bent down slightly so the smaller man wouldn't have to reach up to shake. "I'm Dawn Madison, Frank's daughter."

He glanced at her hand like she was holding roadkill on a stick. Then he turned around, leaving her greeting flapping in the wind.

"'Bout time you got here," he grumped over his shoulder as he walked away. "We've been waiting."

Gee. Color her welcomed.

Had she done something besides getting here as fast as she could to encourage this crankiness? Or, worse yet, what had Frank done?

Dawn stepped over the threshold and, as soon as she shut the door, faint darkness took over, helped only by the waning light fighting through the thick curtains over the foyer windows. There was also a hint of something in the air—a scent that belonged to old houses, places with a story or two behind their walls. Must, wilted roses, aged wood, lemon polish that tried to reduce all those histories to a dull shine.

As her eyes adjusted, she realized that she was standing beneath a sprawling black iron chandelier, complete with gutted candles. To her right, the faint glow of a grand staircase curved to the second story.

"I came up here to fiddle with the fuse box," his Jolliness said. "We blew something downstairs."

She was about to ask him if he'd heard her ringing the bell when he beat her to the punch.

"Uh-huh," he said in response to the non-query. "So I thought I ought to come up here for that, also."

Brows puckering, she started to ask how he'd known what she was going to say.

"None of your biz." His footsteps clomped on the floor.

The snot was walking away from her again.

Odd duck, she thought. Probably some guy with a few psychic moments who made most of his money on the Venice Beach Boardwalk hustling tourists. His parlor tricks didn't phase her though, because L.A. had one of every kind. The city was a bowl that held all types of fruit.

And as a kid who'd been raised in Hollyweird, she'd pretty much seen everything.

Following him through the dimness, she traced a hand along the walls. They were rough, paint layered upon itself year after year. He came to an abrupt halt, and she bumped into him.

"Have any flashlights?" she asked.

"Please. I know this place like the back of my hand."

Sweek, went the sound of a metal door being opened. *Snick, snick, snick,* went the pulse of switches being levered.

A burst of white illuminated the room, compliments of that chandelier. It allowed her to see the humming starkness of the creamy walls, the aged hardwood floors, a massive blackened granite-edged fireplace. A sienna-tinged painting hung above the mantel, featuring a red cape that wrapped like a column of fire around a nude, lushly curved woman. She had a wicked gleam in her narrowed amber eyes—something like an invitation.

Absently, Dawn brushed over her neck with her fingertips, her skin misted with sweat from having been outside.

This place was overkill. *So* L.A. A melodramatic Frankenstein Castle decorated with "LOOK AT ME!" desperation.

"Let there be light," he said.

"Not as much as outside, thank God."

"Oh." The man was wiping his hands together, his gaze trained on Dawn again. "The UVs. Ultraviolets."

Ultraviolets?

While languidly rubbing her neck, she resigned herself to what he was seeing: an average Josey who could never compete with that woman in the painting. A tall brunette chick wearing a long, low ponytail and dressed in a sleeveless black T-shirt with black jeans and biker boots. Tanned skin, light brown eyes, a slim white scar riding one brow. A predilection for leather bracelets and a lone silver armband that circled her bicep like a coiled snake. Her only other jewelry decorated her pierced ears, her right lobe featuring two earrings instead of one. The extra bauble depicted a moon dripping delicate silver chains and ruby gem-beads, a proud souvenir.

Yup, physically honed Dawn Madison, a twenty-four-year-old who was connected to her daddy by her rough-edged looks and to her stupendously famous sex goddess mother in . . .

Well, nothing, except for lineage.

"So you're Kiko?" she asked, running a look up and down his body, too, just to be ornery.

He bristled. "What? You're put off by my kind? Figures. I get it from all sides. Women, casting directors, society in general . . ."

Way to endear yourself to strangers, Dawn.

She started to explain that she had no issues with his shortness. "I—"

He sighed. "Being psychic really stands out."

"Oh." Awkward.

Shrugging, he stood on his tiptoes to close the fuse box. "Luckily, I'm also an actor. Makes me less of a curiosity."

"Yeah. So you must have an understanding boss to be able to go on auditions during work hours," she said, trying to steer the topic back to work. Back to Frank. "What do you do when you're on location or shooting daylight here in town?"

Kiko was frowning, as if wondering why she didn't know dip about her dad's career. "Mostly, the boss uses us at night. Our work isn't always conducive to sunshine hours, you know."

Special schedules. Night hours. Was Limpet and Associates some seedy joint where they spied on unfaithful spouses during nocturnal assignations?

Par for the course, Frank, she thought. Were you the Bluto who crashed in motel room doors to snap a few sleazy pictures?

"Oh, the boss knows more about *that*," Kiko added.

"Would you stop it?"

"What?"

"Answering questions I haven't asked."

"Mmmm." Kiko smiled to himself. "Maybe you're just that transparent."

"If I were, you'd know that all I want to do is find out what's happening."

"Of course." Kiko unsmugged himself, nodding, avoiding her eyes now. "We all wanna know."

Stunned, Dawn didn't say anything for a second, taking in the fact that the agency was as clueless as she was, swallowing back an ache in her throat.

But this wasn't the time to get all sensitive. She could do that alone, where people couldn't feel sorry for her.

"We thought you might give us a better idea about where he is," Kiko added. "That's one of the reasons I called you."

She couldn't ask about the other reasons why he'd gotten in touch, not while she was still slammed by the bad news. If they didn't know where Frank was, who would? "You can't . . . I don't know . . . divine any details?"

"I'm blacked out where your dad's concerned. I tried touching his old clothes, his possessions, to get a read from him, but . . . nothing we didn't already know."

"That's it? That's all you've got? Nothing?"

"Well, we know this. Frank was on a job for us when he disappeared."

"What job?"

He shuffled his black combat boots. She hadn't noticed before now that his feet were too big for his body.

"Do you have an answer?" she asked.

"The boss is gonna tell you."

"I'm sick of hearing about Mr. Limpet. Can't *you* tell me?"

"We don't call him Mr. Limpet," Kiko said softly.

God.

She toned down her temper because she sure as sugar wasn't getting anywhere by losing it. But just as she was cooling her jets, something creaked behind her, moaning, yawning awake.

On edge, she whipped around, raising her hands in front of herself defensively. Krav Maga—street fighting—at its best. Pure instinct.

But it was only a door opening. When a petite woman dressed in an apron peered around the wood, Dawn lowered her arms, stilled her adrenaline.

The interloper was gorgeous, a Hispanic heartbreaker with dusky skin, huge dark eyes, and bobbed, black, Louise Brooks hair. Her features were strong and wide yet utterly feminine.

A soulless *zzzmmm*, like the sound of captured electricity, escaped from behind the door and into the large room.

"Kiko?" she asked in heavily accented English. The words rushed out of her, intense and urgent, even kind of ADD-like. "Just send the girl upstairs and get yourself down here."

"Tell me you got a break." One minute, there'd been sadness about Frank. The next, Kiko was hopped up on whatever this woman had to tell him. He was kind of a schiz.

"A big break." The newcomer scoped Dawn out as thoroughly as Dawn had done to her, then busted out with a blunt, "Frank's daughter?"

Kiko nodded, darting over to the door and reaching up to grasp the fancy iron doorknob. "Breisi, this is Dawn. Dawn, Breisi." He pronounced her name *breezy*, like wind meandering through a meadow on a summer's day.

Irony didn't get any better than that.

Dawn gestured a hello to her, but Breisi visually brushed her aside by making some kind of urgent motion to Kiko.

"Just hurry with this business and get down here," the woman said, then disappeared.

Her tennis shoes slapped on the stone floor, fading downward, as if there were stairs leading to a dungeon. And, truthfully, with this funhouse, Dawn would've expected to see skeletons chained to the walls down there.

"We're on a case," Kiko said.

"Not my dad's, I suppose."

"We're not really sure."

Huh?

He glanced at his watch, flicked his gaze toward the foyer where the dark of approaching night was shading the window curtains, then seemed to come to a decision. "Go ahead to the boss's office. Upstairs and to the left, the door at the end of the hall. Don't bother knocking because he'll be expecting you now, but I'll be up there soon as I can."

She didn't ask how "the boss" knew exactly when she was coming. A Kiko vision had no doubt informed him.

With that, the psychic flipped around the door like a puppy tearing around a tree after a rabbit. The oak crashed closed after him, the heavy thunk of a lock jammed into place.

Dawn gazed up the stairway with its wrought-iron railing and endless distance. It faded into the oblivion of the upper floor. Upon closer inspection, she noticed that the railing sported gargoyles in flight, wings spread like open arms.

Hardly comforted, she started climbing. But halfway up, a shiver traveled across her shoulders.

The sensation tingled, undulating like a heat wave down the rest of her body. Dawn grabbed the banister and slashed a gaze down to the foyer, where the painting of the fire woman stared back, her eyes fixed on Dawn.

Wait. Hadn't she been looking straight ahead before . . . ?

Um. Yeah.

Spending all day on a plane and worrying about Frank had frayed her nerves to a crisp.

Keeping her mind on this meeting with "the boss," she managed to avoid more *Twilight Zone* moments and eventually arrive at the door Kiko had mentioned, a monstrosity that loomed from floor to high ceiling in all its dark grandeur. Surprisingly enough, when she opened it, not a sound was made.

Still, unsurprisingly, the room was black and quiet, minted with a different smell—something she couldn't identify. Not a bad something, either. Old and new mixed together like various colors of paint before they merge. Like . . .

She tried to identify the scent, but couldn't.

Then she heard the voice.

"I'll turn on the lights," it said.

Without warning, an eye-stinging flood of yellow whooshed over her, forcing Dawn to shut her eyelids against it. But she barely had time to hitch in a breath before a gust of chilled air slammed against her. No—*through* her.

Thrown off guard, she startled backward, hitting the wall.

Wha—?

The oxygen rushed out of her lungs as she tried to recover, opening her eyes and lurching into a boxer's stance, swiping one arm upward as if blocking a physical blow. Gasping, heart stuttering, she stood ready to beat off another attack.

Blindside me, you bastard? she thought. Try it again.

But she was stopped by the coldness that had taken root in her chest. It was turning itself inside out, swirling into a warm glow, spreading, sliding down her body, heating and lining her belly with tremors and slick weakness.

Dizzy, she slumped down the wall, her eyes taking in the space around her, seeking a culprit.

But there was no one else in the room.

THREE

The Voice

What the hell?

When Dawn realized the greeting—or whatever it was—had ended, she attempted to stand again. Her pulse wrestled with her veins, tangling with that first ebbing flare of surprise. The heat was still buzzing through her tummy, trickling, melting even lower.

Exciting her.

Oh . . . God . . .

As she panted, confused and overcome, she felt the vibration lingering like a slow thrum of fingers between her legs, stroking her with the pressure of foreplay, stimulating her with a warm flood of fear.

She wilted even more against the doorframe, giving in to whatever was happening.

What had hit her? It was . . .

Pressing her lips together to stifle a slight moan, then leaning her head back, Dawn brushed a hand over her belly. The muscles there prickled, jumped, sensitive and awakened.

It was *good.*

Pulse calming to a cautious thud, she languished until the rush eased away. But even then, she was too lazy, too fuzzy-warm to move.

Almost like great sex, she thought, wanting more.

Almost like a quick erotic fix—the type she depended on to get her through most weeks.

Not trusting herself to stand yet, Dawn warily scanned the room: the book-choked shelves, the sultry paintings of women with bared, smooth backs and heavy-lidded, satiated gazes. Only one of the pictures lacked a female subject: it was red-orange with fire—a burning, lonely landscape. Otherwise, all the windows were blocked by heavy burgundy drapes trimmed with golden fringe; they clashed with a plasma TV that loomed like a Times Square advertisement over the fire painting. A vacant leather chair waited behind a massive desk. The eternal surface of it was clean, as if "the boss" had finished every last case and was biding his time until a new one came his way. Well, he had it.

"Anyone here?" Dawn murmured, wondering if she'd stepped into some kind of demented trap that Frank had fallen prey to, also.

No answer.

Her blood had boiled down to a shivering hunger low in her body. Wet and ready. Swollen with need.

Both intrigued and cautious, she smoothed back a damp strand of hair from her face. God, her hand was trembling.

Okay, maybe she was actually just dreaming on the plane? Or maybe she was so exhausted that she was hallucinating?

Eventually, Dawn felt strong enough to stand, then took a few steps forward, all too aware of the arousal that had left her with a dull ache. Her legs were like two traveling jellyfish, her breathing choppy.

Then she felt it—another huff of wind. After bracing herself, she immediately relaxed when she found that this one was softer, milder. And it didn't come with any below-the-belt thrills, either.

Peeking to the left, she saw an air-conditioning vent that was blowing away on high gear, cooling the room.

She flushed in mortification.

Ambushed by a household appliance? You've got to be kidding. Surely that hadn't been air from a freakin' *conditioner* running through her.

Finally, her host spoke again. "Sit."

The voice was coming out of the speakers of the TV, a low, deep tone filling the room with the tinge of an accent she couldn't identify. Something Latin? At any rate, in spite of the volume, it was still a whisper, a midnight hush.

He could've been here in the room with her, for all the sound quality the system possessed.

Dawn couldn't help rubbing her hands over her arms to chase away the goose bumps. Hot goose bumps, too, like his voice was physically running up and down her skin.

Unable to help it, she nervously laughed at herself.

Even though I'm a sick puppy when it comes to men, she thought, this is ridiculous.

"I'd rather stand," she said, "just to be prepared for any other shit that might come down. Where the hell are you?"

"Dawn."

Her belly twisted at the way he'd shaped her name, drawing it out, toying with it. Without thinking, she took a step.

He continued. "Now make yourself comfortable."

She kept moving, just like she had no mind of her own. Strange.

But . . . hey, since they were going to have a conversation anyway, she found a nice velvet couch and crashed on it. Then, propping her ankle on her knee and slinking down, she ignored her still-singing nerves. They were electric with an afterglow she'd rather forget. And enjoy.

"So." She gestured around the office, toward the speakers. "This is real *Charlie's Angels* of you."

He ignored her sarcasm. "It's good to finally meet you."

Foreign. Yeah, there was definitely some mystique in his buried accent.

"I'd like to say the same thing, but . . ." She raised up her hands and allowed them to flop back down to the couch. "You know. My dad missing. Weird-ass things happening. All that."

"Angry." The Voice paused. "I don't blame you."

"Years in the making." This small talk made her tired. "Why don't you start enlightening me now."

"After a few questions."

Wait. Who should be asking the que—

"When's the last time you talked to Frank?"

Shame suffused her, and she glanced away from the TV, The Voice. So they'd talk about her father first. No prob. "A month ago."

His lack of response said everything.

"We're . . ." She combed her fingertips over the couch. ". . . not the closest."

This time, she was the one who kept her tongue. The quietude traced the air with tension, the urge for her to explain, to make more excuses for her familial relationships.

But *his* silence was needling her.

"Don't goddamn judge me," she continued. "He worked for you. You must be some real crackerjack PIs to figure out he was missing after only four days."

"We wanted to be certain he was really gone before we worried you. Against my wishes, Frank had a tendency to disappear during an assignment—he liked working alone—but he was never out of contact for too long. We had quite a time finding you, out there in . . ." He paused. ". . . Virginia?"

Frank had been doing PI work? This was a joke. Her dad wasn't much for brain jobs, even by his own admission.

"A girl's got to do what she's got to do to survive," she said, ducking the Virginia topic.

"You're not very forthcoming."

"Quid pro quo, man. When you talk, I'll talk."

"Dawn."

Her eyelids weighed downward.

Jet lag, she thought. It's really hitting now.

"We expected to find you on location for a film," he added. "You threw us a curveball by ending up on a contracting job in a beat-up house near Arlington."

This time, his whisper seeped into her, just as the air had earlier. Burgeoning heat flowed to the same dangerous places, making her feel a little restless, like one of those women in the paintings: stretching like a feline after a long, naked nap in the sun, purring as rays of light throbbed through her veins.

Dawn's sight went hazy, and she slipped farther down the couch, sliding her ankle off her knee, angling out her leg and allowing her thighs to part.

Mmmm. God. Warm, nice . . .

She thought she heard soft laughter. Without commanding herself to do it, she coaxed her palm up her hip, rubbed the coarse denim of her jeans, traveled near the juncture of her thighs, where a stiff yearning was starting to burn again.

"Dawn?"

She started. "Virginia . . ." Her tone was slurred, even though her brain was still full speed ahead. "Took a friend up on an offer to earn a few bucks."

And to help her hide her face until what she'd done on her last gig had been forgotten.

" 'A friend'?" he asked. "I didn't know you had many of those. Not of the female sort, at least."

The compulsion to touch herself overwhelmed her, but she resisted, forcing her hand to the couch, leaving her frustrated, craving relief for the sharp anguish between her legs.

"What's going on?" she said, her groggy tone taking the snap out of her demand.

"You're tough to crack, Dawn. I'm glad to see it." He was acting as if he had horny, impulsive women in his office every day. "Let me clarify my questions. Your 'friend' is the wife of one of the carpenters from the last film you worked on, isn't she? A women's studies professor who took pity on you after what happened with Darrin Ryder."

Before she could stop the words, they came out of her mouth—fluid and easy, even as Dawn told herself not to talk.

"She was the first person to congratulate me after I was kicked off the set. There was a lot of satisfaction in the air after I gave Darrin Ryder's family jewels a proper polish."

"Remind me never to make an unwarranted pass at you."

Her sight was veiled by a gray mist, the feel of a man's hand trailing down her neck.

Oh.

Even though she couldn't figure out what was wrong with this picture, she smiled under the mental caress.

Fully sedated, she said, "You sound amused with the current state of my life."

"It can't be that bad."

Perhaps, in his book, being a social leper was good?

"Oh, it's bad enough." Talking was using up too much energy. And she was doing so *much* of it. "Darrin Ryder is a whiny little actor who thinks everything belongs to him . . . including the crew. He pulled me into a closet on location in D.C. Pawed at me during one of those mind-numbingly long breaks between camera shots. He may be the flavor of the month in Hollywood . . . but I didn't want a taste of him."

"So he didn't appreciate that."

Again, her answer came unchecked. "Usually the support staff is like wolfsbane to actors. Yeah . . . we're there to make them look fabulous. And that's where most gratitude ends. But Darrin Ryder had some kind of obsession with the Eva-Claremont's-kid thing. I'm used to it, so I didn't return all the displaced affection. I suppose that pulled his trigger. When he made his move, I just gave him my own love tap. In the balls."

"Effective."

"But Ryder . . . and the director . . . and the producer . . . and his agent . . . and his manager . . . weren't won over."

Wow, she thought, listening through a fog. She sounded flippant, even though the career she loved so much was suffering. But the industry was forgiving. If she could manage to charm her way back from this whole "loose canon" stigma, she could get back to stuntwork—the one fulfilling activity in her life that gave her some actual pride. Hell, it wasn't like she was in it for the pitiful paycheck and zero glitz; what she got out of it was worth any amount of cuts and bruises.

Dawn tried to pep up. "I have questions for *you*, too." She raised a lazy finger to point at him. "Starting with, how do you propose to make an unwarranted pass at me when you don't even have a body?"

The Voice laughed, and she succumbed to the vocal caress. The couch's velvet was soft as she brushed over it, picturing something way more intriguing than upholstery under her fingertips.

"No answer?" she asked, satisfied with being the one who was guiding things now.

"I don't think so," he said, his whisper even lower. "You've got too much of a reputation as a maneater, and I'm into this notion called self-preservation."

So sue me for all the bangathons I've entered, she thought. No shame in the enjoyment of sex.

"You're also very good at your job, very physically adept," he added. "Trained in swordplay and assorted weaponry, fights, high falls, gymnastics, harness work . . ."

"Say, maybe you could continue the list in person, Mr. . . . ?" Limpet? The name just didn't go with The Voice. It was like imagining Don Knotts playing the Phantom of the Opera.

He shifted back into gear with dizzying agility. “How familiar are you with your mother’s films?”

Back to business, then. She knew she could steer him there at some point.

“I know her stuff well. She made some watchable flicks before she was murdered.”

“Yes, she did. I’m impressed with her work. And I’m sorry her life was cut so short.”

“Hey, she was twenty-three,” Dawn said. “We’ve all got to go some time.”

“You seem cavalier.”

Dawn struggled to sit up straighter, forcing out her words so they matched the flow of her thoughts. Her speech was still pokey, but stronger.

“What do you want me to do? Tear my clothes and wail about how much it bothers me that I, the wayward daughter of Eva Claremont, have already outlived the ideal woman, a person who gave so much beauty to the world during her short stay on it? Do you want that sort of tragic eloquence?”

Her throat burned, so she couldn’t talk anymore.

“Grieving would be a start,” he said.

Closing her eyes, Dawn sighed, the sound short, soft, and even a little bitter. “Hate to disappoint you, but she died when I was about a month old, and her blood doesn’t exactly run through me. Unlike her, I’m not much for drama.”

“And that’s why you went into the biz.”

She wasn’t about to allow Amateur Freud Hour here, explaining how her career was a connection to Mommy while simultaneously being a big screw-you to Eva’s indelible glamour. Sure, maybe Dawn was getting rebellious revenge against a parent who’d left too early, and maybe she was even enjoying how lovely starlet Eva wouldn’t have approved of her daughter’s gritty career. But this stranger didn’t have to know any of that—Dawn’s hyper self-awareness provided all the judgmental nitpicking she needed.

"Is my mother's oeuvre that important to my dad's disappearance, Mr. . . . ?"

Once again, he dodged, this time with an appreciation for her tenacity in his whisper. "I believe there are links."

"Then tell me already." She battled through the mental mist to stand, but only got to the edge of the couch.

"I'm not sure you'd believe any of it, Dawn."

"Try me. What are you all hiding around here?"

The soft electronic fizz of the speakers divided them as he stayed quiet. With the last of her strength, she pushed to her feet. The world became a little clearer, as if she'd broken through the surface of a pond and could hear, *see* again. She stood in front of the TV, still wavering, searching for a hidden camera, desperate for a clue.

"You won't find anything," he said, sounding impressed for some reason. "Breisi set this up so that I'm next to impossible to trace."

"Really. Let's see. Since you won't tell me jack about Frank . . ." She ran a hand under the TV, finding nothing amiss. "What's with Breisi anyway? And Kiko?" Gaining lucidity and composure by the second, she kept searching, standing on her tiptoes to get a gander at the underbelly of the screen. "It wasn't like your employees were cheering to see me."

From where she was standing, The Voice fully enveloped her, sending brittle tremors of awareness through her skin, under it. She closed her eyes again, liking this, wanting this to stop so she could concentrate on why she was actually here.

Shaking her head free of its fuzz, she forced alertness.

"I don't understand why Kiko and Breisi would've been rude," The Voice said. "Frank rarely discussed Eva, but he talked about you as if you walk on water."

Peering around, she thought, Screw it, and climbed onto the colossal desk. From there, she got a different vantage point of the speaker. Didn't help.

Too bad she sucked at technology. Even if she had step-by-step directions, she wouldn't know how this setup worked.

"Walk on water, huh?" Dawn breathed in big gulps of air, almost back to her old self now. "Hardly. But I am quite a sight when I'm walking on mahogany."

She tapped her boot on his desktop, daring him to say something.

"Cherry wood," he whispered. "And that surface has withstood a lot more than you."

"Well. Have you been a bad boss man, using your desk for shenanigans with your secretary, Mr. . . . ?"

Another mild laugh, but this one wasn't very nice. It was ragged. Dark. "You can't possibly imagine what's found itself with its back to that wood."

Dawn didn't say anything for a moment, not with all the doubts she was having about Limpet and Associates. There was something creepier than their interior decorations going on here, something way out of her league.

As nonchalantly as she could, she dropped to the carpet and walked around to the side of the desk, where the chair rested. There, she skimmed her hand over the wood, pausing when she found something—a groove. She bent to inspect it.

"I'm not the one being questioned here," The Voice reminded her. *"Dawn."*

She felt that mental pull again, a jarring loss of her senses, but she pushed against it, concentrating on the groove instead. It was sharp, like the scar from an ax that had embedded itself there.

That's when Kiko bowled into the room with Breisi on his tail. Without preamble, Dawn gasped to full attention, roaring on all cylinders again, oddly refreshed.

It was almost as if she'd just woken up, like the past few minutes were pieces of a scattered puzzle and she'd just arrived in the office to fit them back together.

"Thank you, Dawn," The Voice whispered. "You're stronger than I imagined."

Before she could ask what that meant, Kiko spoke.

"Sorry we took so long." He was still in excitement mode and oblivious to everything else. "Our locator turned up something big."

Breisi wore an apron that came to mid-thigh and revealed black parachute pants. Up close, she looked older than Dawn had first thought, with fine wrinkles hugging her eyes and mouth. Dawn doubted they were from smiling, either.

"Nathan Pennybaker just got back into the country," Breisi said. "Kiko and I need to pay him a visit."

"And we should take her with us." Kiko glanced at Dawn.

She blinked, the past half hour of weirdness all but forgotten.

"It's too soon," The Voice said.

Kiko stepped forward, shaking his finger at the TV. Aha—the screen acted as The Voice's "eye," his face.

But where was the rest of him? Dawn thought. Behind the wall in a control room? Down the street in another house?

A chill fluttered up her spine as she focused on the TV, feeling it watching her. . . .

"Remember what I saw?" Kiko continued. "She's key."

"Me?" she asked. "I'm . . . what?"

Again, the psychic brushed his gaze over her, and she felt as if he were actually digging around her heart, trying to pull it out. Tired of feeling under attack, she stepped back, protectively laying her hand over her chest.

He turned back to the TV while Breisi kept an eye on Dawn. Unidentifiable emotion flashed over the other woman's eyes, but she glanced away before Dawn could define it.

"We need her," Kiko said. "So let's just cut to the chase, put Dawn on the payroll, and deal."

"Payroll?" This was all going too fast, a scribbled comic-horror strip. But she had to find Frank, and if they were willing to help, she'd take their offer—no two ways about it. It wasn't as if her job installing cabinets or laying tile in Virginia was going to miss her. *This* was where she needed to be. "All right, I'll do anything, tag along with you, answer any questions . . ."

Over the speakers, The Voice sighed. Harsh. Resigned? "*Anything*," he repeated. "You are telling me how far you would go to find your father?"

Her heart picked up speed. "I'd do *anything* it takes."

Breisi came to stand beside her, parallel to Kiko.

"Frank was working on finding a missing little boy whose mother hired us," she said.

A little boy? Unsettled, Dawn turned away from them. That meant facing a wrecked mom, digging into the possibility of what might have happened to the child . . . to Frank.

She crossed her arms over her chest. But if this was an avenue to find him, she had to take it.

Before she could respond, the plasma TV blipped to life, an eye of Big Brother. In its iris was a scene from *Diaper Derby*, a very bad comedy that had opened at thirty-three million dollars a couple weeks ago at the box office. How The Voice had gotten a hold of it already, Dawn didn't know. Maybe it was a pirated copy. If it was, she might have to give him a good cuffing, because that sort of crap cut into film profits and, thus, her paychecks—if she could ever get another film gig.

The scene played out. In a cozy loft somewhere in a clean, pristine, fictional big city found only in the movies, two grizzled men, who were clearly not fatherhood material, were arguing over a crib that was emanating fake baby cries. They were tug-of-warring a soiled diaper between them.

Dawn didn't want to guess what was about to happen next. But it did happen, a big explosion of . . .

"There," The Voice said, the TV freezing on a most unfortunate image.

Dawn, Kiko, and Breisi all shook their heads.

"Comedy at its finest," Kiko said. "I swear, today's movies—"

"*Kiko.*" The Voice obviously had another point in mind. "Dawn, did you see that?"

"I saw plenty."

"I'm referring to the case. Just focus on the windows in the rear of their room."

When she glanced back, the picture had been rewound and frozen again, this time to a frame in which the men were back to pulling at the intact diaper.

"Watch," The Voice said, and the image zoomed in to focus on the windows in the background.

At first she didn't catch anything. Just a glare, a play of light from a super-powered bulb. But the more she looked, the more she saw in the close-up:

A young boy with big blue eyes and a striped shirt, scratching at the window. He looked like he couldn't have been more than a preteen, but he'd tried to force his age by growing his black hair into a careless mop; there were piercings, too—a diamond stud in his nose, his eyebrow.

He seemed familiar, but she couldn't . . .

"So he trespassed onto a set," Dawn said, and even though she sounded as smooth as dry ice, she was unable to tear her eyes away. "Why is everyone acting shocked about a boy in a fake window? He wandered into a shot. It's not like he's floating up twelve stories. He's not a ghost or something."

Both Breisi and Kiko glanced at each other, then back at Dawn.

She wasn't so sure she realized the full extent of what was going on. Big shocker. It matched the entire Limpet experience so far. Still, she was definitely going to get her answers soon, come hell or high water.

Kiko spoke up. "We've consulted with special effects wizards and they say no movie magic was used. But more important than that, this boy's mom tells us that superimposing the kid's image isn't possible anyway. . . ."

"Dawn." The Voice paused. He'd said her name like she'd already failed him. "You don't recognize him?"

Maybe she did. Or maybe her mind just wasn't accepting it.

But Kiko helpfully jumped in.

"That's Robby Pennybaker," he said. "And you, of all people, should know that he shouldn't be anywhere near that movie."

Her mind . . . not accepting this . . . shutting down . . .

"Not," Kiko added, "when he died twenty-three years ago."

FOUR
The Lost Little Boy

AFTER the meeting, Kiko persuaded his boss to allow Dawn to go with him and Breisi to the Pennybaker home for an innocuous round of questioning with Robby's dad. Although the mysterious Voice wasn't that excited about her riding along, Kiko was adamant—no doubt because, in the psychic's all-knowing mind, Frank's daughter was meant be on this case with them. The Voice had to have a lot of faith in Kiko's talents to go along with this.

And, even though she didn't really buy into the vision thing, she couldn't fly in the face of this opportunity, either.

In any event, the boss had made his employees promise to always keep Dawn in their sights, safe. Truthfully, she didn't feel the need for babysitting, but if she wanted to be there, following directions from the spook crew was mandatory.

And that's how she got to this point: stuck in the backseat of Breisi's 4Runner. There were some wanky features, like the panels that had been built into the floor and the compartments in the doors. Also, in the rear storage area, gray canvas covered something Kiko wouldn't explain, so Dawn had stopped asking within the first few minutes. It smelled like grease and steel. That, mixed with the tropical air freshener attached to Breisi's vents, tumbled Dawn's stomach.

As they roared out of the Hills and along the 405 Freeway to Brentwood, where the Pennybakers lived in a swanky mini-mansion close to where OJ Simpson had performed the last leg of his Freedom Rider Bronco fiasco, she watched the night embrace L.A. Lights shimmered in the valley, winking and seducing as they frosted the dark glass of skyscrapers. Back in the distance, the famous Hollywood sign rested against the withered skin of Mount Lee. It was lit by floodlights, crooked in its dotage but alive with the hope and sparkle of people who still had some dreams left.

In a good mood, Kiko turned around in his seat, wearing sunglasses. God, that chapped her hide. There was no reason to wear those things at night unless you were a poseur.

"Smooth as a Lamborghini, huh, Dawn?"

"I've never had the pleasure of driving one."

"Me, either; but I will. You watch. One day, I'll have a garage full of 'em after I score the right roles. Right now, I'm just a face in the crowd, but my agent's got a few jobs cooking. Something along the lines of *The Station Agent*. Or a stage production of *Waiting for Godot*. I'm up for Vladmir in this production where we would dress like pawns being used in the game of life."

"Interesting," she said, distracted by all the questions she needed answered.

"I'm here to tell you," he continued, on a roll, "that actors of my talent have been fucked ever since *Lord of the Rings* and *Star Wars* ended. Gimme a hobbit to double or an Ewok to play any day of the week, I say. All I want to do is be on that screen. That's how it's always been, too, ever since I was just a rugrat from Phoenix. I was in school plays and all that stuff, but I knew movies were the golden ticket. That's why I came out to L.A., right out of twelfth grade. I was a starving actor for a while, but then the boss came calling one day after this *thing* happened. . . ."

At the way he trailed off, Dawn's interest was piqued. *"Thing?"*

"Yeah." Kiko frowned. "It was in the papers—"

"What *thing*, Kiko?" Man, he liked to flap those gums.

He paused, like this was allowing the memory time to fully form. Then, shrugging, he said, "There was a guy going around my old neighborhood, breaking into apartments and attacking women. I knew who he was. He just lived two doors down and, one day, he left his jacket by the mailboxes. When I touched it, I sensed what he'd been up to."

She hadn't expected such a sobering story. "Seriously?"

"Seriously. I have psychometric talents along with precognition and telepathy."

She wanted to ask more, but he was already talking again.

"I started bugging the police about him before he could ruin another woman's life, but they, of course, didn't believe me. I'm used to that though, so I cut to the chase and told them I was going to do something about the guy myself if they were just going to sit on their asses and let him rape his way through L.A."

Kiko, the vigilante? "So did you do . . . something?"

The psychic smirked. "I didn't have to. This detective who'd already worked with sixth-sense consultants and believed in its value investigated my neighbor. She ended up gathering enough evidence to nail him pretty quick."

"Wow." Dawn just sat there. "You're, like, a hero then."

"Yes, I am."

He rushed on, making her wonder if he actually had the capacity for humility. Small chance, but maybe.

"The press got a hold of the story, and that's how the boss found me. He liked my 'interest in justice' besides all the psychic talent."

"You were in the news? Aren't you afraid this rapist will have a vendetta against you?"

"Not really. He hanged himself in prison."

Silence struck the air. Breisi sighed and inserted a receiver in her right ear and pushed a glowing red button in the middle of the steering wheel. The 4Runner revved, then jetted to a higher speed.

Thrown back in her seat, Dawn recovered, then scooted forward. She gestured toward the button. "What's *that*?"

There. Change the subject, pronto. It helped her to stop worrying about Frank's part in this PI firm that required a "sense of justice" from its employees. It kept her from thinking about Breisi's part in it. Frank's part in it.

Breisi was acting like the backseat was vacant, but Kiko was glad to answer.

"That's one of her antiradar gadgets. It saves us a lot of time." Kiko tapped his ear. "And she likes to monitor."

"Police scanners?"

"Not right now. The Dodgers are playing the Giants, so don't talk to her unless it's highly necessary."

Dawn didn't need an excuse to do that, but she played "nice" instead. Frank would've been proud.

She shifted back into her seat, finally at her wits' end with these people. "So . . . What's going on with Mr. Limpet?"

"Don't call him that."

"Why?"

He took off his sunglasses and gave her a blank look.

"Oh, come on, Kiko. For starters, did you think I wouldn't notice that he wasn't in the room for our entire conversation?"

"The boss just enjoys his privacy."

"You've never wondered? Man, do you guys ever solve anything or do you just run around in that Hammer House of Horror getting your jollies from blowing the minds of people who manage to get past the door?"

Kiko, as compact as he was, turned his entire body around to face her. "We're aces in what we do, but . . . well, our clientele is slightly different from the norm. Breisi and I handle the customer service and aboveboard groundwork. None of the clients gets to see the boss like you did."

"I didn't exactly *see* him."

"At least you made it into the office."

"Yeah, barely." A phantom throb started between her legs again. God. "By the way, it was a really . . . I search for the word . . . *different* experience talking with him."

"Oh? Oooohhh." Kiko nodded. "He put you under. You know, you didn't look like you were that far gone when Breisi and I came into the room. I'll bet *you* were a hard customer."

Dawn was still back at "put you under." As in "hypnosis"? It would go a long way in explaining her inability to stop revealing personal tidbits to The Voice. What an asshole.

Kiko pointed to his head. "Now, I'm no slouch in the mind-over-matter department myself, but the boss . . . He's the best at hypnosis. I've already learned a ton of things from him, but I'm stuck at where you initially read people. That's my forte, I guess—reading. Maybe I'll never go as far as the boss—you know, where he uses his voice to get what he needs, to *really* go inside. Not that it matters. He says the two of us brainiacs have different talents anyway."

He donned a worshipful grin. Aw, The Voice's pet acolyte.

"The boss says," Kiko added, "that mind skills are a good tool against bad guys who're being stubborn or defensive about giving up information."

Her? Stubborn and defensive? *A bad guy?*

She crossed her arms over her chest, as if to block out more attempts at the mind games she'd been subjected to tonight, courtesy of Kiko and the freakin' Voice. "I recall that he asked questions that had nothing to do with Frank."

"Maybe they did and you don't know it."

"You'd better be right, because you know what? I don't like anyone in my head or pulling words out of me."

She didn't add anything about how the apparent hypnosis had affected her body because, truthfully, *that* had been the highlight of her day. It had offered a measure of comfort, pleasure. Calm. But that's just how she operated, no apologies necessary. Sex was her balm, dignified or not.

But had The Voice "read" this about her and used it as a means to relax her?

Anger twisted in her chest. It was an invasion, she thought, and she didn't appreciate it one damned bit.

Kiko was raising an eyebrow, probably knowing exactly what was going through her head. "He was testing you, I'll bet. Seeing how much you'd be able to take on the job. Seeing if you'd measure up."

Bullshit. "I'm warning you, if anyone tries to go where no man has gone before on me again, I will tear you apart. I will draw and quarter your asses. Relay *that* to the boss."

He shrank away from her, clearly knowing she wasn't kidding. "Don't get uppity. He would never go in uninvited. And once he's inside, *you* decide how he's going to function."

"Say what?"

"You . . ." Kiko paused, then shrugged fatalistically. "You have to leave some kind of door open for him to get in, a willingness, whether it's conscious or unconscious. That's what he uses to enter, then to take control. I don't know exactly how it worked with you, but—"

"Unbelievable." Okay, so this meant sex was her doorbell. She was well aware of that. The Voice had just better keep it classified information. "What kind of business do you chuckleheads do, anyway?"

Kiko paused, then lifted his dimpled chin. "We help with life's strange emergencies."

"Which means . . . ?"

"Well, it means things like 'how did Robby get into that movie?' " Kiko hesitated. "I don't know. I could be wrong about you. Still, I really feel it's going to take more than explanations to bring you into Frank's life."

He stopped and turned around, leaving Dawn with a thousand more questions she didn't really want to ask.

A few seconds passed.

Dawn couldn't stand it anymore. "So the agency is . . ." She used her hands to search for a description.

"Paranormally inclined?" Kiko smiled.

She just stared at him. There was no way Frank would've been into this junk.

"I'm not some naïve client who needs entertainment as a side platter to a main course of case solving, so just give me real answers."

"I'm trying."

What a drama queen, she thought. There's got to be a logical explanation waiting right around the corner.

But he wasn't giving it to her yet. "The boss is being cautious about taking you on because I think, deep down, he hates having you walk in your dad's footsteps. But he knows I'm always right in the end. See, that's another thing—I can sometimes grasp the future, and that's just as useful as hypnosis, he says."

Touching. The Voice cared for her. A lot of good that would do Frank. "Kiko, I can look out for myself. And, I swear, Limpet doesn't have to hire me on, not after I find Dad. I'll be going back to regular work."

"I'm sure."

"I will."

"I know you think so. But, in the meantime, a consultation fee wouldn't come amiss for you. Am I right?"

Damn it, it was a bitch to be broke, especially when her dad constantly made so many bad investments with the residuals from her mom's legacy. And if Dawn was going to desert her job back in Arlington in order to find Frank, her pockets would be even lighter. "I suppose I could get paid for my time and effort."

"Good."

Pride stinging, she shut her mouth.

Kiko glanced over his shoulder at the GPS device Breisi was using to get to the Pennybakers', then back at Dawn. In the meantime, Breisi uttered a victorious "Yesss!" while pumping her fist by her side. Score for the Dodgers.

"If we're done with Boss Talk," Kiko said, "it looks like we've got a few minutes for me to catch you up on what's happening with this case."

Good. The nitty gritty. Maybe now Kiko would drop the ghost crap and get down to brass tacks.

"Shoot," she said.

"Okay. The boss approached Marla Pennybaker, Robby's mom, after the publicity hit about her 'dead' son being in *Diaper Derby*. The Internet is what started it all. All the film geek chat rooms were buzzing about the sighting, calling Robby's appearance 'the ultimate Easter Egg.' "

"Ah." An Easter Egg was code for an inside movie joke, usually a scene that's tucked away on a DVD as a bonus. "You told me that Robby's mom said special effects weren't the reason her son appeared in the movie. Why's that?"

"Because about four months before Robby's death, he dropped out of the movies, went through a phase where he refused to work. We'll see why with further investigation, I'm sure. He hid inside the house, even while his mom and dad tried to get him out, but Robby was adamant about not making any public appearances at all. Then he did something out of character: he had someone come in to pierce him, and he grew out his hair so he looked like a little punk. There were no pictures, no recorded images of him during that time."

Dawn sighed and glanced out the window. "I remember Robby in the movies. He was so clean-cut. So cute."

"Right. That's why Mrs. Pennybaker believes something is off. Robby's long-haired, pierced image couldn't have been spliced into *Diaper Derby* because it isn't available."

Her mind wasn't quite wrapping around all of this. It didn't want to. "So, somewhere, he *is* alive?"

But that didn't sound right. She thought about how Robby hadn't aged in twenty-three years.

Don't even think "paranormal," Dawn. Don't.

"I have my doubts about him actually 'being alive.' " Kiko actually used air quotes for that last part.

"Then how can you explain him showing up in the movie with his altered appearance?"

He lifted a heavy eyebrow, all serious. "There're a world of explanations out there."

Okay. Back to the ghoulie talk.

Or were ghosts the reason Kiko and Breisi had traded meaningful looks back at the office when Dawn had commented about the kid's image in the window?

Not surprisingly, Kiko picked up on the negativity.

"Guess I'll talk about what we do know," he said, a patient slant to his mouth. "The kid's sadly legendary for dying from a drug overdose when he was twelve."

Even though she'd heard the story a million times, Dawn still couldn't get over the thud of shock. Twelve. A boy who'd partied and pierced himself. Had Robby been chafing at strict parents? Or had they indulged their little star, justifying his behavior by thinking that kids didn't remain kids for long in Hollywood—especially back in the eighties? Drew Barrymore had gone down the same road: drinking by nine, taking drugs by ten, rehab soon afterward. In this city, children grew up at warp speed, and Dawn hated parents who allowed it to happen. And every once in a while it still did, even in today's more conservative environment.

Kiko had started talking again, watching her closely. "Because his body disappeared from the morgue, there were a lot of different rumors about the CIA killing him or terrorists making a statement about our depraved society by murdering Robby. Maybe he's just a fucked-up Hollywood child who started partying too early, or . . ."

Or maybe he was a spirit come to haunt the earth? she silently added for Kiko's sake. Yeah, right.

Hollywood was full of legends, movie stars who'd expired in spectacular, newsworthy ways, many of their deaths unsolved. Conspiracy theories surrounded every one of them, resurrecting their spirits as urban myths or cautionary tales for the dreamers of tomorrow.

Robby Pennybaker, Jayne Mansfield, Jesse Shane, Marilyn Monroe . . . Dawn stopped there, unwilling to go any further.

Legend or not, Robby Pennybaker was dead. It was ridiculous to think he was out there and somehow ready to return to his mother. There had to be some logic to his appearance in the movie clip.

"You don't have to give me details of Robby's demise." Dawn's chest fisted at her next thought. She concentrated on blocking the memories, mental Polaroids that left her drained and stunned. "He died almost a year after my mom. They were costars in her biggest movie, so it's easy to remember."

Her own words echoed in the car, and suddenly it hit her. Duh. No wonder The Voice had started to quiz her about how well she knew Eva Claremont's films. He'd been trying to ready her psyche for the shock of seeing Robby's image again.

"Ah, Eva's biggest movie." Kiko's gaze had gone goofy. "*Daydreamer*. I still remember her in that one scene, where she was standing on the top of a grassy hill and the sun was lighting the back of her so you could see through her dress. She had flowers in her blond hair. She looked like something out of a dream, all right."

Dawn's heart clenched with the fondness in his recollection. Lots of people loved that scene; it had been the instigator of a hundred thousand crushes. It was the definitive moment of Eva's career—the one shot that encapsulated her flower-child perfection at the start of the Me Decade. She'd been a symbol of more ideal times, a beautiful ghost that slipped through everyone's fingers, no matter how hard they tried to hold on.

"Kiko," Dawn said softly, not wanting to shake him out of the orgasm he was having.

He jolted, then sent her a sheepish grin.

She didn't react. She was too used to random strangers and their impossible love for Eva. The problem came when they wondered why Dawn wasn't anything like her mother.

“Sorry,” he said. “Where was I?”

“Robby’s legend: The Death of a Rising Wastoid.”

“Got it.” He sighed, then went back to being Kiko—whatever that meant. Version 1.0, 2.0 . . . Dawn wasn’t sure who she’d get this time. Happy pup? Sad clown? Rude bugger?

“From talking to Marla Pennybaker,” he said, slipping into Serious Kiko, “we have an idea of what happened after Robby’s death. Their home life broke down. The housekeeper committed suicide. His dad moved out of the country because he couldn’t handle being around anything that reminded him of his son.”

“I’ve heard of Nathan Pennybaker. He was a failed child actor himself before he became Robby’s manager.”

“Uh-huh. And he was devastated when his son died, so he went to Europe to search his soul, to ‘rebuild his life.’ ”

“Sounds like the mom is the strong one, toughing it out here, even if she did mess up the kid’s formative years.”

“I’m not sure if she was blissfully unaware of Robby’s ‘dark side’ or not. She indicated she wasn’t, but my readings weren’t clear. I think her big crime was not being more involved with Robby’s day-to-day activities because she was so into her own stuff—a Red Cross volunteer back in the day. A real bleeding heart who devoted time to the less fortunate. *Un*fortunately, she now regrets not spending more precious moments with Robby. She beats herself up daily about that.”

“And how about the dad?”

Breisi turned onto Cliffwood Avenue, slowing their speed. Everything passed in a dense blur: thick foliage hovering over high walls, iron gates, long drives snaking up to stately homes, red-tinged security signs staked into perfect lawns.

“We haven’t talked to Nathan Pennybaker yet,” Kiko said. “He only came home a few hours ago. It’s the first break we’ve gotten in this case, because, Lord knows, nothing else we’ve done has turned up anything. Not interviews with all the conspiracy theorists, not scouring the soundstage where *Diaper Derby* was filmed, or even going over that celluloid a thousand times—nothing has mattered. Too bad Mr. P. doesn't feel up to seeing us. When Breisi called Marla Pennybaker to request an interview with her husband tonight, he shied away."

The psychic strikes again. "You *read* that from him."

"Well . . . no. I get my readings from proximity, unless I dream a prediction. That means I have to be in the same general area as the mind or items I'm trying to go on, and even then it doesn't always work. People can unconsciously block my efforts—just like *you*—or maybe there's nothing there to read. Sometimes I have to use touch—" When he reached out a hand to Dawn, just as an example, she held up a palm to keep him away. "—in order to go deep inside my subject, to really focus. Like with that rapist dick's jacket."

"Don't you go crazy with all those voices in your head?"

"Nah." Kiko shrugged. "I don't pick up on everyone's every vibe, you know. I'd go bonkers if I did."

He wasn't all-powerful, she thought. Thank God.

"So you're guessing that Mr. Pennybaker doesn't want to see us," she said, slightly more at ease now, but not by much.

"I'm making an educated estimation since his wife was trying to get him to come to the phone and he wouldn't."

"Got it. And you didn't actually *see* Nathan Pennybaker's homecoming?"

"No." Kiko shrugged. "But Breisi had him under watch."

Dawn must've looked confused because Kiko shot a glance to their driver, who was still immersed in her baseball game. Then he leaned toward the backseat, lowering his voice.

"It's something we call a locator," he said.

"And . . . ?"

"It's only totally brilliant and much more efficient than audio taps. All Breisi has to do is run a sample of someone's clothing—or something that holds their scent—through the machine, plant a sensor in the place they're expected to show up and bingo, we know when Mr. P.'s in the house, whether he wants us to realize it or not. And based on how he likes to run away, we guessed we'd need the insurance with him."

Apron technology. Now Breisi's downstairs room was making sense. Sort of. "That's illegal. An invasion of privacy."

"They won't ever know, so we really don't give a crap. So, when we get into the house, don't be surprised if Breisi takes a bathroom break."

"She'll be retrieving the locator?"

"You bet. That sensor ain't no trinket."

"Hmmm." Dawn thought that The Voice might be cheap.

"No," Kiko said, catching her thoughts. "He pays good. If there's one thing the boss isn't, it's a tightwad."

Dawn shot her hand out to grab Kiko's wrist. He tried to whip away from her, but she was on him before he could move.

"I told you I'd do damage," she said through gritted teeth.

"Why?"

Oh, like he didn't know.

Point made, she let go of him and he turned back around, rubbing his wrist and hopefully promising to himself that he would never jack with Dawn's mind again.

"Are we expecting Mr. Pennybaker to be at home when we get there?" she asked.

Kiko didn't answer. Was he pouting? How mature.

"Hey," she said, raising the volume to eleven.

"Mrs. Pennybaker hasn't told him we're coming tonight. He'll be there."

"Thank you."

"My wrist hurts. You're strong."

"I barely touched you." Pussy.

He was still nursing his tender wound when they arrived at the Pennybaker residence.

After pulling up to the gate, where roaring iron lions greeted them, Breisi ditched her earphone with a few, rapid-fire, muttered complaints that she never got to relax, then accessed the gate speaker. A female voice told them to wait while the barrier was opened.

The black grating parted, and Dawn would've felt welcomed if it weren't for a couple of details: the expansive manicured lawn. The landscaped rock waterfalls and bronze statues that danced in frozen action under the flood of spotlights. The fact that there was no one to greet them outside. Hell, even the porch light wasn't on.

At first glance, the Pennybaker residence looked like a museum that carried modern art: two stories, streamlined white facade, boxy with angles and sleek sterility. Bushes and trees surrounded the structure: a copse of oak and pines on the left and a hedged maze on the right. All Dawn could hear through Kiko's gapped window was the lap of water flowing over granite and the night wind keening through the pines like a lonely pack of animals howling, calling.

Breisi got out of the car, but Kiko just sat there.

"Hey, are you mad at me?" Dawn asked.

"Shhh."

As she moved forward to look at him, she saw that he had his eyes closed. Oh, right. Hocus-pocus time.

On Dawn's left, Breisi was hyper-fluffing her bobbed hair. Earlier, she had taken off the apron, revealing a black T-shirt to go with her parachute pants. There was a picture of a teddy bear holding a bubbling beaker on the front.

Don't even comment, Dawn thought. It wasn't like they were trying to get into the Viper Room, so she'd let the wardrobe pass—especially after Breisi shoved herself into a shoulder holster and then a lightweight black jacket.

Dawn kept staring at where the jacket was covering Breisi's gun. A real gun loaded with *real* ammunition, no doubt.

Kiko undid his seat belt and strapped himself into his own rig and light jacket. "Breisi's the good cop. I'm the unpredictable one, like Mel Gibson in *Lethal Weapon*."

Dawn tried not to freak out any more than she was already doing. "This should be fascinating."

Kiko stood on the floorboard, and even he had to duck. He swept his arms out dramatically, dismissing any hurt feelings from Dawn's wrist snatch.

"You're in good hands," he said. "We have trained with the best. It's all in the *acting*."

Shit. "So she's one, too. An actor?"

"Aren't we all?"

Dawn held back all her opinions about what a joke actors were, especially ones who thought they could do their own stunts . . . and carry their own guns.

"Breisi is also a thespian in her day hours," Kiko added. "Up until a year ago, she was on *Bandito*."

"What's that?"

Kiko pulled a superior look out of his arsenal. "*Bandito*? It's only the most popular Mexican soap ever. Breisi was a virgin who got gunned down before the Bandito could ravish her."

No wonder she had such attitude. Lack of sex would sure make Dawn testy, too.

He lowered his voice. "She got written off because they said thirty-one-year-olds make bad ingenues. Ouch. I'm twenty-seven, myself, and I'm scared that I'll get the shaft when *I* reach the big—"

Breisi had obviously been listening. "Kik, could you maybe tell her about my last Pap smear, too, since you're spilling my whole life?"

"Sorry." Kiko opened his door and climbed out.

Dawn followed suit, marveling that a loquacious little person and a teddy-bear-shirt-wearing grump were the ones who'd been appointed to find Frank. She'd already talked to the police about his disappearance, but hadn't been assured by their blasé tone that they were invested in finding him. Maybe she'd call again later tonight, now that there was officially no hope left.

Everyone shut their doors quietly. A dog barked in the near

distance, mingling with the wind, making the night seem that much more unfriendly.

"Just out of curiosity," Dawn asked, "how did my dad fit into a . . ." *whacked out* ". . . place like Limpet and Associates?"

Breisi tucked her thumbs into her belt loops and looked off into the bushes. Leaves rustled, dancing to an eerie song.

"Mr. Frank Madison was our best PR man," Kiko said, his voice still hushed. "He was good at taking people into his confidence, and he could fight, too. Real good, and believe me, that's a nice skill to have handy in this job."

As the bushes rattled, Breisi opened her jacket and slid her hand into a pants pocket at the same time, like she was tuned in to a frequency Dawn couldn't hear. But Kiko was looking at Dawn like she should already know what kind of life her dad led.

She didn't. From what Dawn knew of Frank, he was a good-time guy, a former bar bouncer who'd managed to charm his way into Eva Claremont's pants one vulnerable night. The scandal had rocked the tabloids because this was before Madonna got busy with her personal trainer and made the whole star-falls-for-normal-mortal trend "the thing."

"Yo, Kiko." It was Breisi. She'd gone stiff, one hand poised near her gun, the other near a pants pocket as she watched the bushes. "Be prepared."

Spurred by her sharp tone, he immediately turned into Serious Kiko and stuck a hand in an open cargo pants pocket. There was a bulge there, something Dawn hadn't gotten a bead on before.

"Wasn't expecting this," he muttered.

Both of the PIs were focused on the strangely silent foliage. When had the rustling stopped?

Slowly, Dawn dragged her gaze there, too.

Three pairs of red eyes were staring, blinking.

Waiting.

Holy . . .

"Here," Breisi whispered.

Dawn felt something solid, steely, nudge her left hand. She opened her fingers and grabbed whatever the other woman was giving her. It didn't feel like a gun or a knife, items Dawn had been trained to use.

"And stop looking into their eyes," Kiko added. "Rule of thumb in this business? It's never a good idea to do that."

She followed his advice and glanced just above their steady red gazes. Were they guard dogs? Had Marla Pennybaker gotten defensive about them coming over to see her husband and set the hounds loose on them? Maybe looking into their eyes sent some kind of predatory message that would rile them up.

Dogs. Okay, she could handle this. She'd dealt with canine actors before.

Dawn raised the object she was gripping, ready and willing to fend them off.

But when she saw what Breisi had given her, she froze.

A silver crucifix.

And as one of the creatures moved forward, to the edge of the darkness, she realized that these sure as hell weren't dogs they were facing.

FIVE

THE DAMNED

EVEN before Dawn could choke out a question—*What are these things?*—Bresi shoved what was clearly a gun, a .45-caliber revolver, into Dawn's right hand.

"Listen, you must hold up the crucifix, cover me with the gun—you've been trained to use it, *si*?—and don't you bleeping move from that spot . . ."

Her voice trailed off, and Dawn had the bad feeling that Breisi was hightailing it back to the SUV, deserting them. When she heard a door pop open, her fears were confirmed. But then it sounded like Breisi was rooting around in that back storage area. For what? Shit! She'd left Dawn standing all alone with Kiko, who'd thrust out his own crucifix and gun and . . .

The red eyes were getting closer, framed by the hint of pale faces outlined in the darkness.

Damn it, what was she doing here again?

Dawn's gun and crucifix started shaking in her hands.

Gradually, moonlight revealed three black-clad creatures

hunching out of the trees, moving in a way she'd never imagined possible. It was like they were wildly palpitating heartbeats, stopping and starting in a fluttering stalking motion that iced her blood. More out of panic than anything else, Dawn pushed her crucifix at them, corrected her grip on the revolver.

Closer. Dear Lord . . .

Even bent over, they were hulking, like jittering shadows looming against a pale wall. Their skin was white and shot through with blue veins, their heads hairless, their hands shriveled into sharp claws. When they hissed at the crucifixes—a throaty whistle that rose above the wind—a peek of dull gray caught the faint light: fangs. Iron, sharpened to points.

Dawn's legs wobbled, but she stood, damned if she would back down from anything—even a . . . whatever these were.

Just cowboy up, she told herself. Just do it.

Surprisingly, Kiko didn't seem to be much affected. He took a cool step toward them, brandishing his weapons. "Talk to us before we mess you up."

Talk?

Dawn's head scrambled into itself, dizzy cuts of nightmare flashes. Not real, she kept thinking. Make-up, prosthetics, fake movie monsters . . .

As Kiko took another step forward, the things cringed and shrieked at his crucifix. It was like the silver symbols provided some sort of force field, pushing the creatures back.

Dawn imitated him, emphasizing her own crucifix. In the background, she heard Breisi's feet hit the ground running.

Kiko was mere yards away from the things now. "Not a chatty crowd? Fine. If you're capable, just tell me why you're here, that's all."

That's when Dawn did something stupid.

Out of habit, a split second of forgetfulness, she looked one of them in the eyes.

Red fire, sucking her in.

She dropped her crucifix, helpless.

Kiko and Breisi yelled something at the same moment, but she had no idea what they were saying. She just knew that she wanted to jump into the fire, wanted to end it all because everything was so, so hopeless.

Her dad was missing; she was a pariah in the movie industry; she was a loser . . .

Unable to stop herself, she raised her gun, wanting to point it at her head, wanting to fill all the empty spaces inside of her with lead and peace. Wanting—

A million jagged shards through her mind—the memory of this evening in The Voice's office . . . fighting off the personal intrusion . . . struggling to get back her body, her mind . . .

Get out of my head, you asshole.

With a determined cry, Dawn jerked her gaze away, feeling her sanity rush back. Separating from the eyes had been like tearing away from an umbilical cord that had given her dark serenity and direction, even for a muddled instant.

Stumbling backward, she sucked in a choking breath, focusing back on reality with sharp, growing horror.

Wouldn't you know it? The creatures had backup plans.

Without missing a beat, the things all turned their backs at the same time, and that's when Dawn, even in her fluster, noticed a detail she'd missed from the frontal view.

Tails. Long, barbed, whip-fast.

One tail whooshed out to knock the crucifix from Kiko's hand. The others sang through the air, propelling the remaining two creatures skyward into stop-and-start-motion flight.

One barreled toward Breisi, who was aiming what looked like a crossbow at it.

And the other was zooming toward Dawn.

Tunnel vision swirled around her, blocking out everything but the next second and then the one after that—thuds of time that sped by much too quickly, bringing the monsters with them. Instinctively, she bent her knees and aimed the gun at her own attack creature. But she was too slow.

It'd already doubled its tail back, then sliced it through the air in a stuttering, whistling arc that blurred her sight. Before Dawn could process the motion, it had swept her legs out from under her, a stinging shock of agony cutting through her jeans and to the flesh of one of her calves, the force of its tail-snap crashing her to the ground. Her gun went flying out of her hand.

For a stunned second, Dawn saw something blinking at her from the black sky.

Stars. Those are called stars, and you're on your back looking at them, you idiot. . . .

A swooping sound forced her to spring to a crouch, just as she'd been trained to do. Her leg was smarting, but there was no chance to think about that as a long tail flashed at her. Dawn ducked, glanced madly around for her gun, spied it about three feet away. She was vaguely aware of Kiko and Breisi tangling with the other two things, but that was white noise.

All Dawn could register was that she needed to survive, needed to overcome the thumping blood in her veins, the fast-forward zoom of a fight she didn't know if she could handle since it wasn't choreographed move by move.

Without glancing at the creature, she knew deep in her gut that it had caught sight of her gun, too. An endless moment passed as Dawn felt the thing crouching on the ground, staring at her, daring her to go for her weapon.

Ga-gump, ga-gump . . .

Her heartbeat darted around each chopping catch of breath. Don't look at it, she kept thinking. Don't you dare look at that thing again. Its gaze is like *your* crucifix. . . .

Damn it, she had to get that revolver. Had to—

A drawn-out hiss reminded her that her enemy was only a few feet away.

Get it before it gets you!

Adrenaline bursting, she sprang toward the weapon, ears full of that whipping tail's scream. But before she could get to the gun, the creature flew right next to it, landing on all fours, challenging her.

Fear speared through Dawn's belly: these things could fly with the propulsion of their tails. They could hurt her with the barbed end of them. And those fangs . . . those long, sharp iron fangs . . .

With a flash of white, the creature spit at her.

Swallowing a shocked grunt, she dodged to the side, but not before the stream of moisture hit her arm with a sizzling burn.

"*Ahhh!*" Dawn darted away from another expectoration, while the spit ate away at her flesh. She gritted her teeth to keep from yelling again as she scrambled out of the monster's present range. Just in front of her, grass crackled, charred from the fluids.

"Dawn—duck and cover!"

Breisi's voice. Like a good stuntperson, Dawn followed directions, obeying her gut instinct as well as Breisi, because when you felt fear marching its cold little feet up your spine, you didn't think twice about getting out of the way.

Heaving herself to the ground, she flattened her body, catching a glimpse of Breisi rising up behind the creature, just to its left. The woman was aiming that crossbow, and after doing a double take, Dawn realized that, instead of an arrow, it was loaded with a circle of silver blades, almost like a very long, wide-toothed electric saw.

As the creature straightened up and, sensing a new presence, cocked its head toward Breisi, the woman pulled the trigger.

The blades exploded out of the bow in a flash of sparks, whizzing through the air with a high squeal of friction.

Swick!

Frantically, Dawn used her feet to gain purchase on the ground and launch herself away as the thing's head popped off, serrated by the flying blades. Blood showered outward, barely missing Dawn as she rolled to safety, just in case the blood burned, too.

From the corner of her eye, she saw that the creature's headless body was still on alert, claws outstretched and frozen in its last moments. Then, with almost beautiful ease, the black clothing sucked into itself, the body losing form and disappearing.

Whoa. Whoa, whoa, whoa, whoa . . .

The babbling litany continued in her head as she grabbed the revolver and bolted to her feet, ignoring her boiling wounds. She was just doing a job, right? Another day, another dollar. Nothing but a gig on Quentin Tarantino's set being catapulted through windows and beaten to a pulp by sadists while collecting higher pay adjustments for the stunt's difficulty. She could take it. *Screw* these freakin' mothers, she wasn't going to be deadweight to Kiko and Breisi.

The lies kept her sane—for now.

Breisi was already working on wrenching her circle of blades from the tree trunk where it'd embedded itself. Dawn also noticed that the first creature Breisi had been fighting wasn't around anymore.

Instead of asking what had happened to it—Dawn could kind of assume that Breisi had the superhero rah-rah to have taken it out already—she ran over to retrieve her crucifix, then search out Kiko.

She found him slowly moving among the trees, flashing his crucifix and gun like he really was a cop, except the crucifix made one odd badge. Without even looking, he motioned for Dawn to be quiet and still. He'd "read" her coming, she knew, but she wasn't in the mood to kick his butt for it. Not right now.

Using his chin, he gestured to the trees. Panting, Dawn took that to mean that a creature had whirred up to the treetops with its tail, probably to escape Breisi's death machine.

As the wind moaned past her body, a branch snapped somewhere to the left. Leaves shook to their right. Dawn took one direction while Kiko took the other.

Fake, she thought again. All of this is what you're used to handling on the job. No sweat.

Snap, went another branch in the near distance.

Pop, went another, in back of them this time.

Waiting, waiting . . . Dawn wanted to scream. She felt the

creature's eyes all over her, cold chills that reminded her exactly who the prey was.

But just as she was about to impulsively fire a bullet into the trees and beat the creature out of them, the thing took the initiative, whipping out of a bank of leaves right above them, its body shivering with that creepy stop-motion.

Its barbed tail whished past Dawn's face as she bent backward, barely avoiding its branding sting, even though it did smack her crucifix out of her grip. Expertly she recovered, twisted her body, spun around, and landed a kick to what felt like its head. In one smooth move, she brought her gun around, finally ready for more action.

The force of her kick had jammed it to the ground, but it wasn't helpless. Far from it. With its tail, it had engaged Kiko in taunting combat, wrapping its length around his gun arm and slamming the small guy to the ground as Kiko struggled to regain his balance.

And, lucky her, Dawn got the claws and teeth. The creature bent at the knees, biting at her, trying to scratch the crap out of her face. She dodged it, avoiding more injury only by virtue of her constant training. Vigilant practice had allowed her to read an opponent's intentions—a skill that wasn't tested nearly enough in all her staged fights.

Adrenalized, she rose to the challenge, getting more confident every time she eluded the creature's snapping teeth and flailing claws.

Swipe, feint. Bite, dodge.

Finally, Dawn snapped her gun up to its face, avoiding eye contact this time.

"Heart!" Kiko said. "Aim for the heart!"

She targeted.

From behind, Kiko yelled as the creature's tail flung him away, sending the psychic crashing against a tree. Then, without pause, the tail curved around, zinging and vibrating toward Dawn as her finger squeezed the trigger, and she dropped toward the ground.

The creature only beat her by a millisecond.

The tail smacked against her arm, sending her and the gun flying just as the shot rang out. Dawn ate dirt, but, by some miracle, found herself face to silver with her crucifix.

With a balls-out yell, she grabbed it and rolled to her back. The tail came flying toward her, the end gleaming like the barbs had somehow grown. She thrust up the crucifix, meeting the tail with it, pressing it against the creature, hearing a wheeze of steam as the pale flesh met its comeuppance.

The thing threw back its head and let out a tortured shriek.

Meanwhile, Kiko calmly stepped in front of it, raised his own gun, then fired into its heart.

At the impact, the creature seemed to self-implode, its mouth open in a silent scream, its iron fangs catching a slant of moonlight through the trees as it covered its bloodied chest with a claw. Tail snapping into itself and smacking the ground, the thing stumbled backward. Then, without further ado, it hissed into oblivion, just like Dawn's creature had done.

Its pile of black clothing simmered, bodiless, at the base of the tree as Kiko kept his gun and crucifix at the ready. Soon, the material burned to nothing.

"Breisi's pet ran away," he said, sounding slightly pained as he favored his left shoulder. Still, he was incredibly nonplussed, even with a stream of blood drying on his face. "And, damn, you did some bitchin' good work when you locked eyes with one earlier. No wonder the boss let you come with us. You might have some kind of resistance to mind tricks, Dawn, and he obviously knew that. I mean, jeez, making eye contact is a no-no because they can compel you if they so choose. I thought you were a goner."

In spite of the compliment, Dawn couldn't move from her spot on the ground. Literally. It was like she was in the midst of a quiet panic attack, just like when you hear a sound while you're trying to sleep, alone in the house, at midnight. A footstep down the hall, a shuffle of movement under your bed. A thud that makes you hope nothing has crept into your room.

It was at times like this that a body couldn't do anything but wait, wish, as if not moving will make whatever it is go away.

Dawn couldn't even ask Kiko if he thought Breisi's creature might come back for them, because from the way he was holding his weapons, the answer was obvious.

Moments later, Breisi joined them, all business with her first-aid kit taking the place of that crossbow.

She must've gone to the car, Dawn thought, careful not to move, careful not to disturb this fragile reprieve.

Straightaway, Breisi went to work, snapping on latex gloves, taking a sample of burned skin from Dawn's arm, depositing it in a container and capping it. Before she slathered some kind of stinking gel where the creature's spit had fizzed into flesh, then on the calf that'd been sliced by its tail, Breisi lingered near Dawn's silver arm bracelet. There were black char marks where the spit had hit it but, otherwise, the jewelry was unscathed.

As the older woman wrapped Dawn's leg in gauze, she noted, "Lucky. It didn't get you deep enough to need stitches."

Dawn didn't answer. She'd started trembling, low in her stomach. If she didn't want to find Frank so badly, she'd have burned rubber at the sight of that first crucifix.

But she did want to find him. *Had* to find her dad—the only realistic part of this whole freak show right now.

Through a slow haze, Dawn watched Breisi sit back on her haunches and inspect her. She had a streak of dirt on one cheek, but that was it. Unruffled. A new sense of respect washed over Dawn, a sort of reluctant awe of Breisi and Kiko. A grudging thankfulness.

Kiko, limping slightly, came over to join the proceedings. In addition to the blood on his face, his pants were torn. "Think she'll be okay? She ain't looking so hot."

"She won't turn, if that's what you're asking, fool. That thing spit at her and . . . check it out . . . the stuff *burns*."

"I got hit by its blood and it doesn't hurt." Kiko dabbed at the red on his forehead. "I just hope it doesn't contaminate me in any way."

"Boss says you need an exchange of blood for the change, so don't worry your pretty head about it."

"Thanks for explaining, Van Helsing. I knew *that*."

Breisi went back to fussing, plucking at a glove. And why not—it'd been a whole few minutes since she'd gotten to whirl around like a hurricane.

"Besides," she added, "you're the one who had that vision about Dawn being 'key.' *You* tell *me* if she'll be okay."

Kiko nodded, already convinced. "Well, I suppose being key means she'll man up and stop being in shock pretty soon."

Breisi stopped fidgeting and glanced at him. "We went through the same thing at our first sighting, Kik. And we never had this level of confrontation with a vamp before."

They were talking like Dawn wasn't even there. And maybe she wasn't. Maybe she'd checked out of her mind and all that was left was for her to lay here just staring straight ahead, hearing the conversation like it was being held in an echo chamber.

She saw the psychic poke at Breisi. Back to Happy Kiko. "Did you see me in action? My kill disappeared, just like steam. Sweet, huh?"

"Mine did the same thing after decapitation."

Breisi kept watching Dawn, who merely watched back.

"Oh." Kiko went quiet. "Hell, just because you lop the head off them doesn't make you any more creative, you know."

Something flickered inside Dawn. Annoyance at Kiko. She *was* okay, thank God.

"Jeez, Kik, let's not be jealous of my saw-bow." Breisi was also irritated. "And don't make this into a monster slaying contest, because you'll lose."

"Silver bullet to the heart," Kiko said. "Tell me that's an everyday headline. I'm so good at this."

Breisi was still watching, but Dawn didn't have the strength to physically react just yet. Instead, her eyes started to close, just for a blessed second. . . .

A smack to Dawn's cheek made her start to attention.

Breisi was staring at her, still gauging.

Skin stinging, Dawn lightly smacked Breisi right back by using her good arm. Tit for tat.

"Ooo, girlfight," Kiko said.

But Breisi didn't seem too put out about it. In fact, she smiled a little, then stood. "Get your booty up, Dawn. We've got a lot to do."

Pissed at being challenged, Dawn slowly rose to her feet, touching her arm as Breisi went about tending to Kiko's minor injuries. The gel was tingling on her wounds, reminding her of how close she'd come to being cut into Dawn McNuggets.

"Thank you," she said softly. "I . . ."

Words failed her. She wasn't so great at this, even if she was grateful.

As if agreeing, Breisi paused, then obviously decided to go easy on her, nodding toward Dawn's arm. "Let me know if there's pain. I've used a new balm on you, my own concoction made with a lot of advice from the boss. I just hope it works like it's supposed to. I'll check on it later."

"Vampires," Dawn shook her head. "*Vampires*, you guys."

Currently under Breisi's ministrations, Kiko shrugged. "You're going to get to know more than you ever wanted about vamps, ghosts, ghouls, or whatever hides in every little kid's closet. If you stick with this, that is."

Dawn managed to look offended, partly because Kiko had taken a jab at her pride. "I'm not going to quit."

Turning her back, Breisi bent down and started to pack her first-aid kit.

Kiko gave Dawn another once-over, then motioned toward the lip of the tree stand. They started to walk toward civilization, knowing Breisi would catch up.

"Now that you're a believer . . ." he said, giving her an I-told-you-so glance.

She just blew out a breath.

". . . there're a million things to know, Dawn, starting with the fact that there're all kinds of vamps. All kinds of ghouls. Night to night, we're never sure what we'll be dealing with, and some of them are even good eggs, believe it or not."

Dawn's laugh was cutting. "A decent vampire?"

"They exist, and that's why I tried to talk with these guys before defending."

"Holy mother, Kiko, how did you get involved with this stuff?"

He shrugged. "The boss found both me and Breisi about a year ago, tested us with those mind powers he tried on you today, except our tests were more PG, if you know what I mean."

Even though she was still in the getting-over-the-monster-attack stage, Dawn whipped up a dirty look at his nosiness.

Kiko offered a cheeky grin. "When the boss first hired us for 'odd jobs,' as he called it, it was a good paycheck between auditions. We trained, got educated in supernatural lore, trained some more. Little by little, the boss made the paranormal commonplace, even though Breisi had experienced a lot of it when she was younger. I did, too, but my talents weren't nearly as good before the boss showed up. Then there came a night when he thought we were ready enough to hit the streets, to start searching out 'the unexplainable,' as he calls it. Usually, we just report what we find to him. Well, that and a few tangles with a cranky vamp or a sour ghost. Boss is looking for something real specific. . . ."

He shut up, obviously unwilling to go on.

Dawn's temper flared, surprise, surprise. "Come, on, Kiko, what's he—"

"L.A. is a cesspool of paranormal activity." He was Serious Kiko now. "We've been kept busy, but not like tonight. Jeez, *these* vamps . . . We've never seen 'em before."

Soft footsteps picked up speed behind them. With one glimpse over her shoulder, Dawn saw Breisi, her head down as she followed them back to the car.

"But if they're hanging out here, it looks like we're getting close to something," Kiko said.

“Why didn’t you prepare me for the vamps?”

As they returned to the car, Kiko looked mortally wounded. “I didn’t feel them coming. My talents don’t seem to work on vamps the way they do on everything else. Besides, I was expecting more of a ghost, and I think the boss wasn’t sure, himself. Believe me, Dawn, the last thing we want to do is get you hurt.”

A tiny twinge needled her chest, but she shrugged it off—especially when Kiko glanced away from her, abruptly playing with his torn clothes, distractedly trying to put himself together. As for Breisi, she was performing the same number, concentrating oh-so-intensely on stowing the first-aid kit.

Vamps. Ghosts. Things that went bump in the night.

She nodded toward Breisi. “What about her?”

“What *about* her?”

Dawn wanted to know why the other woman wasn’t as aching and bruised as she was, wanted to know why a petite lab rat had trumped Dawn’s own tough ass during the brawl.

“How can she deal with all this?” she asked.

Kiko seemed to actually weigh the act of revealing more about the private Breisi against his own raging need to verbalize anything and everything.

Luckily, he couldn’t fight his nature.

He lowered his voice. “Breisi grew up in a bad part of San Diego. I guess her dad was in jail half the time, and her mom was one of those suffer-in-silence types. Breisi told me once that three things got her though those years: the determination to get a college scholarship, the conversations she had with the ghost of her *abuelita*, and a good right hook.”

“She sees dead people?” Dawn whispered.

“Not anymore. When she got out of that house on a free ride to USC, the visitations stopped. She could have just been using them as a coping mechanism when she needed it the most.” He puffed up a little, the competitive guy. “That’s what I think, anyway.”

“And The Voice found her . . . how?”

"He saw her on *Bandito*. She got that job when a producer spotted her waitressing, and she used some of her salary to save up for engineering grad school. The producers used to worship her. I mean, why not—she's gorgeous and can work the hell out of a crying scene. But she never loved acting, just the paycheck. Grad school costs an arm and a leg, even with financial help, and she was sending money to her ingrate mom, too. But"—here, Kiko motioned Dawn closer, and she bent next to him, ear near his mouth—"she eventually got fired and our boss was there to take up where *Bandito* left off. He needed someone who was tech-savvy and she needed . . . someone. When it comes right down to it, we're more of a real family to Breisi than her other one ever was—"

Kiko cleared his throat when Breisi brushed by them on her way to the mansion's door. Once there, she knocked and sent her coworkers a piercing glance that made Kiko zip his lips.

The house's front porch light blared on, and an old woman, her shoulders hunched, her skin listless, opened the door. Her mouth went agape at seeing the PI team in such disheveled attire.

"Mrs. Pennybaker," Breisi the good cop said. She was holding a dark duffel bag now, and Dawn could only guess at what the hell was in it.

"That was a long trip up the driveway," the old woman said.

"We had some matters to attend to before we knocked."

Mrs. Pennybaker broke into an anxious fret. "Are you here with more news about Robby?"

"Not yet, ma'am," Breisi said gently. "I'm sorry."

That one faint glint of Marla Pennybaker's hope exploded in the crumbling of her posture; it reminded Dawn of how those vampires had disappeared into themselves, perishing.

When she looked closer, she saw that this wasn't a senior citizen at all. Mrs. Pennybaker couldn't have been older than her mid-fifties, but she'd been so beaten down by life, by the tragedy of her son, that most of her had already died.

A ghost, Dawn thought. Then she pictured her dad—vital and

full of smiles—in all his old pictures with Eva. She remembered the reality of how much he'd changed after her mom had died one month after giving birth to Dawn.

Ghost.

She glanced at Marla Pennybaker again, pitying her. Knowing her.

Because, like this woman, both Dawn and Frank had also lost something along the way.

Making them restless, empty spirits, too.

SIX

Below, Phase One

WORKING the whip with skilled ease, Sorin sent one more lash to the bared back of the pale, massive Guard as it cowered against the stone wall.

"S . . . sorry," the beaten vampire said. "I'm sorry, Master."

Sorin relaxed the whip in mercy as the Guard slumped to the ground of its cell—its home. It had been reduced to groans at its punishment for failing so spectacularly on its mission tonight. The iron of its fangs decorated a grimace; the barb of its sharp tail beat against the stone in pathetic time.

Even though it was Sorin's job to discipline the Guards, among other residents of the Underground, he couldn't bring himself to strike at the poor creature again. It already understood what had gone wrong: the drone, plus his two newly created comrades who had gone Above tonight, had been careless while tracking their quarry. Once they had been detected, they had panicked, attacking when they should have retreated.

That was the problem with the Guards—expendable, lower-rank

vampires. They had limited intelligence, the better to follow orders with. Starting immediately, Sorin would have to improve their skills in judging a situation, as well as in how to fight more effectively Above, *if* required.

"You have learned not to attack any humans who will be missed?" Sorin asked, walking to the corner of the cell where he had set down a bowl of sustenance for the Guard.

At the sight of dinner, the creature's tongue lolled out of its mouth in sad anticipation of the cold, secondhand blood. "Yes, Master, yes. Food?"

Sorin tilted the bowl, watching the discarded blood from the feeding he, himself, had enjoyed not ten minutes ago as it lapped against the porcelain. Disgusting, this cold, leftover meal, but it was what kept the Guards alive and happy.

He set the bowl on the ground, locking gazes with the red-eyed creature as it began panting for its meal. When Sorin left the unlocked cell, the vampire buried its face in the bowl, sucking and growling in pleasure.

Heading for the emporium, Sorin left the creature to its ecstasy and walked the electric lamp–lined tunnels that held the Guards' cells.

His harsh treatment with the whip did not bother him. Now was the time for vigilance, as far as matters Above were concerned; that is why the Guards had finally been sent up. In the past year, there had been a breach of security, an escape, and a crack in the armor of their leadership. During these trying times, it was more important than ever to keep calm, to remain hidden and discreet under the streets of Los Angeles. The Underground had been flourishing for barely over half a century—a speck of time in the history of the world—but what they had established was something worth protecting.

Sorin was not about to allow one wrinkle to ruin it all.

As he pulled open the heavy steel door that fortified the emporium, he was overcome by a veritable misted bacchanal. Sheer veils all but masked the silken beds decorating the marbled floors as incense and loud, primal music laced the air. On those beds, bare bodies, their skin glistening with sweat and exotic oils, twined together. Sorin passed one particular large, circular, pillow-strewn mattress, where a band of Groupies, silver-eyed, lithe, and gorgeous in their preternatural states, were entertaining three human Servants whom they had invited from Above for the night. With slow, predatory grace, they slid against each other, legs spreading, tongues licking, voices moaning. One Groupie, a petite brunette wearing nothing but a belly chain, was crawling toward a Servant from Above who worked as a Wilshire Boulevard talent agent. She kissed her way up his shin, his thigh, his hip and stomach and chest, pausing at his neck. There she sucked at him, toying with him as he writhed beneath her, then—

Pure need clenched inside Sorin as she bit into the Servant, nursing at him while the others scented his blood and nipped at his exposed skin, drawing their own red.

Never enough, Sorin thought, continuing past the mammoth screens that showcased MTV and connected them to the world Above, past a landscaped waterfall pool, where one of their elite citizens lounged under the kisses of a Groupie.

A little blood is never enough.

Citizens greeted him with royal deference, turning from their crystal flutes filled with blood and bowing, touching their fingers to their foreheads as he walked by. It was not until he reached the fringes of the room, where dark met velvet, that he could melt into the shadows behind a heavy red drape. There, he traveled another tunnel until he reached a door that the eye would have to be trained to see. Pressing a stone panel, he entered his Master's domain.

The Master.

As usual, he sat in the dark, in one of his black moods. Sorin's vampire sight caught the red haze of the Master's outline, the emptiness of his soul.

Even his television—the lifeline to Above—was silent.

The Master had been keeping to himself for years now, away from the Groupies and Servants and Guards. Only Sorin, the second in command, and the elite citizens gained audience with the Master, and that was because the Elites' silence was guaranteed through an exchange of blood and money: they did not dare reveal that Sorin was not really the one in charge of the Underground.

Their punishment for that would be swift and devastating.

But, these past few years, the Master's loneliness had reached a peak, and this concerned Sorin.

"News?" the Master asked in a lifeless whisper, one that all but covered a foreign accent that had faded with time and educated effort.

Sorin tried not to lose hope at this further evidence of decline. Over three centuries ago, when the Master had first made Sorin a vampire, he was full of colorful moods and the desire to explore. But gradually that had changed. Sorin had noticed the exhaustion, the almost destructive carelessness with which the Master had been making decisions lately.

He was tired of existing, and that was living death for a vampire.

Sorin could not stand by and watch it happen. Could not bear to see his maker waste away. As a first step to righting matters, he settled on giving the positive news before the negative. "All the Elites, except the one, are doing well."

"Good." He sounded disinterested.

Sorin's frustration welled. That led to anger and impulse. "Would it elicit a reaction if I mentioned that three Guards had a run-in with humans tonight? And these humans happen to be ones our Servants and Groupies have noticed asking questions Above during the last year? They killed two Guards."

A shimmer of movement told Sorin that the Master had become more interested. "I did feel something earlier . . ."

Sorin remained calm, vampire-cool. "You *felt* something a year ago as well, Master, but after the initial scare, you were lax. You have—"

"That's enough, Sorin."

He fisted his hands. He wanted to say so much more. Wanted to remind the Master that his Awareness was the first defense against danger, that if another master was in the area, they needed to discover if his intentions were civil or malicious. A lot had happened since all the masters had separated and created their own secret undergrounds over a century ago. And, once some of the others were discovered, there had been takeovers, wipeouts of entire vampire societies, although it was true that the other masters did not always have ill intentions. Some of them were loners, seeking to join established undergrounds; some wished to wed their own societies with a more dominant one in order to strengthen their numbers.

Perhaps the Master had not aggressively responded to the first throb of Awareness one year ago because he did not wish to face what had occurred with his *first* Underground. Understandable, yet Sorin had attempted time and again to convince his maker to be proactive in any matters of defense. He recalled the terror of losing the first paradise all too well. However, with the threat, the Master had seemed to delve that much deeper into secrecy, avoiding the issue, without taking the precautions Sorin feared they required.

All the same, did the Master not see what could happen? Sorin knew that his maker's mind powers—the Awareness that allowed him to feel those other masters and keep track of his own blood children—had grown weak with boredom and lack of care. In Sorin's opinion, this left the Underground vulnerable, and he had a heavy feeling that the Master was in the process of surrendering, though it was impossible for a master to commit suicide, due to the oath taken so long ago.

But if the Master had lost his will . . .

The older vampire sighed, world-weary and final. "Go outside and play, Sorin. We both know that hunters are legion in this country, in Los Angeles. We've dealt with them and eluded them for years."

"Even so," Sorin continued, risking his Master's further wrath—

an emotion he would have welcomed at this point—"you have already had one notable sign of danger—the Awareness you felt of another and have been shielding against for a year." Here, Sorin heard the Master lean forward in his chair, and the bold gesture pushed him to continue. "And *now* you have these humans who are capable of decimating two Guards. . . ."

Sorin stopped, wondering if he had overstepped his bounds, glad to have done so.

"Go on," the Master said.

Holding back a victorious smile—finally, some concern—Sorin added, "Our surviving Guard told me something disturbing. While listening, they heard the humans mention Frank Madison, and one of their own referred to him as being her father."

"Really." The Master slowly sat back in his chair, then gave a short, mirthless laugh.

There, Sorin thought. Another flicker of interest, a flinch of the sleeping giant.

Ever since the invention of moving pictures, the Master had been enthralled. He watched all the movies, learned from them, even lived through them. Eva Claremont's life was manna to him—her films, her A&E biography, her E! Entertainment special reports.

"Eva Claremont's daughter was at the Pennybakers'," the Master said, as if turning the thought over in his mind, prodding it to see how it reacted under an outside influence.

"I assume she is looking for her father."

"She probably is. And maybe that's all there is to it."

Silence buzzed the darkness as the second in command waited for the Master to filter the information, to command Sorin in his passion to keep the Underground safe.

But when the Master did not say another word, Sorin braved one last comment.

"Keeping track of these humans is a necessity. I request more of a presence Above, even if we have to press more Servants into service, or if . . ."

Sorin gestured to his chest, offering himself up for anything the Master might require.

All the same, black silence reigned while Sorin deferred to his maker, all but raging while the Master decided if he cared enough to protect the Underground. . . .

Or if Sorin would have to take matters into his own hands right here and now.

SEVEN

The Ghost of the Past

THE Pennybakers' air-conditioned parlor was a stark depository for blunt art: paintings and sculptures which were all circles and squares, severe black-cushioned furniture, white walls. The decor echoed Robby's mom, who looked like her soul had been turned into a deadened room ever since the death of her son twenty-three years ago.

Right now, Breisi was poised on the couch next to Nathan Pennybaker, her casual manner disguising what Dawn recognized as building questions. Sure, there'd been some introductory small talk after the missus had expressed her surprise at seeing the bruised and torn Limpet associates at her front door, but it'd only been a formality.

Dawn could see the good-cop/bad-cop pattern emerging. Breisi, uncharacteristically loose and friendly. Kiko, glowering in the corner while holding some of Robby's old clothes, just to see if he could get any new vibes off of them.

In the meantime, Dawn sat quietly on the fringes, sweat drying to stickiness on her bruised skin as she gripped one of the glasses of iced tea Mrs. Pennybaker had served. Since there was no fighting involved in this round, she was *really* out of her element, and that humbled her, made her uncomfortable and frustrated. Still, she was savvy enough to know that watching how Kiko and Breisi worked the room would be way more beneficial than opening her mouth to ask all the questions knocking at her.

There was especially a lot to learn from seeing Breisi finesse Nathan Pennybaker, yet it was all Dawn could do to keep from ripping into him and the missus about how Robby had been allowed to get so out of control.

In contrast to his prematurely ancient wife, hubby was well adjusted and well fed, his stomach rounded under the silk of an Armani shirt. His skin glowed with health and probably a good European facial or two. His graying hair was carefully styled in one of those Roman senator cuts; Dawn guessed that old Nathan had been too busy snacking on gnocchi and manicotti to notice that *Gladiator* was out of the theaters, the hairdo dead and buried in the cemetery of unfortunate trends.

"I'm sure you understand the reason we couldn't contact you immediately upon my return," he was saying to Breisi. He clasped his hands together and stared at his manicured nails. "Being back in this house is hard enough. Talking about Robby . . ."

Nathan had one of those pseudo-Euro accents. It was almost enough to detract from the fact that he'd lost a son just as horrifically as his traumatized wife had. But at least he'd moved on . . . something Dawn had tried so hard to do, too.

Across the room, Kiko traded one of Robby's T-shirts for another. Immediately, his compact body tensed.

Was he feeling something? What was he seeing?

Breisi seemed not to notice the show since she was busy patting Mr. Pennybaker's shoulder. "I understand, Nathan. But I'm sure you see the need for taking another look at Robby's situation."

A pained sigh came from Mrs. Pennybaker. "The film. He was right there, alive!"

When Dawn saw yet another anxious gleam in the woman's eyes, her stomach tightened. Mrs. Pennybaker was never going to get her little twelve-year-old Robby back again, even if he *had* returned as something else. Earlier, before Nathan had come downstairs, Breisi had tried to tell Marla about the red-eyed vamps, but the old woman wasn't hearing any of it. In fact, she was refusing to hear any talk of paranormalcy. But why? Hadn't she thought something was weird when a supernatural PI agency offered to take her case?

At Nathan's appearance, Breisi had backed off, though Dawn guessed she'd be sitting Marla down for another talk later. Instead, the actress had reassured the old woman. "In the end, we're out to see to the peace of Robby and your family, Mrs. Pennybaker, just as Mr. Limpet promised."

Now, Dawn couldn't help relating to Marla's reluctance to hear whacked-out theories. As it was, there was something bothering Dawn—Robby's age, his appearance in the film. . . .

She stirred in her seat, whiting out her brain, still in partial denial about what had gone on tonight, even though she'd seen—*felt*—more than enough proof.

In his seat, Kiko relaxed, peered at Robby's shirt, then laid it down gently. He was frowning, and when his eyes met Dawn's, he shook his head. Not a good sign.

"May I ask," Breisi said to Mr. Pennybaker, "why you left the country?"

Kiko slid out of his chair, coming to a stand, using his intimidator glare as he limped to where Nathan could see him. Dawn could tell the psychic was digging deep into the man's mind, searching for all the words that weren't being voiced.

The dapper manager cleared his throat and focused on Breisi, studiously avoiding Kiko. "I left because I couldn't take the reminders. I *stayed* away because I found a home in Bari, Italy. An old college friend had moved there, and it was far away from L.A. . . ." He closed his eyes. "I couldn't bring myself to come back until now."

All the while, Dawn was cataloguing Mrs. Pennybaker's reactions. She was fisting, then unfisting, her veined hands, spreading them flat against her thighs as if forcing herself to peace. Her face remained a wrinkled mask, emotionless except for the eyes. Dawn tried to decipher what was being reflected in them—anger? resentment? affection?—but she couldn't. She wasn't Kiko, with his skill for understanding how people thought.

A twinge of profound isolation grabbed her again. She just wanted to wake up and find herself back at yesterday, back in Virginia, hammering nails and not knowing that Frank had been hunting vampires.

Yeah. Hunting. Vampires.

How the hell had her dad gotten into this? And why?More than ever, she realized how much of a stranger he was.

The alienation expanded, gnawing at her, dredging up the hunger, the need to feel a part of something. She started to ache, to itch for some fulfillment, however temporary.

As Dawn sat there throbbing away, she realized that Breisi and Kiko were trading one of those meaningful glances again.

Breisi stood. "Mrs. Pennybaker, would it be okay if I used the restroom?"

Ah, Dawn thought. The locator.

"Of course." The old woman started to get up.

"Oh, no, I can find it." Breisi pointed to the hallway. "Through here?"

"Yes."

The room was quiet as Breisi left. Subtly, Kiko took his associate's place on the couch, looking as confident as Mel Gibson, except for the fact that his legs didn't reach the floor.

"We've read the police report and heard different accounts," he said to Nathan, "but we haven't really gotten your side of the story."

"The story," Mr. Pennybaker repeated, eyebrows knitted.

"The story." Kiko glanced at Mrs. Pennybaker. "The night Robby . . ."

". . . left," she finished.

She was watching Kiko, her lower lip trembling. Maybe it was because his small body made him look so much like a boy. Maybe it was because she was seeing Robby in her memories.

At any rate, Dawn thought, Mrs. Pennybaker hadn't used the word "died."

Her husband had stiffened in his seat. "I fail to understand why this will help, Mr. Daniels. Rehashing this is upsetting my wife and—"

"You might know some details that can help us now," Kiko said. "Robby's out there . . . somewhere . . . and we need to do everything we can to find him."

"Please," Mrs. Pennybaker said, still staring at Kiko. "Tell him, Nathan."

Bit by bit, the man wilted, then ran a hand through his neat hair. "It's not going to help. Robby's gone."

Kiko nodded. Then he pulled a Breisi, resting his hand on Nathan Pennybaker's shoulder in "comfort."

A reading, Dawn thought, again impressed by Kiko's confidence and ease, by the talents he so easily wielded.

Mrs. Pennybaker sat back in her chair, closed her eyes, and covered her face with one hand, as if to shield herself. Dawn imagined that her own grief about Eva Claremont would be just as fresh if she'd seen her mom's image in a recent movie, if she'd been given more hope about getting her back, too.

"I wasn't even there when he . . ." Mr. Pennybaker said, forehead wrinkling. "Robby had snuck out to our housekeeper's cottage on her night off and was experimenting with her pill stash. He overdosed back there, and he wasn't discovered until later that night. Ingrid, the housekeeper, found him."

Mrs. Pennybaker was shaking her head, in total denial.

"She's the one who killed herself?" Kiko asked, with more gentleness than Dawn would've ever given him credit for.

"*It's all in the acting,*" he'd said by the car earlier, spreading out his arms dramatically. The talent he'd boasted about was sure shining through now.

"Yes, that was Ingrid." Mr. Pennybaker grimaced. "She felt guilty about the pills and rightfully blamed herself for Robby's overdose."

Suddenly, Kiko seemed to get some kind of charge from his contact with the man's shoulder, because he jerked back his hand, as if scorched. Dawn leaned forward in her chair, but Kiko just shot her a wide-eyed I'll-tell-you-*later* glance.

Mrs. Pennybaker spoke, her voice muffled by her hand. "Robby had an accidental overdose—*he* didn't commit suicide." Her breath hitched in agony.

"Nobody said he did," Kiko offered. "We're not the press, Marla. We don't jump to those kinds of conclusions."

Dawn remained silent. Twelve-year-olds were too young for addiction, for depression. Weren't they? Even in this town?

"I just wanted to make sure that was clear," Marla added. "They never found his body after it disappeared. How . . ." She laughed, a trace of nervous disbelief in the sound. ". . . how does a body disappear from the morgue?"

Good question, Dawn thought, turning her face from a mother's raw grief. And what kind of world allowed Robby's perversely wild lifestyle *and* his missing body to make him a shining star in the annals of Hollywood lore?

Her throat dry, she sipped her drink, the ice rattling in the silence, echoing against the walls and high ceiling.

Luckily, Breisi returned. While Kiko got to his feet again, she kneeled next to her duffel bag. Thanks to the psychic's diversion, Dawn might've been the only one to see her associate slide a small, metal object—the locator—inside the canvas as she extracted two other pieces of equipment.

Standing, Breisi unwrapped a wire from around a white rectangle while holding another palm-sized instrument in her other hand. She came over to Dawn, pushed one of the dealy-bobs at her.

"Here," she said. "Just hold this level to your body as you walk around—it reads from the front only. Look for oscillation in the numbers, okay? Oh, and careful around electrical outlets—they'll mess up the results."

Filled with even *more* questions, Dawn sat there, looking at the foreign doodad.

"Excuse me," Nathan Pennybaker said, "but what are those?"

Breisi stood still, watching the handheld white rectangle as she held the connected wire out in front of her.

Kiko answered, all important-like. "Tools of the trade. Ms. Montoya is using a thermo-anemometer, a sort of temperature gauge. She's taking the base reading of the room right now so we'll get a foundation for comparison as she tests different parts of the house for deviations in temperature. Ms. Madison will be using a magnetometer, which searches for shifts in the electromagnetic field."

Smiling like a *Price is Right* model, Dawn tentatively held out her magnetic thingie to Mr. Pennybaker, not comfortable in doing anything else with it, really.

"What's the purpose?" the man asked, eyes narrowed.

While Breisi tapped her foot, waiting for the base temp to show up, the missus rubbed her hand down her face. "Let them do their jobs, Nathan."

"We're seeing if there's any paranormal activity around here," Kiko said. "We've tested the premises before, but because of what happened outside tonight—"

It was like an invisible puppetmaster yanked Mr. Pennybaker out of his seat. "Para-what? I . . . Turn those things off!"

"Nathan . . ." Mrs. Pennybaker's voice was pleading.

"No, Marla, this is ridiculous. Robby is dead. Do you get that? It's been twenty-three years. He's gone." Wearily, he dropped to his knees in front of her chair.

She stared at him, so cold, so remorseful. "He's back, Nathan. On that film—"

"We'll talk about this later," he rasped. He calmed himself, started stroking his wife's leg. "Just . . . believe me. Okay? Those days are past, Marla. We need to move on, go to the next stage of life. Don't put us through this. . . ."

His voice broke, and he pressed his limp body to his wife's knees, wrapping his arms around her legs. Haltingly, Marla rested a hand on his head, emotionless once again, her gaze a million miles away.

She raised those empty eyes to Dawn, whispered, "We'll continue later."

By silent communication, the three of them agreed to return at another time to use their instruments. They left a shattered Nathan Pennybaker on the ground, shriveled next to his wife.

Even after they'd packed up their gear and loaded themselves into the SUV, they didn't say anything. There was a thread of compassion for the Pennybakers that was holding the team together, stifling their voices. In the quiet rhythm of tires whirring over the driveway as they drove to the bottom of the property, Dawn's loneliness returned full force.

So did her desperation, her yearning for a fix—a human touch of reassurance, a cleansing rush of release and forgetfulness. As they passed the gates, Dawn's unrest only grew, her body keening from more than just the physical injuries she'd sustained tonight.

Once on the road, Kiko's mouth took off.

"I really wanted to talk more about those vampires to them. But Mrs. P.—"

"Maybe tonight wasn't a good time," Dawn said softly, "what with Nathan suddenly returning and all."

"Ah, her reaction wasn't out of bounds. No one wants to believe in vamps." He took a peek at Dawn, then turned around.

Breisi finally spoke up. "Kik, punch the boss's number into the phone. He needs to know about those red-eyes."

Kiko did as he was asked. "And he can tell us how to approach this with the Pennybakers."

The ring tone trilled through the speakerphone, but there was no answer. Instead, after a mere beep, they left a message.

Kiko disconnected. "He always gets back to us."

Dawn wanted to ask what The Voice could possibly be doing besides waiting by the phone, but she knew she wouldn't get anything but the runaround. "So what do you guys think? Was it a wasted trip?"

"Not even," Kiko said. "Breisi planted a few bugs around the place so we can get some unadulterated scoop when Mr. Europe doesn't know we're listening." He caught Dawn's stern gaze. "Don't worry—it's procedure."

"You know what I want to know?" Dawn said as their vehicle roared down the avenue. "Why didn't those vamps show up before Nathan got home?"

Breisi plugged into her earpiece while Kiko shrugged. "Could be that we just haven't seen them before."

"Or maybe Mrs. Pennybaker didn't tell us they've been around," Dawn said.

Silence. Then, "All I know," Kiko said, "is that Maximus Suspiciouses there is hiding something."

Dawn remembered Kiko's flinch while he'd been touching Mr. Pennybaker. "You got a reading."

"Yeah, I sure as Sam did." Straining against the seat belt, Kiko draped himself over the passenger seat in his enthusiasm. "When he mentioned that housekeeper, I saw blood on his hands. I felt him screaming and panicking."

Dawn's pulse jerked.

"Funny," Kiko added. "I also got a reading from Robby's old clothes. Little boy memories—images of him studying with a tutor on a movie set, feelings of him looking out a limo's window at a schoolyard and wanting to be with the other kids. All cylinders were kicking, and I was really getting him." His forehead furrowed. "So if I was so on tonight, why didn't I get a read on those vamps outside the house? Better yet, why can't I sense vamps at all?"

The growl of the engine substituted for conversation.

"They don't have souls," Dawn said, knowing that everyone was aware of that fact. She'd just been the one to say it. "But I don't get how they move like they have something inside of them."

"They're animated," Kiko said.

"By what? Do they just not have consciences? Is that what a soul is?" At the thought, Dawn squirmed in her seat, suddenly uncomfortable with the direction of their talk. Frank hadn't raised her with much religion. In the years after Eva's death, there'd been a lot of "why" and "how could this happen." Too many reasons to lack faith.

Before anyone could engage her in some kind of Big Discussion, Dawn said, "I just wish I knew what was going on."

"We'll talk it out." Kiko turned back around, obviously sensing her funk, even without having to bust into her mind.

Breisi finally spoke up. "We'll meet up later, then. I've got a lot to do before we brainstorm. I need to get into the lab to test that skin sample I took from Dawn. Maybe I can get a hint of what's in that vamp spittle."

"All right. Our new consultant and I can do some more exploring. You up for that, Dawn?"

Absolutely. She'd drop from exhaustion rather than blow the chance to get more answers. Boiling frustration was keeping her awake, edgy.

"Ready if you are," she said.

"Good." Kiko smiled. "I've been checking at Frank's favorite hangout every night, just to see who walks in and who's willing to give me some worthwhile information."

"The Cat's Paw," Dawn said. "I picked Frank's drunk butt up from there more than once before I left town."

Breisi took an unnecessarily sharp turn onto the 405. Dawn slid to the door, her shoulder banging into it. She gasped but squelched the full yelp of her pain.

"*Perdone me*," the older woman said. "The Dodgers bleeping lost."

"Bummer," Dawn ground out.

"Would you just drive?" Kiko said, flicking Breisi in the ear like an irritating sibling.

Breisi shot him a hurtful glance, but stuck to her business.

They kept to their own thoughts on the way to Limpet and Associates, where they dropped off their taciturn driver. During the ride, Dawn had been fending off her disquietude, her body full of fevered wants, her mind conjuring scenarios of what she might find at the Cat's Paw besides information about Frank.

As she took the driver's seat, Kiko gave her a hard look. She blocked him, but it wasn't soon enough.

"We're going to the Cat's Paw to *work*," he said.

A flare of mortification charred her. "I know that."

"Just making sure you don't have any ulterior motives while we're slinking around the bar, Dawn. After we're done, you're going to need to come back with me, not go home with someone else, okay? Besides, you know there's bad stuff out there—AIDS, hepatitis C, and all that."

He angled away from her, probably anticipating a good wrist snatching.

"Is there something wrong with sex?" she asked, unflustered, even if she did want to belt him.

"No, no, you should just watch out a little more, you know? I probably deserve a good hit from you, but your vibes are so obvious that I couldn't shut up." A few seconds dragged by, and he finally relaxed at her stillness, letting down his guard and facing the front window. "We really do need you, Dawn. Be careful with yourself."

She jammed the vehicle in gear and took off, not bothering to answer. Wondering exactly why someone dared to need her.

And not liking it very much at all.

EIGHT

The Other PI

NESTLED on a lonely stretch of Hollywood Boulevard, the Cat's Paw was one of those places that hung rusted license plates on the walls as if they were fine art. It showcased vintage posters with things like 3-D women hefting sledgehammers over their heads, an act that, of course, made their size D breasts the focal point of every uber-heterosexual male within a mile radius. The walls were planked wood, the chairs high, wobbly, and swivelly. There was a polished faux-marble bar—the owner's pride and joy—and brick pillars reaching up to the ceiling. It smelled of strong alcohol and soured ambitions while a broken-down air conditioner and old Johnny Cash tunes created music.

It was Frank's kind of joint, Dawn thought. And for tonight, it was hers, too.

As "Tennessee Flat-Top Box" chugged along on the jukebox, she held a baggie of ice that the bartender had provided against her left wrist. It was an old injury earned from her second movie, when she'd landed wrong on a padded mat during some flying harness work. Clearly, her wrist had belatedly decided that, along with the rest of her body, it hurt. Since she was fairly new to stuntwork, she didn't have a lot of war wounds yet. Sure, a scar here and there, and a number of close calls, but otherwise, the injuries didn't give her much grief.

Unless she'd been thrown around by vampires.

Across the raised, scarred table, Kiko held his own ice baggie against his shoulder as he stared at the broad-shouldered, front lineman–eseque man they were interviewing.

Just having returned from a short engagement at the county clink, Hugh Wayne fumbled off his grimy Raiders cap and cleared the sweat from his forehead, smashing the hat right back on at a jaunty slant. His dull brown eyes, shot through with red, darted around the room as he slurred, "Damn shame what happened to Frank. Yeahyeah, damned shame."

"Hey, Hugh?" Dawn said with all the patience she'd been storing up. "You told us that before. Is there anything else? Are you sure you haven't seen Frank around?"

When his eyes focused on Dawn, the pupils expanded, retracted, then expanded again. He was high *and* drunk, judging from his Wild Turkey cologne.

"I'm tellin' you, Dawnie, he hasn't been here lately. I'm sorry though. Realreal sorry."

Kiko dropped his ice bag onto the table, disgruntled. They'd already talked to three other patrons, plus Maury the bartender. No one knew anything.

She sat back in her chair, kept her eyes on Hugh. He was one of Frank's bar buddies, but that didn't mean he knew squat about her dad. Boozy relationships weren't notorious for their longevity or depth. It saddened her to realize that these were the people Frank called friends nowadays.

"Hugh . . ." She waved her hand in front of his face, attracting his attention again. "That's it. Can you just tell me what Frank was like the last time you saw him? How he acted . . . if there was anything different about him?"

The drunk reached for his beer again but, automatically, Dawn placed her hand over his. She was used to babysitting adults who drank too much.

Kiko's gaze settled on her hand, a smile on his face. It occurred to her that they were in her arena now, that she had some interviewing skills, too, and that, maybe he was just as fish-out-of-water as she'd been back at the Pennybakers'.

"Actin' different?" Hugh wrinkled his forehead in thought. "Frank sat here gettin' cozy with Jack Daniels, told a few jokes, then left, jus' like any other night. Say, Dawnie, you still doin' movies?"

A drunken tangent. How refreshing. "Yes, Hugh, stuntwork. So Frank was his old self? He never said anything . . . off . . . to you? Nothing about any trips he might be taking?"

"Naw." Hugh used one hand to tip back his baseball cap, leaned forward in his chair, fumigating the area with his breath. "You ever wanted to act, Dawnie? Because I got my hands on a great schrip . . . script."

The next thing Dawn knew, Kiko was just about dancing on the table to get Hugh's attention. "What kind of script?"

Knowing this was the end of the line for Hugh's interview, Dawn slumped back in her chair. "Kiko."

"Just a sec. What kind of parts you looking to cast?"

Dawn sent Kiko a confused glance. Wasn't this the guy who was so good at reading people? Or maybe he was just playing around with Hugh, wheedling more information out of him. Yeah, of course, that was it.

Then she took another good look at Kiko's energized body language. If she didn't know better, she might've said that he was so much of an acting whore that he couldn't read a scam when confronted with one.

No. No way. Not the guy she'd seen in action tonight. Not Lethal Weapon Daniels, he of the steel-trap bad-cop mind.

Squinting, Hugh Wayne held his hands in front of his face, like he was composing a camera shot. "Picture this . . . *Die Hard* meets *My Big Fat Greek Wedding.*"

"You know," Kiko said, his tongue practically hanging out, "I *can* play ethnic."

Dawn ran a jaded gaze over his blond hair and blue eyes. Whatever.

Hugh raised his hand to high-five Kiko but lost strength, his palm slapping his thigh. "You got any money to invest, 'cos this's gonna kill at the box office. . . ."

Dropping her ice, Dawn stood, "helping" Kiko out of his chair. "He'll send you his head shot and résumé." She fished her business card out of a back pocket. Sure, it was kind of mushed up from all her rolling around and almost dying tonight, but it was legible. "Call me if you remember anything. It's really important."

"I will, Dawnie, I will." Hugh stifled a burp. "I sure am sorry 'bout Frank."

"Thanks." She blinked, held it together. "Me, too."

As she and Kiko left, she caught Kiko holding his fingers to his ear like a phone and mouthing "Call me" to Hugh.

She stopped by the doorway, facing him. "Hugh Wayne is a hustler, man. The only script he has is probably some scribbles on a cocktail napkin. He's no producer."

Actually, that wasn't true. Everyone in this town produced. Everyone directed movies. Just because they'd never actually done either didn't provide any sort of hurdle.

It looked like the air had been let out of Kiko's happy balloon. "Are you sure, Dawn? Because I don't want to miss a chance. You gotta grab 'em right away in this town or you find out someone else took the role you were born to play."

Dawn rested her hands on Kiko's upper arms, avoiding his wounded shoulder. "So tell me more about how your psychic powers work. Can you read shysters who're selling beachfront property in Death Valley, too?"

He looked shocked. "You really think he was zooming me?"

"Oh, boy. Yeah, I think so."

As he looked up at her, Dawn realized that she was getting awfully close to being protective. Why the hell she wanted to keep a smart aleck like him safe from all the evil producers of the world, she couldn't say. But before she could get too mushy, she dropped her hands from his arms, made a concerted effort to scope out the bar.

When she was done, he was still staring. She fidgeted, playing with her long moon earring, absently drawing his attention away from whatever he might be seeing on her face.

"You might wanna take that off before the next fight," he said. "It'd hurt to have it yanked out."

He was worried about earring yanking. Damn, and here she'd been focusing on getting her throat ripped out. Her bad.

"The design's cool," he added.

The smooth curves of the moon and the shift of the tiny hanging rubies and silver felt more real against her fingertips than anything else she'd come into contact with tonight. She kept touching it, unwilling to let go. "A bunch of stunt doubles from one of my jobs, this low-budget horror fest called *Blood Moon*, got together one night and bought mementos. The guys got their lobes shot with moon studs but I'd already been pierced, so I got something a little more detailed. . . ."

She trailed off, thinking how irrelevant her old life was right now.

Changing the subject, she asked, "You getting any vibes from this place? Is it worth hanging around?"

When he didn't answer, she glanced at him against her better judgment. Kiko was still watching her, like he was reveling in how she'd gone all mother hen on him.

Hell, she couldn't return a favor?

"Truthfully," he said, "I don't get even a quiver of humanity in this place, much less thoughts. Just a bunch of emptiness."

"Interesting." She looked away, crossed her arms over her chest, keeping his gratefulness at bay.

"Yeah, *interesting*."

Did he have to be so bubbly about her being nice to him? "You can stop grinning like a fool now, Kiko."

"I'm going to do that."

His cell phone rang, and he answered it, leaving Dawn to her own devices.

She glanced from table to table, and not entirely because she was searching for more helpful witnesses. No, that sexual stirring—the antidote to a stressful day—was getting to her.

Just something quick and easy, she thought. What would be the harm? If she could find a tourist, a non-regular, someone who'd never come to this bar again. . . .

Kiko flipped his phone shut. "That was Breisi. The boss wants to see us at two a.m., so we've got a couple hours to while away. I vote for going back to the office."

She hesitated. A couple of hours. More than enough time.

"You go on ahead," she said casually. "I have a gut feeling there's something more here. I'll take a cab back."

He paused, threw his hands in the air. "Oh, no . . ."

At the end of her rope, she turned on him, bending down so they were face to face. "I'm not on the market for a lecture."

For the first time, he looked *at* her, not *in* her, and the expression on his face indicated that he didn't understand, wouldn't ever understand.

She was so taken aback by his reaction that she didn't have time to appreciate the fact that he'd kept his promise about staying out of her thoughts.

He shook his head, disappointed in her. Prude.

"Right," he said. "Well, shit, I mean, who am I to think that you have any pride?"

As Dawn stepped back, nicked by his comment, he continued.

"As a big girl, you know how to use that crucifix you stuffed in your boot just in case any more of those fun-loving red-eyes show up. The only reason I'm leaving you here alone is that we've found that they don't like to tangle in public. The boss says vamps value their secrecy too much to open a can of whoop-ass on a crowd. Still, be on your toes. You can't ever be sure about anything." He turned around. Then, shaking his head, he faced her again, skin red. "Damn it, forget it. I'm just going to wait in the car."

With that, he pushed out the door, leaving her alone.

A whoosh of summer night air washed over her as she just stood there, wondering if she should go after him. But what good would that do? What would be the point? She was what she was, and she didn't have to apologize for it.

Still . . . God, was he really going to wait outside as she picked someone up? What, was he going to follow her to a hotel or whatever, too?

Thoroughly annoyed, Dawn strode up to the bar, took a seat. It was midnight, and most of Frank's buddies were either head-down on the table or so tanked that they couldn't see straight. She knew that if he were here it'd be the same story.

The bartender, Maury, appeared before her. He was bald, his two front teeth capped in gold. "What's your pleasure?"

"Just bottled water."

"To flush out those toxins, eh, Dawnie? Comin' up."

As she laid a couple of dollar bills on the bar, Maury served her. She played with her cocktail napkin, tearing at the edges until it resembled the blade-saw in Breisi's crossbow. Freaked, Dawn crumpled it up and sipped at her drink.

Vampires. On top of everything else, she'd met vampires tonight. Wow, when had *she* won the Queen-for-a-Day lottery?

No more than a few minutes had passed when she felt someone watching her on the left.

Tucking a stray hair behind her ear, she turned her head in the same motion, locking onto a man who hadn't been there when she'd ordered. He had short dark brown hair, a heavy brow that was, at the moment, knitted in concentration in front of him, and a cleft in his chin. It was the face of a tough, a man who didn't mind throwing punches or standing in the way of them. Under his dark shirt, she detected sinew and muscle, a body that wasn't stocky so much as retracted in preparation for attack.

He wasn't looking at her now, but Dawn knew he had been.

She played with the label of her drink, just for something to do. She wanted his attention again, longing for a distraction to improve her mood.

Waiting, waiting . . . she willed him to see her.

Nonchalantly, he did glance at her, then away. And in that one heartbeat of a second, her body crushed into itself, then burst back to form. The power of her reaction left her dizzy, discombobulated . . .

God, she needed to feel a man against her. Her demons really needed to be exorcised if she could be rocked *this* easy.

Maury delivered a shot glass full of amber liquid to the man, but the stranger merely wrapped his long fingers around it, spinning it around as he chanced another glimpse at Dawn.

He didn't smile, didn't flirt. He just measured. Pale blue eyes, full lower lip . . . Dawn's pulse hammered away, chipping off the seconds of their silent introduction.

This drawn-out glance was miles from the carnal violence of his other, shorter gaze. Now, her body was gradually warming with sensual anticipation, heating with fantasies of what she shouldn't do with a stranger.

She got out of her chair, slid into the one next to him. "You're a new face around here."

A beat passed between them, loaded with possibility. His gaze brushed over her hair, her face. He didn't smile.

"I just started coming." He turned to his drink, but didn't indulge in it.

Voice low, graveled. Hunger squeezed her lower belly.

"My name's Dawn."

Now he did smile . . . at his drink. "I know."

She sat up in her chair.

So did he, facing her, reaching into his back pocket to take out a wallet. He flicked it open to a license.

Matthew Lonigan.

Private Investigator.

A granite laugh seized Dawn. "Great. Another PI, huh? And here I thought . . ." She laughed again; it made her feel like less of an idiot. "Why do I get the impression that this meeting isn't some chance encounter?"

"It's not." He tucked the license back into his pocket. "I heard that Frank Madison's daughter and a friend were hanging around here tonight. I've been doing the same thing ever since getting this case, so I came running."

She didn't know what to say for a moment, but it wasn't only because of this cruel surprise. It was because she was embarrassed to be rejected. He hadn't been coyly checking her out at all—not in *that* way. If he was a PI, he no doubt had access to pictures of Frank's life, his family. He'd known what she looked like, and he'd honed right in on her.

"Who hired you, Matthew?" she asked.

To save her ego, she stayed on her barstool, still hovering inches from his body, close enough to feel his skin prickle. Close enough to scent the soap he'd used.

Something clean and mysterious, she thought. And it smelled way too damned good.

He sent her a glance that said he was aware of her intentions. Even so, he didn't move away. Uh-uh. In fact, his gaze drifted lower, over her chest, down, back up again.

"People call me Matt," he said, "and it's none of your business who hired me."

"Frank's my dad."

"And I'm not at liberty to divulge anything except to the person who's paying me."

As if she didn't have enough questions, a whole new meteor shower of them came raining down on her. Who else in this world cared enough about Frank to have him tracked? And why would they want to find him?

As the PI watched Dawn, everything pressed in on her, weighing against her brain. She fought to keep the world out, just as she'd been doing half the night with all the mysteries that had swallowed her whole. She pushed right back, keeping her mind in the here and now.

"Come on," she said. "Tell me what you've found out."

Hell, if he could interview her, she could interview him right back.

A laugh of disbelief forced a smile—a sidelong gesture of wry appreciation—out of him. "You're a tenacious one."

"I'm sick of not knowing. From dusk on, it's been . . ." She huffed out a breath, gripped her drink. "Quite the adventure."

"Welcome to detective work."

When he bent closer to her, Dawn raised her eyebrows. Was he working her? Or had she miscalculated his true level of interest? *Did* it go beyond detecting?

He skimmed his fingertips near the bandages over her burns. The faint contact woke up her nerve endings.

"What happened?" he asked.

Sure. Like she was going to spill *that* story. "Just a stunt gone awry."

"That's it, huh?" Matt Lonigan leaned over on the bar, fixing her in his sights, hunter to prey. "I hear you tolerate pain pretty well."

"Yup, my life's one long demolition derby."

She took a slow sip from her drink. A trickle of ice sweat caught her chin, slid down her throat, past her shirt and between her breasts. Deliberately, she wiped the lingering moisture away from her mouth, taking great pleasure in how his gaze stayed on her lips.

Boyfriend was intrigued, all right, even if he was fighting tooth and nail to stay professional. Girls knew this kind of thing. It was one of the advantages of femininity, and Dawn had no qualms about using any of the tools in her arsenal.

Just as a final tease, she licked the corner of her mouth with the tip of her tongue.

Matt Lonigan's eyes went unfocused, but he turned his face away before Dawn could call him on it with a knowing grin.

"You were saying . . . ?" His voice was more ragged than usual.

She rested her elbows on the bar in a pose that stretched her shirt over her chest. "About what?"

"About tonight? An adventure? Those bandages . . . ?"

"Is this the best interview you've got in you?"

He sighed, kept staring at his drink. "You're not exactly the easiest subject, Ms. Madison. If you could just—"

"Oh, I see. You want me to share with you what you won't share with me. That hardly seems like a professional courtesy, now, does it?"

He clenched his jaw.

Hmm. Would he be more talkative about Frank if she persuaded him just a little bit more?

She started to play with the strand of loose hair that had escaped her low ponytail. Winding, winding it around her finger, waiting for him to look back at her.

Which he soon did.

He'd collected himself, but only marginally. Now she was pretty damned sure he was attracted to her: it was in the set of his mouth, the angle of his body.

An old Neil Young song wafted out of the jukebox.

"The first good looking man who walks in here," she said, "and you have to be difficult."

He didn't respond at all.

Naturally, that made Dawn turn the heat up—a challenge always did. Why was he making this so impossible? Or . . .

Wait, maybe he really wasn't into *her*. Maybe he'd seen too many pictures of Eva Claremont and Dawn wasn't measuring up. Was that it? It had to be. It'd happened so many times before.

Out of pure anger, she reached out, slid her hand onto his thigh.

A craving so urgent, so dangerous, seized her that her breath quickened, sharp in her lungs.

Would Eva touch him like this? No—she couldn't, not any more. Dawn was the one who was alive, not Eva. Dawn was the one who could stretch her body along the length of his; she was the one who could satisfy him tonight.

His hand clamped over hers, stopping her from traveling upward, to the center of his legs. When she caught the fire in his eyes, she thought for certain that he was about to give in.

But then something mysterious wavered there, like a flame that was struggling in the wind, rolling to a weak flicker, guttering, dying—

Dawn held her breath, watching him make some sort of decision.

And he did. The flame danced, grew stronger.

Twisted itself back up to a solid stand again.

"What're you doing?" he rasped.

Embarrassed, she jerked her hand away.

A full minute of twanging guitars and Neil Young waxing eloquent about love provided a buffer. But then the PI went and decimated it.

"Let me drive you home," he said more gently. "And maybe we can schedule an appointment to talk tomorrow, when you're in a different mood."

"Why? So you can taunt me with everything I don't know about Frank? No thank you. I've already got a whole lifetime supply of that." She started to leave.

"Dawn, wait."

Standing, he was taller than she'd expected. She had to tilt her head back a little to look at him head-on.

"I . . ." He put his hands on his hips and laughed. "I'm just not sure how to handle you."

Dawn took that in. A normal guy. *She* wasn't sure how to handle one of those, either. She was used to a different breed of male, a fleeting somebody who was willing to take advantage of what she so easily offered.

Dawn didn't know if she could be into normal.

"I'm serious about getting together tomorrow." He gave her his card. It was nice and neat—not a blood mark on it. "And maybe we could also get together with your friend. The one who was with you tonight?"

Taking the card, she knew the right thing to do would be to offer him aid. She wanted to. But, damn it, it pissed her off that he could be privy to information that could help her to find Frank and he was withholding it.

She held up the card, turned to leave.

"Dawn."

The tone of his voice halted her cold, but she knew it was only because The Voice had said her name so many times today, himself. The memory rang through her: soft caresses from the inside out, warm strokes of being loved. Sexual healing.

Exactly what she wanted.

Matt Lonigan had come closer, near her back and just over her shoulder. His breath was moist against her ear.

"I'm interested. But I'm *not* desperate."

When he left, a cool patch of absence lingered against her back. A shiver wracked her, left her empty as she stared ahead, struggling not to look back. She walked out the door.

On post-midnight Hollywood Boulevard, it was drizzling, leaving a sheen of neon to streak the pavement. Without comment, Dawn climbed into the car where Kiko was waiting.

As they drove back in silence, neither of them realized that they were being followed.

NINE

The Hunger

At 2:00 a.m., the team met in The Voice's office, rain tapping at the window like it wanted to enter the insular safety of the room as well.

On Dawn's left, Kiko reclined in a lounge chair, ice packs tucked against strategic locations of his body. On Dawn's right, Breisi sat on an ottoman, straight-backed, one long leg crossed over the other, her foot bobbing with nervous energy.

Dawn adjusted her own ice packs, keenly aware of muscles she hadn't known about before. All of them were whining, too.

And then there was the ache, the belly-deep nudge of a craving she hadn't been able to satisfy back at the Cat's Paw.

She tried to forget it as The Voice talked to Kiko. "In light of the attack, keep your eyes open for vampires hiding behind any corner, waiting for you to be alone."

"So what do you think those tailed things were? They sure were ugly mo'fos. Strong, too."

Outside, a branch moaned against the velvet-shrouded window, and Dawn started in her seat. The covering blocked what was going on out there, and she didn't like that at all.

She just couldn't lose the feeling of being a bug under a microscope, of being observed by a cold, practiced *something* . . .

Her gaze wandered up to the big TV. The Voice's eye.

His disembodied tone moved across the room like seething fog. "I don't know what breed of vampire we're dealing with, Kiko. From your description—iron fangs, barbed tails—I can't place the type. But until I do, we'll step up security for the Pennybakers and keep trying to ease Marla into accepting that vampires exist. I'll put Friends on watch, as well."

"Friends?" Dawn asked.

"Friends." The Voice wasn't elaborating.

Again, something prodded her to recognize its existence: vamps outside Robby's house, Robby's image in the window . . .

She sliced off her thoughts, unwilling to face where they were leading right now. "And how do you propose we find out what those things are?"

Breisi held up her hands in a gesture that said, *Isn't it obvious?* "We identify their lair."

"But you don't go in," The Voice said. "I've taught you to never enter a hidden nest of vampires. *I'll* take care of something that dangerous. Do you understand, Kiko? No more wandering into a copse of trees to track them."

"Frank would've gone for it, too," the psychic said.

Her dad's name forced a wound of guilt to split open inside Dawn. "I'm with Kiko. If those vamps had anything to do with Frank's disappearance, I'm not going to back off, either, even if they do run into their little holes to hide."

Yeah, she sounded brave *now*.

"Listen to me." The Voice's tone grew in volume. "There are some forces I alone will have to deal with."

"That's rich. How can you bring me into this and then—"

"We're all going to find Frank." There was a catch of barbed wire in Breisi's voice. "*Never* doubt that, Dawn."

As Dawn gaped at her, the room went quiet. Breisi glared at the carpet, then started to jog her ankle again.

"And this," The Voice said, back to his normal harsh hush, "brings me to another subject." He stopped, the speaker humming. "Dawn, I'm still not even comfortable with the thought of you being out there at the present time. Not without more training, especially after tonight."

Breisi kept bobbing her foot. "Boss, she'll do great, as long as we're around. As I said before, she's got the basics down—we just need to hone and educate her."

"I'll be fine," Dawn said, "if I know what to expect."

Kiko spoke up. "Everyone's first time with a vamp encounter is a test, Boss. And I suspect you knew that Dawn would be real good at resisting. You should've seen her when that thing tried to get into her head. She kicked *ass*."

Even though Dawn knew she hadn't been quite that phenomenal, she shot Kiko a thankful look. He knew how much she needed to find Frank.

And she knew how much he believed that she was "key" to the investigation.

The Voice chuckled, but it wasn't a warm, inviting sound. It was dark, low, the drag of slow footsteps in the night. "Dawn *is* already an expert at keeping anyone and everyone out."

Was that a compliment? She didn't think so.

"Dawn," he added, "you'll begin training tomorrow in mind blocking until it becomes second nature to you. Breisi, please outfit her with a revolver and an encrypted cell phone when we're done here."

"She can have my forty-five. I've got lots of extras."

One of Kiko's ice packs thunked to the floor as he shifted position in his chair. "There's also the matter of where Dawn is staying.

After those vamps just popped up out of nowhere, I'm thinking we need to watch each other more."

In all the hubbub, Dawn had almost forgotten about a crash pad. She'd planned to check into a motel, seeing as she was a bit of a drifter, just like Frank, and hadn't been renting anything in L.A. Normally, Dawn would shack up with a friend—male, of course—until she needed to move on.

"Were you planning to go to Frank's?" Breisi asked softly.

Dawn flinched. "No."

That house. A reminder of how life with Frank had been a constant seesaw. One day he'd be Number One father, buying her cotton candy at Six Flags Magic Mountain or attending parent conference night at school in a button-down and tie. The next, he'd be a weeping mess, a cheap bottle of whiskey drained and lying on its side next to him as he brought out her mom's old movies and locked his daughter out of their home.

As soon as Dawn had been old enough to leave—Frank had done a couple of stunt gigs years ago and she'd gotten her first job through a friend of his when she was eighteen—they'd gone their separate ways. Sure, there were stilted phone calls while she was on the road, birthday cards he remembered to send, but the two of them had never been your typical Hallmark ad.

She didn't want to go back to that house.

"Dawn can camp out at my place," Kiko said.

Relief seeped through her, and she smiled at him. He nodded back. It looked like he'd come to terms with what had happened at the Cat's Paw. Or was this Kiko's puritanical way of babysitting, keeping tabs on all the naughty misadventures he didn't approve of?

"Is everything settled then?" Breisi half-rose out of her seat, eager to be on her merry way.

"I've got something else," Dawn said.

Breisi plopped back down to her ottoman.

"At the Cat's Paw, there was a PI. A Matt Lonigan. He's looking for Frank, too." She told them almost everything: how he wouldn't give her any of his information about Frank, how he wanted to meet with her tomorrow. She didn't, however, offer any chin music about the complicated little details, like how she'd thrown herself at him and he'd semi-rejected her.

In the aftermath, Breisi and Kiko watched the blank TV, as if for a reaction. Dawn swallowed hard, sensing that prickle of being observed again. Her gaze flew to the velvet-curtained window, where the raindrops kept knocking.

Suddenly, the TV screen pinged on, showcasing a picture of Matt Lonigan. She felt her skin pink with heat and amazement.

"This is the man?" The Voice asked.

"Yeah." He'd probably accessed some database from his hovel. Quick work.

"Don't contact him, Dawn, not until I've checked a few matters out. Leave his number with Breisi, and if he approaches you again, refer him to my phone. There's a chance he could be of some help."

"Or he could be trouble," Breisi added.

For a full fifteen seconds, there was no answer.

Breisi held up her hands. "I hate when he doesn't even sign off. I think he gets bored with us."

"Boss is busy." Kiko started to walk out of the room.

Breisi followed. "Kik, before you two leave, can I see you downstairs?"

"Sure." The psychic glanced over his shoulder at Dawn. "Meet you in the foyer?"

"Yeah." She got up, gathering her ice packs.

With the meeting at an end, she felt like crashing, all systems down. Couldn't help it: even though she didn't require anything more than four hours of sleep per night, she was one of those fast burnout cases when she didn't get decent rest.

She yawned. Alone in the room, it sounded like the wind's wail had been pumped up. It groaned against the window, the tiny scratches of tree branches like claws against the glass.

Dawn, it seemed to say. *Let me in.*

She shook her head, clearing it. Nothing but my stress talking, she thought, turning away from the window.

But then she found herself facing one of The Voice's erotic paintings, and that wasn't much more comforting.

This particular lady looked like she was from Queen Elizabeth the First's court, with her starched, stand-up collar halfway undone, her lips red and moist and open for a kiss that would never come. Her bodice was unlaced, her frizzy hair unfurling from its pins. Her heavy-lidded eyes were latched onto Dawn, searing into her.

A sound filled the room—a woman's sigh of pleasure, barely discernible over the wind. Dawn's body tightened, blood heating and pumping into that hunger she could never seem to appease.

Clearing her head again, she left the office and ambled into the hall. She couldn't escape the sense that the woman looked as if she'd been feeling sorry for Dawn, even in the midst of her passion.

I've got to get out of this house, she thought. It isn't good for my sanity.

Darkness escorted her, one step, two steps . . .

The drift of soft glass chimes halted her progress.

Dawn . . .

Warmth flowed into her, trickled downward, relaxing her for the first time since . . .

A door creaked open, revealing a slit of amber light.

Lured, she dropped the ice packs, pushing open the door as it moaned on its hinges, then wandered into the massive room.

It looked like a boudoir, complete with divans draped with sheer gauze, a changing screen etched with Asian patterns, a chandelier that tinkled in glass-graced song, and three more paintings: one of an exotic lady whose veils were being unwound from her body by the gentle wind, one of a half-nude Japanese woman with kanji symbols painted on her bared back. The third picture was out of place, featuring a pristine landscape: the shoreline of a beach, the water blue and pure.

Dawn sank against a satin-lined couch. It smelled of jasmine. Like an afterthought, the door closed.

The Voice came to her, even though she didn't see any speakers. "I noticed that you're weary. In so many ways."

"Didn't you disappear for the night?" she whispered, lacking energy.

"I'm right here."

Shivering, she glanced around, finding nothing.

Weary, she thought, her eyes drooping closed. He's right. So, so weary.

"That's not going to stop me," Dawn whispered. "I just need a little . . ."

"I know."

A light breeze dusted near her.

Was it happening again? Was he coming into her, hypnotizing her?

The mere thought raised her hackles, but she was also remembering how nice it had felt, how satisfying. How much like the physical release she'd been longing for tonight.

She closed her eyes. "Peace would be nice."

The breeze swirled closer. "Why aren't you resisting, Dawn? I want you to get used to doing that."

"I will, but there's a difference between resisting a vampire mind meld and . . ." Her body clenched, so needful.

"Then I have your permission?" he asked.

Was it her, or did he sound eager?

A battling pride made her hesitate, but the temptation was too overwhelming. *Peace. Contentment. The addiction of forgetting everything else.*

"Yes," she said, relieved now that she'd allowed herself to give up. "But when I want you out, you'll go out, ri—?"

The next thing she knew, she was soaked with his mind, hot and heavy with damp gratification. Warmth licked her skin, in between her legs, like a tide pulling in and back, lulling her.

When she opened her eyes, she found herself staring at the sky, wet sand sucking at her back. An easy roar built, approached, splashed and covered her with wetness as the sun stroked her body.

In dreamy shock, she realized that this was the scene from the painting. It was like she'd become one of his women, caught by oils and textured by an artist's hand, preserved in a langorous pose.

Or maybe this was some kind of exhaustion-fed fantasy . . .

She heard his voice as if it were part of the air.

"Tell me more about this Matt Lonigan, Dawn."

This wasn't the reason she'd invited him in. She didn't want questions. She wanted escape.

Burrowing further into the sand, she opened her legs as the tide lapped at her, bathing her thighs, her sex.

Matt Lonigan.

She conjured up an image of him hovering over her, sand and sun glistening on his skin, emphasizing his muscles as water dripped down from his body onto her own. Her mind forced him to lower himself, to fit his length over hers and slide down, lower and lower, until his mouth reached her belly.

He kissed her, using his tongue to glide southward. With it, he separated her, delved inside, making her swell and grasp at the sand.

She craned her neck to watch him, turned on by seeing his head moving between her legs. But when he looked up—

A wave crashed, pounding him into nothing.

She heard The Voice laughing, a cruel sound of revenge.

"Jealous?" The tide hissed, retreated.

His laughter faded, too. "Yes. I am."

An incoming wave tickled her thighs, gurgling against her, and she gasped, closing her eyes again.

Another light breeze combed her skin, and she knew it was him this time. The Voice.

"None of your pictures do you justice, Dawn," he said.

She thought she felt fingers threading through her hair, unbinding it from the ponytail, allowing the strands to float in the rush of water, free, like a mermaid's.

He continued. "I didn't realize you would be so . . ."

"Don't." She couldn't handle the inevitable comparisons, the new heartbreak.

"No, you shine with spirit. You have no idea how that affects someone like me. Ah, Dawn, I have so much to teach you, to bring out in you . . ."

A heavier pressure moved down her body, as if hands were on her, shaping her, memorizing her. The scars she'd earned from her work didn't exist anymore, only the touch, the sensations.

Even though there was no one there, the sensuous homage made her feel womanly. She loved when that happened; she thrilled to it on the movie sets when she moved among the stuntmen, was always aware of it when she caught the glances that acknowledged her femininity in a world dominated by males.

Until she remembered she could never be as perfect as Eva.

But that's not how it was now. Here, she wasn't competing against a ghost. Here, she was wanted for what was inside of her, for what was . . .

Emotion—fluid and combustible—churned, building, stiffening as the invisible climax tingled against her sex. Powerful, strong; damn it she couldn't hold it back . . .

With a whoosh of release, she arched up against it, moaning, biting her lip to keep it inside, failing as she reached up her arms to hold on.

Finding nothing.

Hands empty, she panted, looking around. "Who are you?"

Without warning, the pressure lifted from her body. The seductive tide thrashed back into the ocean, leaving her on the shore, alone. Little by little, the boudoir lifted into focus around her as she sprawled on the recliner.

He was gone.

Finally, sated, she sighed into the cushions, exhaustion catching up with her as she burned with something else now.

Languid curiosity.

"Why won't you tell me?" she slurred as the room continued to change. It faded to darkness while the melody of the chandelier dragged her into unconsciousness.

As she was consumed, she fought to stay awake, especially as the door creaked open again.

Letting someone—or something—in.

TEN

The Lesson

Dawn woke up late the next morning on a strange couch with a new crucifix hanging around her neck.

As things came into focus, she saw a pin-neat living room, complete with a TV, a TiVo box, a stereo system, and about a thousand CDs and DVDs stacked against the walls. The reason the place was so clean was that these were the only things in it.

Well, besides a framed poster of Pam Grier as Foxy Brown, the ultimate cool badass.

Slowly, Dawn sat up, her body tender with cuts, bruises, and dull pain. Like a one-second newsreel, it all came back to her: the plane ride back to California, the nouveau gothic dollhouse of Limpet and Associates, the vampires, and then . . .

Her skin flushed, heat flowing inward.

Thanks to The Voice, she'd actually slumbered well last night. In fact . . . She glanced at the digital clock on the TiVo. 9:11. She hadn't slept this long in years.

"Morning!" called a cheery voice.

Kiko burst into the room from the hallway, tossed a PowerBar at her and deposited a glass of milk into her hands. He was already showered, shampooed, and shined for the day, his blond hair dried into slight curls, his soul patch neat and trimmed.

He pointed at the crucifix. "Happy birthday."

"You're about three hundred days off, but thank you." She touched the sleek safety of it. "I appreciate it, Kiko."

"Don't get too sentimental. You're gonna need it."

"I'm gonna need some information, too." She gestured to the couch. "How did I get here?"

"Here?" He half-grinned. "I drove you last night. You were out cold in one of the rooms. The boss told me where you were, so Breisi helped me carry you and your baggage out to my customized car. Your hunk of junk is back at the office, by the way."

Even though Dawn was thankful that Kiko didn't know about her and The Voice, it left her feeling stranded, isolated in her struggle to understand everything that was going on.

While she thought about the wisdom of telling her associate what had happened in the boudoir last night, Dawn unwrapped the bandage that had been covering her burns. The bindings were nasty with remnants of Breisi's wonder gel as well as spots of burn goo, but Dawn was stunned to find that the wounds themselves were already healing. Pushed by curiosity, she started taking off her jeans to check the cut on her leg, too.

"Hey." Wide-eyed, Kiko turned his back.

"What are you, a virgin?" Jeans on the floor, Dawn glanced under the bandage, finding that the slice from the vamp's barbed tail had mended together. "Say, what's in Breisi's voodoo gel? She could market this stuff and become a zillionaire."

"Maybe after we take care of our other priorities." He was still facing away from her. "So, when you're done with your Pussycat Dolls routine, we'll do some training. You need it before we get back out there tonight."

"Speaking of which—when am I going to get all that education I'll need to fight these vamps, if they show again?"

"We'll start today, but I have to be honest . . ."

Kiko peeked behind him, yet when he saw that Dawn was still pants-less, he turned back around. Aw, a gentleman. Dawn covered herself with the sheet just for his sake.

"We're all still feeling our way around these vamps," he said. "The boss tells us that different types have different powers, just like human races have various skin colors or cultural mores. He says to always expect *anything* to happen, whether it's hypnotic powers, shapeshifting, or even flying. That's why you've got to stick with me or Breisi from now on, all right? We have more experience than you."

From the set of his shoulders, the tone of his voice, Dawn could tell he was absolutely serious. She didn't need to see his face to figure that out.

"Besides," he added, finding that she was tucked under the sheet now, then turning all the way around, "all you have to do is find Frank and stick around until we crack this case, then you're out of here. We'll take things from that point. You can drive your pop to bum-fuck wherever and settle in a place like Kansas where there aren't any vampires." He paused. "I think."

Dawn massaged her temples. He made it sound so easy.

"*Capisce*?" Kiko asked.

"I got you." Dawn became suddenly aware of how sticky she felt under all the grime she hadn't had the chance to clean off yet. "But before we save humanity, how about a shower?"

"Please."

She speed-ate her PowerBar and chugged the milk, cleaned up, and told herself that her body wasn't hurting. And, really, it wasn't too bad. Even her sore wrist was cooperating.

Then, after checking in with the cops to find that they'd made no progress on Frank's case, Dawn decided to hell with them. She extracted sweats and a T-shirt from her luggage, slung her hair back in a low ponytail, and armed herself for some mental warfare, investing fully in the hope that Limpet and Buddies would be her ticket to getting Frank back.

For the rest of the morning, she and Kiko sat on the worn carpet and faced each other as she practiced blocking him.

"Push against me with your thoughts," he kept saying. "Do it from the inside, like your mind is a wave."

It got to the point where he was throwing surprise attacks at her. As the afternoon passed, she became pretty decent at fending him off, even if she still had a way to go.

"As the boss said, you're already good at this." Worn out, Kiko slumped onto his couch. "Isn't it nuts that in our normal, daily lives, we don't even tap a fraction of what our minds are capable of? Imagine if everyone just admitted that the sixth sense isn't all about con men and Gypsies."

She remembered The Voice's comment about her being an expert at keeping people at bay. Was her habit of ignoring what she didn't want to deal with actually her own sixth sense at w—

A dart of invasive confusion parted her thoughts.

Out! Dawn said to herself, pushing mentally.

Beaming, Kiko gave her a thumbs-up. "Good reflexes."

"Is this going to be the extent of our day?" she asked. "Me dodging your psychic bombs?"

"Actually, I thought I'd start you on some reading. *Vampires, Burial, and Death*, for one, and some writings by Montague Summers. He was this famous supernatural expert."

"Can't I just watch *Buffy the Vampire Slayer*?"

Kiko looked intrigued. "That might be surprisingly valuable. Maybe later. I also thought we could go through some of Frank's paperwork—you know, bills and such. Maybe you'll see some sort of pattern in his spending habits. Something weird."

"You mean *relatively* weird."

Kiko pursed his lips, as if wanting to ask a question, but then he seemed to think better of it.

"What?" she asked.

"Your relationship with Frank . . . If you two don't get along so well, why're you going to such extremes? I mean, yeah, I know he's your dad, but there're a lot of people in this world who would leave the finding to us instead of dealing personally with all this crap that's hitting the fan."

She thought about the gleam of pride in Frank's eyes after she'd shown him some arm bruises from her first stunt gig. Thought of how she'd once caught him bragging about her to a table of drunks at the Cat's Paw.

Her words were like blades in her throat. She couldn't say the rest out loud: when it came right down to it, she couldn't tolerate the thought of never reconciling with her dad. Remorse was driving her to make up for the estrangement between them, because she'd had so many chances to correct things while she'd been in L.A. before. He'd been only miles away from where she'd worked, where she'd played.

Now he was out of reach, and in some karmic manner, she deserved the bleeding punishments.

Kiko looked sympathetic. "Sometimes it takes a tragedy for everything to become clearer."

Dawn nodded, busied herself by toying with her crucifix.

Neither of them said anything for a bit. Kiko got up, went down the hall, returned with a couple of vampire books and shoved them into her hands. Then he thumped back to the couch and turned on his TV. The impersonal blather coated Dawn's inner wounds, a temporary balm that would disappear just as soon as she looked at Kiko's compassionate gaze again.

At loose ends, she shifted her weight from foot to foot. Vegging out in front of the tube during the day wasn't her style. For a girl who was used to working out everyday, whether it was at the gym or at a training session, sitting in one place while sunshine burned wasn't her preference, especially when there was so much to deal with now.

She took a gander at the clock again. 3:15. "Kiko?"

He'd stopped channel surfing, lingering on the one show that was bound to take over the earth: *Cops*.

"Uh-huh?"

"Where are we?" she asked.

He laughed. "In low-rent heaven on Franklin Avenue near the Hills."

Hell, she knew the perfect place to go: somewhere close and useful.

She hovered nearer to him, nudged his leg with her shin. "You'd probably agree that it's important to get some physical training in, right?"

"Definitely. But I'm tired. Just read."

She prodded him again. "I thought I might get in a workout at my fencing studio. Do some networking to see what's out there day job–wise at the same time. I mean, it's not like I'm going to be working with you guys forever. I need to look toward the future, too."

"Networking?" Kiko sat up on the couch, circling the hook.

Dawn set about reeling him in. "A trip to the studio really is justified. I mean, surely we can take one hour out of the day for free time, don't you think?"

"But your books—"

She gave him the Scout salute. "I promise to be a good study bunny when we get back."

"I don't know, Dawn. . . ."

"Come on, Kik. We've worked all morning, and I ruled at mind blocking. You can't deny that. A little recess is definitely in order."

He sighed, but she could tell she had him.

"Fencing," he said, trying very hard not to be into it.

"I worked on some episodes of *Blades of Spain* a year or so ago." And, after the TV show had gotten cancelled, she'd continued going to the studio, partly because the more skills you had on your resume, the better. Also, fencing was a killer workout. But Dawn planned to take it easy today, go over some basics like footwork, see if Dipak, her coach, had a line on any productions that might be requiring her talents soon.

You had to keep up with the game in this town, she thought, because it sure wouldn't keep up with you.

"I'm pretty sore," Kiko said, making a tragically obvious last-ditch effort to be a pain in the ass.

"Aw, that's too bad. My coach is in touch with who's looking to cast what project." Dawn turned around, strolled away, all coy. "If you're into that."

Suddenly healed, Kiko tested his shoulder. "I suppose I could stand to master more skills. Are you sure *you're* up for a workout?"

Excellent. "What are you? A dandelion? I've fenced the day after a bookshelf landed on me during *Slay Shay*."

"Yeah?"

"Yeah. Unless one of my limbs has fallen off, I'm all over a bit of strenuous effort."

Well, that certainly did it for the male of the house. Kiko accepted the tossed gauntlet, donned a pair of new tennis shoes and sweats—which, of course, had pockets big enough for a small crucifix and a cell phone. Like Dawn, he was carrying a gym bag to hide the gun. They still had to get her registered, so flashing the weapons around wasn't on the agenda.

Off they went to the studio, leaving the old-school seventies cheer of his apartment complex and traveling to Gower Street.

Once inside the studio, nostalgia hit Dawn with the overpowering stench of stale sweat. The echoes of shoes scuffing the gymnasium-wood floor and steel clashing against steel surrounded the masked fencers. They were dressed in white jackets and wielding their blades, sparring.

Kiko was wearing his damned sunglasses, and Dawn motioned for him to take them off. Using them inside was dopey.

"Ditch your shades," she said.

"Nope."

"Listen, if you're Jack Nicholson, you get to wear sunglasses anywhere you want. If you're Joe Blow, Struggling Actor, you look plain pathetic. Everybody who thinks they *should* be somebody wears them inside. Taking them off at this point is the new cool." She put her hands together in prayer. "Please do the right thing."

"Nope."

Dipak, a tall, lean man in his late thirties who hailed from Calcutta, welcomed Dawn with the relish of a long-lost cousin, hugging her and "where have you been"ing her. After they caught up, he turned to Kiko, dark brown gaze assessing the little person's physical attributes.

"I suppose we will need children's gear for you."

As Kiko opened his mouth to respond, Dawn rushed to cover the possible awkwardness. God knew when Kiko would decide that he'd been offended.

"We can rent equipment here," she said smoothly, as if continuing a conversation. "Come on, let's gear up."

She pulled him away, waving to Dipak.

"I will be back to coach you." He donned his mask and moved on to two foil fencers who were hooked to a machine that beeped when one of them hit their body target and scored a point.

"I've always wanted to be a pirate," an unaffected Kiko said as they went to the equipment room.

Happy Kiko. And it was good.

They picked out their jackets and masks. Dawn had to use a breastplate, so she secured one of those, too, as well as a rancid glove that'd seen better days.

"You don't own your own stuff?" Kiko asked, sniffing at one of the gloves. He tested a tiny jacket, also, but those were frequently washed, so he looked more optimistic after that olfactory experience.

"Owning is too expensive." After taking off her long earring, Dawn chose sabers for both of them, even though she knew he wouldn't be using the blade today. But sabers were way more exhilarating because you got to cut and thrust as opposed to merely getting points for contacting the target areas with a foil's tip.

As they went back to the floor, Kiko said, "I wonder how many little people can fence. Maybe I can corner this market."

"Hell, yes, you can." She dug Kiko's enthusiasm. "We'll chat with Dipak about it."

Kiko gave an excited hop. "See, I knew meeting you would bring great things. And I'm not just talking about . . ." He glanced around furtively. "You know."

Damn. And here she'd forgotten about vamps for a blessed minute. But that probably wasn't a good thing. "I know. Take off those sunglasses, please."

He did, probably thinking that pirates didn't need shades.

Sans masks and gloves, they stretched, Kiko complaining about his soreness and then getting all google-eyed at Dawn's flexibility as she eased into the splits. The more limber she was for lunging, the better. Soon, she got him started on the proper en guarde position, adjusting the bend of his front leg, the angle of his blade arm. He sucked in a breath every time she touched him, but . . . whatever. Kiko could tough this out as much as she could. She taught him how to advance, then retreat.

Dipak finally made it over. He pointed at Kiko's feet. "Oh, this footwork, my tiny friend. It is not satisfactory, not satisfactory at all."

Knowing what a drill sergeant Dipak could be, Dawn stiffened, waiting for Kiko to freak out at the blunt criticism. But he didn't. Nope, instead, he good-naturedly went along with the coaching, grinning at Dawn the whole time.

Cool.

"Dawn," Dipak said, "a favor, please?"

"Sure."

He jerked his head toward the other side of the room. "Run to the washer and put the jackets into the dryer? Later, perhaps we can cross blades and chat while your friend practices what he has learned."

Dipak the taskmaster. How she'd missed him. "Done."

Leaving a now-focused Kiko, Dawn hustled to the small laundry room and finished her assignment, eager to return to the floor and see how rusty her skills had gotten. The last time she'd fenced was about a month ago—dog years in this sport.

She'd crossed half the room on her way back when she was stopped by another student.

"Excuse me? Can I . . . ?" The woman gestured to her jacket. She had it on backward.

She was a redhead, her long hair braided, her body toned and long-limbed. A starlet, Dawn thought, hardly taking a second look at her.

Dawn's favorite Hollywood creature.

"New to fencing?" Dawn asked, impatiently getting the girl out of the jacket and buttoning her into it the right way.

"Yes, I am. My agent wants me to do some training because there's this part in the new Will Smith movie that requires some ability. Can't hurt to try it, right?"

The breathing mannequin—early twenties, probably, though you never knew—waited with friendly patience for an answer as Dawn inspected her work. Dawn could sense the the girl's neediness for recognition out of the corner of her eye.

Wiping her hands of the girl, she remained distant, walking away without another glance. "Good luck with that audition."

She could feel the starlet watching her leave, probably cussing her out for being such a pill. Dawn told herself it didn't matter.

When she got back, Dipak had already left to yell at two épée fencers with sloppy technique.

"I'm Captain Jack Sparrow," Kiko said in a purring British accent, using his new footwork and slashing the air with his invisible sword. "Savvy?"

"Savvy." Dawn bent down into her own en guarde position. Ooo—a little pain in the barbed calf.

"So who's your new friend?" Kiko pointed his air sword at the starlet. "Boy, Dawn, could you have been more rude? You practically rolled her in and out of her jacket like it was a carpet and she was a stowaway."

He was giving her a chastising look.

"What?" she asked.

"Minute by minute, I'm finding out that you're kinda antisocial."

She laughed. "Antisocial or picky? Tom-ay-toes, tom-ah-toes."

Then she went back to position, advancing, retreating. Footwork in itself would make you sweat. And that was before you got into the mask—the fencer's sauna.

Kiko came to stand in front of her, hands on his hips. "Jeez, you barely even looked at her when she was trying to be friendly and engage you in a conversation."

Dawn gave up. "Kik, she's a starlet. They're here today, gone yesterday. What's the use?"

Even as she said it, she knew she was being too harsh. But excuses were so much easier than getting down to the truth: the anguish of knowing that her mother had been one of them. The fact that the gorgeous masses, like Eva, made life hard for the average girl in America by creating an impossible standard of beauty to compete with.

Dawn would rather ignore them than know them.

"Starlets are people, too," Kiko said.

"Are they?" She lunged forward, her heart pattering, her breath coming faster.

Kiko didn't move from his soapbox. "I notice that you manage to get along with guys all fine and good, but when you have to deal with a female . . . whoo."

"I get along with Breisi," Dawn said, panting.

"Watching you two interact is like hearing nails screeching down a blackboard. What's your deal? You're warming up to me just fine—because who *wouldn't*—and you get along with the boss. . . ."

She blushed, tried to control it. "Maybe I'm just used to hanging out with guys. Did you ever think of that?"

"Not good enough."

Dawn held up her hand, and he stopped. She didn't want to get into the nuances of her inner mechanics.

Glancing over at the starlet, Kiko dismissed Dawn with a wave. "Too damned bad. She's hot. You could've introduced us but nooo. . . . Now I'm *never* gonna meet my future wife."

Dawn had to stop her footwork because she was laughing, more out of nervous thankfulness that Kiko had ended his diatribe than anything. As Kiko asked her what was so funny, she couldn't help peeking at the redhead again. And why not? Since she hadn't looked at the girl long enough to get a reading on a beauty queen scale of one to ten, now was her chance.

But Dawn was too late. She caught the starlet sliding the mask over her face. Then the girl stood still for a moment, watching Dawn before turning to shake hands with Dipak as he welcomed her.

"She's going to sweat to death," Dawn said to herself, thinking she should maybe go back over there just to tell the girl to wear the mask only when necessary. *And* to keep Kiko off her case. Shouldn't she?

Kiko's sweatpants started ringing. He unzipped a pocket and took out his cell phone, checking the number first.

"Breisi," he said, suddenly Business Kiko.

Hardly in the mood for something as irrelevant as social niceties anymore, Dawn listened to the one-sided conversation.

"We're on our way." He cut the line, taking off toward the equipment room as Dawn kept up.

"What happened?" she asked, a heavy feeling dogging her.

"We're going to talk to one of Robby's last costars, Klara Monaghan. Breisi just tracked her down."

Dawn's pulse picked up momentum. "Why is she important?"

Kiko glanced at her, his cheeks going a little pale. "She's saying Mr. Pennybaker was some kind of pimp."

ELEVEN

The Informant

KLARA Monaghan sat in front of the mirror in a makeup trailer on location in Santa Monica, where a TV show, *Manic Five*, was shooting on the amusement park–studded pier. She sat still under the deft touch of the production's cosmetic artist, who was turning the actress into a prostitute.

"It's only a bit part," Klara said apologetically, "but it's better than nothing."

In spite of her smooth face, the skin of her hands was getting wrinkled, showing a middle-forty age range that she would never admit to. Her tinted auburn hair was cotton-candied up into a mockery of a beehive.

As Breisi crowded the chair during her "good cop" act, Dawn and Kiko sat to the side, out of the way. The make-up artist kept shooting their associate irritated glances, and Dawn couldn't blame him. The area was cramped with chairs and supplies, including a variety of wigs.

When the man finished his makeover, Klara led everyone outside.

She'd wanted privacy while telling them the most sensitive information about the Pennybakers.

They all stood at the back of the trailer while the lighting was set for the next scene. Summer heat waned as the ocean shimmered and winked at the coming of twilight.

Stretching her arms over her head, Klara leaned against the trailer, her aging body aerobicized and yogacized. "I hope you don't mind me warming up while we talk."

"Please, no, go ahead," Breisi said. She was wearing another cartoon bear shirt under her light jacket, this one featuring Teddy with a baseball bat. "We're very interested to know more about what you told me on the phone. It could help us to get a better idea of Robby's circumstances."

"I hope so." Klara worked the kinks out of her neck. "When I saw the news about Robby on *Entertainment Tonight*, everything I know about him started to bother me again. Not that it ever stopped, really, but it seemed tawdry to dwell on it after the kid died. What would be the use? I kept my mouth shut for years, but then, a couple weeks ago, I saw his poor mom on TV giving a statement to the press, and I realized that Robby isn't dead—not to her. She seemed desperate to find out what's happening, so I contacted her from a friend's phone out of town—to express condolences and support as one of Robby's coworkers, you know? But I didn't want to discuss . . . *everything*. I couldn't bring myself to. Luckily, that's when you called."

As Kiko worked on his bad-cop glower, Dawn touched the crucifix under her T-shirt and jacket, her eyes scanning the area. With the sun making its way to the horizon, she was on alert, thinking about those vamps from last night.

Were they going to show themselves once darkness fell?

Breisi took an affable, one-hand-on-one-hip stance. "You were referred to us by Mrs. Pennybaker. We check all recent contacts, but it took us a while to find you."

"My cell got turned off and I was out of state. But I'm all paid up now." Klara embarked on her diction exercises, stretching open her mouth, as if chewing on a really big piece of taffy. Then she paused. "Maybe what I have to contribute won't matter, but at least I'll have it off my conscience."

A crewmember carrying props—oversized stuffed animals—hustled by. The aging actress waited for him to pass.

Then she slowly eased into it. "When I first met Robby, during the read-through for the movie we did together—his final one—he was such a little doll, so scrubbed-up and huggable. He could've been Theodore Cleaver, don't you know. 'Can I get you any food from the service table, Miss Monaghan?' 'I really loved you in *Benji Goes to the Dogs*, Miss Monaghan.' Sweet." Klara looked off into the distance, smiling. "Charming as the dickens. But"—the smile disappeared—"his dad was enough to make you forget about that. Mr. Pennybaker was the biggest stage parent I've ever seen. He drove the director nuts with his suggestions about how to put Robby into more scenes or how to compose a shot so it would flatter him. Once, I caught him watching the kid act as the cameras were going. Nathan was saying every line along with his son—just like he was Robby."

A failed child actor, Dawn thought. It made sad sense.

She'd seen stage parents on set before. Nightmares. More often than not they were living vicariously through their children, and it sounded like Nathan wasn't any different. Sure, he'd put on some great waterworks last night—losing Robby had probably been as traumatic as losing his own career.

But what about the rest of the story, like the pimping part that Kiko had mentioned? And how would all this lead to Frank?

Before Dawn could ask, Klara continued. "About two weeks into production, things started getting . . . I guess you'd say, *icky*. Me and Robby had become friends. I was just starting out, fresh-faced and all that." She had a faraway glow, a glory-day melancholy about her. "Robby liked to get close to you physically, hold your hand, the like. I was his big sister—don't you know how relationships form on the set? You become a family, because nothing much exists outside of the production most times. Besides, I heard he ran around with older friends; he related to adults better than kids. But then . . ."

Breisi and Kiko waited her out, probably because they had trained to be effective listeners, tuning in to body language as well as what was being said out loud.

But Dawn's balled anger made her impatient. "Then what?"

Her question took Klara Monaghan out of her reverie. A sea breeze huffed at her vivid beehive as she focused on Dawn, almost as if just realizing that she existed.

Kiko pinched her, and she took the hint. Shut up and allow the well-oiled machine that was Kiko and Breisi to perform.

Couldn't they hurry it up?

"You were saying?" Breisi asked, giving Dawn her own chiding pinch of a stare.

The cotton candy–haired actress blinked, her hand going to the looser skin of her neck. It clashed with the surgery-enhanced tightness of her face.

"This is a little embarrassing," Klara said.

Breisi put her hand on the older woman's arm. "We appreciate your honesty. Marla will appreciate it."

That did the trick. Klara rested a palm against her throat, covered her chest with the other arm, cocooning herself.

"One day, when we were waiting around for our next scene, Robby leaned against me. He . . ." Klara's fingers fluttered against her skin, finding the proper way to say this. ". . . he put his cheek against my arm. At first. But, well, then he moved over just a touch, putting his lips on my . . ." She motioned to her breast. "He started nuzzling me, looking up at me with this . . . this kind of come-hither invitation. He was *twelve*."

Although Dawn tried not to change expression, something inside of her cracked. Shit like this was par for the course on a movie set; entitled behavior, even from a kid, wasn't a big shocker. Good public relations work and a delusional need to put movie stars on a pedestal kept the general public in the dark about the real Hollywood, but that didn't make it right.

It didn't make it easier to stomach, either.

"Do you think you misinterpreted his actions?" Breisi asked, undetered. "Maybe he accidentally brushed you and that look he gave you wasn't what you thought it was?"

"If it'd happened once, yes. And if I hadn't seen Nathan nearby, watching, I probably would've been less disturbed. Kids his age get experimental, don't you know? They start wondering what sex is all about. But Robby got more persistent day by day, and his dad started inching closer and closer to us while it was happening, sort of like he was coaching Robby or . . . God . . . even getting off on the sight of it, I suppose. You could tell that little kid was going to grow up to be a lady killer, I tell you, and I wonder if Nathan Pennybaker lived through Robby in that way, too . . . If he liked to see how off balance it made me, if he felt like he was dominating me through Robby."

She tightened her arms around herself. "I ended up shutting myself in my trailer to avoid them, but I still had to work with Robby. I still had look at him and get creeped out about what he and his dad were up to."

Dawn couldn't hold back. "Did you report the harassment?"

"No, no. I wanted a career, not a reputation for making trouble. Not that it mattered though. The jobs dried up during the next few years anyway."

Steam whistled in Dawn's head. When Darrin Ryder had felt her up during *her* last gig, she hadn't done dip officially. She was no idiot. Initiating sexual harassment charges against a powerful star would only result in him trotting out twenty witnesses who'd say Dawn was lying. Better to give the pervert a banzai smash in the groin and hope that he associated the pain with making the same mistake in the future. Better to take a chance on securing justice herself than to be ridiculed and, as Klara had said, banned from this small entertainment community.

Yup, Dawn's way had merit, because there were stunt coordinators and directors out there who would choose skill over hard-assedness any day. There were friends of friends who might admire a tough-as-nails stuntwoman and appreciate that she could discreetly solve her own problems—as long as she was good enough for them to take the risk of hiring her.

In fact, she knew that there were a few maverick directors who would name a holiday after her for quietly going vigilante on Darrin Ryder.

All they had to do was look at her headshot and résumé. . . .

Klara was talking again. "Unfortunately, Robby's advances didn't stop there." Her fingers worked at her throat, long, lacquered red nails like clamps. "With a week left on the shoot, Nathan Pennybaker began asking me strange questions. What kind of men did I like? Older ones? Young ones? He was saying it like he was joking around, but I got the feeling he wasn't, so I told him to bug off. Later, after we wrapped, I found out that some other actresses—and *actors*—had gone through the same treatment with Robby and Nathan."

Breisi looked miffed. "Why was this never made public?"

"Are you kidding?" Klara said, her hand dropping. "Robby was a big star. Teflon. A crazy story like mine wouldn't stick to him. A child commodity with a Golden Globe who had the world at his fingertips. No one would believe even a hint of what was really going on."

"The Hollywood code of silence," Dawn added.

Klara nodded at her, her gaze catching Dawn's in understanding. "But that's not the worst of it. Rumor has it that a few women and older men—studio heads and producers—with a certain fetish had taken Nathan up on his offers."

Holy crap. "Do you know that for sure?"

Now nobody was shutting her up.

"You bet I believe what I heard," Klara said. "And from what I went through, I can't say I'm stunned."

"Damn," Kiko finally said.

He wandered closer to Klara, shaking his head in consolation, then put his hand on her lower arm.

The action was twofold. First, Dawn knew he was reading the woman, seeking the veracity of her claims. Second, he was playing a psychological game, too. She'd seen that clear enough with Mrs. Pennybaker's reaction to Kiko last night.

He had the power and appearance to act childlike, evoking trust, recalling what Robby's career was built on: innocence.

When Klara's gaze settled on his hand, Dawn was pretty sure she was picturing and reliving Robby just like Mrs. Pennybaker had done, that she was taking Kiko back on a mind journey to what had happened during his final film.

After a moment, Kiko let go, stepped back to his place next to Dawn. He nodded at her.

Klara Monaghan was on the up-and-up.

"There's something else," the older actress said, suddenly shy and probably even slightly confused by what had just happened. "Word was that Nathan Pennybaker made a habit of encouraging Robby to be aggressive, with females and movie bosses alike. That kid knew more about the biz than people twice his age, and he knew how to act, that one. He was so good. Good enough to take everything he wanted, whether it was a meaty part or a starlet. I shudder to think what Robby would be like today."

Right. Maybe Robby would've grown up to be another Nathan. Maybe it *was* best that the world remember the lie of Robby Pennybaker as a cute, lovable boy and not as the ugly truth.

Yet that was impossible after his scandalous death, after this new image of him had come out in *Diaper Derby*. Now, to the public, Robby was a drugged-out recluse, a freak of the media who made the masses long for the return of the sweet-faced, perfect child he'd once been.

Klara had started running through a slew of tongue twisters in preparation for her dialogue.

"One more thing," Breisi said. "Mrs. Pennybaker doesn't seem to know anything about these rumors."

Klara segued from "Mary sells seashells by the seashore" to "Noooo." She was waving her hands around emphatically. "No, she sure doesn't, and I hope it stays that way. Robby's mom wasn't so much into the Hollywood scene. She never went to the parties, never had power lunches. She spent a lot of time away from home, traveling with the Red Cross, far away from Robby's glittery world. Besides, you have to remember that these rumors were whispers, and they never crossed that invisible line between Hollywood and the rest of society."

That's right, Dawn thought. Movie sets, lunch at the Ivy, cocktails at the Sky Bar—they were different planets in a solar system that existed apart from reality. It's what made stars larger than life, beyond normalcy.

Footsteps came stomping toward them. A production assistant stuck her head around the trailer as Dawn's old phone vibrated in her pocket next to the new one Breisi had given her. And it wasn't for the first time that day, either.

"We need you in five," the young PA said to Klara.

"All right." The actress stretched everything in earnest, her body, her mouth.

"Thank you," Breisi said. "If you think of anything else . . ."

"You're not going to spread it around that I told you this? I wanted to help his mom, bless her heart, I don't want—"

"Our lips are sealed," Dawn said, ready and raring to find Nathan.

Klara took a couple of steps toward the set, then stopped. "There are some places . . . Bava on Vine, The Lei House, Deacon's, and a list of hotels I can give you. People used to say that Nathan Pennybaker took Robby out to be seen in the social scene. Bava was their favorite. It's a hole in the wall, dark, discreet. A lot of underaged actors get in. The same management owns it today, even though it's changed clientele. Maybe they can tell you more about this?"

Nathan took Robby to bars and clubs? Nice. Dawn couldn't wait to *interview* the man for real this time.

"We appreciate it," Breisi said. "I'll call you for those hotels later."

"Good luck getting to the bottom of this." Klara took a couple more steps backward. "I can't imagine why that kid was in *Diaper Derby*. He didn't even look like the Robby I knew."

Then she took off in a clatter of high-heeled pumps, wiggling her way to her job.

Dawn watched her leave, feeling the same way she had after the vamp fight: drained and beaten. But there was still that something about Robby that was mentally jabbing at her. . . .

She pushed it by the wayside. "Goddamnit, I can't wait to hear what good old Mr. P. has to say."

"Copy that," Kiko said.

"Twelve years old. T*welve*! God, if Frank hadn't . . ."

She shut herself up. Sure, her dad had done some good by distancing her from the Hollywood scene, but he'd done a lot of bad, too. Nothing this unforgivable though.

Nothing that made her want to forget him.

"Did it sound like Nathan P. was kind of avenging himself on the business through Robby?" she asked.

"He felt superior as he watched the actresses squirm," Kiko noted. "And I'll bet he got off on renting Robby out to those powerful men, being the supplier of something they needed."

"The glamour of his son's presence," Dawn added. "Do you realize how much blackmail material Nathan P. has? Think *that* was a part of it? Wow, what a big man, using his kid as his goddamned tool of power."

"We'll check into possible blackmail." All business, Breisi pulled out her phone and called information to get Bava's hours. Kiko followed suit, checking his messages in the hope that his agent had called.

Still stewing, Dawn opened her own cell, taking a guess as to who had been making it vibrate during Klara's interview.

It was just as she expected: another call from Matt Lonigan. She'd gotten one earlier, on the way from the fencing studio to the pier. And, as instructed by The Voice, she hadn't returned his message.

"Kiko," she said as he closed his phone in disgust. No summons from the agent, evidently. "Lonigan called."

"The guy's a bull terrier, huh? We'll just have to leave another message for the boss. He'll get a hold of our persistent PI tonight, I'm sure."

Unable to keep her feet still, Breisi ended her call, shuffling back and forth. "We'll head to Bava around nine, when they open. That'll give us a chance to mingle while things are slow, then to hang around when the night gets going. And as for Matt Lonigan, Dawn? I've got some news. While you and *Señor* Pirate Dingleberry here were jabbing swords at each other—"

"There was no jabbing involved," Kiko interrupted.

"—I was actually working."

Dawn's hackles pinged. "We *were* in training."

"Training for leaving the boss once this ends," Breisi added. "We need to be concentrating on this case. And Kiko, honestly, I'm disappointed you didn't have more self-control."

Speechless, Dawn couldn't believe that Breisi was testing her determination to find Frank. Just . . . couldn't believe it.

Kiko lifted his chin. "Fencing promotes agility. You just watch how I dust some vamps with my new footwork."

"I await that on pins and needles." Breisi shoved her phone in a pants pocket. "Anyway, about this Matt. He's legit. His agency says he's been active since the mid-nineties, and he checks out with his licensing."

"How thorough," Dawn said, still smarting from Breisi's tongue lashing. "What do you think he could be, anyway? A vampire slave or something? Like Renfield?"

"The boss would call him a servant," Kiko said. "Not vampire, but still human, because they haven't exchanged blood with a real vamp and lost their soul, supposedly. Next time, Dawn, look for bite marks. That should tell you. Was he wearing a turtleneck?"

"In the middle of summer—no."

Actually, he'd been wearing a black T-shirt that'd hugged his muscles. At the thought, Dawn's mojo started to tingle.

Breisi was tapping her fingers against her hips. "Bite marks can be anywhere. Boss says a servant is fixated with pleasing his or her master, the vamp who takes their blood. They'll do anything for them."

"But they're still human," Dawn repeated.

Kiko shrugged. "For the most part."

"Maybe we should do a body search of Nathan Pennybaker tonight for bites." She strolled away from the trailer. Breisi and Kiko followed. "Not that exploring his body is my fantasy. My fist has just got some questions it wants to ask him."

Breisi cupped her knuckles in her other palm. "I'd like to take that cocksucker by the *cojones* and hear him squeal, too."

At the unexpected cussing from Breisi, Dawn glanced at her. The two women locked gazes, a deep understanding cementing something unspoken—a primal instinct, an urge to defend a child, even if you told yourself over and over again that you weren't ever going to have one.

In acknowledgment, Dawn jerked her chin at her coworker, who returned the gesture. They looked away, continued walking.

"What do you say we get some takeout before we go to Bava?" Kiko asked. "And Dawn needs to catch up on some reading after she fills out her concealed weapon permit."

Pulling a face at the thought of bookwork, Dawn patted the revolver that was hidden in its shoulder holster beneath her own sweatjacket. "Could I do some shooting practice instead?"

"Not a reader?" Breisi asked.

"Not so much. Aside from a stint at UCLA for a few months, I'm not exactly the studious type."

"Good to know." Breisi veered off toward the 4Runner, leaving Dawn and Kiko to go to his small car.

Dawn sent one last look at their tech geek as she disappeared into a shadow of twilight dimming the sky. Stymied, she shrugged, not knowing what the hell to make of Breisi.

Meanwhile, from a car parked two spaces away, a pair of eyes watched Dawn with their own intense scrutiny.

With the desperation of an obsession.

TWELVE

Below, Phase Two

LATER, Sorin watched a contingent of Groupies readying themselves to journey Above via the deep canyon caves that had once been used as a rock quarry and were now forgotten. The young vampires were dressed in what was known as their "Gothic" finery, primed to blend with humans as well as any other ghouls and stray, non-Underground vampires who wandered the city.

The leader, who called herself Galatea, came to the front of the black-clad crowd. As she faced Sorin, her eyes held the silver tint of all Groupies—vampires who had joined the society for the honor of providing food and amusement for the Elites. Above, they would hide their preternatural appearances and abilities, just as chameleons would camouflage themselves in drab surroundings with far less spectacular colors.

As the young vampire bowed her head, a thicket of dark, braided hair fell around her moon-white face. Her high cheekbones were decorated with slashes of blue paint, warlike. She wore a blackened Native American bone hairpipe breastplate that showed a hint of her small breasts, tight leather pants with knee-high boots and spurs. Holding her fingers to her forehead, she saluted Sorin.

"Protect your home," he said. It was an order.

With the arrogance of one who has not lived more than a century, the beautiful creature smiled. "Don't worry, Master. We'll fit right in at Bava." She winked. "We always do."

Accompanied by the faint jingle of her spurs, she left him, disappearing with her flock into the darkness of a tunnel where the lights forever stayed black.

Sorin had assigned Galatea and the Groupies to go Above based on what he had gleaned from the spywork he had convinced the real Master to initiate last night—spywork that troubled him more than it assuaged his concerns. But there was no contradicting his parent, especially after the work had confirmed that Dawn Madison and her investigator friends had been visiting the Pennybaker residence on a clue hunt. Evidently, they wished to discover a reason for Robby Pennybaker's appearance in that ghostly film clip.

And, since Sorin must also admit that their spywork had already led them to Bava tonight, he would tolerate the Master's plans until he had the leverage to protest.

Bava was a bar where Groupies and Servants occasionally gathered, their identities blurred by the fine Goth line between imagination and reality. Like most haunted bars in L.A., one of the Underground Servants was already employed there. He functioned well as a spy who reported back to Sorin.

Tonight, the Groupies would take spywork even a step further, masquerading in human form, focusing on Dawn Madison's group from anonymous positions in the crowd. They would use their mild mind powers in casual conversation to gather whether the Guard killers were garden-variety mercenaries or indeed connected to a more powerful individual, as Sorin feared.

He hated having to depend on the Groupies, who were normally fun-loving beings who served in the Underground of their own free will. But since they were dedicated to keeping their vow of secrecy when they mingled and fed among humans, Sorin had agreed to assign them to this important work. They loved the Underground as much as he did, so he would trust them.

In any case, it was imperative that the humans not uncover any information about the Underground; unless the Groupies were compromised, the scheme required mere reconnaissance. Passive intelligence. That was all.

With a cynical growl, he turned around, his presence needed elsewhere. He meant to visit the Master in person, mainly to persuade him to rethink their strategy, yet also to do business.

As a stream of wind howled through the tunnel and gathered Sorin in its embrace, his dark clothing chopped around him.

Night wind, he thought, and it was drenched with the scent of humanity.

He shivered in hunger but moved on, knowing a meal—a Servant who voluntarily offered blood without the expectation of exchanging it—awaited him after he took care of his Master.

All the same, he kept his mind where it should be: on security. Vampire secrecy was prized above all else—it was essential to living in peace among the humans—so Sorin had also sent a patrol of Guards Above to quietly resume the hunt for their quarry.

Sorin would do anything and *everything* to find out if the Underground should risk revealing more of itself in order to stamp out a possible threat. But the threat had to be valid to take such a serious risk. Neutralizing Dawn Madison and her friends now could be costly, especially if other humans noticed their absence and took up the search for their missing loved ones, peeling back the layers of carefully cultivated vampire myth and mystery, one by one.

Like a lighted pathway home, Sorin's Awareness of his maker—their lifeline between a vampire and the child he had created—led him to a hidden room off the east tunnel. He scratched at the stone, coaxing open a slab, which allowed him to surreptitiously slip through and enter the room.

There, he found a sight that chilled his blood.

In the darkness, he could see the red-hazed outline of his Master. Yet now, instead of a black void filling the inside of his body, a burst of color—violet, green, white, a menagerie of shades—swirled inside the ancient vampire. A hushed sound, much like the whispers of a million voices crying into one, filled the room, emanating from the Master.

He was indulging again.

Sorin could hear his parent's breath coming in gasps, could only imagine how his body was shaking and shuddering in ecstasy. In sheer, wracking pain.

Had the Master not been expecting him?

Seized by a mixture of mortification, curiosity, and—was it also thirst?—at witnessing this private moment, Sorin bowed his head, waited for the Master to finish.

Yet, a morbid fascination riveted his lowered gaze to the vampire.

As the colors pushed against the old creature's outline, seeking escape with an urgency that increased by the second, he stirred, moaned. Then, when the colors grew in frantic intensity, the Master grunted, cried out, and gripped the table.

Without warning, the colors ripped out of him in a scream of terror, circling overhead, darting with an ear-shattering sucking groan into the vial that Sorin knew was waiting, open, on the table. A tiny screech wept out of the container, sounding every bit as traumatized as a victim who was cowering from whatever was stalking him.

Weakened, the head vampire collapsed, his red-neon outline fizzing out, lacking energy while he grasped the table as if it could keep him afloat. His breath rasped out of him, yet Sorin kept his peace, knowing from experience that the Master would not want pity or aid.

Even if Sorin feared for his parent's safety, he knew silence and lack of worry was prudent. Instead, he moved forward, then corked the vial, keeping the contents inside.

Keeping the soul contained for the Master's future use.

"Sorin . . ." the other vampire uttered while crashing to the ground.

The younger vampire did not answer. He wanted no part of feeding this addiction beyond cleaning up after the mentor he had so admired over the centuries.

By now, he could hear the Master's breath rattling as he recovered from imbibing one of those souls in his extensive collection. In the dark, Sorin's vampire sight caught the gleam of a hundred more vials stored in boxes on the wall's shelves.

He asked no questions, because he knew precisely what had transpired. His Master was a Soul Taker, feasting on the only tie to humanity he possessed anymore. Souls mattered more than blood now—it was a rush for the Master, the drinking of them making him feel temporarily alive. And if Sorin had not believed that this was one of the only ways to keep the Master interested in existing, he would have campaigned for a stop to it long ago.

"My shell of a body . . ." the Master said, his breath catching. "It never fails to reject what I need the most."

"A soul is foreign to you," Sorin said, feeling as if this were a vicious resurrection replayed week by week, the words frayed and useless from too much repetition. "You lost your own when you took the oath, Master. There is no reclaiming it."

The older vampire's teeth chattered. It was the only sound hitting the stone walls.

Sorin often wondered if the souls so violently departed from the Master because he had not earned the right to one.

"None of us has them anymore," Sorin added stoically. "It is the price we paid." He eased toward his parent, unable to withstand the suffering. "In spite of your greater powers, you are no different from the rest of your brood in that matter."

"Sorin." It was painfully uttered, yet still an ecstatic command. "A . . . moment . . . more."

Hands clasped behind his back, Sorin obeyed, allowing the other vampire to wallow in his anguish. A masochistic luxury.

"Innocence . . ." The Master heaved out a long breath. "This one had such . . . innocence . . . before it was corrupted. Remember what that was like, Sorin?"

"No, Master."

Sorin saw no use in the Master's insistence on taking the souls in. But the old vampire often said that each spirit had its own properties, and that he was a little in love with them all. Each allowed him to lose himself, if only for a sublime minute, in an intimate stranger's essence.

To be human for an agonizing burst of stolen joy.

And the Master could never get enough of escaping himself. Not lately.

Still quaking, the old vampire drew himself up, propped himself against the wall, cradled a leg and rested his arms over a knee. Sorin was puzzled at this new wrinkle in the process. Normally, this was when his parent shed enraged tears, when he pulled into himself and escaped to his own separate world until Sorin attempted, once again, to pull him out.

But this was not the way of it tonight. No, the Master seemed more reflective than usual, even restlessly content.

"Master . . . ?"

"A miracle." He laughed, the sound edged with disbelief, happiness. "It's possible. This time, it doesn't hurt for me to come back. A *miracle*."

Thankfulness welled inside Sorin, a muted celebration at finally seeing his Master interested in his surroundings again. He wondered how much this had to do with what was transpiring Above—if these desperate times had finally jarred the rightful ruler back into form: the vampire who had tasted all the pleasures the world had to offer.

The ruthless warrior who had created a powerful Underground that, until this point, had run smoothly and effortlessly.

Seeing the change in his parent, Sorin knew that, in spite of all of his doubts and concerns, perhaps he had done well to challenge the Master last night. He held a hand to his chest.

Long live the Underground.

Long live this blink of interest from the Master.

"I am so very pleased," Sorin said, saluting his superior with his other hand, fingers to his forehead. "Welcome back."

A well-fought grunt, a sigh of renewed anguish from against the wall, gave Sorin pause. Had he spoken too quickly? Had he made too many assumptions?

In due haste, he moved on to the business at hand, keeping the Master engaged. He extracted a manila envelope bulging with money from his coat, set it on the table. The Master's breath hitched at the scent of it.

"It is a payment from Tamsin Greene." A human who wished to become an elite citizen. "I have completed her preliminary procedures, and we await a time and date at your pleasure."

"Tamsin Greene," the Master said.

Sorin knew that his parent recognized the name. He had been privy to her interview tapes, her vows of maintaining Underground secrecy at the cost of her life and dearest desires.

"She seemed anxious about her decision." The Master's voice, still shaky with spent passion, had gone wary. "Is she convinced she wants to be here? Based on recent events, Sorin, we need to be careful."

"We are."

Now the Master's tone sounded strangled, choked with an emotion Sorin could not readily identify.

"I'm *never* taking anyone without their full permission again. Not unless they want what I have to offer with *all* of their soul."

Perhaps he was smarting from the trouble Above?

"She is willing." Sorin rested a firm hand on the money, a payment of millions. "And she has no qualms about giving more."

Sorin tried not to glance at the capped vial on the table, the boxes lining the walls.

"Then schedule her to join us as soon as possible." A pause. "I trust you with this, Sorin."

"Yes, Master." Yesterday, Sorin would have entertained grave doubts as to whether or not his Master would have been up to the exhaustive ceremonies and celebrations required to welcome a new citizen. Today, he was slightly more reassured based on what he had just witnessed as well as the Master's decision to initiate spy-work last night.

A decision that Sorin still wanted to discuss. There were elements that concerned him, especially—

"Leave me," the Master rasped, reading Sorin's mind and cutting him off. He slumped against the wall, the aura around his body fading as he rested.

Without another word, Sorin bowed and saluted once again, going about his work.

Leaving the Master alone in his beloved darkness so he could go about his, as well.

THIRTEEN

The Gathering

SMOKE and mirrors. That's what this place was made of, Dawn thought as she, Breisi, and Kiko sat at Bava's crumbling altar-bar smelling of the garlic they'd rubbed over their skin like insect repellant. If it worked, great. If not, she'd be tasty scampi for some lucky set of teeth tonight.

Kiko had been the first to note that this cramped Goth hangout was named for Mario Bava, a noted Italian horror director. It was an homage to one of the artist's best-known movies, *Black Sunday*, *La Maschera del Demonio*. The color scheme was stark gray and white; the inside gutted like a ruined chapel with iron grating, stone coffins, and gnarled branches and weeds creeping over the walls. A tinge of white light rose up from the bar, casting shadows under the faces of the black-garbed bartenders, lending them nefarious attitude to go along with the dyed jet hair and heavy eyeliner. Dog collars, see-through netted shirts, and piercings were the order of the night in here. Throbbing music drowned out conversation and identity in a mist of sweat and darkness.

Dawn sipped at her glass of water and moved her fingers in time to the heavy bass. Sliding a hard look around, she took in the small dance floor choked with customers who swayed in haunting, studied rhythm under the shifting lights.

During the last hour and a half, their attempts at engaging the management and then the patrons in conversation hadn't worked so well. The owner didn't know squat. To make matters more difficult, the customers were skeptical and unwilling to help, their painted looks discouraging queries. If they weren't on the dance floor, they were huddled in the dark corners, where a few underage, famous faces lurked, too. Dawn had already spied a "new punk" eighteen-year-old pop singer drinking from a martini glass of blue-tinted Hypnotiq and snorting coke from behind the shield of her bodyguards. No one was acknowledging that she even existed.

Breisi leaned toward Kiko and Dawn, yelling, "We need to isolate these bartenders and waitresses and convince them to talk. They've got to take breaks sooner or later."

Sounded doable to Dawn. Responding to the idea, she raised her glass to Breisi, then downed the rest of the liquid.

The older woman's face didn't change expression; she disengaged eye contact, tapped her foot, and began taking inventory of the bartenders.

Dawn followed suit, resting her hand in her jacket pocket and feeling a holy water vial for defense. Before heading out here, Breisi had smeared more of her wonder goo on Dawn's rapidly healing injuries, then armed her with a cluster of vampire weapons: garlic, a stake, an additional crucifix, and the holy water. Dawn had asked Breisi when she would get to use that bitchin' crossbow with the blades, but Breisi had just gotten all pissy and shoved a garlic clove into Dawn's hand for a rubdown while muttering, "In your next life."

But Dawn was set. Besides her pocket arsenal, the silver bullet–loaded revolver was in its shoulder holster. However, the stake would've been too obvious, so it was back in the car.

They weren't at Bava for a rumble anyway, right? Still, if the vamps showed up, they'd be ready.

They'd also changed into appropriate attire for clubbing. Dawn had no problems: she'd just thrown on her earring, boots, heavy makeup, a clean pair of black jeans, and a dark skull-and-crossbones tank top to wear under her jacket. Breisi and Kiko, on the other hand, had needed some coaching.

Kiko had on a pair of leather pants and a jacket—all black, of course. Oddly enough, he looked like one of the underage kids in Bava, so he fit right in. But Breisi . . .

Jeez, Breisi. She'd shown up dressed in black, thank God, but she'd been wearing one of those damned bear shirts—this one of Teddy doing a cartwheel. Dawn had made her take it off, rip it in a few fashionable places, then turn it inside out so the picture didn't really show beneath her jacket.

Breisi was not amused.

"For this kind of place," Dawn had told her, "black-lace teddy—okay. Teddy *Ruxpin*—not so much."

Now, as the music transitioned to an old song by Siouxsie and the Banshees, Kiko hopped off his bar stool. He indicated a magenta-haired waitress and darted away to corner her.

That left Breisi and Dawn. They just stared at each other for a second, then yelled over Siouxsie at the same time.

"I'll work the bar!" That was Dawn, pointing to her glass.

"I've got to make a call!" That was Breisi, pointing to her phone then heading outside.

Dawn knew she was going to give Nathan Pennybaker another try. God, she couldn't wait to bruise all the parts of him that were pink and justifiably poetic.

And as for Mrs. Pennybaker . . . they'd decided to hold back on telling the mom anything until they could approach Nathan first. Hell, was it so wrong to have their facts straight before ruining the poor woman?

Too bad they weren't having any luck reaching her husband. To make matters even more frustrating, Breisi had told them that the bugs she'd planted weren't even picking up Nathan's voice.

As Dawn wondered if they were going to have to find Robby's dad now, too, she hunkered down over the bar. She thought of her own father—where he might be right now, what he was . . .

Coldness shivered over the back of her neck.

Immediately, she straightened, on guard, eyes locking on a woman at the end of the bar.

Asian-featured, she was pale, with Adam Ant war paint on her face and braids all over her head. Like the flash of a mirrored ball, the woman's eyes went silver, and Dawn jammed her hand into her pocket for the crucifix. But . . .

There was nothing—no fire, no mind screw.

Dawn hesitated. A vamp would've worked its gaze, like those red-eyed things, yet there'd been nothing with this woman.

The Adam Antette turned away, leaning on the bar and watching the dance floor.

The hair on Dawn's arms was standing on end, and she let go of her crucifix, not sure what to think. Too rattled to think.

Was she getting paranoid? That'd be awesome.

Someone yelled at her, and she jerked back to find the bartender waiting for her to answer him. Wearing a black vest, long dark hair, and makeup straight out of *The Crow*, he resembled the ghost of Brandon Lee, the actor who'd died during a tragic shooting on the set of his last movie.

Her pulse stopped, screwing into itself at the eerie resemblance. But when she looked a little closer, she realized that he was merely a wan imitation of the rising star who had shown such potential.

Forcing herself to recover, Dawn took a wild guess and determined that he was asking her if she wanted a refill.

"No, thanks."

Some Nine-Inch-Nails Betty who was way too eager for a vodka on the rocks smashed against Dawn's back in a bad rendition of party etiquette, sticking out ten dollars to attract the bartender's attention. Dawn subtly forced her shoulder against the woman, making her back off.

On a whim, she glanced at the Adam Antette again, but she was gone.

The bartender handed over the vodka to the pushy customer. As he moved forward, his vest gaped open, and that's when Dawn saw it: two wounds above his pecs.

Her blood tugged at her veins, her head going woozy. Good God . . . bite marks? A servant?

Or maybe it was just that paranoia. And, really, who could blame her after last night?

Keeping cool, Dawn kept him in her sights, easing from her stool the second he scooped up two handfuls of empty bottles and headed toward the back of the room.

As she threaded her way through the dance floor toward him, she saw Kiko. He was near the restroom pay phone, where it was quieter, though not by much. The magenta waitress he was talking to had her head tilted back in laughter, her dominatrix-garbed body aimed straight at the psychic in open invitation. *Go, Kiko.*

He reached toward the woman's arm.

But before he made contact, Dawn rested her hand on his healthy shoulder. As he followed her with his gaze, she jerked her chin toward the back, and he nodded, acknowledging where she was going.

Then, as his interview subject sighed in post-laugh recovery, he touched her. She didn't make another sound.

Dawn entered the far more utilitarian back hall, with its blasé walls and red tile. The faint clatter of glass led her to a storage room, where she found the bartender picking up full liquor bottles to replenish the spent ones. At the sound of her entrance he did a double take, his *Crow* face, threatening and pale, caught in a frown.

"You're not allowed here."

The music was more background than hindrance now.

"I got lost." Dawn shot him a smile, came a bit closer. "But while I'm around, do you mind talking to me for a few?"

He relaxed, ran a gaze over her. When he got to her face, she marked the typical reaction: "Unimpressive, but she does have a thumpin' bod."

She battled back the twinge of inferiority, of being second-tier attractive.

"I've got to get back soon," he said, gaze still roving, contradicting his words.

Then he propped the bottles on a stainless steel table. Good sign. He also gave her one of those looks: the smirk of a bartender who kind of resembled a legend and was kind of used to getting laid because of it.

The air snapped between them. Dawn's body reacted, restless, ever-hungry. Used to being fed.

She walked nearer, taking advantage of his weakness. Of hers, too. "How long you been working here?"

"A couple weeks, give or take. It's a gig—not permanent."

Of course. He'd get his break soon, leave bartending behind, become a star. "Pay much attention to the customers?"

Adjusting his lean body to face hers head-on, he laughed at the strange question. "What's this about?"

She was two feet away from him now, close enough to smell the cocktail of his skin. She heated up under her jacket as he continued checking her out.

Do men look at you this way now, *Eva?* she thought.

She caught herself, feeling her nails crush into her palms.

Concentrate on questions, she thought. Find Frank.

She relaxed, bolstered her strength. "Can you remember the faces of the people who come in here?"

Laughing, he clearly thought she was leading up to something entirely different. She'd done too good of a job stringing her pick-up lines together and tugging him closer.

"Can you remember any of them?" Dawn asked, focusing on the interview now . . . pushing, *pushing* back at everything else.

"Sometimes I pay attention to the clientele." He lowered his voice, grinned. "Certain ones in particular."

Her gaze instinctively wandered over his chest, the pale expanse of flesh over gym-honed planes. She beat back the attraction: a cadence of warning that drummed beneath her skin.

As she listened to the pulsing in her temples, she identified what the sound was.

Anger, not lust. Anger at Eva, at Frank. At herself.

Goddamnit, get it together, she thought. Be strong, be tough. *Concentrate.*

With difficulty, she backed off, started circling the bartender. "I'm looking for someone."

"No shit." He laughed again, obviously growing wary as she crossed to the opposite side of the room.

Ignoring his double entendre, she kept moving, stalking, gauging him, growing stronger with his increasing anxiety and her increasing distance.

As she came around the table, he slanted his body toward her again, but it wasn't exactly in lust this time. Now it was more like a man who didn't want to keep his back to an open door without his guns drawn.

He sniffed. "Jesus, do you work in a pizza factory?"

The garlic. Interesting that he wasn't strongly repelled.

More composed now, she showed him two pictures of Robby that Breisi had given her—one of the clean-cut superstar, one of a pierced and shaggy boy.

"Has this kid been around?"

The bartender reared back. "That's Robby Pennybaker."

" 'No shit.' I hope you don't mind me quoting you. Your words were so profound."

He started at her change of tone, no doubt wondering where the aggressive flirt had gone. "Hey, what's your issue?"

The anger inside her went up a notch.

Issue. She could probably redefine the word for him.

"My issue is . . ." She shoved the pictures at him again. ". . . this kid might be in trouble. If you could find it within your heart to help, you'd earn a Brownie point or two."

He stared at the photo for a second longer, and it was enough time to allow Dawn to see a hint of helplessness. When his gaze met hers, she held her breath, knowing he was about to say something. . . .

But then he abruptly turned back to the table and reached for the bottles, a long flow of black hair conveniently hiding his face. "I've gotta go."

In an implosion of undiluted frustration, Dawn forgot about all her sore muscles, cuts, and scrapes and grabbed his arm, whipping him around to face her.

"What aren't you telling me?"

He bolted back, holding up his hands. Peace, man, peace. "You need to get out of here."

She smiled—a razor-thin line singing with impatience. This guy might lead to Robby. Robby might lead to Frank. Frank might lead to . . . She didn't know, but she had to find out.

"You just became much more intriguing." She tucked Robby's pictures away and took out Frank's. "How about this man? Ever seen him? It might be more recently."

The bartender's Adam's apple worked in his throat as he tried to swallow. He'd seen Frank. His eyes told her so.

Relieved, happiness lit through her at the possibility of getting a lead. Then a memory intruded.

Her smiling father, pushing her on a playground merry-go-round when she was a little girl. Faster, faster. He grinned down at her as she squealed in delight, laughed with her as her hands grew sweaty against the bars.

"Hold on, Dawn."

Her hands were slipping, but she was laughing so hard she couldn't tell him.

Faster, faster.

"Isn't this fun? Look how fast you're going! My little girl can take anything!"

Slipping . . .

Her fingers loosened around the paint-chipped bars; the rust smelled like blood.

"Daddy's so proud of his rough-and-ready girl! Kids twice your age can't take this kind of speed!"

Her mouth formed around a cry of "Daddy!" but the word wouldn't come out.

The bars slithered out of her grip, colors melding, flying in front of her face . . . an expanse of green . . . grass . . . zooming up to meet her—

Everything stopped, her face an inch from the green.

The next thing she knew she was in her father's arms, trembling, nausea rising up in her throat. He smelled like gin and he felt like home.

"Baby . . . oh, little baby . . . I'd never let my little girl get hurt." He was close to sobs. "Daddy will always be here for you. He'll protect you from falling again, he'll make sure of that. He won't let anything . . . not the playground, not the awful people that got your mommy . . . anything hurt you, Dawnie . . ."

In his embrace, she had tried so hard not to cry, because her daddy wouldn't want that. He was proud that she wasn't a wimp, and Dawn lived for his pride.

As his tears dampened her cheek, little Dawn looked at him, wiped the moisture away.

"I'll protect you from all the bad things, too, Daddy. . . ."

She glanced down at the actual photo. His dark hair was windblown as he posed, jaunty and carefree, on a dock at Marina del Rey. In the background, fishermen waited for their latest catch. The colors dredged up a shadow below the surface of so many things she didn't like to think about. . .

Throat tight, she pushed it at the bartender. "This is Frank Madison. He's . . . a PI. He went missing about five days ago."

"I haven't seen him. Now get out before I call the cops."

His resistance was a needle-sharp poke to her swollen grief. Patience exploding, Dawn flew at him, caught him in a headlock, and slammed his body face-first against the table. Bottles went flying, shattering to the tile. She levered her weight onto him, forgetting her usual practice of holding back. In her biz, she'd been taught to pull punches, to "sell" a fight and make it all look real without injuring anyone.

But she didn't have to do that right now. Not with this callous motherfucker.

Nope. Instead she jammed the side of her forearm against the back of his neck, making him cry out like a prissy little girl who'd torn her pinafore.

"If you know something about Frank, you'd better tell me before I get angry."

He squirmed under her, but she rapidly cleared the table of cut glass with her jacketed arm, saving a fragment. As alcohol dripped to the tile, she held the shard to his face, knowing how to really threaten an actor.

With his disfigurement—real or imagined.

The picture of Frank, happy and healthy on the pier, swam in front of her eyes.

Rage muddled her judgment, drove her heartbeat until it pounded in her ears. "What do you know about Frank Madison?"

The bartender didn't move.

Smart guy. He realized he couldn't overpower her without the risk of getting cut first.

"Take the glass away!"

"Tell me!"

"All right." He was panting, his face smashed against the table. "He was hanging around here near the time you said he disappeared.

A big guy, asking a lot of questions about Robby, too. He . . . never came back."

"Bullshit!"

"I swear, I swear! That's all I know. Please, let go!"

With her other arm, she increased the pressure on his neck, then let up when his face reddened. "And what about Robby?"

"The kid hung out here. They say his dad used to party here, too, but Robby ran around like it was his playhouse while his father lurked in some corner. It was a long time ago, back before this was a Goth hang out, but the staff still talks about it. It's history though . . . Please, my face."

Something wasn't ringing right here.

Dawn inched the glass over him, the edge dancing on his smooth cheek. Rage squeezed at her, choking her conscience.

A voice yelled from behind her. "Dawn, what're you doing?"

It was Kiko.

"Interviewing." She didn't take her eyes from her subject. "And just wait 'til you see me with Nathan Pennybaker."

"Get off of him," Breisi said.

"He's a servant," Dawn announced.

She felt the bartender go stiff beneath her.

"Aren't you?" she added, tone jagged. "You've got bite marks on your chest, and you're not careful about hiding them."

"I like to be sucked every once in a while," he said, words muffled by the table. "Go back into the bar and you'll find a hundred other people just like me."

A fine tremble wavered in the pit of her stomach, where her memories of Frank had settled. The glass grew unsteady in her hand, so she pulled it away, but not by much. She told her associates what the bartender had relayed so far.

"Dawn," Breisi said again, "we're going to have to teach you how to finesse an interview from now on."

"I don't know." Kiko walked to the other side of the table

where Dawn could see him. "Her way seems to be working just fine." He climbed onto the surface, put his hand on the servant's back. "Are you a servant to vampires?"

The man closed his eyes, as if darkness would make them all go away. He sniffed again, probably digusted—but not broken—by their garlic.

Kiko sat up. "Yes."

"Good," Dawn said. "Time for some turkey carving."

"Stop! I'll tell you anything! Just don't . . . oh, God." The bartender looked like he might weep.

Breisi came to Kiko's side of the table, arms crossed over her chest in displeasure.

Concentrating on the servant instead of Breisi, Dawn moved the shard ever so slightly. It did the trick.

"Okay—Robby's been around," the bartender moaned. "That's really all I know!"

The vibration of the bass from the club's music buzzed the room, jittering around the outline of her heart. Slowly, Dawn glanced up at her cohorts. Kiko's and Breisi's eyes had gone wide.

"Don't you mean *Frank's* been around?" Dawn asked the servant, needing to hear it again.

"No, Robby. Robby Penny—"

The jangle of something like spurs interrupted.

Tossing aside her shard, Dawn flew up from the table, her hand going for her revolver instead. Kiko and Breisi did the same, crouched for action, their weapons aimed.

Adam Antette was standing in the doorway, her hands up. A crowd of Goths stood behind the woman.

"This isn't the bathroom, I take it," she said.

Hand to his face—probably to check for damage—the bartender scuttled away from Dawn. He crashed through the back entrance, a blast of outside air washing into the room.

"Facilities are down the hall." Breisi's gun was still poised.

"No worries, babe, I'm just a drunken lout who stumbled into this on her way to a leak." The woman glanced at each of them in turn, as if committing their faces to mind.

Dawn felt ready to explode, loaded with frustration and the remnants of Frank's memory. Vamp paranoia reaching a peak, she reached her free hand into her jacket pocket. Then, with quicksilver speed, she whipped out the crucifix.

Everything flew into fast-forward motion.

All of the Goths reacted, jerking backward. A change licked over them, like pale flame rushing up a curtain. Sharpened nails, metallic eyes, white fangs, and skin with such a moon-glow that Dawn choked in a breath.

Before her gaze could take in their strange beauty, they all raised their hands at once, because Breisi and Kiko had followed Dawn's lead, brandishing their crucifixes, too.

But while the others hid their faces, the braided woman reacted by glaring at Dawn, her eyes folding into red slits of fire, just like the vampire from last night.

Mental fury scorched into Dawn, a flash of hopelessness, a reminder of failure. Her body weakened, crumbling to ash . . .

Lessons. What did you learn in your lesson—

With a burst of wrath, she used her mind as a wave, flinging the hypnotic energy back at the vampire, making the woman clutch at her chest.

She hadn't expected Dawn's lightning-fast parry.

Like an atomic shudder, the vampires broke apart, leaving faint imprints of a black cloud that had dissipated. Dawn took off after them.

"Are you crazy?" Breisi yelled, grabbing Dawn. The older woman was digging her fingers into Dawn's healing burns.

Snarling in pain, she gathered all her strength and wrenched herself away, revolver and crucifix in front of her as she blazed into the hall.

The empty hall.

"Shit!" Dawn kept aiming around, hoping to find them.

Needing to find them.

I had something, Frank. Damn it, I had something!

Breisi and Kiko marched into the hallway, the tech geek taking hold of Dawn's jacket and dragging her toward the club and the exit. "We're no good to the boss if we're dead."

The look on Kiko's face almost echoed Breisi's sentiments, but Dawn couldn't be sure.

His expression was as fleeting as the silver in those vamps' eyes.

FOURTEEN

The Haunted House

ONCE they were in the car, Breisi turned around in her driver's seat and let loose. "You're out of control, Dawn."

"We had them." Dawn held up her hands in impotent fury. "We should've given chase before they disappeared."

"No. We gather information for the boss. We don't exterminate, not unless we're attacked and we have to. Besides, that's how Frank got into trouble—not thinking and pursuing things at a whim, the fool."

Scolding was bringing out the mother in Breisi, or at least, close to what Dawn thought a mother might sound like. The fine wrinkles had deepened around the older woman's narrowed eyes, her tone final and nonnegotiable.

But Dawn didn't need a parent—never had. As soon as she was old enough, she'd assumed that role in a household where Frank needed someone else to take care of the bills, cook the meals, tuck him into bed after he passed out.

Staring out the window, Kiko wasn't saying a word, so Dawn

didn't know whether or not he was agreeing with Breisi. Hell, it'd be nice to have an ally here, seeing as Dawn had done some good and gotten them major information, right?

Robby's been around, the bartender/servant had said. But he'd uttered something else that had disturbed her much more. . . .

A big guy, asking a lot of questions about Robby.

He . . . never came back.

Frank. Dawn closed her eyes, dug her nails into her jeans. Her dad had been at Bava earlier this week. She could almost still feel him in the air. So close. So goddamned close.

Finally, Kiko said something. "Those silver-eyed vamps weren't as tough as the red-eyes. Think they know each other? They both like to hang around Robby's turf."

Dawn opened her gaze to find Breisi still glaring at her, jaw tight as she answered her associate.

"It wouldn't be a leap to think they're somehow connected."

"And they all ran away." Kiko motioned to the window, outside. Somewhere, the vamps—and the servant with the answers—were on the loose. "Wimps."

"We should've gone after them," Dawn repeated, like saying it again would give her another chance at them.

Breisi held up a finger, the terse gesture demanding silence. Slowly, she allowed her hand to drop as she spoke.

"There are times when weakness covers desperation, and that's even more dangerous than strength or skill. We might be very lucky that those creatures ran away. Very lucky." She turned to Kiko. "Maybe the boss is right about giving Dawn more training, or maybe . . ."

"Maybe what?" Dawn sat forward, her hands on the front seats, frustration skimming her nerves.

Breisi hesitated. "If Frank knew you were involved with this business, he would've made you stop anyway."

"I am not quitting." Dawn sat back in the seat, assuming the determined, easy posture of a person who was going to stay around a while, even if she knew she was in over her head. Even if she knew, deep down, that all her fake fighting skills might just be succeeding on borrowed time and that, one day soon, her showy talents might not stand up to a bigger crowd of vampires who stayed to face the rock music instead of running away.

The other woman wasn't letting up. "Now that it's come to this, I don't know how many times Frank told me how *loco* he'd get if you found out what he was doing for a living."

"You know my dad well enough to speak for him, do you?"

It was like Dawn had cracked a whip over Breisi's head, missing by inches. The woman flinched, then remained still, her dark eyes suddenly explaining more than Dawn wanted to know.

There was a softness there, a tenderness. As Dawn recalled the strange flash of emotion on Breisi's face when they'd first talked about Frank's disappearance with The Voice last night, livid shock tore through her. Then she remembered more: Breisi angrily jerking the steering wheel after Dawn had mentioned that she'd often picked Frank's "drunk butt" up from the Cat's Paw; the emotion in Breisi's voice as she vowed to Dawn that they would get Frank back, no matter what.

Breisi's eyes got watery, like she was holding back tears. Dawn slumped, numb, the strength sapped out of her.

Frank, she thought, who else have you hurt? What other damage did you do while I was gone?

In the face of Dawn's non-responsiveness, Breisi glanced at Kiko for aid. "I know we have to go along with this, but . . ."

Kiko touched her shoulder, and she bit her lip.

"Drive," he said. "Just drive for now."

She ran a hand through her bobbed hair, gave a clipped nod, wiped at her face, then started the SUV. It squealed onto the street, mingling with the traffic.

Dawn barely heard Kiko trying to melt the ice that had frozen the air. He was saying something about the waitress he'd talked to at Bava, how he hadn't gotten much information from her. . . .

God, Frank.

Dawn's mind drifted, hiding in the memories that had been triggered by the bartender.

He . . . never came back.

So where was he, huh? Where was the widower who'd taken responsibility for a newborn baby as he mourned his young, dead wife? Where was the father who'd invited over friends he'd met during a couple of light stunt gigs for football Sunday—men who'd enchanted little Dawn with their laughter and exciting stories while making her dream of getting paid to have such fun someday, too? Where was he, damn it?

Dawn's voice came out in a battered whisper. "Take the one-oh-one." The highway.

No one in the car had to ask where she wanted to go. Breisi merely headed there, shooting toward Studio City and the modest two-bedroom house that had been waiting for Dawn for so many years now.

"Should we leave her alone in . . . ?" Kiko started to say.

Breisi interrupted him, her voice raw. "It was protected enough for Frank while he lived there."

"I know," he continued, "but we've already gone through his place. Dawn, you don't need to go there tonight."

"Yes." In the pocket of her jacket, the corners of Frank's photograph chafed her, ever-present. "I do."

It didn't take long to arrive and, once there, she noted that nothing much had changed. Same cul-de-sac, same magnolia trees and bushes huddling over the whitewashed wood, same carport lending to the sense of false security.

Already in the habit, Dawn grabbed her stake to go along with all her other weapons, then exited the car.

Kiko rolled down his window. "You need us?"

Dawn shook her head, then walked down the short drive, aiming for the front door. The SUV idled behind her. She knew they were watching to see that she got safely inside.

A flood of light—UV? she wondered—consumed the porch, and she noticed an iron cross hovering over the doorway. She got out her anemic set of keys and let herself in. But, as soon as she entered, the past rushed at her, and it was all she could do to lean against the slammed door while it overwhelmed her.

The smell of must and hardwood floors that had been around since the mid-1950s, the stench of whiskey. Home. A place Frank had bought shortly after Eva's death, a hideaway that wasn't supposed to remind him of her.

As shadows floated through the windows, moonlight slanted over his favorite worn easy chair, where Dawn pictured him sitting, ready to welcome her with his weather-beaten cowboy boots propped up on the shabby coffee table and his hands clasped behind his shaggy head.

"Welcome to my sanctuary," the nonexistent Frank said, grinning as he disappeared from her imagination.

It was hard for Dawn to swallow past the lump in her throat.

Home. It was the only thing he'd managed to hold on to through the years, maybe because he'd been aware that Dawn had needed a place to be raised near the grandparents who loved her, near the bar that had employed him at the time. Frank had gone back to being a bouncer after Eva's tragedy. He'd never been much for ambition.

The growl of the SUV taking off made Dawn take in a quick breath, reach for the lights. They still worked, which seemed strange, considering her dad was gone. Yet the electric company didn't know he was missing, and he'd obviously managed to keep up on the bills. Miracle. Limpet must really surrender a decent paycheck.

Her gaze touched the same furnishings, the same TV and stereo he'd used for decades. Faint music played on the turntable of her memory: Frankie Valli and the Four Seasons, "Sherry." The ghosts of a young Frank Madison and a small girl in cutoff overalls danced across the room with each other.

A twist of sadness wrenched through Dawn, almost made her slouch to the ground. Pushing the images away, she forged toward the television, turned it on. Company. She needed voices, sound, something to keep her from going crazy.

She knew exactly what she should be doing: rifling through paperwork, seeing if Kiko and Breisi had missed any clues, but she couldn't bring herself to deal with that. So she sank down on the overstuffed couch, resting her sore body.

The TV's reception was fuzzy. Frank had probably tapped into the cable service illegally. Shocker.

She laughed, but there was a thrust of hysteria behind it.

Stop, she thought. Stop, calm down, and think rationally. Freaking out isn't going to help. Seeing ghosts isn't going to do anything, either.

She didn't know how long she sat facing the TV. *Cops* was on. Then *Celebrity Justice*. Then a repeat of *Access Hollywood*.

Procrastinating, Dawn watched them all, absorbing nothing, seeing the images, hearing the words: *red carpet movie premiere. Who are you wearing? Valentino. What's your next project? I'm taking some time off. That's nice for you. Have fun inside. Wait, here comes Chad Robb, the new James Dean. Star of the film. Did you do your own stunts? Of course, I did. . . .*

Dawn stood, ambling down the hall to her dad's bedroom. She stared at the bed for what seemed like hours, the murmur of the television haunting the background. She went to his closet, found a stockpile of grenades and heavy-duty rifles behind his clothing. Turning aside from evidence of his secret life, she touched his shirts, just like Kiko had said he'd done.

But she felt nothing. Nothing at all.

She wandered to a set of drawers, where she shuffled through more clothing, taking out one of his sleeveless undershirts. On a whim, she took off her jacket, her gun holster, her tank top, then slid his shirt over her head. It was too big, but that was fine. It felt like a security blanket that carried his familiar scent.

Breathing it in, she saw another conjured image of him waiting in the corner, arms folded over his wide chest, disapproval in his frown.

"You're wearing too much makeup. Wipe some of that off or you're not going anywhere tonight."

Teenage angst revisited her, mingling with her present bottled rage. She kicked the drawer shut as the mirage fell apart. A scream welled up, seeking release. She fought it, her body tight, building toward an explosion.

Damn you, Frank, for getting into this. Damn you, damn you . . .

Escaping, walking it off, she stalked to the kitchen table where she'd caught a glimpse of papers strewn over the surface. Bills, documents. The paperwork Breisi and Kiko had sorted through. A quick search told her that they'd missed a lot of his effects though. Missed—

Sprinting back into his bedroom, Dawn dove to the floor, pushing at the bed where she knew there were some loose floorboards. Once they were revealed, she worked them apart, reaching inside without a thought as to what might be in the dark hole besides the bootbox she knew was there. Taking it out, she spilled the contents. Bundles of money—Frank didn't trust banks—mingled with faded pictures and more documents.

She needed to tell Kiko about this secret stash. Maybe there'd be a clue, somewhere, anywhere.

Growing more frantic by the second, she scanned the papers. Marriage license. Newspaper clippings about Eva's career as well as Dawn's sports achievements. Frank always had a sentimental side.

Pictures. Frank and Eva beaming in front of a small chapel in Vegas where they'd quietly gotten married, away from her agent and manager—everyone who would've told her she was committing career suicide. Frank and Eva staring at each other during a candid moment at Griffith Park, her mother's stomach swelled with Dawn, their love child.

Fighting tears, she turned them face down, one by one, struggling to hold herself together.

But then, like a plank blindsiding her with a blow to the head, she came to an image that jarred her with such ferocity that she threw it away.

The picture landed in the corner of the room, face down.

Her hands shook as they remained poised in the air.

She'd forgotten he'd kept it. God, she'd forgotten.

Even though it was hidden now, the contents icepicked into her skin, prickled around her heart until it felt like it was going to squeeze into itself and freeze the life out of her. She felt ten again, reliving the time she'd been poking into places she never should've been looking and finding that nightmares weren't something that just happened in your sleep.

That was the day she'd seen Frank putting the box away, wondered what was in it, then waited for him to leave so she could dig it up and explore what was inside.

She wished she never had, because that's when she'd seen the picture, the image she'd blanked out until this moment.

Why had he kept it? Dawn had never confronted him. It wouldn't have done any good; it would've been just another thing to scream at each other about, to hide from once the initial burst of shock had worn off.

Once she'd blocked it out.

Now, she did the same thing she'd done when she was ten, hugging her knees to her chest and rocking back and forth, erasing what a camera had once captured.

She must've been forcing herself to forget for a long time, because when the doorbell rang, Frank's digital bedside clock read 3:00 AM.

Even though Dawn wanted to move, she didn't. Her muscles had iced over with the same white she'd used to blank her brain. She heard someone—Breisi and Kiko from the sound of the voices—enter anyway, their footsteps stopping at the bedroom.

"You okay?" Kiko asked. "You left the door unlocked."

"Sorry."

She found her associates standing in the doorway. They had a distance between them, like they'd been arguing. You could always tell, could always catch the snap of tension between two people after they'd had words with each other.

Glancing at Frank's shirt on Dawn, Kiko walked forward first, Breisi trailing behind like she wasn't so sure Dawn would be happy to see her. He sat on the floor, started sifting through some photos then depositing them in the shoebox. He smiled at one, held it out to Dawn.

In its time-preserved colors, she was maybe thirteen, dressed in a leotard and holding out a trophy she'd won during a gymnastics meet. Her pigtails and bright smile clashed with the heavy eye makeup she was already wearing in a fit of rebellion, making sure she distanced herself as far away from the "naturally lovely" Eva as she could. It made life at school—a place where reputations were based on parents—easier. Her vehement denial of her legacy, her passion for sports and for keeping her body fit and healthy, had made her an outsider early on. While the other brats had been getting stoned every day, Dawn had been practicing in the gym, hanging out with baseball-playing boys, avoiding the life of a star's kid.

She cradled the picture in her hand. "Good times."

Breisi had crept next to Kiko, staring at a photo, her face ravaged. When she carefully laid the picture in the shoebox, Dawn saw that it was the one of Frank and Eva at their wedding.

"Frank lived here an awful long time," Kiko said, pointing to a photo of him in the backyard in a hammock. "I'm surprised he never moved from L.A."

"He always said that he wanted to raise me somewhere else, but his parents lived here, and he liked to stay near them. They died a few years ago."

But, Dawn added to herself, even though Frank had been good at getting close to some people, he'd managed to put a canyon between Dawn and Eva. He'd raised his daughter to be a tomboy, emphasizing how she was nothing like her mother at all. In return,

Dawn had created the same space between her and the Hollywood kids, knowing she really wasn't a part of their scene because Frank had repeatedly told her so.

The positive side? She'd avoided the suicides and drug problems that plagued many stars' kids.

The negative side? Last night at the Cat's Paw when she'd been in heat, competing with the ghost of her mom again.

Just then, Breisi gasped. Dawn stiffened, instinctively starting to reach for her revolver that lay on the bed, but that wasn't necessary.

It was only the picture. The one that Dawn had heaved across the room in the hope that it would somehow go away.

Breisi was holding it in front of her, eyes saucer-wide, hand over her mouth. Kiko took it from her, looked at it, glared up at Dawn.

"Dear Lord," was all he said.

Already on her feet, Breisi stumbled toward the door. Her footsteps faded toward the direction of the kitchen.

Again, Dawn shut it out. She tasted bile in the back of her throat.

"Dear Lord, Dawn," Kiko repeated. "Why's *this* in your dad's damned bedroom?"

"I have no idea."

"Dawn?"

Reluctantly, she met Kiko's gaze. He was looking at her like she was a freak show, probably wondering why she wasn't screaming in sheer terror, even now, years after the picture had been taken.

"I don't want to talk about it." She felt sick. Sick and tired. "Not now, not ever."

"I understand." He sounded like a therapist, not that she'd know.

In the background, they could hear Breisi's voice on the phone, her tone high and wobbly, on the precipice of tears.

"Is she okay?" Dawn asked.

"I doubt it. We're not all troupers like you." Kiko hesitated. "You probably figured out that she and Frank were . . . close."

Dawn packed up a few more pictures. "Close."

"Damn it, Dawn, would you stop it! Look at me!"

Don't do it, don't do it, said the glue that had been holding her together for years.

But she did. She met Kiko's big, kind blue eyes and tried not to break down.

"With all that's been going on, she wanted to wait before she told you."

"Were they . . . ?"

"Serious? Uh-huh. They were serious enough to be arguing about how Frank needed to get Eva out of his system if he wanted Breisi to stick around. It got to the point where they broke up the day before Frank disappeared."

The news crashed into her solar plexus, a sucker punch. Why? Was she expecting Frank to always love Eva? And why would Dawn even *want* that?

"Breisi's coming to terms with a lot of things, Dawn. Like having you around. We knew we had to contact you about Frank, but she was making herself ill about meeting you, along with everything else. She was angry because you'd left Frank. Love made her protective of him."

Love. Dawn's temples throbbed, and it wasn't just because of this bombshell. She felt for Breisi, knew exactly what she was going through and wished there wasn't another person on earth who had to suffer through the horror of fearing for Frank.

Kiko wasn't done. "She knows how much you care about him, you've proven that you do. So maybe . . ."

Dawn allowed her hand to fall away from her head. "What? Maybe we can be best buddies and go shopping for back-to-school items together? Maybe we can have a Jamba Juice at the mall then go slay some vamps afterward?"

Harsh. But she didn't know how else to take this. Any other reaction was an effort, an act.

"Listen, I'm not going to sit here and watch Breisi go through this." Kiko's face reddened. "That woman is like a sister to me, and I'd do *anything* to help her get Frank back."

When Dawn met his eyes again, she could see the potential for the same kind of support for *her*. The desire to grab on to it almost shattered the fragile bones that propped her up.

But habit, year after year of rebelling, preserving, died harder than that. She knew she had to take care of herself without weakening, without glomming on to someone else.

Meeting him halfway, Dawn nodded, her thanks unspoken.

"Why don't I finish cleaning up in here," Kiko said softly.

His request was an encrypted one. He was actually asking her to go to Breisi. And he was right. Damn it, he was right.

Rising to her feet was like pulling herself out of a tar pit, difficult and slow.

"I'm just going to . . ." She gestured toward the door.

"Good." Kiko smiled to himself and picked up another photo. "That's good."

Footsteps heavy, Dawn went to the kitchen, where she found Breisi sitting down, her phone laid neatly in front of her clasped hands. She was staring at the family room, her eyes red-rimmed, her face a blank, just like she was seeing the same memories Dawn had encountered in this house. When she spied Dawn, she blinked, jerked upright in her chair, started to say something and then stopped.

But even the forces of nature couldn't keep Breisi from being Breisi.

After wiping her eyes, she started to spin the phone around on the table while launching into a quivering update.

"There's lots to talk about, so listen. First, Marla Pennybaker left a message saying that she doesn't know where Nathan is, either, so she'll contact us when she hears something." She swallowed, but kept on going, hell-for-leather. "Second, I got results from that skin sample I took from you last night. There were no traces of acid or burning agents in the vamp spit, so the temperature of it was actually *that* hot. And I was thinking I might be able to adjust those locators. I can see if they'll sense that vamp spit, working on a temperature gauge or . . . something . . ." She faltered, but her hands kept going, waving around. Her voice followed. "That's only an idea. And the boss—he'd like you to set up a meeting with that Matt Lonigan. And—"

This time her words crashed to a halt, a massive sob taking her over. Breisi buried her face in her hands, weeping.

Dawn walked to her, laid a tentative palm on Breisi's head. The other woman grabbed on to her wrist.

In an effort to stay strong, Dawn glanced away, her gaze sweeping the house, taking in the family room where Breisi had been fixating her gaze: the couch, the TV, the coffee table, the stereo system with the old turntable. Another record that Frank used to play skipped over and over in her mind:

Big girls don't cry . . .

Pressure built from her chest, to her throat, creeping upward in hard, tense heat. . . .

Then she saw the ghosts again: her and her father dancing in the family room together, laughing.

Big girls don't cry . . .

As a gush of moisture rolled out of one eye, Dawn pummeled it away with a slash of her fingers, reducing it to nothing.

"We'll find him, Breisi," she said, stroking the woman's hair. "No matter what, we're going to find him."

Breisi wrapped her arms around Dawn's waist, burying her face against Frank's shirt and taking in his essence as his daughter held her.

Meanwhile, the night breathed, watching through the window.

Fogging the panes of the only fragile barrier that was keeping it from Dawn.

FIFTEEN

The Standoff

Seven bucks for an iced tea," Dawn said to no one in particular as she perused a menu the next day at Chez Rose, a bistro near the trendy Farmers Market.

She was seated outside, an umbrella fighting the waning sun, misters spraying huffs of moisture over her garlic-rubbed skin as she waited for Matt Lonigan. At Breisi's urging and The Voice's go-ahead, Dawn had called him early this afternoon to finally make an appointment with the PI.

The day had been another full one. She'd sent in a concealed weapons permit application that might not even be approved since the L.A. County Sheriff's Department wasn't exactly known for giving out a lot of those. Afterward, she'd arranged to take a class for the permit and had done some shooting at a range with a supply of lead bullets—not the customized silver ones Breisi made—then arranged to meet Matt. Yes, Dawn Madison was turning into a regular *Magnum, P.I.*

"Seven ducats? That glass better come as big and roomy as your head," said Kiko's voice in the earpiece Breisi had given Dawn for this particular occasion.

"Cut the chatter," said the techno geek herself.

Dawn changed position, facing Breisi, who was at the outdoor bar. Wearing a long black wig, she held a virgin strawberry daiquiri like it was a prop, yellow-tinted Tomb Raider sunglasses hiding eyes that would be trained on Lonigan. She was Dawn's backup, extra help in case Lonigan got feisty, she supposed. As for Kiko, he was biding his time near the SUV in the parking lot, monitoring until Matt arrived.

And, somewhere in this town, The Voice was listening, too.

His deep, lulling tone nestled into Dawn's ear, wrapping her in the remembrance of their last meeting: the lick of the ocean's tide, the crash of a climax.

"Don't mind the prices, Dawn," he said. "Find out who hired him and see if he reacts to your garlic and crucifix. I want to know if there's more to this man than first appears."

"Got it."

There was a pause, filled with a thousand chances for Dawn to guess what he was thinking. Then, "I'm going silent now."

As the correspondence died, Dawn glanced over the top of her menu at Breisi, who subtly tipped her drink to her cohort, then made an effort to play barfly.

Dawn bit back a smile. There was a certain morning-after type thing going on with her and the older woman, an embarrassed tip of the hat to what had happened at Frank's last night. There, after Breisi had cried it out, they'd all returned to business, knowing it was the only thing that would make them feel better about Frank.

So they'd double-checked his paperwork, confirming that he'd no doubt used cash for all his purchases so as not to leave paper trails. Thus, there were no spending patterns to give them a hint as to where he'd been lately besides Bava. At their wits' end, they had returned to Limpet's, believing that tracking down more of Robby's old coworkers and visiting the places on Klara's list to place locators for detection—all the while keeping an eye on Bava—would yield the best return on their investment of time.

When all was said and done, Dawn had crashed on Kiko's couch again, laden with the question of whether or not she should move into Frank's. Even now, she still had no idea if she could handle being there. The closest she could come to it was wearing one of the undershirts she'd filched from his room. It just felt right to have it on, the subtle weight of it an albatross, a second skin.

Dawn's earpiece came to life.

"This should be our man," Kiko said.

Oh so casually, Dawn set down her menu, pretending to tuck back a strand of hair over her ear at the same time she fixed her eyes on the entrance to the patio. Smoothness.

Moments later, Matt Lonigan sauntered to her table. Every stride reminded her of a boxer moving to the center of the ring, checking out his opponent from beneath a lowered brow. His light blue eyes assessed her, determining her mood, predicting her reactions far in advance. He was dressed in new blue jeans, Doc Martens, a white T-shirt covered by an untucked short-sleeved khaki shirt that was unbuttoned. Dawn guessed that the last item was hiding his gun.

Her foot rested next to the bag she'd brought for her own weapons.

A veil of awareness—as thin as the water from the misters—fell over her, melting into her with waves of heat. Maybe it was Matt Lonigan's talent for self-control, or maybe it was just because she was constantly on the prowl, but it was all she could do to bite back an inviting smile, a raging come-on.

"I was half afraid you wouldn't show," he said, arriving at the table.

He was holding out his hand, expecting her to shake it. Such the professional.

Dawn couldn't help herself. She took her fingers, placed the tips of them in his palm, ran them gently over his skin. "Have no fear—I'm way better at showing than telling."

In her ear, Kiko sharply cleared his throat, but The Voice's silence was much more of a welcome scold.

Jealous?

But that was stupid. Sure, she was intrigued by her boss, but playing games with him was useless *and* inappropriate, even if it was engrained in her nature.

She forced herself to cut it out, concentrating on the fact that Matt hadn't reacted to the garlic on her skin yet.

He'd ignored her spunkiness, too, folding himself into his chair, adjusting his seat so that his back was to a wall. Then he opened the menu, his gaze occasionally encompassing the patio, searching, never resting. It was almost like he knew he was under watch.

"How's your case going?" Dawn asked, starting her mission in earnest.

"Rolling along. Yours?" He put down the menu.

Like she was going to spill all the beans. "It's all diamond nights and caviar dreams, you know. Weren't you the one who told me something about detective work's lack of glitz?"

Before Matt answered, the waiter came to take their orders, then left them alone at a stubborn impasse.

During the silence he scanned her arm with the burns that had healed so quickly, then he continued to inspect the patio.

"So no sharing today, either." She arranged herself in her chair so that his gaze was lured back to her and not the rest of the area—especially Breisi. He'd been checking out the bar, where her associate was listening. It made Dawn nervous.

Her ploy worked. Almost unwillingly, he locked onto her, the hint of attraction darkening his eyes.

There. The carnal interest made her feel a little more complete now. She had just enough time to hate herself for that before he answered.

"Listen, Dawn, I'd give anything to tell you what's going on. But you're never going to find out who's retaining me. I mean it. Don't waste your energy."

Taming her disappointment, she took her time in tucking her hair behind her ear. His gaze followed. He shifted in his seat, obviously uncomfortable, desperate to get back to business.

It struck her that he might be kind of shy. Or was he just so damned one-track-minded that his life didn't allow for diversions like giving in to what she was obviously offering?

Shit, she had no idea how to deal with a guy like this.

At that point, a sunglassed Kiko wandered into Chez Rose, right over to Dawn's table. Damn it, she'd begged him to leave those dipwad lenses in the car.

"Hey," she said, feigning surprise at seeing him.

"Hey, Dawn, I forgot to give you . . ." Kiko handed her a credit card, then acknowledged Matt. "Lunch money."

Acting! she thought. Kiko was in his element right now.

"I've got the bill covered," Matt said.

Like a real pro, Kiko stuck out his hand in greeting. Dawn held her breath, anticipating the reading he might get.

When they shook, Kiko's expression didn't change. Instead, he turned to Dawn. "I'll be at the office, waiting. Paperwork, paperwork, you know."

"You're not joining us?" Matt asked.

"No rest for the wicked." Then, with a wave, Kiko left, completing his cameo appearance.

Dawn shifted in her seat, dying to know what Kiko had come up with. "My associate."

With a whisper, Kiko's voice came over the earpiece. "Clean as a whistle. His mind's all on you, Dawn. But still be on your toes with him—you never know."

She sank down in her chair, halfway relieved.

"What would help," Matt was saying, as if Kiko hadn't even made an appearance, "is if you'd tell me about Frank and your family. And was there any reason for him to disappear?"

"You mean run away?"

"Sure."

Oh, boy, poor PI. He was so far off base it wasn't funny. And she wouldn't even entertain the thought of Frank going all 'fraidy cat and taking off once he realized that Robby's case wasn't just another muscle job.

In an effort to be halfway helpful, she told Matt some personal details about her father, things that weren't necessarily in the newspapers: his wham-bam courtship with Eva, the surprising love that had followed the sudden news of a pregnancy, his grief after his wife's death, his raising of Dawn . . . She assumed Matt had done his homework on Eva and knew her own much-publicized details.

But when she mentioned her mom, she saw how his gaze went a little dreamy, just like Kiko's had in the SUV that first night. Jealousy tore into her, leaving a bitter taste on her tongue, something even her seven-dollar iced tea couldn't chase away.

Instead, she leaned even closer to him, competing for his attention. When she got it, he smiled at her, and her body relaxed to a low thrum, begging her to feed it.

Later, she thought, assuaging herself. Later.

By the time she'd finished, their food had arrived. Matt didn't say anything. He'd come to stare at the bar, where Breisi was lingering. Dawn still didn't know if he'd somehow identified her associate or not.

At any rate, just as a warning for Breisi, Dawn said, "Did you want a drink from the bar? You're pretty interested in it."

"No. I'm just taking your story in." He turned back to Dawn without even another glance across the patio.

Thank God. "You have any more ideas about Frank now that you've interviewed me?"

"I *am* wondering if—" Matt cut himself off, poking at his pan-seared steak with a fork.

"Wondering what?"

He kept poking for a second, then grabbed a knife to cut into the meat. "I wonder if his emotions about Eva finally got to him. Was he really upset before he vanished?" Uneasily, he looked at her.

Her stomach knotted up, her mind refusing to give his question any credence whatsoever. "Are you asking if he committed suicide?"

Matt nodded, seeming sorry to have mentioned it.

His sincerity got to Dawn. And since she wasn't sure what to do about that, she simply answered.

"There's no way he did himself in. Things were going better with Frank." She thought of Breisi, hoped she'd made him happy. . . . Besides, "He had a good job making better money than he'd ever made before."

Matt put his utensils by his plate, eyes fixed intently on her. "He had a good job, you say. I know he worked with Limpet and Associates."

At his steady gaze, her pulse beat double time. They'd strayed away from Dawn's mission: to discover the identity of his client. Way too far.

She became extremely interested in her Cobb salad. "Yeah, that's where he worked."

"And you're with them now."

"As a consultant. I'm helping with Frank."

"And not with . . . any *other* cases?"

She had the feeling he was talking about Robby Pennybaker. Was that because he knew what Frank had been investigating?

"I'm working with them because of my dad, and that's it," she said, stuffing some lettuce into her mouth so she wouldn't have to continue.

He sat back, arms crossed over his chest, eyes narrowed, not so shy anymore. Talk about feeling like she was about to be pounced on. In spite of her turmoil—or maybe because of it—her body warmed up, smoking with adrenaline, the thought of being chased and caught.

"Funny," Matt said. "Mr. Limpet. No one knows him."

Tell me about it. "He's a private guy."

"Have you ever met him?"

Kiko's voice sounded in Dawn's ear. "Get him off the subject."

Just what she'd been thinking. "*You* can give Limpet a call, you know, have a nice chat, talk about the latest in investigator chic, that sort of thing." Hell, earlier, during a briefing, The Voice had told her that he and Lonigan had talked, but she was running interference here.

"I've got no interest in chatting."

His intense gaze was still on her. Out of pure habit, she summoned enough strength to block him from her mind—

Get out!

—but all he did was tilt his head, like he was wondering why she'd scrunched up her face.

Great, she thought. She'd just crossed the line into overkill. Was she so desperate to keep everyone out?

Dawn stared at the table. Yeah. Yeah, she was.

But that didn't mean she still didn't want him inside of her in another, more physical way. She wasn't even sure why she craved him so much. And, if she was honest with herself, it was more than the usual longing for contact.

Was it because he was a challenge? A hard-to-get wish?

She went back to her salad, hopefully making Matt think she had no more suggestions about getting to know Limpet.

She could feel his eyes on her.

"I have talked to him on the phone," he said. "It was all very civil and uninformative."

Time to get back to *her* agenda now.

As she set down her fork, she started to toy with the chain around her neck, drawing out the small crucifix attached to it. She braced herself.

He glanced at the silver and . . .

Nothing. No cringing, no hissing.

Okay. So no response to a crucifix or garlic. But the servant at Bava had shown the same reaction. So was Matt just an unfortunate human participant in a case that was getting weirder by the hour? Or was he really a servant, immune to these items because he still had a soul?

Matt's phone trilled. He took a glimpse at the call screen and grunted. "I've got to take this."

"No problem." Dawn offered another smile, dropped her chain.

Again, kind of shyly, he grinned back at her, then got up and wandered to a secluded area while answering.

She tracked his exit, more intrigued than ever, more unsatisfied, too. These working hours were going to put a real crimp in her lifestyle. The night before last, The Voice had soothed her, filled her up for a short time, but now she was hungry again.

Dawn heaved her napkin to the table, burying her face in her hands. Even if her body was as taut as a rubber band pulled to its limits, she didn't want to go back to The Voice begging for another encounter. Sure, the experience had left her breathing easy afterward, but it had also alienated her, given her more self-doubt.

But, if she really admitted it, her personal life was the pits anyway. She'd always made excuses, said she'd settle into a normal relationship someday, just as soon as she'd sowed all those ever-lovin' wild oats. Problem was, she seemed to have an unlimited supply in her silo.

Her face was flushed from just dwelling on all this. Shit.

"I'm going to the restroom to cool down," she said to her audio friends.

"Does Dawn have a crush?" Kiko asked.

Ignoring him, she got up, made her way to where Matt had disappeared. She really wanted to tell Kiko where to stick it, but she didn't want to talk to herself and advertise that she was hooked up on Spy Satellite, Inc. Then again, this was L.A., so holding a one-way conversation might actually come off as pretty normal.

Yet the choice was made for her when she found Matt pacing near the bathrooms, phone to his ear, looking mighty upset. When he saw her, he ended the call.

"I hate to do this, but—"

"You've got to go." She tried not to feel bruised by the brush off. "Excuses, excuses."

"I'm really sorry."

"It's not like this was a date." She stuck out her hand, a gracious loser. "Best of luck with Frank, okay?"

That was their cue to shake on it and leave everything at the status quo. But he wasn't walking away. No, he was standing there, mouth in a line.

"P.S.?" she added.

He spread out his hands, like he was surrendering. "I'm trying to figure out how to do this gracefully."

Ugh. She didn't like the sound of that, so she crossed her arms over her chest, preparing herself.

"I . . ." He ran a hand through his short brown hair, making it stand up. "Here's the thing. I haven't had much of a social life, and I'm out of practice."

Now she was confused. "Seriously. Don't worry about leaving."

"It'd just be . . . well, I suppose a real conflict of interest to see if you'd want to go out sometime."

She loosened up, arms falling to her sides. In spite of herself, she broke into a dumb grin. "Go out?"

He was talking about a date, right? Wasn't he? Had she really ever been on one of those? Oh, God. How did they work?

"It's probably a bad idea," he said.

"I'd go." What the hell. "I mean, on a date. Or. Whatever."

He seemed surprised. "You would."

"When this is all over, of course. After I find Frank."

"Or when I find him." He smiled, but it wasn't shyly or nicely. For one splinter of a moment, she pictured herself in the sights on a hunting rifle.

Then he moved closer, reaching out to her, and the smile turned into that reticent gesture he flashed whenever he was comfortable enough to do it.

Sniffing, he pulled back.

Garlic. The oxygen lodged in her chest.

But then—light of all lights—he smiled again, an oddly knowing gesture. Then, hesitantly, he brushed his knuckles over her cheek. His touch skimmed upward, pausing over the bare white scar she'd earned just above one brow, then downward, to touch her long earring.

She remembered her audio earpiece. He's gonna call us on our games, she thought.

But then . . . miracle.

After the longest tick of the clock in history, his hand trailed back to her cheek and, smoothly, with the slow speed of a yearning caress, he slipped both hands under her jaw, pulled her to him, completely throwing her off guard.

When he kissed her, it was soft, explosive. On the backs of her eyelids, she saw the flow of sheer red curtains in a breeze, the hems whispering down over the curve of one naked body that was poised over another. Dawn flowed with the motion of the material, of the bodies, with their sweat, their slick rocking movements, their low moans and cries.

But, too soon, Matt was pulling away, leaving her with just a taste of him: an unidentifiable mélange of possibility. She bit her lower lip, wanting more, dying to ask for it.

So this is normal, she thought. First-date sweetness. Is this what it's like to get only one kiss?

He backed away. "You fascinate me."

Then with an embarrassed shake of the head, he left her, as if too mortified to look back. He retreated to the hostess desk where she saw him take out his wallet and present the girl with a wad of bills to cover their check.

Dumbstruck, she wanted to follow him, to take what he'd teased her with. But then again, there was a part of her—a new angle—that gleamed with the infatuation of wanting to be discovered, inch by slow inch, day by long day.

Kiko's voice came over the earpiece. "I'm calling nine-one-one because there's a three-alarm conflagration going down."

Breisi shushed him, her "*Shhh*" chopping off mid-scold as

Dawn wandered back out to the patio. At the bar, the older woman was tapping her headset, as if it had suddenly died on her.

Then Dawn heard a familiar voice in her ear. Ten to one he'd disabled Breisi's and Kiko's equipment to speak to Dawn privately.

"Good work," The Voice said, his tone so jagged that it was almost disguised. "Now come back *here*."

The vibrations of his words called to her, even as she fought the pull of what he was no doubt promising.

SIXTEEN

Below, Phase Three

THAT night, the Underground rang with the presence of all its members, save for those who had been released Above. They had been gathered into a community meeting to pass judgment on a threat that could steal their utopia.

On the top tier of the stone theater, the elite citizens sat next to Sorin in cushioned throne seats. The top vampires shone in all their unfathomable beauty, their skin rosy from feeding, their eyes a swirl of colors that did not exist on the surface of earth. Males were bare-chested, dressed only in loose-fitting silk pants. Females decorated themselves with the finest of embroidered materials that seduced Sorin with thoughts of a mighty old world.

Then came the Groupies on the lower tiers. Dressed in thin silks, their skin shining with scented oils and glitter, they lounged like cats, rubbing against each other, draped over the stone in lazy luxury. Some had been chosen by the Elites to sit at their feet, the lower-ranking vampires leashed in jeweled collars as they nuzzled against their masters' legs. Amusing, tasty pets. That was the niche of the Groupie.

Guards and human Servants were generally not allowed at any gatherings. Their opinions—if they had any—were of no importance since the manufactured Guards were merely puppets who, unlike the Groupies or Elites, did not even have the ability to change from preternatural creature to blending, quasi-human being. And as for the mortal Servants? Food. And, more importantly, they were the extremely willing worker bees who facilitated the vampires' needs Above, rewarded for their efforts and kept loyal through their addiction to the Underground's decadence and glamour.

Sorin stirred in his throne chair as he listened to the speaker who had been lending testimony from her position on the stage, her voice amplified by the stone acoustics. Next to her stood a coiffed man with graying hair and glasses. He was dressed in a black suit and maroon tie, the only human Servant in attendance.

"After being shielded from Dawn Madison's mind and failing to get any information," said Goth-laced Galatea, the Groupie who had been charged with spywork at Bava last night, "we chased the human Servant Lee Tomlinson, who took sanctuary in a church where we could not get to him."

Sorin grimaced. They were talking of the bartender from Bava, a man who resembled a deceased actor from Above—Brandon Lee had been the name. Under the threat of having his pretty face harmed, Lee Tomlinson and his massive ego had gone against the code of secrecy by surrendering information about Robby Pennybaker to Dawn Madison and her friends last night.

Damage control was now called for.

"And what say you?" Sorin directed this at the man standing next to Galatea, a lawyer whom the cowardly Lee Tomlinson had contacted Above as a liaison to the Underground—a man who was pleading his case.

He bowed to Sorin, fingers to forehead. "Lee is genuinely sorry for what he's done, Master. We ask to take into account his service to our community. First, he's a loyal visitor to this Underground, providing consistent sustenance for the citizens with his disease-free blood. He'd planned to stay here a very long time, aspiring to become an Elite one day after 'making it.' He's only had this one misstep."

"A most costly misstep," Sorin added, leveling a terrible glare on the advocate.

The polished man frowned ever so slightly in admission. "The justice system Above allows for everyone to be fairly represented, Master. I'm only living up to my duty in the hopes that it's the same way down here."

Sorin laughed to himself. Such a quaint observation. And this particular lawyer, Mr. Milton Crockett, had been a trusted member of the Underground for a decade and a half. He aspired to be no more than a Servant, because he loved his family and home. He was also paid well for the referrals he brought to them; Mr. Crockett was responsible for guiding the last two elite citizens here, plus the new candidate Tamsin Greene. He had an eye for choosing those who fit the profile—beautiful, magnetic, ambitious to a fault.

"You do your job well, Mr. Crockett," Sorin said. "But Lee Tomlinson showed an appalling lack of discretion."

Galatea's voice filled the theater. "And there're other people Above with loose lips. Rumor has it that a woman named Klara Monaghan talked trash about Robby to those PIs. Maybe Lee felt a little too comfortable with sharing after he heard about her."

Murmurs burbled through the theater—anxiety from the Elites, excitement from the Groupies who were stroking the higher beings in worshipful compassion.

Sorin held up a hand for silence. It was immediate.

There was no erasing what this Klara Monaghan had evidently told the investigators. The aging actress was only a part of the bigger problem: Limpet's detectives. Sorin was not certain whether they were merely defending themselves from dangers while following leads about Robby Pennybaker and Frank Madison, or if there was a much more perilous reason for their meddling.

"We will discuss additional safety precautions after we have finished with Lee Tomlinson." Sorin rested his hands on the throne. A calm appearance was paramount. "Mr. Crockett, for what your client has done, he must be banished."

A gasp from the crowd did not sway Sorin. Banishment was worse than death. No one wanted to have their minds wiped of memory like a pitiful Guard or to be separated from the paradise of the Underground.

The lawyer stepped forward in supplication, hands in front of him. "Master, Lee Tomlinson has promised to do anything—*anything*—to return to your graces."

"Then he will come to us peacefully, and we will go about banishment in a congenial manner. If he refuses, we will hunt him down and destroy him."

"He can't be imprisoned down here?"

"And give him the prize he wishes for? No."

Mr. Crockett looked conflicted. Even he knew that violence was the last option. The consequences for his beloved Underground would be unthinkable. Lee Tomlinson might be missed by someone Above, such as the human lover he had taken within the last two months. So if the bartender disappeared, there would be hell to pay.

All the same, how could they tolerate a Servant who had gone against his vows? The punishment could not be ignored, or else a pattern would be established, a weakness in authority. Excusing this crime would mean ignoring the next, and the next, until the Underground crumbled under the crushing blow of discovery.

Best to establish fear through caution now.

He rose from his throne, and every vampire responded with a bow, a salute. "You are free to discuss your ideas for security. I will return with a clear mind after I have fed."

One of the Groupies stood, a woman clothed in a wispy skirt that fell around her hips and revealed her long legs through the material. She was intending to supply food. Sorin's groin tightened at the sight of her full, golden breasts. Juices flooded his mouth at the thought of sinking himself into a spot below one of them, piercing the skin just under the sensual weight of a rounded globe.

"Not now." He waved her off, ignoring her hurt gaze. His loose, dark clothing flared around him as he made his way to an isolated room where he knew the Master was working.

There, he found his parent and another vampire sprawled on the expanse of a cushiony divan. They were participating in the monthly infusion of blood that an Elite required to survive, especially after they were released.

The Master was always careful to give the Elite only enough to lend a fraction of his powers, but it was sufficient for what the top citizen required. However, the Elite's own vampire children—if they cared to have any—would not have access to the Master's powers through an infusion: the blood would have become too weak, too diluted in the recipient's inferior body. The only reason the Elites *had* a hint of the Master's abilities was because they drank of him regularly, else they would be powerless and bereft.

Sorin attempted to ignore the Elite, the inferior vampire. Unlike them, he was a full-blooded son, not requiring any more of the Master's infusions since his father had not held back at his birth. In fact, he was the only one of this type, a source of great love for his maker.

His face buried in a pillow, the Master affectionately stroked the Elite's hair back from his forehead. As the male Elite sucked greedily from the older vampire's wrist, the exhausted slump of the Master's body reflected boredom. Sorin panicked at the sight.

Or perhaps he was merely tired, Sorin thought. He had been working much harder lately, thank the day.

The glow of the television—Sorin thrilled to see that it was on—reflected the closed-circuit video images of the meeting in the theater. He had been watching.

Sorin's spirits lifted high above the room at this indication of the Master's renewed interest. In decades past, the head vampire had taken great exhilaration in games—hunting and being hunted. Was his old love of chaos resurrecting him?

"You were watching?" he asked, studiously keeping the joy from his voice.

The Master's words slurred together. "I was. You did everything perfectly, Sorin."

A stain of pride spread through his chest. Sad, that he still depended on the Master's approval. Sad, that Sorin suspected he would never be able to discard the need for it.

"Now, to deal with the PIs," Sorin said.

"We *are*. From what's been gathered in intelligence, I think they might be useful to us. If there really *is* another master directing them, they could lead us to the source itself."

The male Elite tilted his head back, gasping for air, blood on his chin as he opened his eyes and smiled.

"Ahhh," he said, wavering back and forth as if dizzy. "My very own Dr. Feelgood. Or . . . sorry . . . *Dr. Eternity*." He chuckled. "It's a little bit like calling out the wrong name after you come, huh?"

At the mention of the nickname that the Elites had invented for the Master, the head vampire patted the young creature's head, ending the infusion.

Balancing to his feet, the youngster stood by the television, wiping his mouth. One of the oldest of the elite class, this one's humanity had died in an automobile crash a half century ago, and he was awaiting a second release. He was strung together with fine, slender bones, his hair a golden brown fluff that was punctuated with long sideburns. Lanky and sexy—that is what the Groupies said about him.

"It is time for you to leave," Sorin said.

"Aw, hell, you're going to see me around the emporium and whatnot." He strutted to the entrance. "I'm going to visit the baths tonight for a real, real long time. Get me some *pussy*, and then I'll be set to leave."

He laughed as he exited, and Sorin scowled. He could not deny the Elite. These vampires were allowed full use of the Underground because they paid enough to ensure the privilege.

The Master was still buried amongst the divan cushions, his wrist already having healed from the infusion.

"He is arrogant," Sorin noted.

"All of them are." He sounded weary now. "But that's part of their charm, now, isn't it. You weren't that different from them back when I found you."

Just as Sorin was becoming worried about his tone, the Master reached for his television remote control, flipping through channels. "*Alias* reruns will be on in ten minutes. Sit."

Relieved beyond measure, Sorin laughed. The media-loving Master. "I must see to the meeting's close. Shall I report to you later for details regarding Tamsin Greene's welcome?"

The Master sat up, his red-outlined aura stronger than Sorin had seen it in years. "I'll be prepared."

As the television's screen revealed the faces of lovely young people, Sorin rethought his plan for the night. "Perhaps I *will* stay. Only for a few moments though."

His aura beaming, the Master made room for his child on the divan.

But soon, after the news of the murder reached the spies of the Underground, the television was turned off.

And the vampires were forced into action, once again.

SEVENTEEN

The Body

CAUGHT in a limbo between reluctance and satisfaction, Dawn lay on the couch in Limpet's office somewhere around midnight.

Newsflash: she'd been with The Voice again. Yeah, it was true. Dawn wasn't about to admit to having a lot of restraint when it came to him or the way he made her feel with his talent for soothing her neuroses. He'd become something like a bed buddy, a comforting return to real life.

At least, sort of. If they'd actually been having flesh-to-flesh, wolf-howling *sex* sex, it would've been just like old times for her. But this kind of loving wasn't so normal.

Even *she* knew that.

Still, there was one indisputable fact: instead of just entering her from the inside and working his way out tonight, The Voice had kept her overtime, switching from mystery *luv-ah* to mentor without intermission. Even during the aftermath of the Big O, he began coaching her on mind blocking, seeing to the fine details of what he called her "greatest weapon."

It'd been a puzzling transition for Dawn, who couldn't make heads or tails—literally, in a locker room sense—of what the hell was happening.

"Every time I'm with you," The Voice was saying, "I realize how much you've repressed. You've shoved many things to the back of your mind, as though they've been packed into boxes and rarely opened, if at all."

Kiko had obviously told him about *the* picture.

"And why can't it just stay packed?" she asked, her gaze stuck on the painting that had caught her attention last time: the Elizabethan woman. The ageless beauty watched Dawn right back, a perceptive smile on her pink, parted lips.

What was even more odd, though, were the other paintings in there—the ones Dawn thought had contained women also. All they showed now were landscapes, backgrounds, just like the one with the fire setting.

But The Voice wasn't exactly giving her much opportunity to gab about the difference in his décor.

"You cannot stay so tightly wound, because you *will* implode. A fine example of that was last night, at Bava, then again at the restaurant with that private investigator."

At the mention of Matt Lonigan, his tone sounded scraped, rough with something that could've been the jealousy she was always hoping for. She couldn't help being a little happy about that. Freaky girl.

"So I got nervous and threw a mind block at Lonigan." Dawn turned her gaze from the Elizabethan painting to the speakers where The Voice was coming from. "He didn't react to that, the garlic, or the crucifix. So, in effect, didn't my blocking overkill actually result in getting even more information about his responses? Shouldn't you be stoked about your growing dossier on him?"

"Perhaps. But you're misdirecting our discussion again."

"I sure am." She grinned, but it was more about defensive cockiness than anything else.

As he sighed, she could almost see him tossing his hands up, done with her. "Dawn."

"Limpet."

There was a stretched pause. "At least there's this: in spite of your amazing ability to consistently sass back, I'm at least satisfied that you're now relaxed enough to go out there and function rationally."

He was teasing her about the sex . . . or . . . whatever it was.

"Don't sound so proud of yourself. We've got a good, symbiotic deal going. You get to tour the dark closets of my mind, and I leave happy. It's not like you've become my personal savior because you're diddling my noggin or something. Besides, if you ask me, whatever's going on here is just one therapy session away from masturbation anyway."

She could almost feel him get angry; his silence was that eloquent.

What—did he think he was actually helping her by mind screwing her? Dare to dream.

Out of the corner of her eye, Dawn thought she saw movement in the Elizabethan painting, a twitch from the lady. But when Dawn rounded on it, she only found the woman's gaze to be locked on her again, unwavering and sympathetic.

When The Voice resumed speaking, it was with maddening calm. "I understand. So when another chance presents itself, we'll practice your mind tricks again—but without the masturbation, as you call it."

Dawn opened her mouth to protest, then shut it. She couldn't bitch at him for entering her and then flip right around and say that it was okay for him to do it again. That would make her a cocktease, and she'd always considered herself everything but. And hadn't there been a time when she'd been pissed about him coming into her in the first place? Yeah, it'd lasted for about an hour, and then she'd gotten randy.

Man, she was confused.

"In the meantime, Dawn, practice what we went over tonight—how to relax, how to *sense* when you're in true danger. I don't want you wasting your precious energy on blocking everyone you meet. Also, try doing it in a mirror, so you can perfect your facade. During your attempts to block, we want to hide it. We don't want to give the impression that you're . . ."

He searched for a phrase.

"Giving birth to a bowling ball?" she finished.

"Earth-shatteringly poetic, but yes."

A knock on the door brought things to a close. Kiko poked his head inside. "Is it safe in here?"

Without waiting for an answer, he bounded into the room, giving Dawn a better look at him. His eyes were wide and his face was red, so her systems went on alert.

"Breisi just got a call from our cop source," he said. "She'd asked Sergeant Brighton to keep an eye out for anyone connected with this case and—"

"Kiko," The Voice said.

Uncharacteristically, the psychic huffed out a long breath, unable to talk. Was he nervous?

"Kik?" Dawn asked.

Finally, he chilled out. "Klara Monaghan's dead."

"What?" Dawn sprang off the couch.

"They got a call on her body a few minutes ago. She's already been identified."

"How?" The Voice quietly asked—quiet in a bad way.

"Looks like a big neck wound, a blood drain." Suddenly back in action, Kiko motioned for Dawn to leave with him. "We're on our way, Boss. She's just down Highland. Sergeant Brighton is making sure we'll at least get a peek, if we can get there before things go nuts."

"Be careful," The Voice said.

Having grabbed her weapons, Dawn was already halfway out of the room, strapping on her shoulder holster then a jacket as Kiko jogged to catch up with her long strides.

When they got downstairs, Breisi was just coming out of her

dungeon. A dull blue light shone behind her, casting her in shadow. A grinding hum made Dawn wonder just exactly what the hell Breisi was up to, what she was hiding behind that door.

But this wasn't the time for that.

They all sprinted to the 4Runner, Breisi popping it into high gear, engaging the antiradar gadgets and a very illegal opticom that would manipulate the traffic lights so they could get to Klara's location ASAP. Breisi insisted that the boss would take care of matters if they were caught with the emergency vehicle equipment, so it was no skin off Dawn's back.

On the way, Kiko caught her up on what she'd missed during her tutorial with The Voice: he and Breisi had made a late-night visit to Marla Pennybaker, who was just as concerned about the missing Nathan as they were. Based on recordings from the bugs in Marla's house that The Voice and "Friends" had monitored, they now had evidence confirming the woman's innocence in not knowing where her husband was. Even though he'd called her a time or two to tell her he was safe, he never revealed his location.

Her veracity was further supported by The Voice's "Friends," who were watching over the Pennybaker home and had been ordered to remain there as protection against the red-eyes. God knew who these buddies were, but they'd seen Mr. P. leave the premises shortly after they'd been assigned there. And he hadn't returned since.

Dawn groaned at the news. They were almost back to square one with Nathan Pennybaker. But, in the hopes of turning things around again, Breisi had planted more locators in the home, thinking that would pay off once more. In fact, she'd adjusted one of the tools to pick up on Robby's presence inside the house.

When Kiko started telling Dawn about how Breisi had again broached the red-eye vamp visit with Marla, Dawn could emphathize with Marla's continued reluctance to hear any of it.

Repression, right? It had its uses.

"And what about tonight?" Dawn asked. "How're we going to get into the murder scene?"

Kiko crossed his fingers. "Connections. Brighton is the patrol sergeant in charge, so he's got someone waiting there for us. I doubt we'll get beyond the crime-scene tape because of contamination issues and all that. But just a gander at Klara will help, and we've got pals in the coroner's office who can give us autopsy reports and photos."

"And a secret visit, if we're lucky," Breisi added.

Thanks to the traffic-cheating equipment, they arrived at Klara's apartment complex without much fuss. It was a stucco-tan bundle of buildings, unremarkable except for a couple of broken streetlights around a parking lot littered with neon-green flyers and fast-food wrappers.

They exited the 4Runner, passed three lone cop cars, then approached the yellow crime-scene tape that established a perimeter near a carport. The tape circled around a Dumpster that blocked their view and ended on the opposite side of the roofed structure.

"You can't go any farther," a young officer near the Dumpster said. He had an accent tinted with Mexican flavor like Breisi's, a caterpillar mustache, sunglasses, close-cropped black hair, and a chewing-gum habit.

"Hold up, Santos," said a female whose voice made her sound like she ate nails for breakfast. A patrolwoman came to stand next to him. "I'll take care of them."

She wore her long, curly blond hair back in a haphazard bun, her uniform clinging to an athletically slim body, her nametag telling them that she was Burks. Sunglasses were perched on her head, and there was a beauty spot near her upper lip, adding some femininity.

Santos gave Kiko a curious you're-not-very-tall look while he wandered to another area of the tape, where some neighbors had gathered, craning their necks to get a better look.

When he was out of earshot, Burks whispered, "Her roommate found her under here." She sent a subtle nod to the carport. "She says that Klara had been taking out some foul trash that couldn't wait until morning. When Klara didn't come back, the roommate checked by the Dumpster to see what was happening. No one was around, so we don't have a suspect description yet."

Walking toward the spot of the murder, Burks motioned them to follow. "Hurry up with your rubbernecking. Detectives are on their way, and I'll be watching to see that you don't go in. No matter who your boss knows on the force, I have *some* pride in upholding my reputation."

They reached the morbid location to find one other uniform comforting a woman who was sitting on the sidewalk, hunched over, weeping. The roommate? Burks talked to the other cop for a moment, and he took her original position on the other side of the Dumpster. Then she signaled that it was clear, and Breisi took out a digital camera while Kiko opened up his phone.

For her part, Dawn watched the crying woman, noting that her face was purposely turned away from the sight of a body lying prone on the white pavement.

God.

Under the blinking lights of the carport, its arms were open, palms to the sky. One leg was bent back like the corpse was about to kick, its hair a cotton-candy mess melting in a pool of blood, its neck torn to shreds, its skin bled of color, its mouth open in a scream that would never be heard.

It was Klara Monaghan.

Breisi pressed a camera button, extending its lens to close-range. A flash shed pricks of white over the body.

Sn-a-nnnzzz.

Next to Dawn, Kiko was taking pictures with his phone.

Dawn couldn't tear her eyes away. Blood . . . *red* haloed Klara Monaghan's body.

Red on white.

Sn-a-nnnzzz, went Breisi's camera. *Sn-a-nnnzzz.*

Nausea crashed through Dawn, and she closed her eyes, wanting to blank it out. She'd never seen a neck ripped open like this, had never imagined it could happen to someone she'd talked to only yesterday.

A plain white car roared into the lot, and Breisi and Kiko hid their cameras. Two men in rumpled suits got out. Detectives.

Breisi and Kiko made like gawkers, launching into an unscripted lament about the dead woman. An acting class coach would've been proud. They ambled off to the left, near some bushes, then slyly crouched down for a better view.

But Dawn went to the right, ignoring the corpse, trying to get herself together. That's when she heard a whisper.

"Dawn."

She told herself it was just a sputter, a wheeze from the exhaust of the dying engine that was her body. A brain burp. But then she heard it again.

"*Dawn.*"

Hands darting toward her revolver and pocket-bound crucifix, she moved closer, near a wall that separated Klara's apartments from another complex.

She glanced back at her partners, caught Kiko's eye and motioned toward the wall to show them that there might be something back there. At the same instant, one of the detectives pointed to Breisi and Kiko.

"Hey, you're too close!" he yelled.

Beyond the crime-scene tape, Burks made her way over, probably intending to distract the detective and earn her kickback.

But just as Kiko and Breisi stood to greet the detective, someone grabbed Dawn's arm.

She couldn't do much more than gasp as she was tugged behind the wall. A big shadow greeted her.

Without thinking, Dawn swung at her attacker. He raised his palm, caught her fist in his hand.

But she'd already whipped her body around the opposite way, twisting, leg flying out to connect with his knee.

Hellelujah. He keeled sideways, thudding against the wall.

"Dawn!" His familiar voice was muddled with pain.

Breath rasping, she held back, took a good look at her assailant.

"Matt?" She relaxed out of her fighter's stance. Anger turned her fear inside out, exposing her nerves. "You dipshit. What're you doing here?"

He was pushing himself away from the wall. Something—a cat?—scuttled past them, setting Dawn on edge again.

"I wanted . . . to ask you the . . . same question." He touched his knee, then frowned, tested it. Took a few seconds to compose himself. "Not that I should be worried about you."

She started to be glad to see him, recalling what had happened this afternoon at Chez Rose. The kiss. Mmmm.

It reminded her, though, that one kiss didn't mean he could tell her where she could be and couldn't be. Or that he could grab her and yank her behind walls when he felt like it.

"You couldn't just come out to say hi?" she asked.

"Trying to keep a low profile."

A tame fog grew golden under the clank and fizz of a streetlight that was struggling to stay on. Groaning and favoring his knee, Matt leaned back against the wall, his light blue eyes narrowing, containing a low fire—the deepest part of a flame. Nearby, a cat yowled.

Dawn stayed on guard, arms curved at her sides. She felt the night tingling at her back, up her spine.

"I'm wondering," she said. "If you're on my dad's case, why're you at Klara Monaghan's murder scene?"

He clenched his jaw, immovable.

A terrible thought hit her. "Are they connected? What do you think Frank did?"

Again, not a word.

Furious, Dawn reared back her fist again, ready to strike out at anyone, anything. Just as her hand hurled toward his tight lips, she pulled her punch, keeping her wrath contained.

"Damn it. *Damn it.*" She pressed her fists against her forehead.

Frank. What did you do, Frank?

"Hey . . ."

She felt Matt's hands on her shoulders, heard him sniff at her eau de garlic. Too drained to brush him off, she sank against him, used him to regain her strength so she could fight her doubts. Meanwhile, she took in the scent of his shirt: musk, spice, unidentifiable headiness.

Spreading her palms against his chest, she parted her lips, breathed against him, tasted him with every intake of oxygen. As he talked, she felt the vibrations of his words run over her skin.

"Still wearing that garlic," he said. "What do you think you're protecting yourself from?"

"Maybe I just had a nice Italian dinner."

"Dawn, go home. It's safer. You don't need to be around all this."

Tell that to Kiko, The Voice, and their predictions, she thought. Hell, even this PI who she barely knew realized she was out of her league.

Yet . . . Dawn exhaled against Matt. She hadn't even told Frank "I love you" back when he'd said it to her during their last phone call a month ago. They'd been arguing about some dumb thing—take your pick—and she'd hung up on him.

As if pushing away from the thought, Dawn distanced herself from Matt, building herself back up to the big girl she'd trained herself to be. He just stood there, his arms awkward, like she'd robbed him of something.

"When you said you wanted to get together again, I was picturing a whole other scenario," Dawn said, trying desperately to get back her emotional footing.

"I'm not joking around here."

"And what do you mean by 'all this'? What do you know?"

Behind the wall, a car peeled out of the lot as a few more peeled in, ushering in a collage of red-blue cop car lights on the face of the apartment buildings. Closer, another cat screeched, its cry strangled to a fading wince.

"You and your partners saw the body." His mouth curled down at the corners. Anger? "Tell me why you're here and I just might share my theories."

A devil's bargain. Even if it was tempting, she knew that Limpet would kill her if she sang the tune of their investigative details. But . . . hell, what if she broke this wall of silence between the two parties? What if, in spite of all this game playing and secrecy, Matt Lonigan really *was* an ally?

But if that was true, why wasn't The Voice allowing the other PI to come on board?

Logic told her that she'd better just go with her growing bond with Kiko and Breisi . . . and whatever she had in The Voice—the devil she *already* knew.

Shit. "I'm here because Klara was a friend in the biz," she lied, taking the easy way out. "Her roommate called."

Matt glared at the ground. The muscles in his forearms bunched, veins rising to the surface of his flesh as he went taut. His anger pulsed between them.

"Matt, are—"

"Do you believe in vampires?"

Dawn took a step backward. Did he just say what she thought . . . ?

"Do you?" When he raised his head, his eyes were a cool, cutting blue.

Her new cell phone vibrated on her belt, but she had more important things to deal with instead of answering it.

"Believe is a pretty strong word," she said, still hedging.

"Do you think they exist?"

Part of her needed to talk to him about this, needed to hear that he was ruling *out* vampires in this case. Hearing it from someone relatively sane would've done a lot for her desire to cling to delusion. After all, Matt never mind screwed her. He didn't go around with bladed crossbows or stakes. And up until a few seconds ago when the word "vampire" had entered the picture, she'd thought he was the most normal thing going on in her life right now.

Up until a few seconds ago.

But, once again, common sense told her to pretend that she thought he was joking around, to blow him off for the sake of keeping their investigation to themselves. *Acting!*, as Kiko would've said.

So that's what she did. "You're talking about Dracula and Lestat—things with fangs that run around with capes and bloody appetites?"

Wonderful performance. Applause, please.

"Did you see Klara's body, Dawn?"

Again, her stomach dipped, grew heavy with a red-tinged illness. "Not in detail."

"She bled out through a neck wound, and I'm not talking about two neat little punctures, either. I'm talking about a tear, like someone was feasting on her."

"God, okay, I've got the gist of it." Pain sharded through her temples. Was he testing her, trying to shock the truth out of her? "You think a vampire did that?"

Somehow, she'd again succeeded in making it sound ludicrous.

After giving her a long look, Matt walked to the end of the wall, thumbs hitched in his belt loops. From there, the beat of cop lights swirled over his body as he fixed his gaze on the crime scene. The wall was blocking her own view, thank God.

"Let me tell you something," he said. "When I was a boy, my parents and I left the theater one night . . . I was ill . . . and when we went out the back door, into the alley . . ." He stopped, cleared his throat. "We ran into this man. He was crazed. My dad tried to hand over his wallet—he didn't want any trouble—but the man . . . he . . ." Matt looked lost, like he couldn't believe what he was saying. He tilted his head. "He took my dad, and with these . . . teeth . . . *fangs* . . . he ripped out his neck. Then, while I sat there like a coward, he did the same thing to my mom. I finally found my legs and ran away. I screamed and screamed, but . . ."

Stunned, Dawn walked closer to him, but Matt evaded her. The patrol vehicles' lights seemed to grab at his clothing, unsuccessful in their attempt to hook him back as he returned behind the wall to the dim lighting.

"It happened a long time ago," he said, tone flat.

"I'm sorry. That's beyond awful."

"But useful. It gave me the incentive to become a detective. I took criminal justice classes in college, discovered that the police academy didn't agree with my . . . point of view . . ." His laugh was etched with hard finality. "And here I am."

How could he talk about this so rationally? "So you think . . . a vampire . . . killed your parents?"

"The police reports said it was some raging psycho who belonged in a mental ward. But they didn't see the guy, his bared teeth, the inhumanity of him. That's why I decided they were full of crap and I was going to work my way around the system. PIs have a lot more freedom to maneuver than cops."

"Matt . . ."

He held up his hands, warding her off. "Really. It was years ago. You know how it is."

His clear-cut reminder of a parent's death weighed her to the spot. But it also linked her to him, because they were both struggling to shed a child's misery and loss.

"And now you're a vamp hunter, is that what you're saying, Matt?"

He laughed.

"Right?" she repeated.

"Are you able to come to that conclusion through personal experience?"

He knew about the red- and silver-eyes?

Panicked, she brushed past him, searching her way out of the trap he'd so carefully built around her. The cop lights bathed her as she came to the end of the wall.

"Wait." He grabbed her arm below where she was wearing the jacket sleeves pushed above her healing burn wounds.

Was it her imagination, or was he checking them out a little too closely?

She yanked her arm away.

It didn't stop him from finishing. "The best way to stay safe is to stay home. I mean it. This isn't your area of expertise." He shrugged, his gaze shyly going to the ground, then back up to her. "I want you in one piece, for selfish reasons."

"Because we're going to get busy after this is all done? Flattering. But I'm not one to wait around for other people to take care of my problems. Frank's *my* responsibility."

"That's noble, it really is." He came to hover above her, his body blocking the streetlight. He was all darkness and heat. "But there's something more going on that you really don't understand. I don't know exactly what it is yet, but I'll find out. You should ask your boss about it. Demand some answers. Then *stay out of it.*"

"I've already asked questions until I'm blue in the face."

"Then dig a little deeper into Mr. Limpet yourself."

"So I can help you with your detective work?"

He backed up a step, smile flashing. "When you're ready and willing, I won't turn you down on that. I'm just waiting for you to come to me when you've sorted some things out, Dawn. That's all."

Cutting him off, she raised her hand in an abrupt good-bye, walking back to the crime scene and leaving him in the dirt.

Demand some answers. Yeah, like it was that easy.

As she took in the news vans that had just arrived, the ever-growing crowd of onlookers, the fear lancing the night air, her heart rate picked up.

Where were Breisi and Kiko?

Accessing her cell phone, she headed toward the street, finding a message from them. Nearby, a large dog barked behind a dilapidated fence. As she dialed Kiko's number, Matt's words hammered into her.

I won't turn you down on that.

Was that some kind of snide comment on what she had already

been offering him? He could turn down her body but not her help, huh? Ass.

Yet what niggled at her even more was his talk about The Voice. How could she check into him? Where would she even start? Damn it, she was really some detective.

Behind her, a scream of tires signaled an approaching vehicle. She saw headlights making their way toward her. When she realized it was the 4Runner, she disabled her call to Kiko and waved the vehicle down.

It heaved to a stop.

Through the open window, Kiko yelled, “Get in!”

And she did, without question.

Which bothered her a whole lot more than it had earlier tonight.

EIGHTEEN

The Bait

Breisi was making record time through the streets as Kiko leaned over the seat, asking Dawn what happened to her.

"Lonigan," she said. "We had an intense tête-à-tête behind that wall. He was hanging out there."

Her coworkers exchanged a significant look.

"What, it's not like I was making out with him in our special hidden spot." Dawn hesitated. "Did you . . . I don't know . . . ever wonder if the guy is just after the same things we are? Or if he's following the trail of vampires and not just Frank?"

"Wondering about it now," Kiko said.

"He wasn't happy to see me . . . us . . . there. Not even remotely."

Kiko raised his eyebrows. "Hey, maybe he's a PI who has a bit on the side, one of them mercenaries who doesn't want the competition. You know, Breisi, those people we've heard about who travel the world bagging vamps for big cash? There's this website where you can contact them. I've been on it."

"It's possible." Breisi kept her eyes on the road.

"You should've heard this story he told me about his parents." Now that Dawn wasn't near Matt, caught in the mind-spinning web of his proximity, she suddenly got a strange sense of having heard the details of his parents' deaths before. Weird. Why? "He saw them murdered by what he thinks was a vamp, and that's what drove him to PI work. And you know what else? If he's, like, this 'hunter,' what the hell does that make the client who hired him?" She didn't dare ask what that also might make Frank himself. . . .

Instead, she forged ahead. "If I do the math, it adds up to trouble. If Lonigan is involved with the paranormal *and* he's investigating Frank, it sounds like he might know more about Robby's case than we first suspected. Things you guys might not want public."

"Could be," Breisi said.

"And Lonigan said . . . more."

Kiko waited for her to go on. Serious Kiko.

"He pretty much said it's a bad idea to trust Limpet," she said, watching her psychic coworker just as closely. "Said I should be investigating his intentions."

"That's not a good way to spend your time," Breisi said.

"Why?" Dawn scooted up in her seat. "How much do you two really know about your boss?"

Kiko faced front, like he was hiding his reaction. "We know enough."

She wasn't going to get anywhere when it came to The Voice. Kiko was loyal to a fault, even if Dawn suspected he wanted to take more of a lead when it came to hunting monsters. But Breisi . . . ? Her face was still emotionless as the streetlights whisked over her broad features.

Behind that facade, was she actually pissed at Dawn for doubting the boss? Or was there something much deeper going on: resentfulness about Frank's disappearance—maybe because of something The Voice had ordered him to do?

"So," Kiko said, "I assume Lonigan got a load of Klara, too. He must've been doing his detective thing before we got there. I wonder who he pays off in the department."

At the mention of the victim, jabs of red taunted Dawn. She slammed them away.

"Me and Breisi barely got out of there with the telephoto pictures," Kiko added. "Burks helped when that detective started harassing us, but he caught a glimpse of Breisi's digital camera and told us to hand it over. That's when we made a run for it. Luckily the 4Runner is outfitted to flip its license plates, so it'll be hard to trace us. Needless to say, we got real worried about leaving you, Dawn, but we called to see where you were so we could pick you up."

"Sorry for the trouble."

Breisi shrugged. Wow, she clearly gave two shits about Dawn, didn't she? Yup, they'd *really* bonded last night.

"Klara's neck," Kiko was saying. "It was like some kind of frenzied animal got to her. No punctures, like vamp bites in the movies."

"You said that we can't depend on a certain set of vampire rules," Dawn said. "So it's par for the course."

"That's what the boss tells us."

Matt's last words came back. *Demand some answers.* Good advice. So why wasn't she being more aggressive about it?

Red, blood, an image turned to a slab of white nothingness . . .

Dawn cleared her mind.

"By the way, we talked to the boss," Kiko said. "I sent him those cell phone pictures already. He's wondering if Klara got caught by one of those red-eyes with the iron teeth."

"What if Klara is just some unfortunate soul who crossed paths with a random cretin on a regular L.A. night?"

Even as Dawn asked, she knew it sounded foolish. The fact that nobody answered just proved it.

God, you knew your shit was messed up when a vampire attack turned out to be a more logical explanation for a violent death than regular old murder itself. After all, they had just interviewed the actress about Robby. And vampires had been loitering around Robby's old property.

One plus one equaled a connection. Not a satisfactory answer, but a definite coincidence.

And that meant . . . Klara could very well have been killed because she'd talked to them. Dawn leaned her head against the window. It was cool against her skin.

So what exactly did that mean? Was there some greater power—a vamp who had ties to Robby—who needed to shut Klara up? And what did Robby and Frank have to do with it?

In the back of her brain, on the white, white screen of thought, a film reel spliced itself together and flickered to life: Robby in *Diaper Derby*, a kid who hadn't aged in twenty-three years.

The packed box of her mind blew open, setting free an obscene possibility that had been lurking for days. A possibility she'd fought tooth and nail.

"Robby's a freakin' vampire," she said.

With a guffaw, Breisi held her hand out to Kiko. Muttering under his breath, he dug into his pants, fished out a twenty-dollar bill and gave it up.

"Excuse me?" Dawn said.

Kiko smiled at her, as if welcoming her to a rite of passage. "Breisi said you'd admit what was going on in under a week. I told her you were too bullheaded and it'd take at least two."

"Nice." Dawn shook her head. "Thanks for sharing all your theories with me, guys."

"It wasn't about theories. Remember when I told you that you'd have to see to believe? That's what it was about, Dawn. *Telling* you that Robby might be a vamp wasn't the point. Part of your training is to come to accept what's happening, and that's not easy. But you're getting there, even if we have no proof about what Robby is or isn't."

"Hopefully Marla will follow your lead," Breisi said.

Dawn wanted to lay into him, but he had her nailed. It was true that she'd scattered all the pieces of Robby's story in her mind, never allowing them to come together. Not wanting them to, even after everything she'd seen, experienced.

Demand some answers, Matt had said.

Trouble was, she was pretty sure she couldn't bear any more of them. Robby was hard enough. What was she eventually going to find out about Frank . . . ?

She told herself not to think about it.

Dawn was still unnerved when they arrived back at the office, where she decided to go ahead and approach Breisi instead of Kiko. Five-to-one that his unswerving devotion to the boss would make him a harder person to question.

Or maybe Dawn knew that strong-and-silent Breisi would actually be the last person to give up answers, and that's what she *really* wanted—to remain clueless.

In the foyer, she pulled the older woman aside. "Can we chat?"

Since Breisi was all but rolling back and forward on her heels, raring to get to her dungeon, Dawn predicted the answer. The massive door of Breisi's private domain loomed behind her, like a black hole she was only too happy to be sucked into.

"Maybe later," the other woman said, gravitating toward the door/hole, caught in its pull. "All right?"

Dawn followed her. "Can't I just talk to you while—"

"No," Breisi snapped. She placed a proprietary hand on the door's iron entrance handle.

As Dawn gave Breisi a please-extract-that-pole-out-of-your-ass look, the other woman deviously relaxed most of her body. But Dawn could tell Breisi was only *acting!* again—she was still white-knuckling the handle.

"I'm sorry." She worked up a smile . . . or whatever. "Dodgers lost, Klara's dead . . . my conversation is not flowing right now."

"Got it." Dawn backed off, hands up in the air. "Thought we could talk about Robby—like how him possibly being a vamp means that they can be seen on film and all. You know—just want to continue the education."

"Later then."

Breisi didn't move. Dawn didn't budge, either—not until she realized that the tech geek wasn't going anywhere until Dawn herself took off.

Foiled again. As she moved toward the stairs, she risked one look back over her shoulder, finding that Breisi was still guarding the door.

Man, what was down there?

On her way up the stairs, she ran into Kiko.

"Hey," he said, "grab a mattress. I know it's late, but I've got a million things to do before we head out."

"Who can sleep right now anyway?"

Demand some answers.

Even if she didn't like what she heard. And, truthfully, Limpet wasn't the only person she needed to know about.

There was still something about Lonigan's parent story that was nagging at her. Something that she wasn't necessarily hiding from, either.

They reached the second-floor landing. The soft hush of an old house at rest mingled with the shaded hallway, making Dawn a little cold, inside and out.

"Are there any computers with Internet access?" she asked. "I wanna look up a thing or two."

"You're kidding, aren't you?"

Kiko led her to the right, down a part of the hall she hadn't explored yet. He pushed open a door, revealing dark wood, the ticking of a small Swiss mantel clock, and a bank of computers lining one side of the room. All of them stared out with black gazes, like the eyes of carnival dolls.

"No paintings of wanton women in here?" Dawn asked.

Kiko laughed, showing her to the first computer. "Nope."

"What are those about anyway?"

He used the keyboard to wake up the system. "They're just portraits that the boss collects."

Portraits. "They must be worth a lot. Some look old."

"Some of them are."

"And . . . ?"

"And what? They're pictures."

Whatever. They were more than that. And she'd find out what, even if she had to take one apart.

As she sat down, Kiko gave her a push to her bare arm, just for kicks. Unfortunately, it was exactly where her burns were still healing. She gave a tiny grunt, but only because she was remembering how much the wounds used to hurt. Really.

"Sorry 'bout that," he said. "I have impulse control issues, I think. I need to talk to my therapist about it."

"That won't be a short conversation."

Giving a fake laugh, he motored to the door. "Just click on Firefox. No passwords needed for the Net around here."

"Thanks."

He took off to do his thing, and Dawn followed directions, navigating to Google for a search. Meanwhile, snippets of Lonigan's story pinched her.

They'd been coming out of a theater . . . attacked by a man . . . Matt had seen his parents dying . . .

While she tried to figure out why it was so familiar, she ran a search on his name. Typical stuff that The Voice and Breisi had already ferreted out: a PI employed by a firm called Janus and Patrick. She skipped over most of the information because it seemed redundant and, besides, it wasn't what she really wanted to know.

She searched for any clue to his parents' names, found nothing. Tried some newspaper databases to check for murders that might match what Matt had told her tonight.

Theater . . . left through the back door . . . my dad tried to hand over his wallet . . .

She was striking out all over the place here. But she continued, never giving up, even as the clock struck three.

Theater . . .

The long day had mushed her brain, reducing rational thoughts to goop and forcing her to blink to stay awake. The scenario for the Lonigans' murder kept replaying in her mind as she tried to reconstruct it. She even cast it with actors, slightly familiar faces . . . Oh, God.

Oh, God, oh, God, oh, God.

Their murder. She'd seen it before. Not tonight, not in her head . . .

. . . but on a freakin' cineplex screen.

Not even bothering to shut down the computer, she sprinted out of the room, down the hall, calling for Kiko.

Unbelievable, she kept telling herself. Does Lonigan think I'm some kind of idiot? What kind of mental chess is this guy playing with me?

"Kiko?" Clumsy with fatigue, she came to a slide on the carpet, her leg bumping against the stair railing, right where the vamp-tail injury was healing. Pained, she almost tumbled down the steps, her calf bubbling with a slight throb.

"Kiko!"

Downstairs, the only thing she saw was Breisi's precious door. She flew to it, banging on the thick oak with her fists.

Theater . . . alley . . . handed over his wallet . . .

The door whooshed open to reveal the aproned mad scientist herself, her eyes red with either a lack of sleep or the frustration of being interrupted. Dawn went with the last one.

"What is it?" the older woman ground out.

"Is Kiko down there? You need to hear this, too. I found out something about Lonigan—"

Kiko, somehow still looking as fresh as dew, brought up Breisi's back. It seemed like both of them were blocking the door now, barring Dawn from seeing anything but stone walls bathed in blue light. Behind them, there was the sound of that hum, a metallic heartbeat.

"What're you talking about?" he asked.

"*Batman*," Dawn blurted. "Matt Lonigan's parents died almost like Bruce Wayne's, just without the vampire crap. I remembered it from the movies. He—"

"Breisi, we're gonna go." Kiko bent under Breisi's arm to step upward, past the door. As Breisi shut it behind him, the slam chopped through the house, hatcheting against the high ceilings.

"Come here," he said, guiding her to a plush loveseat in the foyer. The portrait of the fire woman—the one who'd frayed Dawn's nerves that first night—reigned over them, keeping her eyes on Dawn once again.

"Kiko, why would Lonigan do it? Why would he give me such bullshit, I mean, aside from the fact that this is Hollywood and just about everyone here has a manufactured biography, but—"

"I don't know. Maybe it's a true story that happens to be similar to Bruce Wayne's. I've heard—and experienced—crazier things. So have you."

Dawn didn't have the umph to argue. She'd run out of gas. Her reasoning had shut down. Complete overload.

"We should probably just go back to my digs, get some sleep," he said.

Maybe that was the best idea. Maybe she could figure everything out tomorrow, when it would all make more sense.

Yeah, Dawn thought, eyes burning with fatigue. She needed the information to settle in, didn't she? Nothing would make sense until she allowed it to.

Breisi's door creaked wide. She emerged, head down, coming toward Dawn and holding a mahogany box. It was open, revealing a set of very small *shuriken* set against a blue velvet bed.

Throwing stars. Ninja weapons.

"More tools before you leave." Breisi showcased the silver. "I just put the finishing details on them."

Dawn reached out to touch one, avoiding all of the eight star-sharp points. There were tiny etchings, words. "What's written there?"

"Latin incantations from the Catholic Church that banish evil.

I know one of your first stunt jobs was on *Ninjutsu: The Movie*, so I thought you might be comfortable with using the *shuriken*."

At that, Breisi shoved the box at Dawn. But she wasn't being unkind; no, she was actually being awkward, and it was sort of touching. In a Breisi kind of way.

"They're for me?" Dawn asked.

"Well, yes. Since I knew you were trained in the use of them, I've modified the weapons for your needs. There's some silver, but I managed not to allow that to affect the throwing balance. And each is tipped and blessed with holy water, though you'll want to keep up on that maintenance yourself. If one of these gets buried in a vamp's skin . . . poof. I hope. The holy water might travel through their bloodstream and inflict internal damage."

Dawn didn't really know what to say. She wasn't used to gifts. "Thank you," was all she managed before she did something dumb like cry. She was just about to, too. The past days had been long, throwing one punch after another at her head and guts.

"*De nada*," Breisi said.

Shoulders tight, she speed-walked back to her dungeon before Dawn could even glance up again.

Kiko was oohing and ahhing over the weapons. "These are what stealth is all about. Oh, boy, oh, boy." He pretended to pick one up and throw it. "Screw close range fighting—that's for stakes. Screw loud fighting—that's for guns. This . . . *this* is da bomb. Ninjas forever!"

Good old Kiko and his geek-asms. The appreciation of his weirdness got to her also, welling up and making her eyes sting.

She really did need sleep. Just a few hours of it would get her back to normal.

He must've noticed her inability to control. "Dawn?"

"Long day," she said in a strangled whisper.

"Yeah." He reached out to pat her shoulder.

But when he touched her, he froze.

"Kik?"

His mouth was primed for a scream. A faint gurgle rattled from his throat, his eyes full of cold fear.

She tried to grab him, help him, but he was gripping her shirt with all his strength, holding on to it like it was a branch he'd grabbed during a fall off a cliff.

Shirt. Oh, God. Frank's shirt.

"Breisi!"

She must've heard Dawn's screeching loud and clear, because it didn't take long for her to emerge from the door way again.

When she saw Kiko's terrified pose, she kicked the door shut, ran over to him and helped Dawn to pull him off.

With a strenuous yank, Breisi was successful. Kiko tumbled back into her arms, shivering in the aftermath.

"Is he okay?" Dawn asked. Frank's shirt gaped away from her chest, stretched, revealing her black bra. She was afraid to ask what'd happened, because she knew.

He'd gotten a reading.

Breisi lightly slapped at Kiko's face, but he just stared straight ahead, jaw slack.

"Frank," he said. "Alive."

Breisi cried out, and Dawn clutched at the shirt.

Alive? Was she hearing right? Please, God, please . . .

In spite of the tense moment, she and Breisi exchanged hopeful glances, chained together in this endless waiting.

Then Kiko jerked, choking out his next words. "Screaming . . . Hahh-h . . . h . . . hurts, hurts too much."

Dawn dropped to the floor next to him.

He squirmed against Breisi. "Pain . . . pain!"

Breisi started to weep, rocking Kiko back and forth in her arms, as if he were a substitute for Frank.

But Dawn didn't lose it—not now, when she was so close. Not when she couldn't do anything but sit here and listen to the terrible progress report.

"Pain, pain . . . Dawn, where is Dawn?"

She finally realized what was happening. Unlike the calm aftermath of his previous empathic visions, Kiko was in an agony-induced trance this time. A trickle of moisture wiggled out of the corner of his mouth and Dawn wiped it away, oddly concerned for his dignity.

"I'm here, Daddy," she choked out.

"Dawn." Kiko turned his eyes to her, but it was clear he wasn't seeing her. Not at all. "Looking for Robby, went to Bava, and . . ."

Kiko shuddered, then shot out of Breisi's arms. Dawn caught him, holding him in front of her.

"Bava," Dawn said, needing him to continue. "And . . . ?"

"Bait," Kiko said, gaze finally focusing on Dawn.

On her hands and knees, Breisi backed away, looking the same way she had last night, after she'd seen the photo.

The psychic shook his head, his eyes going soft and apologetic as he held his arms out to Dawn in supplication.

"I was the bait to get you here."

NINETEEN

The Mirror

KIKO'S last comment stripped her of comprehension. It was almost like he'd spoken a foreign language and she was taking forever to translate it, the seconds ticking by in a vacuum.

In this slow-motion draw of time, Dawn noticed that Breisi was hiding her face. Had she known about Frank? Had she and The Voice—

Dawn's attention whipped back to Kiko when he hauled in a sharp breath. He blinked his eyes, his pupils contracting to normal size, as if gradually coming back to consciousness.

Back to Dawn who, in spite of her nature, had naively started to trust him.

You idiot, she thought to herself. See what happens when you let down your guard? *See?*

Her sense of betrayal must've announced itself on her face, her whole body, because as Kiko wiped away the sweat that had popped out over his upper lip, he scrambled to explain.

"Wait, I know everything that just came out of my mouth,

Dawn, and it didn't sound like the way things really went down." He glanced at Breisi, as if she could explain.

Trembling. Anger. An urge to tear around this house to find the goddamned Voice.

But she couldn't move, as if iced nails were bolted through her limbs, pinning her to the ground.

"You people used my dad as bait to lure me here? Why?"

She could've answered her own question, but Kiko did it for her.

"My prediction," he said. "You're the one who's key. I saw you . . ." He glanced at her, sheepish. ". . . covered in the blood of a vampire, victorious. It was the end of our struggles, Dawn. I *felt* that everything would be fine after that."

"You *felt* it."

Kiko got to his knees and tried to move closer to her, but she pushed him away, her spine pressed to the loveseat.

"Bait." Breisi barked out a humorless laugh. "Frank decided he was the bait to get Dawn here and he now thinks that's all he was good for."

"He's wrong," Kiko said. "He's searching for a reason for what happened to him."

Dawn had endured enough. She used the seat to lever back to her feet. Her fingers were clawed and ready to strike out. "Where is your boss?"

"Wait, Dawn . . ."

"Where the fuck is he!"

Breisi looked up, her face scrubbed with red streaks. "Resting, I imagine."

Dawn sprang into motion, dashing for Breisi's dungeon door. She heard Kiko behind her, chasing her down.

"It's locked," Breisi said lifelessly. "Kiko, just let her go. Let her try to find him."

Heat covered Dawn's sight, anger turning her vision into bleeding colors that melded together in unstable waves. She had no control over where she was going now—something deep and wounded had taken her over, forcing her to mercilessly shake the iron handle on Breisi's door. Unsuccessful, she pushed away from it, went to another door, then another. All locked.

Hardly fazed, she barged up the stairs, down the hall to The Voice's office.

"Come out!" she yelled at the threshold. "Or do you know how much I want to kill you right now?"

The words rippled down the hall, through the house, against the ceilings, bouncing off the walls and banging back at her. From the two portraits that were still populated, the ladies watched Dawn, their eyes following her as she entered the office.

As her head closed in on itself, she thought she heard a soft "*Shhhh*" in her ear.

She brushed the sound away, stalked near his desk, circled, then stood in front of the TV.

"You come out and talk to me, goddamn you. Get out here!"

"*Hush . . .*" The request brushed over Dawn's arms, silk over flesh. She smelled jasmine.

The tinkle of a chandelier—the one that had drawn her into the boudoir the other night—called to her. A lullaby of gentle crystal.

"Stop playing me," she said.

"*Everything will be alright.*" Now it sounded like a multitude of souls woven together, whispers in a vortex. "*Hu-uu-sh . . .*"

Although she wanted to keep her rage in the open, Dawn could feel it receding into a tiny, destructive ball of packed hatred, small enough to fit into one of those boxes she supposedly had in her soul. As the soft voices tried to soothe her, to douse that ball with cool words, Dawn fought to keep her enflamed emotions on the surface, like living armor.

But she couldn't. She was too weak, successful only in pushing the quelled wrath to the center of her stomach, where it glowed, revolved. Waited to explode full-force again.

Out of nowhere, gentle, invisible fingers began drifting over her arms, pulling her out of the office, stroking her hair, her neck.

"Shhh," the voices said again.

Discombobulated, Dawn struggled against going anywhere, but it was as if she was moving at the command of another force, being led out of the door and into the hall.

With one look back at the office, she saw that the painting of the Elizabethan woman was empty.

How . . . ?

"Shhh . . ."

She was brought to a dusky room at the far end. Candles flickered inside long, gem-cut tubes of glass, the light casting wicked shapes on the beige walls. A writing desk stood open, a pen resting over stationery marked with large, elegant writing. Next to it, a bookcase opened away from the wall at an angle, like a door left ajar; it allowed a slat of darkness, a steady stream of crisp wind that made the candle flames dance. In the opposite corner hung a mirror, sheer black material shrouding everything but a peek of reflection. The invisible hands—more than one pair—continued to explore her shoulders, her neck, her back, their touch like a twilight breeze.

"No." Dawn shoved at the air around her, angry that the sensations were making her skin tingle.

She thought she heard a faint giggle.

"Leave us," said a dredged voice from the dark slat near the bookcase.

It sounded real, unfiltered by a speaker, immediate.

The maddening laughter stopped at the command. A flow of jasmine perfume whooshed past Dawn and out the door. It shut, shaking the walls to a slight vibration.

Dawn took a step toward the slat. "Is that you, asshole?"

"Stay back, Dawn."

She stopped, fought her way forward, but she couldn't seem to advance any more.

Yelling, she finally gave up, reduced to a panting wreck. Her buried ire grew, burning through the serenity that the invisible hands had tried so hard to cover her with.

"I won't blindly obey directions," she said. "Not anymore, *boss*. Not since I found out what you set Frank up for." She faced the darkness, hoping he was right there, feeling every lash of her disappointment. "How could you do this to him?"

"Dawn . . ."

And it started again. She could feel his presence, the calming entry, The Voice, slipping into her body through the pores of her skin. Part of her welcomed it, craved it because it would make her forget that much easier. But another part of her battled him out with all the force she could muster.

"Stop," she whispered.

Her resistance built, heaved against him, stronger, stronger . . .

"Dawn, I need you to listen—"

With a last-ditch explosion, she cried out, clawed at him with her hands, swiping through cold air.

She heard a grunt, felt him pull back.

"Don't touch me. Don't . . ."

Her body finally seized up, tears wrenching out of her in a violent squeeze of terror, helplessness, sorrow. She sank to her knees at the force of them.

I've lost it, she told herself. Damnit. I've lost, *period*.

She could feel The Voice hovering near, in his dark opening by the bookcase. She wanted to rip into him, tear him open, make him feel as vulnerable as she did right now.

"Not only did you lie to me," she said through clenched teeth, "you lied to Frank. Kiko said . . ."

"I already know what Kiko said." He sounded beaten. "I wish you had allowed him to explain further."

"Explain? Can't I hear even a syllable of truth from *you*?"

Stop crying, you wuss.

And Dawn did, though she was so worked up that she couldn't

even moderate her breathing. Her lungs stung with the unnatural efforts of holding back, holding together.

"I've never lied to you," he said. "There's been some omission, but no lies."

"Same thing."

"No." A long pause cut the room in two, putting them on opposite sides of a chasm. "It's not the same. I want to keep you safe, but there's so much more at stake. Matters that are worth the sin of omission. Matters that will have an effect on this world much longer than the span of your lifetime."

"So it's all for the greater good, huh?" Bitter. God, so bitter. "You're such a hero, Voice."

The nickname struck an odd chord, like a grandfather clock whose chimes had warped and accidentally announced a secure hour at midnight.

"I'm known by a lot of names, Dawn, but that's not one of them. Please, call me . . . Jonah."

Cold air from the dark slat seeped into the room, surrounding her, coaxing her to understand his reasoning.

"Why don't you just come all the way out?" she asked.

"As lovely as that sounds, it's not wise. Would you like to hear about Frank?"

"What do you think?"

A caress of air dragged over her cheek, an invisible hand stroking her in compassion. Dawn jerked away from it, wanting so badly to accept it, too.

The Voice . . . Jonah . . . continued, sounding wounded by her rebuff. "You certainly have Frank's passion and conviction."

"I have his temper, too." She glared at the darkness. "What are you exactly? Who are you?"

In the resulting pause, she thought she heard a shift behind the bookcase, like a body—his?—had settled itself in for a long talk, crouched in readiness in case it had to flee.

Or maybe it was her overactive imagination. And why not? It had served her pretty well lately.

"What am I?" he repeated. "That would be up to interpretation. But I know what your father is. He's a good man, Dawn, and I regret that he went missing."

Smooth, she thought. He was just as adept as she was at manipulating a conversation.

"I didn't plan for him to disappear," he added. "You must understand that. But I did track him down and hire him a few months ago, with an eye to convincing you to join him in Los Angeles again. He even knew about Kiko's vision—"

"The one where I'm 'key'?" She put sarcastic emphasis on the last word.

He withstood her abuse. "Yes. I place great stock in Kiko's emerging prescience. He has a developing talent I haven't seen since . . ." He sighed, resigned again. "I'd be a fool to ignore his visions. When he mentioned you by name and advised me that he felt you'd be reluctant, I wasted no time in contacting Frank. It was a devious way to get to you, yes, but he jumped at the salary, and had no problem acting as our 'hired muscle.' When we trained him for PI work, he didn't hesitate there, either. Then we approached him with his biggest purpose."

"Getting me here? So I could be some dreamt-up savior? I think you've got the wrong woman."

"No, I don't. We believed that he could persuade you to return, to work with us, but Frank didn't want you involved with the paranormal."

"Probably for good goddamned reason, *Jonah*."

"As I said, our work is more important than any individual. But what you don't know is that Frank began coming around. As he got deeper into the investigation, he saw how important it was to 'save the world,' for lack of a better description."

Dawn was already shaking her head. "My dad. A crusader. Right, tell me another one."

The Voice's silence was more powerful than any comeback.

"So while he was detecting, *Jonah*, did he find out anything useful? Or were you just keeping him busy until your key came?"

"Dawn, Frank turned out to be very valuable to us. He was hitting a lot of walls in his work, but he did discover . . . something. He called me from what I now think to be Bava and said that perhaps it *was* time for you to come out here and fulfill your place. Yet before he could continue, the phone went dead, and I didn't hear from him again."

She still didn't understand the part about him changing his mind about her working with Limpet. It wasn't like Frank to go against his beliefs. He was as stubborn as she was.

"Are you lying to me about his turnabout?" Dawn asked.

"No." The cold breeze angled again, even as his voice was still anchored from behind the bookcase. "If you hadn't been called now to come to Los Angeles because of his disappearance, you would have been called soon anyway—by Frank. He had come around, I'm certain of that. His disappearance was a tragic surprise—and it wasn't designed to get you here."

"I still don't see how he would've agreed to recruit me."

Pause. "Before he disappeared, I asked him what he would do to make the world a safer place for you. Do you know what he answered, Dawn?"

She knew, because she'd said the same thing to Jonah that first night. Anything—she would do anything. But, back then, Dawn hadn't known just what that meant, how far it would go.

"Frank," Jonah added, "started to realize what 'anything' entailed. I believe you're at the same point."

Her armor wouldn't allow her to believe him—not yet. Especially with Matt Lonigan's words embedded in her brain.

Demand some answers.

Answers about what? Did the PI know that Frank had been hired by Limpet so they could get her back to L.A.?

"Does Matt Lonigan know about all this?"

The air seemed to quiver at the mention of the name.

"I'm not certain *what* Lonigan knows. Not certain at all."

She shuddered. What if Lonigan had been referring to other secrets that Jonah was playing close to his chest? What else wasn't The Voice telling her?

She thought about the reason Lonigan might have been at Klara's murder scene.

Summoning all her courage, she unsteadily got to her feet, asked one of the questions that was bothering her the most. "Do you think Frank had anything to do with Klara's murder?"

"I don't believe so."

She exhaled, profoundly relieved, but not entirely. Also, she wasn't sure *how* to react to the simple truth from The Voice. It'd taken so long to get to this point that she wasn't sure Jonah was really on the up and up. Nevertheless, she rode this opportunity.

"Do you think Frank somehow became a . . . a . . ."

"A vampire?"

She managed a nod.

"If he is, he wouldn't have done it without regret."

No. Please, that couldn't have happened. . . .

"We have no proof of his change, Dawn, it's merely a possibility to consider."

Her defenses down, he flowed right back against her, the cool air pressed against her arm like a face buried there and asking forgiveness. She didn't have the strength to be angry anymore. She had to save her rage for more important fights, fights she knew were inevitable.

"Kiko said Frank's in pain."

"And pain could very well be a sign of humanity."

Pure relief had her slumping backward, turning toward the half-covered mirror, but a pair of invisible arms caught her. More powerless anguish wracked her, threatening new tears.

"If you're going to help him, you must rest." His voice was gentle in her ear, fluttering the loose hairs around it. "Rest, Dawn."

He was soaking past her skin, cell by cell, becoming a part of her, feeding off of her just as she fed off of him. And as much as she knew it was wrong to welcome him, she did, loving the joining too much, needing the comfort.

"Rest," she said in agreement, tired of the struggle. "Please."

The request allowed him all the way in, her limbs heavy, shot through with sexual yearning.

In victory, The Voice's essence swirled around her, scented with familiar mystery, tasting of things she recalled only in the back of her mind—things stored tightly away and mourned by her unconscious self. In the lone, unshrouded corner of the mirror, she could see her jeans-covered thigh, and nothing else.

Closing her eyes, she felt the tips of ghostly fingers running up and down her arms, pausing over her burns, then circumventing them. In the background, the hinges of the bookcase creaked, then stopped.

"I can keep us safe, Dawn," he whispered, his voice mere inches from her ear. "With your help, I can finally do it."

With a heady thrust, he came into her.

Gasping, she tingled, her body like a shower of cinders. But this time, he was on the outside, too. Somehow, he was in both places at the same time, using the physical touch of his hands, his mouth.

The pressure of his lips traveled to her neck. At his urging, she leaned her head to the side. She felt the silver-and-gem strands of her earring shift, felt him pause as if memorizing it. Then she felt him against her throat, running his mouth over a vein, exploring the scent of her skin.

Languid, animal instinct got the better of her. She wanted to hurt him as much as he'd hurt her, wanted to punish, so she ground back against him, feeling the stiffness of an erection. With a swipe that seemed to play out in slow motion, she reached back, her fingernails catching a face. Or what felt like a face. Moisture—his blood—immediately dried under her nails.

He groaned against her ear, driving her to erotic madness, getting her damp, ready.

"I'm going to make you tell me everything," she said.

He bit her ear, hard, eliciting another gasp from her. Then he laughed at her pain, knowing damn well how much she liked it.

Inside *and* outside, she thought. This isn't a mind probe. It's something . . . different.

Still, she wanted him within her, thrilled to the pulse of him under her skin. It drove her crazy to have a man in her veins, possessing her. She grabbed for his hair, intending to wrench him around. But he knew her too well.

Anticipating her violence, he maneuvered her arm behind her back, arching her spine. Her distended nipples brushed against her bra, agonized and raw.

"Bastard," she said, a low, hungry wince telling him that she was lying.

Physically, he eased up on her, but, inside, he was now pooling around her stomach like a jet of warm cream, sliding downward, bathing her sex. With warm, lapping strokes, his essence licked at her.

She cried out.

He laughed again.

In heightened response, she roughly reached behind her, feeling for his erection. When she found it, she rubbed, hard and slow.

Groaning, pushing her forward until she bent at the waist, he buried his face against her neck, nipping. One hand entangled itself in her hair as he carefully undid her ponytail, proving just how much he could take of her torture without giving in. As she continued rubbing him, anticipating the moment he'd glide into her, she felt the strands lift from the sensitive spot where neck met spine, felt the weight of him settling his mouth at her nape, forcing heat and tightness to pull at each other in her belly.

Exerting his control again, he deliberately removed her hand from him, guided it to her stomach, slipped her palm beneath her undershirt so she could touch her tender skin, trace the bared plane just above the line of her jeans.

Responding, she swelled, throbbed, grew even wetter.

God, the texture of his hands . . . The undulation of his mind swirling against her . . .

Suddenly, with a whoosh of cold air, his essence retreated from her body, then plunged back into her, making her stifle a scream because of the driving sensation, the simultaneous inner pressure of a nearing climax.

In his flurry of movement, the material shrouding the mirror had flared away, falling to the floor like wings guiding a raven to a landing.

Moaning in her haze, she looked into the mirror. She had to see him, see what he was doing to her.

But . . .

She blinked, bucked back against him.

The mirror showed a woman flushed and writhing, her eyes passion-flared, like one of the seductive portraits in The Voice's collection. Her shirt was twisted upward, showing her own hand rubbing her belly, moving as if it were being guided by another. Her hair was flying free, suspended in air and wavering up and down as if held by fingers.

But there was no hand over her hand. No fingers in her hair. No one behind her.

He was there, but he wasn't there.

A flash of terror and excitement blinded her, seeping downward, through her skin, into the center of her, wet and furious. She started to slide downward, her knees unable to hold up any longer.

In the mirror, she was floating, her body braced by invisible hands that were holding her up.

"What the hell are you?" she repeated.

Caught, he sought escape: her hair dropped, and the rest of the pressure lifted off of her body. Fighting for balance, Dawn stumbled around, reaching out to grip his arm, his shoulder . . . anything.

Nothing.

Popping out of her stupor, she frantically searched the room for any sign of him. Nowhere. The bookcase creaked, and she noticed that it had gone back to its original position, revealing only a dark slat between it and the wall.

Mirrors, she thought. What did movies say about vampires and mirrors?

Turning back around, she looked in the shiny surface again, seeing only herself, posture steeled with ire.

"Jonah!"

A frenetic breeze whipped around the room, a prelude to a storm. On the traces of the wind, she thought she heard a cry of fury that mirrored her own emotions.

Smash.

Books tumbled out of the case as the wall crashed back into itself, closing up the slat.

"No . . ." She ran to the wall, pounded on it, tried to force it open, but she knew it was useless.

The Voice . . . Jonah . . . had left her.

She whipped around, using the bookcase to hold her up. As she tightened her fists by her side, she focused across the room on the mirror again.

But what she saw there made her do a double take.

It was her, all right, yet not her.

Her mind—she *knew* it was just her mind—had conjured up an image of Dawn with blond hair, bigger brown eyes. It was what she would've looked like if she'd inherited more of Eva's DNA.

As Dawn stared in horrified wonder, heat soaked her body, beating to a mortifying afterglow. But the vision stared right back, broken-hearted and disappointed in how she'd turned out.

"I'm so sorry . . ." she said.

She was apologizing for a lot of things: being weak, never being good enough to warrant the title of Eva Claremont's Daughter.

Like a fatal blow, deep, bone-searing grief broke Dawn in half, reducing her to exhausted tears again. The image hushed to black, and she felt her own soul going along with it.

Fading to wherever movies die after the ending credits have rolled.

TWENTY

Below, Phase Four

Sorin, the Master, and a guest were in a secret room watching through a trick window that was mirrored on the side of the citizens. Steam from the spa, where the Groupies waited on the Elites, fogged the glass's edges, yet a view of the bacchanalia was still clear.

Male Groupies massaging female Elites, female Groupies bathing female Elites, or any other combination of pleasure they could dream up. As if to provide a beautiful garnish, Groupies huddled in the room's misted corners, stroking each other, giggling, as they waited to be called.

The hidden Sorin and Master were focused on the nearest of the raised beds, where an Elite was bent forward, naked, his arms propped on a column of harem pillows while he rested on his knees. Three female Groupies attended him: one rubbing her fingers over his scalp, one spreading oil over his broad shoulders, one positioned on her back beneath him, in between his parted legs. Her mouth worked at his penis, taking him in and out as she lightly squeezed his scrotum with her fingers.

"They are glass gods," Sorin said, ignoring their cowed guest, who was huddled on the floor by the Master's feet. Sorin could scent the nervous sweat from the human's skin. "I find it unsurprising that the Elites enthralled Lee Tomlinson to such an extent. You have created fragile monsters."

In the darkness, the Master's aura pulsed with contained wrath at the mention of the errant Servant.

Due to the spywork Above, they had already seen to Lee Tomlinson's punishment. He had been caught by a patrol of Guards an hour ago, charged with the flagrant murder of Klara Monaghan. Though the Servant's intentions had been noble, he had done much harm. He had confessed and genuinely believed that quieting the aging actress from speaking of Robby Pennybaker for good would only benefit his Underground. Yet Lee Tomlinson had forgotten his humanity while attempting to prove how much of a vampire he was meant to be: he had ripped out his victim's throat in his passion for Underground redemption.

When the Servant had first been caged, he had even then maintained his loyalty to the Underground and petitioned anyone who would listen to believe that he *was* vampire material. His yearning for Klara's blood had proven it, he had cried.

Unfortunately, Sorin and the Master had learned that the murder had indicated vampire activity Above; it had excited the humans who already believed in—and were prepared for—"monsters."

Humans such as the private detectives.

If there were any monsters, Sorin thought, Lee Tomlinson was the epitome. Did he not understand that they were civilized? Indeed, food came from Above, but they did not feed like crazed creatures. At the risk of penalty, they took a prey's volunteered blood. It was their code.

But there had been no need to explain this to the former Servant after he had secretly been brought to the Master's chambers to have his mind wiped.

Afterward, they had released Lee Tomlinson to the Servant lawyer, Milton Crockett, "The Fixer," as he was known up Above to the Hollywood community. Crockett would see to it that his client settled in to a normal life outside of Los Angeles, devoid of Underground memories. He would make certain that no one—not Lee's lover or *anyone*—found out about the incident, as well, at the risk of having to perform yet another mind wipe.

After all this, the Master seemed inclined to face the inevitable. "We've withstood more than Lee Tomlinson in the past," the Master had said. "Much more. And if this Servant's carelessness leads to a confrontation, then come what may, Sorin. Because the day *will* come when we have to defend our Underground, but we would be fools to force it to happen without absolute cause. If we reveal ourselves Above too early, that could bring a premature end for our paradise. You've said it yourself—we *must* use stealth to preserve our secrecy, then, if everything else fails, it's war."

Had the Master become too arrogant recently? Granted, he had abilities not even Sorin could summon, although Sorin had inherited a great deal of his parent's skills through the initial long and proper blood exchange that had birthed him.

All the same, each generation's blood grew weaker, the progeny in need of more protection. Such a pity to lose power as a breed, Sorin thought, remembering his own children.

"Sir?" It was the shaking voice of their guest. "Master?"

Still bruised from the memory of his missing progeny, Sorin reared forward, knowing the human could not see him, but could feel the threat of his blood-laden breath, his hair-splitting power in the dark. "You are not to speak unless spoken to."

"But I've paid—"

"You are making *us* pay, human. Remain quiet."

The man shrunk back, chastised for now, his once-neat, finely manicured hair flat with perspiration.

Experienced in the ways of mental torture, Sorin forced the human to wait a few plodding moments before addressing him again.

"You solicit entrance to the Underground, where no human comes unless he is willing to be fed upon. You come without the intention of offering yourself or ever becoming one of us. You plead an audience with the Master you call Dr. Eternity."

Sorin knew the head vampire was listening, though he seemed enchanted by the trick mirror instead. But he was a vampire noble who need not pay respects to this underling when Sorin was his proxy. His shield who preserved his safety from the public. His devoted bodyguard.

"I need your help," the human said. "That's why I came. And you summoned me back to this country in the first place because you needed me, too."

"I find it odd that you so fear ever becoming a vampire, yet you chose this path for your son."

Nathan Pennybaker looked up at Sorin, his face sorrow-ravaged. "Robby knew his time in the Underground was going to keep his name alive forever. He knew that getting the help of Dr. Eternity was the only answer to his career. That's why we sought you out after we were approached by your Servant-agent."

A man who had left them long ago when his usefulness had expired, may he rest in peace. "Yes, Robby's career *was* on the wane, even though he was at such a tender age."

"That's what happens with child stars," the human said, angry. "The audience doesn't want to see them grow up."

And Robby had been growing up, all too fast, Sorin thought, knowing this story—and all the stories—by heart. Nathan Pennybaker seemed to take no responsibility for his reportedly awful part in Robby's fleeting childhood, and that disgusted Sorin all the more, for he had loved his own children once. He had lost them, too. And, unlike Nathan Pennybaker, Sorin would have moved mountains to alleviate anything his daughters might have suffered; never would he have introduced pain to them.

In effect, he enjoyed toying with this bad father, making *him* suffer.

The Master agreed, his aura reddening.

"True, it is not easy watching your children mature," Sorin said. "It would also not be easy to see them loaned out to the highest bidders—unless you have the soul of a demon."

The human choked on his own rage, seeking the words to defend himself, failing.

But Sorin was too occupied with memory to mind the human. Both of his daughters had gone missing years ago, though he knew they still survived somewhere; after all, their own children remained alive here, thus testifying that their parents had not perished. After they had reproduced here in the Underground, they had left for more thrilling adventures in the Old World, wishing to "explore their roots." Perhaps it had cost them dearly.

The first so-called Groupies had been the result of their fledgling efforts to exchange. More Groupies had followed, each generation losing abilities, the bloodline growing anemic. There had been times that Sorin had pondered the possibility of *his* exchanging with a human again, but the loss of his daughters was still fresh and agonizing, and breeding became too painful an act to consider.

However, if the Underground required more power, he would reproduce in a heartbeat. His own progeny would be strong. Perhaps the time had come to reconsider, with all the threats circling from Above. . . .

"Perhaps," Sorin said to the human, newly scathed by his old loss, "you should get your *own* career to ruin."

Nathan Pennybaker, the failed child star, responded as if slapped across the face with a fine kid glove. Sorin had known that the insult would sting.

Yet he sensed genuine sadness, as well. Curious, how a man like this could still feel for the son he had manipulated so thoroughly.

"I'm begging you," said the human, "please find Robby. I can tame him, just like you asked me to."

Sorin thought of the Guards who had been tracking Robby ever since the child star had permanently escaped from the Underground in order to avoid the final phase of release.

"We are making every attempt to discover his whereabouts," he said, anticipating that fine day. Because after Robby's recovery, the Underground would be that much more secure, the Guards Below in their own area and waiting for another situation, should one come. Then Sorin's worries could be rested.

Tellingly, no one had ever escaped the Underground before Robby. That was a testament to everyone's willingness to be here. Yet the Master had made an error with Robby, believing he would agree with the career advice of his father once he grew older and less rebellious. In spite of his youth, the child had been career savvy, so it did not seem at all improbable.

Besides, the Master had wanted Robby, had been utterly intrigued by his precocious soul, by the relationships he had developed during his stellar career.

"I've tried to find him myself," Nathan Pennybaker said. "These past few nights, I went everywhere I could think of—hotels, bars we frequented—but he's not around. I thought he'd come right back to me. We were inseparable before his . . . death."

"As I suggested previously, perhaps you should stay with us and lure him back *here*." Sorin expected him to refuse, knowing how much the human feared being turned into a vampire, although he had given Robby to the wonder of it. He had probably done so believing his son would never turn to him for blood. And there would never have been a cause for it, either, had Robby not escaped. "You might be the incentive he requires to return."

"I told you—I can find him."

"Yes, you have proven that to be true, have you not?"

Under the withering sarcasm, the human surrendered, his posture deflating. "My wife will still stay under your protection while I'm away from my home? She doesn't know anything. She won't be a problem."

"The protection you have already purchased for your family

remains a part of our contract. But if Robby is sighted, we will send you to your son to gently persuade him to return to us . . . along with a squad of Guards."

Fright laced the human's perspiration. "No Guards—"

"They will follow your commands within reason, human. You need not worry about them turning on you for the prize of your weak blood. Frankly, they are used to better quality."

Even with the derogatory comment, the human seemed placated, as did the Master, who had been agreeing with Sorin via their Awareness.

They had allowed Nathan Pennybaker an audience with the sheltered Master only because Pennybaker had spoken as Robby's parent and taken the oath of secrecy upon buying the boy's place in the Underground. Sorin knew the human would not betray the real Master's existence and cause a breach of security. From stories Robby had told during his stay here, Sorin knew that the human feared torture and fangs; he would not chance being exposed to either that or to the relinquishing of Robby's resurrected career.

Their business finished, Nathan Pennybaker lapsed into silence, awaiting his dismissal. But Sorin was not feeling so kind as to give it just yet.

The Master leaned forward, hardly deigning to recognize the drama between his child and the human. He had been tuned in to the spa as if it were a television or movie screen.

The interest boded nicely for the welcoming of Tamsin Greene, which was set to take place tomorrow at nightfall.

"They're beautiful, aren't they, Sorin?"

The Elites. They were the only ones the Master gifted with his blood these days. Certainly, hundreds of years ago, Sorin had been the Master's first and only child, but the Elites had held a special place in the Master's world for half a century now. He worshipped them, loved them—especially a certain one—with passionate intensity.

But that did not mean the Master was blind to their Allure. Even though the Elites were able to use their powers to convince the humans Above of their perfection, to draw them in, to make others want to *be* them, the Master had always understood the danger of the Elite crowd. They had unstable egos, narcissistic tendencies. Thus, at the birth of the Underground, the Master had decided to allow them one monthly infusion of blood—and that was all—to keep their Allure strong. Controlling their intake of the Master's blood was a safety precaution, keeping the Elites in line through the leveling of inferior power.

Not that they seemed to care who had control and who did not in the Underground. Life Above was all that mattered to them in the end, even if they enjoyed the pleasures here. After an Elite was released, they often returned for a night or two when they became lonely, but they were always drawn back to the surface by the compulsion, pure need, ego . . . and perhaps the restlessness of spending too many years Underground in the first place. For, during their required time here, they hungered to reemerge, anticipating the day they mastered their Allure. In order to accomplish this, they practiced hiding their abilities: when they arrived Above, they would be able to use only enough Allure to hypnotize humans, allowing their powers to emerge in full force strictly around fellow vampires.

At least, that was the mandate. Robby Pennybaker had shown much difficulty in controlling many of his new talents—except, of course, for blocking the Awareness between Master and child. He had perfected that all too well, even though they never used the power Above, for fear of detection. Though he was an adult in years, he was still an adolescent in his emotions. In fact, six months ago, he had even taken to sneaking out of the Underground for secret trips, but he had always returned. Sorin had put a stop to that, but this, among many reasons, was why Robby required taming before his release.

"Yes, Master, your creations are beautiful," Sorin said, always ready to please. He fixed his gaze on the male Elite with his Groupies. "Magic, if I do say so myself."

"You would know."

The Master gestured toward the show, where the male Elite had seized the Groupie who had been massaging his scalp. He had her by the waist, forcefully positioning her over the pillows that had been holding up his torso. Spreading open her thighs so that her legs framed the Groupie who was still servicing him from below, he bent and latched his mouth to the dark red flesh between her legs, laving her there as the Groupie braced herself and warbled in encouragement. The Groupie below him accommodated his accelerated thrusts with her mouth and throat, taking him deep and fast.

With a roar of satisfaction, he came, once, twice, into her. As she eased out from under him, wiping her lips, the rest of his Groupies purred, stroking him in the afterglow, turning him on his back and revealing his breathtaking face.

"My children," the Master said with a sense of wonder and awakened joy. "Gods."

On the other side of the mirror, the Elite closed his eyes. His face shimmered in the steam. A face that had been so adored by the multitudes over eleven years ago.

Back when he had been known as Jesse Shane.

TWENTY-ONE

The Healing

Now there was definitely no way Dawn was getting any sleep, especially after what had happened with Jonah. And, worse, just knowing that Frank was somewhere out there, in pain, needing help, was even more reason to get a load of caffeine into her.

After she left the room where she'd been with The Voice, she engaged in a marathon coffee-drinking session and then went with Kiko back to his place. All the way there, he stumbled over the same explanations about Frank. Having already heard enough from Jonah, she told Kiko to stop apologizing, but she *didn't* tell him that she was never going to forget that he was on the boss's side, so she just let it lie.

Nonetheless, she enlisted him in a ritual that would carry her through the day.

"Can you . . . ?" She motioned to Frank's undershirt.

Kiko seemed to understand. As she drove, he touched the material. This time he didn't go into convulsions; in fact, he didn't even react.

"Nothing," he said. "But we can keep checking."

That last part appeased Dawn a little. Strange as it was, the undershirt was her conduit to Frank. Earlier, Kiko had theorized that maybe his daughter's skin was adding power to the shirt, the item on which Kiko focused his energies. As a result, he was able to conjure Frank's thoughts with more effectiveness than before.

But she wasn't interested in technicalities. She wanted results, no matter what the hocus pocus involved.

While the sun blasted awake in the sky, they arrived at Kiko's, and Dawn decided she needed some exercise to stay awake. Aside from fencing, she hadn't really worked out since returning to L.A., and it was driving her crazy. Her muscles and skills felt flaccid. When all this trouble was finally done, she was going to contact Jerry Aberly, a stunt coordinator she'd worked with three times before. He had his own private workout, and Dawn was hoping he'd invite her to join him sometime, that he would remember how hard she'd labored for him on previous gigs and that he would see how hungry she was for another job.

After a jog during which Kiko trailed her in his car "just in case"—lazy bum—she went into an alley next to his place to practice throwing her *shuriken* while he sat by an open window, going through the *Hollywood Reporter* to see which movies were going into production. It was early enough not to attract much attention as she refamiliarized herself with the art of throwing.

She stacked the blades horizontally in her left hand, sliding one at a time to her right, where she would position her thumb tip in the *shuriken*'s center hole. By shuffling the blades from one hand to the other, she would be able to fire them rapidly at her target, her fingers and wrist tensing just slightly at the moment that the blade slipped away and sang through the air. She was careful not to fling or heft the *shuriken*; the procedure required a lighter touch than that.

For close to an hour, she practiced, getting back into the ninja *taijutsu* method she'd been trained to use for throwing the *shuriken* back when she'd just been learning the ropes of stunt work. By rocking forward and back with each throw, taking care to breathe in then out with every motion, she gained power, accuracy. Pretty soon she was lengthening the distance between her and the fence she was aiming at.

Now she imagined a real target: one of those red-eyed creatures. They'd been wearing clothes, so she'd want to get them where the flesh had been peeking out—the neck, the bald head. Small targets, but doable.

But would her blades be quicker than those tails?

That kept bothering her. She wished she had a weapon that was the equivalent of those long, barbed whips. . . .

"Yo! What're you doing out there, girl?" It was some harpy yelling at Dawn from behind her screen.

"Sorry for the noise," she said, wanting no trouble.

In his window, Kiko kept reading, probably used to the neighbor lady.

"You get out of there before I call the cops!"

Dawn gave a neighborly wave, just for karma points, and went back into Kiko's. Then she showered, allowing the cold spray of water to keep her frosty. Afterward, she applied garlic—she was kind of getting used to the stink—then some of Breisi's goo to the scarred-over injuries on her arm and leg, and then dressed, wearing another of Frank's undershirts. Finally, she joined Kiko on the couch, multitasking by anointing her blades with holy water and downing more java.

"Guess what?" he said, jacked up on caffeine, too.

"Your neighbor is the sentinel charged with guarding the gates to hell—and both of you are living over the mouth of it."

Kiko actually looked like he might consider this and should check it out when he had time. But then he gave her an aw-that's-a-reference-to-a-seventies-horror-movie glance and said, "Breisi got us a date with the coroner at around one o'clock tonight. Looks like Klara is a priority homicide. I can't wait to hear their theories about how she got all . . ."

He stopped, noticing the wan expression on Dawn's face.

She bucked up. "Okay, until then we've got an hour before our first interview." Breisi had set up a day's worth of them yesterday; afterward, they were going to hit the location list that Klara had given them. "Who's this first one?"

"Another child actor, but this guy wasn't half as successful as Robby. Now, he develops scripts over at Universal. Since Breisi's back at the office working on refining those locators, we're going to meet her on the production lot to talk with him."

"Hope it's over lots of coffee. Until then, you up for breakfast?" Here, her ulterior motives crept into play. "I know an Internet cafe near the fencing studio where they make pastries to die for."

And where they had more Web access. This time, she wanted to research Jonah Limpet, and it couldn't be done in his own office. She had the feeling her every activity was monitored there, noted for future reference.

"Just as long as you don't talk me into fencing, I'm there," Kiko said. "I don't want Breisi chewing my ass again about fooling around on the job."

"Man, you made an appointment on Saturday for a private lesson with Dipak. What're you talking about?"

He made innocent eyes. Shyster.

They weaponed up and drove to the cafe in Dawn's car, the sun peering through the smog. Daylight. It gave her a false sense of safety, even with her Vampire Repellers 'R' Us kit. Every hidden corner, every manhole that hissed steam from under its cover introduced the possibility of an ambush.

Kiko slid on his shades, no doubt to fight the L.A. glare of menace. Really. It had nothing to do with being a poseur.

After parking at the curb a block down from the cafe, they entered the brightly lit place. Fishbowl screensavers animated the computer faces, and a ceiling fan danced above their heads, giving the room a sense of neutrality. A pre-work crowd lined up at the glassed-in pastry shelves, girding themselves for the morning commute. Ninety percent of them were wearing sunglasses, too.

"Are yours going to stay on?" she asked Kiko.

"Yup."

L.A. God.

Feeling it was time to check in with Frank, Dawn pulled her shirt away from her waist. "Touch it, please."

Kiko did, but he still had no vibey reaction. Damn.

He offered to buy Dawn's breakfast, which was sweet since she thought he was kind of smoothing things over from last night. But then she realized that he was using the boss's cash to pay. Hey, big spender.

All the same, she was thankful that his absence allowed her to get on a computer and Google Limpet. She'd just have to be careful Kiko didn't get a load of what she was doing. That would be bad form.

As the hits blurbed over the screen, Dawn felt someone coming to stand behind her—the hairs on the back of her neck were an accurate alarm system.

Jumpy, she closed the window.

When she turned around, she found a young woman wearing the requisite sunglasses and a plain white baseball cap, her long red hair held back in a braid. She was holding a large coffee, dressed in pink Juicy sweats.

At first, Dawn didn't recognize her.

The girl seemed put off. "Don't you remember me?"

Dawn's mental Palm Pilot was working on it.

She glanced at Kiko, who was parting the crowd with his garlic stench. He was carrying a tray with his own meal and Dawn's bear claw plus her black-with-no-sugar coffee. Phone to his ear, he placed his java and a plate of two huge muffins and three cream puffs onto one of three open tables, this one near the window. Then he came toward Dawn with her grub.

Meanwhile, the redhead was laughing a little uncomfortably. "I guess I'm incognito without a fencing jacket on backward."

"Ah." It all came back to Dawn now—the starlet from Dipak's studio. Hurrah.

Done with that social interaction, Dawn nodded and turned back to the computer. As Kiko dropped off her meal, he chatted away happily on his cell.

"My agent," he mouthed to Dawn as she glanced at him. Then he took off to his table for some privacy.

The starlet casually took a seat next to Dawn, just like they were buddies and Dawn wasn't getting all bristly about the assumption. Then Dawn caught the girl's nose wrinkling, probably because she'd gotten wind of the garlic. Heh, time for her to scram.

But . . . no. Unfazed, the actress held her beverage, crossing her long starlet legs. "Going over to fence after this? I am."

"Right, you've got some part you're up for in the next Will Smith movie." Dawn was fascinated by her computer, tapping in the site address for the Stunt Players Directory, looking extremely busy and hoping the starlet would get the clue.

"Fingers crossed," she said, all chirpy.

"Mmm-hmm."

"Dipak tells me you're real good at your job. I'd love to have your talents. I'm afraid I'm a klutz when it comes to action, and you have to be versatile these days. An adventure movie here, a drama there, a comedy after that." She leaned closer to Dawn, her perfume overcoming the garlic and striking a note so low that it could've been an olfactory sigh of delight. "But listen to me talk. I've only had a couple of supporting roles. It's just that the chance for this Will Smith gig is making me giddy."

Surfing the stunt site, Dawn ate her bear claw and wished the girl would just leave.

She felt the actress lean a little closer, waiting for Dawn to answer.

Too close. Dawn coughed, subtly scooting her chair away at the same time.

"Your name's Dawn Madison," the starlet said, still clueless. "Dipak told me. He brags about you."

"Good ol' Dipak."

"I'm Jacqueline Ashley. But you can call me Jac." When she laughed again, it was melodic, the sound tickling the line of Dawn's jaw.

She'd gotten too close again.

Dawn took a wild guess at what might be happening here. "Listen, my door doesn't swing to that side, if that's what you're thinking."

When Dawn faced her, she was struck by the curious furrow of the starlet's forehead, like she didn't understand what Dawn had just insinuated. This close, Dawn didn't have any choice but to take in every other detail of her face: the delicate chin; the French-ingenue pout; the high, graceful cheekbones; the Nicole Kidman milk-fresh skin kept safe from the sun by that ball cap.

Okay. Jacqueline Ashley had a certain "It" that defined a movie star. Maybe it was her sparkling laugh, maybe it was her perfect smile. But "It" was there—the unexplainable, impossible chemistry of someone who was going to be loved by the camera.

Hate.

It had taken a few seconds for the girl to process what Dawn had said to her. And, whether Dawn liked it or not, the starlet's obvious naïveté was disturbing, because she'd seen all too often what this town did to darling homecoming queens.

Why did girls like this have to come out here? They weren't tough enough. This one was going to get skewered; she'd probably be talked into doing a porno within the year, and that was only the beginning. Her dreams would die one by one, victims of the biz.

"Don't tell me," Dawn said. "You got off the bus from Podunk two months ago."

"Pahrump, Nevada." Her cheeks had gone pink. "I don't really know anybody here, so I'm trying to meet people. Sorry if you thought I was . . . you know. I've got a boyfriend back home, so I wasn't hitting on you. Wow, how embarrassing."

Dawn's asshole quotient shot straight through the roof at the girl's mortification.

The starl . . . okay . . . *Jacqueline* continued. Dawn could at least acknowledge that she had a name as a brief apology.

"My boyfriend entered a photo of me in some modeling contest because he said he wanted everyone to know how . . . well, pretty I am. What a boyfriend will say, right? Then Barbara Hammer, an agent over at ISM, got a hold of it and she called, wondering if I'd thought about a career out here. I've got a single mom, and she has a hard time making ends meet, so I came because it sounded like I'd be able to send money home to her."

"You'll want to be careful." Nice, Dawn thought. Frank would've wanted you to be nice to this girl. "Don't trust people unless they earn it. Nobody's in this town to be your friend."

"I'm sorry to hear that. Can I ask what your experiences have been like? It'd help me a lot. I don't want to pry, but . . ."

God, this girlie was *so* green. Giving in, Dawn told her about the Darrin Ryder numb nuts incident, being careful not to name names. In spite of the population, this was a small town.

"That kind of stuff happens?" Jacqueline asked. "Really?"

"That's nothing." Dawn pushed the rest of her bear claw away, not hungry anymore.

"You okay?"

"Yeah."

"Can I help? You look like you're going to get sick."

Dawn ran a hand over her hair. "I don't have time for getting sick or small talk or . . . I've just got a lot to do."

She was about to get up and get out of there, fueled by coffee and frustration, but then Dawn felt a hand on her arm, the touch warm and comforting, like a blanket you could burrow under during a thunderstorm. Normalcy. It sounded so nice. Before last night, she'd thought that maybe Matt Lonigan had been her best chance at it, her strongest link to the real world—a place that seemed so far away now.

" 'When the itch is inside the boot, scratching outside provides little consolation.' " Jacqueline laughed softly, with the reassuring levity of someone who hadn't seen the worst yet. "It's a Chinese proverb that my mom used to say to me. I think it's got something to do with taking the time for small talk . . . or big talk. Opening up."

What, was this girl Dawn's Best Friend Forever?

Belatedly, she realized that she hadn't shrugged off Jacqueline's hand yet. Hadn't thought to do it.

Instead she just sat there, the little abandoned girl inside of her kind of wanting to hear more. "Must've been nice, having a smart mom like that around."

"It was." Jacqueline smiled. "It's sad about what happened to your mother. I would've been a complete wreck in your shoes, but you've grown up strong, haven't you? Dipak admires that about you, too."

"You and Dipak talk an awful lot."

"The man's a social butterfly. He likes to chat about his wonderful students, except when he's telling me how bad my posture is."

In spite of herself, Dawn grinned, but only slightly. "You've got good posture. You carry yourself well."

Sad. It was just a matter of time before this decent girl became one of *them*.

For some reason, Jacqueline was beaming. "Was that a compliment I just heard from you?"

Dawn shrugged.

"Wow. That first day, I thought you were sort of a . . ."

"Bitch," Dawn supplied. "I still am."

"Dawn!" Kiko hopped over to her side, grabbing her good arm and demanding her attention. "Guess what?"

She took in his excitement. "Your upstairs neighbor is the devil's handmaiden and she's preparing you to have his child."

"That one's *Rosemary's Baby*!" he blurted without even missing a beat. "Listen, I've got an audition!"

Jacqueline, who didn't even know the guy, clapped her hands.

"When?" Dawn asked, pretty excited, too, even though she wasn't going to go all pep squad about it.

"Monday at ten in the morning. Some kind of fantasy miniseries, so I expect lots of prosthetics and makeup."

As she congratulated him, she wondered how the hell he was going to shoot around their PI schedule. Surely Limpet had to have contingency plans for this sort of thing.

He'd already stuck out his hand to Jacqueline. "Kiko Daniels, actor."

"Jacqueline Ashley, actress."

They started in with the chatter—Kiko so smitten that he was just about to drown in a shower of his own saliva and Jacqueline not seeming to realize it.

Dawn checked her watch. She and her love-struck pal needed to get going if they were going to be on time for their appointment with Robby's old costar.

She stood. "Time," she said to Kiko.

He looked disappointed because the conversation with his future wife was going so swimmingly. Suddenly, Dawn wondered if he'd been serious about the phrase back at the fencing studio—if he'd had some vision about her marrying him.

"Gotta go," Dawn said to Jacqueline, rushing things along.

"Maybe I'll see you fencing sometime?" she asked hopefully.

"Maybe."

"Wait, wait a sec, would you?"

Dawn did, slipping her shoulder bag in place. It was heavy with her stake and gun.

Jacqueline had gotten to her feet, too, an inch or so shorter than Dawn, but a whole lot more slender. Instead of a stuntwoman's streamlined muscles, she had a willowy grace that came with balletic limbs and natural assurance.

"I was thinking," the girl said, "that maybe we could even meet at the studio. You're into sabers, Dipak said, and I know I'm not that good, but if you ever need a partner to beat up on . . ." She laughed. "And I'm not asking you out, either."

Dawn thought that maybe, after she found Frank, she could spare some time to keep an eye on this girl—from afar, you know.

If she didn't, she'd have a hard time forgiving herself when Jacqueline Ashley got eaten by the Hollywood machine, and the last thing Dawn needed was more regret. Besides, a safety check didn't have to happen more than once every two months.

She gave Jacqueline her business card. "Call, and we'll sweat it out sometime."

Then, with short wave, she went to the car with Kiko.

And, as they drove to the production lot, someone followed, keeping an eye on Dawn, too.

TWENTY-TWO
The Pain

That night, hell came to L.A.

It started around a quarter after midnight, when Dawn, Kiko, and Breisi were back at the office after a long day of interviews plus bar and hotel visits. At the very least, they weren't getting any evidence to support the theory that Nathan had been using Robby to gather blackmail material against the more powerful players in town. This gave weight to the possibility that he might've been lending Robby out to further his career even more. Or was it even more personal than that?

Hell, all Dawn knew was that today's first interview with Robby's old costar had revealed a viper; all morning, as they'd strolled around the Universal lot, he'd sniped at his fellow child actor, seeming to revel in Robby's misfortunes. The man was clearly taking out his own failure to succeed in the biz on Robby, but he'd confirmed what Klara Monaghan had told them about Nathan and Robby's passes at the older costars, and he'd noted that his competitor seemed to be getting tired of his little-boy roles. He'd also given them more names to interview.

Accordingly, they'd hit a fraction of that list, plus the one they'd already developed. The highlights included a producer who'd supposedly taken Robby up on Nathan's offers, although he wouldn't admit to it; a childless Hollywood wife who'd brought Robby home to pretend he was her own child for one night—or so she said (and Dawn believed her, even before Kiko had taken her reading and given her the thumbs-up); and a silver-haired actor who'd been accused of hiring the child for an entirely different reason. Much to Dawn's shock, he'd even related the nauseating details of what he'd done to the boy.

"Sick bastard," she said, even though it was hours later in the foyer of the Limpet offices. Having just updated with The Voice himself, they were getting ready to go to the coroner's office for a closer look at Klara. Word had it that there'd been good DNA evidence collected at the scene. Should be interesting.

But what was even more interesting was the way Jonah was treating her. Strictly professional, even deeply respectful, without any hint as to what had happened last night. Hell, she was used to the morning-after amnesia of sleeping with someone, but that wasn't exactly the case here.

She recalled the scream of rage she'd thought she heard before he disappeared.

Maybe it was smart to give him a time-out.

Presently, Kiko was agreeing with Dawn's assessment of the "sick bastard."

"Wouldn't it be great if the Marquis de Sade could travel forward in time and get a hold of that guy? Match made in hell." Getting out of his chair, he adjusted his shoulder holster, readying himself to leave. "He and Nathan Pennybaker probably got along real well back when they were doing business. Like our fugitive friend, the perv liked watching you two women while he told us all about his adventures in Neverland."

"He didn't like it so much when I got up in his face." Dawn meant to scowl, but instead she yawned. "God, I couldn't stand to hear any more of his putrid stories."

"Yes, Dawn," Breisi said, standing and jotting notes to herself on a clipboard. "Your interview-ending temper will go a long way in getting us more sources of information. I'm sure the word is out about your happy hands."

Kiko laughed. "Are you kidding me? Perverts like that love a little who's-your-daddy action. Dawn's phone'll be ringing off the hook."

Speaking of phone calls, Dawn remembered that Matt Lonigan had left a message on her old voice mail an hour ago. "Call me," he'd said. Short and sweet—just the opposite of how she usually liked her men.

"Gotta ring Lonigan," she said, standing.

Breisi speed-walked for the door. "Let's go."

Instead Kiko, being a general pain in the bupkis, came over and nudged Dawn's waist with a pointed finger, obviously intending to rib her about Lonigan. But the second he made contact with Frank's undershirt, he hitched in a breath.

"What?" she said, on alert.

Ever since twilight had hit the horizon, Kiko had been getting stronger vibes whenever he touched the shirt, as their ritual demanded. It was almost like Frank's consciousness was awakening with the growing darkness. Dawn didn't like what that foretold at all.

"Scraps of last night's vision," Kiko said.

Breisi wandered back to them. "Do it again."

Tentatively, Kiko laid a hand on the shirt. Who could blame him for being reluctant now that the night was at its darkest?

He jerked his hand away.

"What?" Breisi and Dawn stereoed.

"Bava. I saw Bava."

"Jonah said that's where he disappeared." Dawn bent down to Kiko's height so she could peer into his eyes.

Normal, focused. Steeped with concern for Frank.

"Jonah?" Breisi asked.

Dawn ignored the question of why she was using The Voice's first name. "What else, Kik?"

She grabbed his hand, put it in the center of her chest, over the shirt where her heart kicked, as if wanting to get out.

Kiko flinched. "Music . . . dancing . . . shock, so much shock because of something . . ." He shook his head. "I'm not sure what he saw, but it got to him."

"Go on," Dawn said.

He squinched his eyes. "He went to call the boss . . . storage room . . . something behind him—?"

Crying out, Kiko stumbled away from Dawn.

"And . . ." He calmed down, regulating his breathing. "There's nothing after that. It's like some presence came up behind him with a two-by-four and turned out the lights."

Dawn sprang to her feet, headed for the door. "I'm going to Bava."

"We're going to the coroner's," Breisi said. "Our friend in that office won't be so understanding about rescheduling."

Kiko beat Dawn to the door, opening it and running outside. "Bava," he called over his shoulder. "It's our best chance! You can handle Klara on your own, just try to get a hold of any of Klara's clothes, even a scrap, so I can read it!" Softer, he muttered, "I ain't so sure I can read dead people anyway."

"To Bava then," Dawn said. "I'm checking out that storage room. Maybe there's something . . . a clue? Frank wasn't there too long ago. Or maybe we can sift through the liars at Bava and find someone who saw what really happened."

Probably knowing she had no other choice, Breisi rolled her eyes. "Keep in contact. The boss won't—"

"The boss will *deal.*" Dawn took off after Kiko.

He was already inside her car. They'd left his at home since he'd rather be chauffeured around town in his sunglasses with

I'm-a-budding-star grandeur. Forget that she was driving a beat-up Corolla, it was all in the entitled attitude.

As they roared off, it felt odd to be without Breisi. Sure, they were used to meeting her at the sites of interviews, but this was different. She wouldn't be there to baby-sit, and Dawn hated the fact that having Breisi around made her feel a little better about whatever they might encounter.

It was the bladed crossbow, no doubt. God, Dawn really had to get one of those, too.

On the way, Kiko compensated for the lack of antiradar gadgets and opticoms by pumping up Dawn's lame radio. The sound system conjured thoughts of a symphony in a tuna can.

"I have a jittery feeling," Kiko said, messing with the radio dial until he hit pay dirt. "Like this is going to be huge. I almost feel like Frank was begging us to go back to Bava, like he's dropping bread crumbs as clues."

Swallowing down her anxiety, Dawn gripped the steering wheel as it shuddered. Hitting thirty miles per hour did that to her ride.

While a hot/cool jazzy song tinned out of the radio, Kiko relaxed against the seat, as if meditating. He *was* nervous. Was it because he'd channeled Frank's fear and he hadn't been able to shake it?

The voice from the radio was as smooth as a balmy night, as elegant as Spanish moss and as dark as bayou swamps. *The* Tamsin Greene, a young legend whose career had blossomed from singing to movies. A superstar.

The music did nothing to calm Dawn, so she floored the gas pedal, eventually screeching onto Vine, where parking was at a premium. They pulled onto Argyle Avenue, found a place, then hoofed it to Bava.

The quake of musical bass stamped the air as they approached. At this time of night, and on a Friday besides, there was a bouncer sitting on a metal stool outside, collecting a twenty-dollar cover charge and checking IDs in a parody of law-abiding cooperation. The guy was huge, with Muscle Beach written all over his hard body.

Ignoring the line to get in—it consisted of a few guys who looked like shadow versions of Ziggy Stardust—Kiko walked up to the bouncer with a dick-in-the-hand strut. Dawn was impressed.

She took up his back, putting on her mean face. With her well-practiced glare, her obvious eyebrow scar, and her biker boots, she gave good pissy attitude.

Her associate flashed his PI license so quickly that Dawn doubted the bouncer had time to read the info.

"We'd like to check out a back room for a case," he said.

The bouncer looked at them both, then busted out laughing. "This isn't midget night."

"Little person," Kiko said with great dignity.

"You're still a short shit. And guess what? We're closed. Nobody else can go in." Amused with himself, he gestured for one of the pseudo-Ziggies to come on over.

They all laughed—*tee-hee-hee*—at how the bouncer was being so politically incorrect.

"Hey . . ." Kiko began.

Muscles took his time with the Ziggy's driver's license. "Dude, if you're under four-ten and have pubes on your face, you're not getting in. And what's that stinkin' cologne?"

"Listen—"

"Is your brain the size of a pea, too?" The bouncer made a fly-swatting motion. "Get out of here, sideshow."

At the brain comment, Kiko had reddened, started to stammer; it only increased his embarrassment. Dawn remembered back when she'd first met him, how he'd seemed more defensive about his psychic abilities than his stature.

She stepped next to him, putting a hand on his shoulder. "You're not letting us in then? Even if we paid a cover and waited in this pathetic line?"

Muscles shrugged. "We're clo—"

Knowing that this guy wasn't worth even bruising her knuckles for, Dawn cocked back her right elbow and crashed it into his jaw. Down he went, but not without some difficulty.

The bigger man reached out, dragged her with him to the ground. Behind her, she heard Kiko say *"Dawn"* with the same exasperation as The Voice.

Drawing back her knee, she drove it upward.

A plastic *dink* told her that the bully was wearing a cup.

Shit.

Out of nowhere, Kiko dove into view, his hand coming down onto the back of Muscles' neck. As the bouncer groaned and slumped over Dawn, the psychic performed what she would have called an amazing sleight-of-hand trick, whizzing his gun out of sight before the Ziggies could even comment on it.

Da-amn.

"That was exceptional," one of the Goths said in a flat voice. Still, it sounded like he'd been won over.

Without further ado, he and his friends barged past Kiko, Dawn, and her steroid luggage, and into the bar.

"Thanks for saving us the cover charge," one of them said, sticking out his pierced, plaque-ridden tongue and wiggling it at Dawn.

"You know," she said when they were gone, "he might have just killed all my sexual urges."

Kiko was wagging his finger at her. "Why'd you do that? This guy is gonna to wake up and hunt us down." Kiko took a second look. "Actually, he ain't gonna wake up for a while."

"Then we'll be gone. We needed to get in." She shrugged. "Besides, he ticked me off, talking to you like that."

As they caught their breath, Kiko grinned. She busied herself with levering this Sephora-fragrance-of-the-month-wearin' guy off of her so she wouldn't have to get mushy and grin back.

"I guess you're about ready then," Kiko said.

She stood, glanced down at Muscles. "Let's get it on."

After Dawn peeked inside to see that the entrance room was empty, they dragged the bouncer over the threshold, finding the darkest corner, then propped him up like he was a drunk. No worry—he blended.

They wove their way through the packed, humid space, heading toward the back. On the way, Dawn inspected the crowd, finding the normal dispassionate glances from the Goth clientele, the usual underage suspects snorting white lines from mirrors in the corners, the bartenders and waitresses working their asses off to serve.

And speaking of serving . . . Dawn glanced at the bar.

No Brandon Lee/Crow look-alike. Maybe when the human servant had run away the other night, he'd never come back.

Too bad. She scanned some more. Tall guys, short guys, all kinds with black hair like Robby's who mingled, pierced and sullen. The sight left her prickly, dreading what she might discover here.

In the relative quiet of the back area, a line for the women's bathroom stretched out the door. Typical. But all the employees seemed to be working the weekend-crowded floor, so Dawn and Kiko took advantage of the freedom and started down the opposite side of the hall. They were checking storage rooms, going past the one where she'd encountered the servant the other night—the one that housed the liquor.

"This is it," Kiko said when they came to the next room. It was just as big as the other one, but it looked like they stored food in the refrigerators, paper products like napkins on the shelves. "I recognize it from the vision."

From his zippered cargo pants, he took out a pair of latex gloves, gave them to Dawn, but didn't cover his own hands. He probably needed them uncovered for readings.

"What're we looking for?" she asked.

He began searching the shelves. "You look for blood spatters. It'd give us a better hint as to how Frank was abducted—by physical means or mental. Damn, I wish Bava had security cameras. That would make this ten times easier."

While she went to work on the shelves, she remembered being attacked by the Goth vamp the other night. "Do you think one of those silver-eyes mind screwed Frank? I imagine *that* could feel like a two-by-four."

She didn't hear him working anymore.

"Ah, Dawn?" he whispered.

"What? You see something?"

She flared around to find Kiko staring at the door. His face was leeched of color, his mouth in an O.

Slowly, Dawn turned her head, her pulse quickening, beating until it took over the tattoo of faint music from the bar. Her blood lurched.

Robby Pennybaker stood there, his skin flushed with life, his ears glinting with piercings, his eyes like pools of fascinating colors Dawn couldn't even identify.

"Are you looking for my dad?" he asked.

TWENTY-THREE

The Child Without

"ROBBY?" Kiko asked.

"No-brainer," Dawn whispered. Her closed throat made her sound like the tense, quick drag of a record needle when it's yanked off the vinyl.

At first glance, the boy looked absolutely human, but there was one big difference—his indescribably colored eyes. They were as magnetic as envy. They made her want to get closer to him, touch him, cry just because he was standing there and he was *the* Robby Pennybaker from the covers of magazines and the heaven of movies. Was Kiko unable to look away, too?

"You've been over at my house," the boy said, tilting his head in curiosity. "You've talked to my dad. You know him?"

Not a child, Dawn kept telling herself.

This boy, who was dressed to go outside and play in a striped soccer T-shirt and jeans, would be a thirty-five-year-old man by now. She wasn't talking to a kid here, even if he still looked twelve.

Robby repeated himself. "So are you looking for my dad?"

"No." Dawn's fear gathered itself in anger. "I'm looking for mine."

Seeming to consider this, Robby entered the room. He moved in such a way that you weren't aware he was walking at all, you just knew he was coming closer, and you were the luckiest soul in the world to be in his presence.

Though Dawn resisted, her skin fluttered, awakened by his force, his steady gaze.

Vampire. Mind screw. Shut him out!

Behind Robby, the door moaned closed, leaving only a strip of the hallway visible. He sniffed the air, cocked his head at Dawn, Kiko, then wrinkled his nose.

A garlic reaction? Was it working?

He took a step forward.

No. *Not* working.

"Your dad's gone, too," the boy said, his gaze caressing her, making her feel wanted, loved. "Was it because he ran away? My father did."

Frantically, Dawn summoned a stronger block, forcing inner energy outward. Robby stopped in his tracks, as if held back.

There!

Maybe he wouldn't be so hard to face after all . . . not like those red-eyed vamps.

Kiko had casually put his hands in his pockets. "So you've been following us, Robby?"

"No." In spite of his stature, the boy/man seemed larger than life. "When I saw you the first time, it was the night Dad came home and you paid my parents a visit. I'd been waiting near the maze the past couple of nights, looking for my dad, watching my mom. But then the Guards came." Robby stiffened. "They just happened to get to you before they got to me."

"Guards." Dawn clenched her teeth to keep them from chattering. She was shivering in her gut, her limbs.

"Those vampires with the iron fangs and the red eyes," Robby added.

Guards . . . so they *were* connected to Robby. How?

"I was running from them," he continued. "But they always found me at night, and I had to run faster, then hide in a place they couldn't get into. You haven't seen any around, have you? They're trying to take me back, but I don't want to go. I *never* want to go back."

"Go where?" Kiko asked calmly.

Robby cocked his head to the other side, suspicious all of a sudden. "Are you with them? Are you Servants?"

"Nope," Kiko said. "No bites on this body. Me and Dawn here aren't associated with vampires, Robby. We're investigators, and your mom hired us to look for you. She'll be real happy to see you again."

"Mom." It was like Robby was tasting the word, the concept, then discovering he had no emotional link with it.

Dawn was straining under her mind block, but this mom talk was testing it, seeing how much she could stand before her barricades crumbled. "She's been crying over you, Robby."

"And my dad? Has he been crying?"

The question was petulant, a preteen sulk.

"Your dad's very upset, too," Kiko said.

"I doubt it."

A zing of heat flashed through the terrible colors of Robby's eyes. Automatically, Dawn held up a hand, as if it would help her retain the integrity of her block. And it did, for the time being, at least.

"My dad abandoned me," Robby said. "He might pretend to be upset, but all he wants is to get me captured again."

"What do you mean?" Dawn asked.

Robby fisted his hands and closed his eyes, wiping out his attempted hold on her. It was like someone had released her mind from a net of chains. Stumbling under the relief, Dawn dug into her jacket pockets, just like Kiko. Crucifix and velvet-wrapped *shuriken* were waiting for her to come and get them.

"I mean that I want my dad to suffer like I did all these years," Robby said, voice crackling.

He opened his eyes, but Dawn didn't gaze into them this time. Hell, no.

"I know he's out there looking for me," he added. "I watch him go from place to place, searching, but he's not going to catch me. I'm not going back to the Underground. Not ever!"

Underground?

The word provoked images of a nest, a lair of vampires. It made the tile beneath Dawn's feet seem like a thin line between herself and a dark pit. Suddenly, her footing wasn't so stable.

"Robby, we just want to take you to your mom." Kiko was walking forward, drawing his hands out of his pockets.

But before he got them all the way out, Robby screamed.

"I said no!"

With the speed of a whirlwind, the boy vampire's body seemed to spin into itself, white streaks of feathered coldness enclosing him.

Dawn heaved in a breath. Move, damnit, *move*. She began taking out her weapons.

But the vampire was faster. With a snap of roaring thunder, a screech ripped through the air, and a new Robby emerged out of the compact storm.

All-encompassing, he floated on air, half transparent misty beauty, half seething fallen angel. The glow of his body blinded Dawn, and even as she squinted her eyes against him, it was too late. The invitation of his gaze was irresistible, pulling her in again with sweet promises of fulfillment.

Frank. His image wavered, then solidified in front of her. He was healthy, grinning. Then Eva materialized, holding hands with him. They both reached out to their daughter.

Longing tore at Dawn's chest, biting, ripping.

"We can be together now," Eva said. "Will you come to me?"

Dawn had wanted to hear this all her life, craved it while watching other children with their moms in the park, resented it at night when she raged against the unfairness of life.

For a wonderful moment, Dawn went to her parents, her heart so full that she thought it might drag her down to her knees.

"Mom?" she asked, reaching out to them, sorrow scratching at the wonder in her voice.

"Dawn!" Kiko broke into her head, his voice like a brick shattering a window, destroying the illusion of the perfect family that never was.

Crying out in grief, she jerked back into herself, grabbing her crucifix and yanking it out of her pocket.

But Kiko beat her to it. He already had his out, pushing it at Robby. The translucent vampire bared his fangs, long and pearly, his awful eyes fixed on the crucifix.

"Come home, Robby," Kiko said, repeating the phrase over and over, an incantation. But Dawn knew he wasn't trying to save Robby's soul. Who knew if that was even possible? Kiko was persuading the vampire to come with them, to The Voice.

To the mysterious unknown.

Dawn joined him, blasting a mind block at the vamp at the same time. "Come home, Robby. . . ."

Rebelling, the vampire reared back his head, crying out in a voice that combined the chill of a graveyard wind with the plea of a lost child in the night.

"Come home, Robby!"

Their voices were growing in strength as they advanced, crucifixes flashing against the luminescence of the vampire.

Another screech. Robby glared at the crucifixes again and then . . .

He stopped screaming, the sounds echoing like broken icicles falling to the ground.

Robby smiled, white fangs gleaming.

What . . . ? Oh, God.

Immune? Unlike the red-eyes, was he immune to religious imagery?

Fear pressed against Dawn's ribs. She thrust her crucifix at the vampire again, concentrated all her mind power against him.

But it seemed like the initial shock of the silver item had worn off. Dear God, is that what Robby had been talking about when he'd said he'd escaped the Guards by hiding someplace they couldn't go? Like maybe a church?

"Oh, oh," Kiko said, flashing his crucifix at Robby again, then one more time . . . and once more after that.

In slow, warped thought, Dawn pictured a man attempting to start a car that was dead.

Survival instinct kicked in. She reached for her *shuriken* because they were closer than the gun, and she would sooner kill this vamp and suffer Jonah's anger than die here tonight. Like the bullets, the silver on the blades might do some kind of fancy Breisi-inspired alchemy in his bloodstream, even if the holy water didn't.

Yet she wasn't in time.

Robby wailed, reared back, swung forward with a tentacle-like hand. It all happened so fast . . . a blur . . . the smack of contact . . .

With a yell, Kiko went flying backward, spine arched.

Dawn screamed as he zoomed toward the back wall—the only one without shelves.

Crrrrr-unnnch.

The crash was bone-breaking, her body shriveling into itself at the painful sound.

"Kiko!"

As she jumped in his direction, she perceived—but couldn't process—that his body lay twisted on the floor, crumpled, eyes wide with disbelief. His mouth worked, trying to form words.

He shuddered, head hitting the tile, his gaze going blank.

A sob tore out of her and she tripped over herself to get to him, but something—a freezing hand on her ankle—was holding her back. In the next instant, her body was flipped upside down, hanging, her heart pounding in her head as she lost hold of her weapons.

In the horrifying silence, her vial of holy water fell from her loose jacket pocket and smashed to wet pieces. Her *shuriken* tingled to the tile one by one, like silver snowflakes.

Robby growled and sped back to the nearly closed door, Dawn still in tow. In his displeasure, he swung her around, her vision fast-forwarding with the speed.

Her body recognized a stunt gone wrong, and she fell into evasive maneuvering, balling up before her body hit—

Bam! Her right arm blasted into a burn of agony as it caught the metal shelves. Thankfully, it went numb before she could acknowledge the full pain.

No time for it, because Robby was already rearing her back for another beating—

She grabbed on to a nearby table with her left hand to slow herself, but he still got the best of her. As the table screeched over the floor, she lost hold of it. The corner of the shelves rushed toward her head, and for a sick, flashing moment, she remembered that day with Frank on the merry-go-round, the green of the grass flying up to meet her. . . .

Hollering in denial, she averted her face, expertly twisting around—

Boom! The shelving caught her in the right shoulder, and that, too, went dead. God knows what she'd look like now if she hadn't grabbed that table. . . .

He started to swing her again.

"Eva!" she screamed.

It hadn't been a plea to the mom Robby had lured her with, the prodigal lifegiver whose image had comforted Dawn in this room only minutes ago.

Or had it?

At the name, she sensed Robby pulling back his strength, and her head glanced off of the shelves, her sight going white, then exploding into a multitude of patterns and colors. She felt her cheek opening up with bloody heat.

Even though she hadn't realized she'd still been holding it, her crucifix clattered to the ground. When Robby let go of her, Dawn's body followed, crashing next to the silver weapon.

She came to a crouch, oxygen chopping out of her. Blood began to wet her face.

Kiko. She had to get to Kiko.

"Your mom," Robby said, referring to the cry that had released her. His head was cocked in curiosity again—but this time it was that beautiful, ghostly head, not the visage of a little boy. His voice sounded like it'd been spliced together from a thousand painful days. "*Daydreamer* . . . Eva was my friend."

"Yes, yes, she was, your friend and costar. Please, can I go to *my* friend?"

Kiko . . . God. In her line of work, she'd seen injuries before—had seen a fellow stuntman almost get his neck broken with the force of a high fall once, had come close to breaking her own back, too—so she knew her partner was in bad shape. Damn it, she needed to get to him.

With brutal efficiency, Robby sucked back into his former facade. At this distraction, Dawn used her good arm to unsnap her gun holster. But when the vampire angled his head at her again, as if trying to see Eva in her, she left it alone, not wanting to provoke him unless she was confident she could draw. And she *wasn't* sure about her chances of success—not until she got a hold of herself and got her shooting hand back in working order.

He sniffed, scenting the blood from her injury. His eye-color began to swirl.

Carefully, Dawn gathered a batch of napkins from a bottom shelf, held it to her face to stanch the bleeding. She wanted to hide the blood from Robby, even though she knew it wouldn't matter, because vamps were vamps, and she was a meal. Nonetheless, she started to move toward Kiko.

"He's not dead," Robby said. "I hear his heart beating."

She glared at him, so disturbed that she forgot about mind blocking, forgot about almost everything but her friend.

With an invasive swish, Robby attacked her memories, his eyes blazing into hers, bolting into her with invasive discomfort. Dawn tried to cuff him off, but—

Helpless, she felt him sifting around in her, violating her secrets, her most tender possessions.

"No!" She mentally pushed at him with desperate futility. She didn't want him inside, hadn't given him permission. . . . Her left hand covered her heart as he tore through her.

"You're like me." He smiled again but didn't release her. "You didn't want to come home, either."

Through her anguish, she saw Robby's nostrils widen again as he came closer.

"Can I drink from you? Please?"

"No."

Surprisingly, he didn't force himself on her physically. Mentally, he was still attacking.

And she was still fighting.

Yet, in spite of her turmoil, she wondered why he wasn't just taking her blood, too. What was holding him back?

"I'm hungry," Robby said. "Can't I please—?"

"*No.*"

As if angry with her, he forcefully rooted around her mind some more, finding images of Eva, of Frank. He seemed thrilled with these discoveries.

"I said no, you little . . ." She took a deep breath, then yelled, "*shit*!"

The force of her rage thrust him back, crashing the vampire against the shelves, his head banging against metal. Dawn felt a cleansing rush of vengeance and pressed it forward, keeping him back, daring him to screw with her again.

How'd she manage that? Hell, now wasn't the time to hypothesize.

"Stay *out*," she said, glaring, right above his eyes.

Touching his cut forehead, he looked stunned to feel the blood, then inspected her as if she were an intriguing specimen. Most importantly, he'd backed off, and Dawn was going to make sure it stayed that way.

"You miss your dad," he said, acting as if they hadn't just thrown down. Maybe it was because he was more interested in relating to her own daddy situation. Or maybe it was because he knew he could kick her ass at any given second and he was in no hurry. "You want to see him again more than anything."

Even while she was mentally pushing at him, she had the presence of mind to realize that Robby might be able to help. "Then take me to Frank."

Robby thought for a moment. Then, "No." It was a parody of her refusal to feed him.

"You're not going to help me? Or are you saying that you weren't the one who took him from Bava?"

"I . . ." The boy seemed puzzled. "I really can't help you."

Why? Wouldn't he, or couldn't he?

She felt his hold release a little, probably because his emotions had gotten the best of him, distracting him again.

Make Robby talk more, she thought, shielding her body with her left hand, ready to fight him off if it came down to it again. Her right arm and shoulder were still robbed of feeling, her left cheek dulled by cutting pain. *Take advantage of his fragile temperament. Mind screw* him. *Control him.*

Her best weapons were her words right now.

"Why'd you stop loving your dad?" she asked, vying for the upper hand. "What happened, Robby?"

Behind him, one of the Bava workers opened the door. With a flick of his wrist, Robby shut it, never even glancing back.

"I told you," he said. "He left me."

"Why?"

"It was for the best, he said. He would send me away, and years later, I'd make a comeback. Then we would be together again." Robby's lips attempted a smile, but his mouth lost the struggle. "My dad and I were close, a long time ago."

"I know." She wouldn't bring up the pimping, the abuse. It would probably agitate him, and she was doing so well without that kind of brain-dead strategy.

Nerve sawing against nerve, she snuck a glance at Kiko, who was still in a pile by the back wall. A hitch of overwhelming worry pulled at her, but she kept it at bay. She had to.

"Dad made me a man," Robby said, touching his head wound again. The slight bleeding fascinated him. "He taught me how to rule Hollywood one day."

"Is that what he was doing?"

Robby seemed taken aback by her venom. "He wanted me to be strong. He showed me how to dominate people by offering, then withholding, then giving them what they wanted at a bigger price than they could've ever imagined paying. Lots of money. Lots of opportunity. I had half of Hollywood dying to be with me."

Even through the vampire bravado, she saw a flicker of human shame. Both of them knew he was lying to himself, failing to make Nathan's actions seem more acceptable.

At her steely silence, his expression fell, and he stared at the ground.

"I don't know how to function without him," he said softly. "Can you imagine that? Thirty-five years old and I still need him to tell me what to do. But it's not going to be that way for long. I kept telling him, even back when I was twelve, that I wanted to move on and stay out of the spotlight for a while until I could start getting adult roles, like Jodie Foster. Yeah," his voice lifted with rekindled dreams, "just like her. I did everything I could to show him I wasn't a little boy anymore—got piercings, turned down parts in family movies, all because I knew I could reinvent myself."

"He didn't like that you weren't daddy's boy anymore." She could feel herself getting dizzy, but she sucked it up.

Again, Robby leaned closer, scenting her blood. She didn't dare make eye contact.

"Robby?" Dawn needed him to keep talking. She wished she could drop the napkins and grab her gun. It'd be awkward, and her left-hand aim wasn't as sharp as her right, but still . . .

The vampire reared back, tone sharp and self-mocking. "*I'm* the one who didn't like that I wasn't daddy's boy anymore. I was afraid not to be, even if I couldn't help rebelling." He grinned. "I used to sneak out of the Underground, you know. Used to go to my old hangouts and workplaces, then slide right back into my room before anyone knew I was gone. That's how I stayed in touch with my sanity."

"*Diaper Derby* was filmed on the same set as one of your movies?"

"Yes—*Bug Hunt*. When my caretakers saw that I'd been accidentally filmed, they punished me by keeping me locked up. That's when I escaped for good, before . . ." He looked afraid. ". . . the final phase of my release."

"And you couldn't help returning to all the old places again."

"Places my dad and I used to go. First I went home. Dad still wasn't there. Then I came to Bava, and it was the same deal. I kept visiting both places, but then the Guards followed me home, and Groupies were infiltrating Bava more than usual, looking for me. I could tell they were present before I even went in again—they have a different scent than the regular vampires and ghouls that hang out. But they're not here tonight. That's why I followed you in when I saw you."

She couldn't quiz him about what Groupies were before she detected the self-disgust creeping back into his gaze.

"After all these years of being away," he added, "there was comfort in these places, like returning would take me back to being the normal Robby Pennybaker."

This guy was confused, Dawn thought. He wanted to resume his little Robby life, and he didn't. He obviously loved his father, and he hated him. *Had* vampirism affected his brain? Were all of these creatures a little tetched?

As he gauged her compassion, he came close enough for Dawn to see he wasn't showing any fang. Obviously, that happened only in his vamp state. In this form, he could pass for human—it was only the mind screwing that revealed him as a vampire.

"When my dad came back home," Robby said, "I realized how much I hated him. Seeing him in the flesh, strolling through the door like he'd never deserted me, made me want to hurt him."

Pulled to Daddy out of habit. Sounded familiar to Dawn. "So what're you going to do if you have no place to go?"

"I'll make a new life Above no matter what. I told you, I'm never going back."

"Even if your mom loves you?" Dawn thought he'd been talking about going back home. Or was he talking about that other place? The Underground.

Robby's mouth tightened, and Dawn shifted, upsetting her arm and shoulder. Who cared though? She just made sure her good arm was ready to grab her gun.

"I never thought . . ." Robby's lips broke into a tremble. "She didn't pay much attention to me when I was human."

"She regrets that."

"Really?" His voice was thick. "I didn't try to contact her because I thought she'd care as much as she used to—which is not at all."

"That's not true. If you saw how upset she is . . ."

He grew contemplative, giving Dawn too much of a chance to think about Kiko. She had to get to him. Had to find out more about this Underground, too.

"Please," she said, taking advantage of this peaceful lull. "My friend."

Seeming to come to a decision, Robby stood, moved to the door before she could ask more questions. Then, as if he hadn't wrecked havoc in the supply room, he zipped out, leaving the door open.

She didn't have the opportunity to wonder what the hell had just happened, how she'd made him leave.

Instead, Dawn groped in her jeans for her phone, calling 911 for an ambulance. At the same time, she gimped over to Kiko.

Hearing her, his eyes fluttered open, and she laughed in pure relief, reaching out to touch his cheek.

But when he spoke, it wasn't with the lighthearted humor she'd come to expect.

"My back," he murmured. "Help me."

TWENTY-FOUR

The Visit

THE ambulance got to Bava in good time. From there, Kiko was whisked to Lady of Mercy Hospital, and despite the overflowing ER, the staff saw to him as quickly as possible.

Though she'd refused to leave Kiko's side, keeping a hold of his fingers while he bravely smiled then alternately winced, Breisi, who Dawn had called from Bava, had pretty much manhandled Dawn into being taken care of, too. So after Breisi had quietly offered the staff a hefty donation to see Dawn quickly—and to ask no probing questions about Kiko's injuries—Dawn had caught Breisi up on current events while a doctor stitched up the gape in her cheek. He pronounced that her arm and shoulder were severely bruised—nothing broken, due to her stunt-experienced maneuvering. Then the medical staff handed her some painkillers, but when they weren't looking, Dawn pocketed the pills. Nothing was going to put her out for the rest of the night; damn the pain.

When further news of Kiko came, it was a mixed blessing.

Dawn and Breisi were in the bustling reception area, where people cried out for attention. Down the row of seats, a drugged-out woman had vomited on the floor, and an orderly was rapidly—and not so happily—mopping it up. Across from them, a little African-American girl was stretched out over a few seats, her head in her mom's lap. The older woman, who was hooked into an iPod, probably to block out the cacophony, stroked her child's hair, singing "Hush little baby, don't say a word . . ."

The song made Dawn turn away.

"A broken back," she said for what had to be the hundredth time. She'd removed her shoulder holster due to her new fashion accessory: a sling with ice packs attached to her injuries. She barely felt their wet chill over the throbbing. "It's my fault. I should've made sure Robby went after me before Kiko. I could've taken it. I've crashed into a lot of walls, and I know how to do it without getting hurt. Once, during some harness work for a flying stunt, I flipped wrong. I almost broke my back, so I know how to handle this kind of—"

"Don't." Breisi had her legs crossed, her ankle bobbing at top speed. "Pain comes with this job."

Dawn didn't doubt it, but . . . God. Limpet was having Kiko transferred to the Cedars-Sinai Institute for Spinal Disorders, where he'd be diagnosed in more detail. Now, as they prepped him for departure, Dawn felt useless.

She fought to stay cool and distant, but exhaustion and then the tremors of Robby's violation started to creep back into her.

No problem, she told herself. She could deal with the trauma. Right?

But when she realized that someone had to cancel Kiko's big audition Monday, it was all over. She coughed, but she and Breisi both knew it was actually a tight sob.

She felt her associate's hand on her good shoulder—way above the vampire-spit burns. Strange. She was getting too used to being touched like this—caringly. But, somehow, it wasn't as terrible as she'd imagined. Especially right now.

"We need to get back to work," Breisi said gently.

For a second, Dawn thought she was joking. But then she remembered that Breisi wasn't much for humor.

"Believe me," the other woman added when she saw the look on Dawn's face, "Kiko would kill us if we hung around fawning over him. He's got an ego, to be sure, but he's also dedicated to this job and would want us out there taking care of it. The boss is sending over a Friend to look after him while we—"

"What?" Dawn said it with such rancor that the girl across from them grabbed her mother's hand and held it to her ear.

Even over the hubbub of the waiting room, Dawn had been too shrill. She lowered her tone. "Are we going to run around town chasing Robby? Why? We know from Jonah's buddies that they haven't seen vampires around the Pennybakers' tonight, so Robby probably cut his losses and went into hiding. Maybe that's why he left me intact—he doesn't want more trouble."

"Klara Monaghan gave us a list that we still need to cover. This isn't over yet."

Wasn't it? With resurrected agony, Dawn remembered what Kiko had looked like at Bava: a pile of flesh and clothing; a bad imitation of the vital guy she'd come to know.

Breisi decided to get even more maternal, resting a cupped hand on the back of Dawn's head. "We've made headway. Think of what the coroner's office told me."

Sure, okay. They'd already known that Klara had bled out from her injuries, but now they'd also been informed that the damage to her throat had been caused by human teeth—not fangs. They'd also discovered that there hadn't been a case similar to this in L.A. County for the last fifty years.

So was Klara's death the work of a weirdo, not a vamp? Did that mean Robby wasn't even a suspect?

Come to think of it, Dawn hadn't even questioned him about it. Hell, she'd been busy with a few other things at the time.

And there was more than that to worry about. Was it possible that the people at the coroner's office were lying when they said that the culprit had been human? Were they trying to cover up a case that would cause the public to get hysterical about monsters in their midst?

Dawn had asked Breisi this earlier, after the initial urgency for Kiko had abated, but the older woman thought the coroner's office was on the up-and-up. After all, she'd seen the autopsy reports and had gotten a peek at Klara's body, herself. There was nothing obvious indicating subterfuge.

So the killer was human, Breisi insisted. And she was betting the DNA results would confirm that.

A nurse, dressed in scrubs and with her dark hair slung back in a high ponytail, bustled over to inform them that Kiko would be transferred within the next half hour. They thanked the woman as she took off toward the administration desk.

"There shouldn't be any more for us to handle. The boss has taken care of all the paperwork that will keep anyone from investigating Kiko's injuries."

Dawn got up. "When's Jonah coming to see Kik?"

"He's not. He's a shut-in."

"He can't come out," Dawn asked, "even for Kiko?"

"As I said, Kik will have no problem with that. The boss has always told us that he'll go outside when it's absolutely necessary; not before. That's why he employs us—we do what he can't beyond the walls of his home right now."

The term echoed in Dawn's head. A shut-in. It almost gave some humanity to the voice Dawn had gotten to know on such a superficial level.

Superficial versus . . . intimate.

Out of nowhere, Matt Lonigan's kiss—the warm, sentimental simplicity of it—came back to her, and she touched her lips. She'd left a message for him earlier, as well as one for Jacqueline Ashley, who'd also called. In her return messages, she'd told them both where she was at, what her new phone number was, and that she would to get back to them later.

And, ironically, there'd also been a summons from a female stunt coordinator who was wondering what Dawn was up to. But she hadn't had time to return that one yet.

Shouldn't she be dancing around like a fool at the contact? Dawn sighed. The career that had seemed so all-important this afternoon was nothing compared to what was going on now. All the same, no matter what time it was, she should leave a message with the coordinator out of professional courtesy. Who knew when she'd have another chance.

"I've got to make a quick call outside," Dawn said. "Too noisy in here."

"I'm running to the girls' room." Breisi got out of her chair. "Keep your gun handy and stay by the doors, around people. I'll be out soon."

With her good hand, Dawn patted her jacket pocket, where she'd transferred her piece, then headed toward the doors, dodging and not even glancing up at a man who was on his way in. He said something, but she kept right on moving.

Then, finding a spot at the side of the building, near a couple of paramedics who were taking a cigarette break, Dawn awkwardly got the gun out. When she realized she had no other choice but to hold it with the same hand as the phone, she crouched, setting the weapon near her shoe, hidden from the workers. Then she extracted the encrypted phone from her jeans pocket, tried to dial it. But her left fingers weren't as dexterous as her right, and she couldn't manage the easy task.

Frustrated, she made another attempt at dialing, failed. She ground her teeth together as her right side blazed with growing awareness of its injuries.

"God-*damnit*."

"Need help?"

She glanced up to find Lonigan leaning against the wall, dressed in a long leather jacket. His gaze was bright, his body alert, as if he was the one who was caffeinated. And maybe he was. It seemed to come with the territory—along with the pain.

"I was just going in as you were coming out," he said. A shadow covered half of his pugilistic features. "Been standing here waiting for you to recognize me."

"I wasn't looking. You know, Matt, you're going to scare the life out of me with all your sneaking around."

She stowed her phone but kept the gun out, nestling it under the right side of her jacket as she stood, then turned to him. To his eyes, she probably seemed to be warding off the cold, one hand hugging the other side of her waist.

"An associate was monitoring the scanner," he said, his tone making it clear he wasn't giving a lot of credence to whatever he was about to say. "She heard a strange story: that a midget had been messing around at Bava—practicing stunts with his friend in a supply room?—and had fallen from a table. Funny how Bava just happens to be a rumored location for vampires. I remembered your partner, tried to get a hold of you to make sure, but then started worrying that you'd gotten hurt, too."

Brushing a gaze over her cheek, her arm and shoulder, he took a step away from the wall. Dawn's flesh came alive, but she quelled her excitement, thinking that this couldn't be filed under her "save the world" reason for running out on Kiko.

With an unreadable look, Matt redirected his footsteps away from her, so that he turned a corner, darkness closing over him as he disappeared around the other side of the building.

What was up with him? Dawn gripped her revolver, glancing at the hospital's exit. She'd keep her eye out for Breisi.

Then she followed.

When she went around the corner, she stopped abruptly, almost running into him. He'd rested his body against the wall and underneath a golden light, back stiff, as if there was something bracing his spine. He had a strange electric air about him, a secretive smile that made her wonder why he was so . . . *ecstatic* wasn't exactly the word—too optimistic. But then again, she couldn't define Lonigan for nothin'.

"You looking for a private conversation or something?" she asked, a tiny pulse wavering in her neck.

"I know what did this to your partner."

That beating in her neck seemed to stop.

She advanced a few inches, but stayed near the corner and the safety of the exit doors. "How do you know?"

"I just do." Matt looked at her cheek again, and a muscle started to twitch by his jaw. He seemed as angry as she was.

Dawn responded to their shared, heightened emotion, grabbing at it like it was an outcropping on the face of a cliff, one that would hold her up and take her to another level where she could see a little more clearly.

"He did this to you," he said, his voice gravelly as he moved a hand toward the bandage that covered her stitches.

Was he remembering what "happened" to his parents?

Right. Before he could lay a hand on her, she lifted her chin, avoiding him. He hesitated, the same look in his eyes that she'd seen back at the Cat's Paw—the indecision, the battle for control.

But then, in spite of her blow-off, he made his choice. He reached out, tucked a strand of hair behind her ear.

Damn him and his insistence on being a nice guy. His politeness made her the loser in their control game.

Easily giving in, she shuddered, rubbing her cheek against the heel of his palm.

But . . . Kiko. She shouldn't be out here fooling around with Matt while her friend was suffering. Slut.

She backed away, leaving him miffed. Leaving her a pained mess as her right side began to thump under the ice packs.

"I've been wondering, Matt. I looked into your parents. Puttered around the Internet, tapped into databases to read more about it. But . . . weird. The only match I found was in a comic book story."

His brows came together, but then he laughed, the sound short and knowing.

"You think this is funny, Bruce Wayne?"

"You don't believe me."

"You're making it hard."

"Did you ever stop to think that I might've changed my name after the murders?"

Hope flinted against her doubts.

He reclined against the wall. "Did you ever stop to think that I didn't want to hear my given name again? Hell, Dawn. Just do another search, but use the name 'Destry' this time."

Before her remorse fully hit, Matt gave her a yearning glance, as if her suspicions didn't mean squat. But maybe this went along with his entire "question what's going on" thing. Maybe that's why he was being so accepting of her skepticism—because he'd encouraged it in the first place.

He'd placed his fingertips on her jawline, turning her bandaged cheek toward him. His breath warmed her, ruffling her hair as he tenderly inspected her.

"It's nothing I won't live through," Dawn said.

"I want to kill this thing. Where did it go afterward?"

"Not sure yet, Matt. Do you have any ideas?"

"No." Now he was stroking her temple with his other hand, running the pads of his fingers over her skin, as if mapping her journeys through all the bruises and cuts that had come and gone. He floated his fingers over her long earring, pausing. Then her lips.

Needing something to help keep her standing, she reached out to grab his arm with her left hand, but the gun was in it.

"You can put that away when you're around me," he whispered.

He unthreaded her fingers from around the weapon, slid the metal against her waist as he stored it in her jacket pocket.

The strum of fantasy played her, pulsating low and deep. After seeing Kiko, she needed a human touch, the reassurance that life was still available. That's why Matt's proximity was pulling her in, making her feel, even for a second, that she didn't need to worry about a thing.

"I'm going to make sure you never get hurt again, Dawn," he said. "Can you trust me to do that?"

She wanted to say yes, but Dawn wasn't built that way. All her life she'd depended on herself and on her talent for mothering Frank. Trust in anything else wasn't easy.

"And why should I trust you and not Limpet?" she asked.

"Because you already *don't* trust Limpet."

Somewhere, an ambulance wailed, headed for the ER. It brought Kiko back to her full-force. She shuddered.

In response, Matt kissed her forehead. As he brushed his lips to her brow, she felt the heat of his smooth chin on her mouth, smelled the warm, spiced scent of him. He kissed his way down her nose, then her uninjured cheek, to her lips. Dawn bunched his shirt in her left hand, pressing closer.

Blood churned in her lower belly, urging her to force him against the wall and increase the tempo of their interaction. But this man didn't respond to that—she'd tried shortcuts to intimacy before and had come up empty with him.

But what else could she do? There was too much emotion here to deal with. How could she plug up all the holes in her soul with something she didn't know how to manipulate?

As he kissed her, a low sound of confusion stuck in her throat. But she was still lured, sucking his lips against hers, long and slow pulls of longing. He was being careful not to hurt her, edging his fingertips along her cheek, her neck. There, he traced the center of her throat, the sensitive line that dipped to the cove between her collarbones. His fingers traveled to a vein, stroking her as if it could be as damp and primed as the swollen flesh between her legs.

"I really don't know what to do about you," he said between kisses.

"Tell me about it." Breathless, she rested her forehead against his jaw as he ran a hand up and down her back. Soothing; the cure for her ills. "You're throwing me into a tailspin here."

The siren was getting closer. Kiko.

What the hell was she doing?

Reluctantly, she inched away, holding up her hands and turning around. "It's time for me to get out of here."

"Dawn."

The timbre of his voice jolted her with dark familiarity.

Thrown for a loop, she rounded on him, finding that his intensity level had ratcheted to the extreme. His body was as tense as rope strung between a dangling victim and the savior who was trying to pull him back to safety. His eyes had gone wide, hunter-hot.

Now this was the type of man she understood. Dangerous. Animal desire. They were on her terms now.

With two long steps she went back to him, using her good arm to pin him against the wall. She rocked her body against his, grinding herself against his groin, biting at his neck in the sheer desperation to get Kiko's pain . . . Frank's pain . . . her *own* pain out of her mind.

"Dawn," he said again, ragged and excited.

"I came to you," she said, dragging her lower teeth against his throat. "Just like you wanted—willing and ready."

He tasted so good; warm against her tongue, with that tinge of spice . . .

When he buried a hand in her hair, she knew she had him. As the siren filled her ears from around the corner—a place of refuge and safety only a few steps away—she bit into him, making him grunt and dig his fingers into both of her arms. As she gasped, he lifted his hands in apology for getting carried away.

But she didn't care. She bolted him against the wall with the plane of her left arm, then slipped that hand toward his back to arch him against her. Her bent cravings were proof that he really was like all the other men she'd been with—conquerable, easy to leave behind.

But then her fingers found something unexpected at his spine, something that felt like a blade in a sheath.

Whip quick, he grabbed her hand, then glared at her, his blue eyes full of wrath.

"That's enough," he said.

At his rejection, she didn't feel anything. She'd already closed herself off from giving a crap. That's how prepared for his damned chivalry she was.

"You get a rise out of taunting me?" she asked. "What was back there, Matt? What's—"

As she reached for his spine, he maneuvered out of position. Within a few breaths, he'd regained the composure of the gentleman she'd come to expect . . . and resent.

The struggle of regret had fallen over his features, softening them, making him look like he'd gone thirteen rounds and lost in the end.

"This isn't the way I want it." His laugh was serrated. "I don't know—maybe I'm the only guy left on earth who needs something meaningful, but I'm not going to change. Instead, I'll wait. And if I'm waiting into next week, next month, next year, I'll do it."

"You're nuts. You've known me for, like, what, a couple of days? And—"

"I know you better than you can ever imagine."

She froze. "What?"

Laughing dryly, he rested his hands on his hips. "I mean I've had access to files, Dawn. I've done surveillance on you, watched your films, talked to people you've known. And, bit by bit, I . . . I liked what I found."

Another ambulance siren shot through the night with red panic. Dawn felt the wail in her veins.

"That sounds bad," Matt said, shaking his head in embarrassment. "Damn, the last thing I want to do is scare you."

Was she scared? Or was he truly the most dangerous man she'd ever known?

The vibration of her phone shook her.

Thankful for the interruption, she answered it, turning her back on him, wanting to talk about this now while not really wanting to.

"Hello?"

"Where are you? Are you okay?" It was Breisi.

"I'm just outside the exit." As Dawn walked into view again, she looked over her shoulder, preparing to make her apologies to Matt.

But he wasn't there. Gone. *Pffft.*

Scanning around and finding no sign of the PI, Dawn turned toward the entrance where Breisi was standing.

She tucked away her phone, hands shaking. Where had he gone? Now that he'd made that confession, it seemed more important than ever to keep tabs on him. She wasn't sure if that was because he'd unsettled her or turned her on. God, she was a sick pup. Really.

Jerking her head toward the parking lot, Breisi said, "Let's go."

"Where?"

She was already heading for the car. "Robby came home."

TWENTY-FIVE

Another Rising

At 3:15 AM Pacific Time, an Internet broadcast aired to an audience of millions. TV executives would have died for numbers like that.

But Tamsin Greene actually *did*.

Worldwide, screens revealed the beautiful, ultra-famous woman who had recorded her first CD at age fifteen. Her voice had been hailed by critics and fans alike, her star shooting into the night sky so rapidly that films had followed, as had champagne-filled hot tubs, Grammy and MTV Video Music Awards, and a thousand fan sites devoted to her majesty.

Now, at twenty-six, Tamsin was still perfection. Her skin was smooth and dark, her eyes almond-shaped and almost black in hue. Her midnight-dark hair was short, sophisticated, and seductive, revealing a lovely nape and curls gelled to the skin of her sloped cheekbones.

As she sat in front of a computer camera in what was obviously her plush, *InStyle* bedroom, Tamsin allowed the tears to fall. She was wearing a creamy satin sheath. A candle burned next to her, making her sadness gleam. Her newest CD, released three days ago, emoted softly in the background.

"Before I start, I want to thank my fans, especially if you ever came to my website to check up on me. I love each and every one of you sincerely, truly, deeply." She looked down, toyed with something off-screen. "And if you really love me, you'll tune out now, understand? But if you're one of those people who slows down on freeways to get a good look at an accident, then stay where you are, because you're the reason I'm doing this."

She held up a scalpel. It snapped like a deadly bite in the candlelight. Her voice took on the same edge.

"I'm talking to you, the paparazzi. You chased me with cameras. You made me less than human. Yes, I knew what I was getting into when I started in show business, but I never realized it would ruin my life. So in honor of you, the scum of the industry, I'm going to do something that'll make you hate me for all time. No exclusive pictures, no more hunting me down the streets and to the gates of my house in your cars just for a picture. You can gape all you want now, but you won't profit from it."

She got up, took the candle. With her trademark grace—like sand rolling over itself in a soft wind—she moved to her bed and set it on fire. As flames licked at the comforter, she returned to her seat.

"This is a condemnation of what the media has become, and I hope when you leeches watch this, you'll realize what kind of damage you did to me and to many other celebrities. And in your quest for a taste of fame, I hope a little part of you dies right along with me."

The fire spread.

She held up the scalpel, paused, then smiled, her lips quivering as her dark eyes overflowed with tears.

The flames whooshed, gaining in destruction, eating their way around the room.

"As for the rest of you, I love you. Remember that. Bless you all."

Then, with fluid violence, she slit her throat, the skin yawning open as blood gushed downward.

Tamsin Greene gurgled, clutched at the computer camera in tragic appeal, then slumped to the floor, ripping the camera from its holder. On computer screens all over the world, the blurred image trailed her fall, completing the awful arch of a swan song as she crashed to her death.

For several horrifyingly peaceful moments afterward, the stoic eye of the lens recorded the fire as it grew, as it swallowed everything in view, as it obliterated her home.

As it continued to record the blood-curdling last moments of a beloved star's mortal life.

TWENTY-SIX

The Reunion

In order to sneak up on the Pennybaker mansion, Breisi parked the 4Runner at the bottom of the hill, where the gates were open. It was a far cry from that first visit, when they'd been shut and secretive.

As night echoes sought refuge in the darkness, the fighters silently armed themselves: among other toys, Breisi had her death-dealing saw-bow for backup, while Dawn wore whatever she could manipulate with her left hand. This meant that her weapons didn't include *shuriken* or a stake. She didn't think she could summon enough power to pierce a vamp's heart with the sharpened wood, so she stuck to carrying the gun, putting a new vial of holy water and a crucifix in her jeans for any other vamp breeds that might show, plus wearing a silver-edged machete from the weapon collection under Breisi's tarp in back of the car. Dawn slid *that* beauty into a sheath at her right hip, believing that she'd be able to swing the blade with enough force to do some damage if the need arose.

As she rubbed more garlic on her skin—for all the good it might do—she focused on Kiko and Frank. Especially Frank.

Would this next encounter with Robby yield any results about her father? If she had to, she was going to *chop* some information out of Nathan Pennybaker and his son.

If they knew anything.

"I can't help you," Robby had said earlier when she'd asked him about Frank. So what the hell had that meant?

Dawn turned on the earpiece both she and Breisi were wearing so the boss could monitor. Her sling-ridden right side was chewing at her, demanding to be recognized for its dull nagging. Screw it.

Ready to go, she turned to the other woman. "Let's do this for Kiko and Frank."

Breisi's jaw hardened, and when she looked at Dawn, it was with conviction—the gaze of a comrade in arms. In her eyes, Dawn saw a love so deep that it could drown. A love for Frank.

Overcome, Dawn held out her hand to her partner.

Breisi grabbed on, gripping Dawn's wrist in something that felt like a sisterhood promise.

Another voice joined them, the sound in Dawn's ear a million miles removed from emotion.

"Try not to harm Robby, if possible," Jonah Limpet said. "I want to talk with him myself. And if you can persuade him to leave the premises and come to mine, that's even better."

"How can we do that?" Dawn asked, releasing Breisi's hand.

"Normally I would recommend a crucifix for binding a vampire in fear and controlling him, but that doesn't work with Robby. He's a creature from a line I've never encountered. Hypnosis is our best risk. That's why I want you to put him in a position—*alone*—to hear my voice on the cell phone. Or if you can get close enough to fit an earpiece—"

"I'm thinking Robby won't let us do that," Dawn said, on the cusp of asking why the boss couldn't just come out here to hypnotize the vamp himself. But then she remembered that he hadn't even been able to get out of the house for Kiko's emergency, so she knew there had to be a good reason for his absence. Too bad nobody was bothering to tell it to her.

Why? And was the possible escape of Robby worth preserving The Voice's isolation? Evidently, yes.

Breisi was holding her cell phone like it was another weapon, readying it for Robby. "With the loss of the crucifix's powers, I need to work on some sort of binding weapon."

"I'll look into it." Jonah's tone had gone even darker. "But for now, protect Robby *and* Marla. And . . ."

"Yes?" Breisi asked.

Dead air crackled. "And . . . go with God."

He abruptly signed off, leaving them to their own devices, even though they knew he'd be listening in.

Ruffled by his closing, Dawn fell into step with Breisi and embarked up the hill.

Try not to harm Robby, Jonah had said. But the specter of Kiko's pain-steeped eyes kept haunting Dawn.

So did the vampire's savage attack on her memories.

She brushed off the dread, instead trying to concentrate on the information she needed to get through this night: The Voice had told them that his "Friends" had seen Robby come home. However, these mysterious pals didn't have enough strength to protect Robby from any possible Guards for an extended period of time, so Dawn and Breisi had to hurry. To make matters even more urgent, Marla Pennybaker, who'd been so eager to find Robby in the first place, was rejecting her son's otherworldly form, refusing to invite him inside the mansion. This left Robby—the vampire they needed for questioning—vulnerable to attack.

As the imposing roof came into view, Dawn wondered if *she* might've triggered Robby's homecoming by telling him how much Marla missed him. Had she actually convinced the vampire to return to Mommy? Was that why he'd left Bava so suddenly?

Earlier, Marla Pennybaker had called Limpet from a closet in her room, wailing that her son was watching her through a window. Despite Breisi's previous hints to the woman that Robby might turn out to be a vampire, Marla was still in denial. But now she was going through that surreal process of accepting the truth that Dawn was enduring. Seeing was believing.

The mansion loomed before them, looking as paralyzed as it had been the other night. Wind made doubtful murmurs while it combed over the trees plus the hedged maze that Robby had confessed to hiding in.

The scene was too peaceful for Dawn's comfort.

"Where is he?" she mouthed to Breisi.

The other woman shook her head, her dark hair brushing her jawline.

Without warning, a gust of wind barged into Dawn, and she aimed her revolver at . . . Hell, at *nothing*.

As a shaky breath escaped her, she realized that it had only been a false alarm, a ghostly taunt trailing a low, chilly howl and a trace of . . . perfume?

Jasmine—reminding her of the invisible hands that had guided her to Limpet's—

Crash!

Something hit the window near the front door. Both Dawn and Breisi targeted the sound, only to find Marla plastered against the glass, her face a mask of panic. The woman darted toward the door.

"Someone came out of her closet," Breisi said.

Before Dawn had time to process that her partner had actually made something resembling a joke, they made a run for the entrance, which Marla Pennybaker was now pulling open.

"Mr. Limpet called to say you were near!" she screeched. "Hurry, get in here!"

When Breisi sprinted to Marla, Dawn guessed that they would quickly return outside to secure Robby after they'd calmed his mother. Unfortunately, that might expose them to the Guards who'd been chasing Robby on previous nights. Dawn only hoped they could contain the young vampire for questioning before those red-eyes showed up.

Following Breisi, Dawn started for the door, too, but was halted by another blast of air. At her jerk of surprise, it swept back, as if it'd only been inspecting her, leaving the scent of jasmine to linger like a delicate threat.

"Dawn!" Breisi was waving her in and watching the lawn.

Behind her, a cry shattered the darkness.

She'd heard that screech before. Tonight. At Bava.

Shit.

She took off, flying across the threshold. The door slammed right behind her, leaving Marla hugging the oak.

"I can't stay in here alone. I—"

Interrupting herself, Marla rushed to the window, peeking past the wooden frame and into the black of nothing outside.

"Robby's fighting off the boss's protection," Breisi muttered to Dawn as she scanned the room. "And they aren't going to be able to waste their energy on him forever."

They. Jasmine perfume. Dawn was getting an idea about just who these Friends were.

Discomfited, her gaze roamed over the nooks and crannies with their hidden shadows; over the modern iron sculpture that watched the foyer like a mercenary with a honed sword extended at a severe incline from its blob of a body; over the stark paintings; over the hushed staircase.

"What did Robby look like?" Dawn asked Marla. Forget the gentle, now-do-you-believe-your-son-is-a-vampire? talk.

"He looked . . . like Robby." Her wrinkled face slack with fear, Marla turned to them, her back to the window. "My God, he hasn't changed a bit. He kept asking me to let him in, kept asking me if I really did love him."

Just as Dawn had thought. If Daddy didn't want him this time out, maybe Mommy could take Nathan's place. Robby was dependent on parental care.

"What's going on?" Marla added. "I don't understand . . ."

But before Dawn could begin the Nosferatu 101 lecture that Marla was now ready for, a scream lodged in her chest.

Behind the fragile woman, Robby had strolled into sight, cocking his head at his mother through the window, eyes glowing.

A bash of terror lit through Dawn: Kiko, splayed over the floor. Dawn, fighting off the mind assault . . .

Cowboy up, damn it, she told herself.

Cautiously, she went to drag Marla away from the glass while avoiding Robby's gaze. Yet, even then, she caught a glimpse of the head wound she'd inflicted on him earlier. It'd already healed to a gummed scar.

The vampire pressed a hand to the glass, his voice muted but audible. "Mom?"

Marla yelped, but Dawn shoved her toward Breisi before Robby's mother could spin around. In turn, Breisi kept Marla from turning back to the window and witnessing her son's pleas. In fact, Breisi set down her saw-bow and secured her charge in the corner by that mercenary sculpture, as if it could guard her. Then she took off her jacket and threw it over Marla Pennybaker's head to block her sight and soothe her.

The Voice sounded over Breisi's open phone and in the earpiece. "We need to invite Robby in, Mrs. Pennybaker. My friends tell me it's not safe for any of you outside now."

Dawn's body washed into itself, recognizing the lulling tone—the hypnosis. She pushed against it, mostly because she wasn't enjoying this "invite Robby in" change of plans. Was it because Jonah knew that his "Friends" were being overcome by the vamp? Or was he anticipating the Guards' arrival within the next few minutes?

Could they even protect Marla from Robby inside the mansion while they were trying to keep the vampire himself safe?

"I won't have Robby near me!" Marla yelled.

Blinking, Dawn didn't fully understand at first that the woman had refused Jonah's hypnotic command. But then she recalled what Kiko had once told her about The Voice.

You have to leave some kind of door open for him to get in.

Marla was shut tight. Jonah had no access.

Would it be the same with Robby, too?

Oh, man, they were up *merde* creek.

As Marla wept in fright, Breisi came to Dawn's side.

"I wonder if Robby'll change to that form you described," she said. "The angel of death. He'd be harder to control."

"And he'd be inside this room with us."

"But the Guards could be on their way. And"—Breisi gestured toward the window—"Robby won't be able to hear the boss on the phone through this glass."

The Voice spoke up. "If Marla won't invite him in, you need to at least try. Guards are coming."

This was really going to happen. They were going to issue an invitation for a monster to join them.

And what did Jonah mean by "try"? Couldn't any person invite a vampire inside?

Robby tapped at the window, tangling her nerves.

Ttch, ttch, ttch.

Then, out of nowhere, the vampire's body jerked, twisting as he fought off an invisible force. There was a boom against the house's exterior, an ear-splitting yowl, then . . . Silence.

"Jonah's 'Friends'?" Dawn asked, pulse twittering.

The Voice didn't answer, but Breisi nodded, gave her a look that said, "You're already acquainted with them, I believe."

Man-oh-man-oh-man. Limpet's paintings. Did they really contain spirits—ghosts? Ones that could step in and out to help "the boss"?

"They can't fight off Robby's unwillingness much longer," Breisi said. "Not with the limits of their powers."

Dawn didn't have a chance to dig deeper, because Marla Pennybaker was getting anxious under the jacket.

"What's he doing?" she asked.

Stalking closer to the window, Dawn chanced a glimpse outside. Leaves waving in the night. Moonlight peeking over the treetops. The calm before a storm.

"He's gone for now," she said, reaching for some curtains. But the window frame was bare. Damn this modern décor.

"When he comes back," Breisi said, "we'll get him inside and have the boss start talking to him and binding him right away while we cover Robby with our weapons. That way we'll at least keep any Guards out of the house."

"No!" Marla was quaking under the black jacket. "Keep him away! He wants revenge, that's all. A ghost's revenge. He's a mean, justice-seeking spirit. He knows that I know . . ."

Dawn gripped her revolver. "What're you talking about?"

Marla's words were muffled. "I . . . I left Robby up to Nathan." She sank lower against the wall. "And by the time I found out about the 'dates' and the parties, it was too late to undo any of it. Oh, God help me, God help me."

Numb, Dawn took in what she'd just said. This woman hadn't been an innocent party in all this? Another victim?

But . . . damn it. In all the vampire confusion, she'd temporarily forgotten. No one in this world was innocent. How could she have unlearned that lesson, even for a few days?

Self-hatred spiked Marla Pennybaker's weeping, but it didn't make any difference to Dawn. Not now.

Are you taking this all in, Jonah? she thought. Are you happy with who you chose to help here? Why did you select her?

"I didn't know what else to do," the older woman continued, "so I kept my peace. 'Do *something*,' I kept telling myself, and I tried to get strong enough to talk to Nathan about my suspicions, but I couldn't. And then . . . then Robby was gone." She sucked in a pained breath. "But now he's back, and this should be my chance to make up for my failings as a mother, shouldn't it? I've been trying to face every truth, but I can't. I just can't. If I let him inside, he'll destroy me because he won't forgive me—and I don't blame him."

"And here we were trying to save you from the agony of knowing all the dirty secrets until it was unavoidable," Dawn said.

"I just wanted you to find him, that's all." She sounded ashamed, cowed by Dawn's comment. "I even understood that he might not be . . . human, based on what Mr. Limpet explained. I was expecting that spirit though. And when you experts tracked him down, I thought that you'd take care of him. That you'd keep him away from me. That's what paranormal professionals do—destroy the ghosts who come back, right?"

Breisi frowned. "We told you we'd give him peace, if that was what he needed. You seemed to want your little boy back so badly, Mrs. Pennybaker. You seemed to want comfort for and from him. But now that Robby's knocking at your window, you're scared, finally telling us information we should have known up front. You were more interested in extermination than saving him, yes?"

"Yes. No . . ." She shook her head under the jacket. "Maybe."

Now, as Dawn recalled Kiko's faith in Marla, it ate away at her. He'd thought she was a decent sort, too. The psychic had picked up on the matron's desperation to find Robby again; he just hadn't interpreted her buried motives correctly.

He'd be devastated to know he'd misconstrued them, because he was too proud of his talents not to take the failure to heart.

Dawn tried not to think of other visions that might have been misinterpreted, too.

"All Robby wanted was a mom and a dad," she said instead. "And he never really had either one."

Marla shrunk into herself, as if stabbed.

But Breisi kept her cool, even as Dawn boiled.

"In addition to Robby's lifestyle," the other PI asked, "did you know about this Underground Nathan took him to for a career overhaul?"

"Underground." Marla pulled the jacket from her tear-stained face. She had a glaze of apology over her eyes, the confusion of someone who knew they'd done wrong and was trying to compensate by doing right this time. "What's Underground?"

Dawn's gaze went red. "Stop jerking us around, Marla."

"I really don't know! Believe me. Nathan was in charge of Robby's career. I only heard a fraction of what was happening, I'm sure. It's all Nathan's . . ."

Behind Dawn, the *ttch, ttch* tap of nails on glass returned. Marla stifled a scream, then burrowed under the jacket again.

Robby was back, and it looked like The Voice's buddies had lost their custody battle. Marla could be taken care of later.

Breisi seemed to be thinking along the same lines. "Dawn, do you remember what you did to Robby earlier? How you mind blasted him across the room at Bava?"

How could she forget? And, more importantly, how the hell had she even managed it?

"If you're asking me if I can do that kind of thing again, when it's needed," Dawn said, "I'm gonna say no."

Breisi gave her an assessing glance, then turned back to Robby. That's when Dawn realized something.

What if mental warfare was the only way to contain this vamp? What if bullets and blades weren't enough?

Ttch, ttch, ttch.

Like a Greek chorus that had taken Marla's story into quiet consideration on the sidelines, Jonah spoke. "Let Robby in. He's about to have company."

Blowing out a breath, Dawn wiped her sweaty palm on her jeans, then prepared her revolver. Breisi turned to the window.

"Robby," she yelled, "come in."

Marla burbled out a string of "no"s from her corner.

And . . . Robby didn't move. He just continued staring with those don't-you-dare-look-into-my eyes.

"The invitation was useless," Breisi said.

The Voice made a thwarted sound. "So it remains that only someone with ownership can issue the invitation. It's no different with Robby."

At the back of the house, a door slammed shut. Footsteps banged on the stark flooring.

"Company," Dawn murmured to Jonah.

Both fighters gunned up, aiming at different entrances to the room. And when a disheveled Nathan Pennybaker ran into the light, neither of them put their weapons down.

Immediately, he raised his hands in surrender. "Marla?" he asked without taking his eyes off the bullet-toting women.

Keeping the jacket on, Marla bolted up in the corner. "Don't look at the window, Nathan!"

Ttch, ttch, ttch.

Snubbing the warning, the man whipped his gaze there anyway. He froze in abject terror.

At the sight of Daddy, Robby began pounding on the window, the glass quaking. *Bam. Bam. Bam. Bam.*

"Lord," Nathan said, his tone thin and trembling.

"Don't you recognize the vampire you made?" Dawn asked. "Where've you been and how'd you get in here without Robby knowing?"

"I . . ." Nathan gulped, turning his back on the window while still keeping his hands up.

Bam. Bam. Bam. Bam.

"Where—have—you—been?" Dawn yelled.

Nathan cowered. "I've been looking for Robby, too. You know I kept in contact—Marla always knew I was safe, even if she didn't know my location."

Bam. Bam. Bam. Bam.

"Dad!" Robby's voice was warped by hatred. "Let me in!"

"Robby," Nathan yelled, refusing to look back. "Just . . . stay where you are! Please!"

A shiver forced Dawn to face the window. And that's when she saw the eyes in the near distance. Red eyes, bobbing up and down, moving to the cadence of a demented heartbeat.

"Guards. They're behind him," she blurted. A connection sparked. "Nathan, did you bring them? Are you taking Robby back Underground?"

The vampire must've caught what she said; he probably had really good hearing, being a child of the night and all.

"Call the Guards off, Dad! Call them off!"

"And invite Robby in," Breisi said to Nathan. Then she glanced at the boy's mother. "You can still do it, too, Marla. Don't you want to make it up to Robby?"

When Marla began shaking her head under the jacket, Dawn reached her limit. "Help your son!"

Neither parent spoke, and Dawn listened for The Voice to offer advice about what to do. But he'd gone silent. Why? Why wasn't he trying to persuade Nathan to invite Robby in?

Had Jonah deserted them?

Nathan stayed facing away from the window, as if he couldn't bear to see the outcome. "We're going back, Robby."

"I don't think so," Dawn said.

On the same pissed-off wavelength, Breisi yanked Nathan to the window, her gun still trained on him. He kept his head down, refusing to look at his son. But he did hold up a hand.

It was an obvious command, because the red-eyes halted, pulsating in place.

"Look at me, Dad!" Robby yelled. "Look at what you made!"

Nathan shook his head, his palms now covering his face.

The vamp didn't seem to mind the Guards—after all, he was finally facing his father, his biggest nemesis. "See me? I'm never going to be a man, no matter how quickly I grow up. But you never wanted me to be more than a little boy, did you." *Bam, bam, bam.* "You hated that my body was maturing, hated my ideas for a new image, so you charmed me into a 'program' "—he mocked the word—"that would reinvent me. And since you knew I wanted to transition into adult roles, I trusted you. I thought it was just what I needed for the change, and I went along with it. I *trusted* you."

Dawn was trying to grasp Robby's accusations, hold them long enough to match them with her questions and meld them into answers. But things were going too fast, and it was all she could do to wonder why Nathan had made Robby into a vamp . . . why he'd forced Robby to stay a child . . . and what good it did to even send his son to this Underground.

Why? And when would everything make sense?

Robby started pounding again, but he gave up, fists slipping down the glass with a suicidal yelp. Nathan wasn't giving any indication that he'd heard a word.

Not knowing how to maneuver things into their favor, Dawn simply targeted the red-eyes in the background. They were waiting patiently, stalkers in the night.

More than anything she wanted to shoot Nathan Pennybaker. And maybe even Marla, too, but . . . there was something about the way Marla Pennybaker was acting now, almost like she was sorry about her neglect.

But Robby wasn't done. "Do you know what a nightmare the Underground was?" He bent down, trying to snag his father's gaze. "After I was initiated, I fought them. But perfect son that I am, I gave up and went back to trusting you again. I don't know why. Seemed easier that way, I suppose. And, for years, I lived the program, but I couldn't follow through—especially when the final release got closer. I just wanted to stay the same, Dad—I wanted to be *myself*. So I started to take some field trips away from the program, to find you again, to recapture the hopes I used to have, to get back the excitement of a normal son who had ambitions for the coming years—a human who could buddy around with his dad and become a *real* man someday. That's when they locked me in. And I answered that by escaping for good. But what did I actually escape?"

His flesh began to glow. "Look at me, Dad! What else can I ever be now but a child star?"

At the sight of his skin, Dawn stiffened—from trepidation and puzzlement. Nothing made sense, nothing was fitting together. . . .

"Look at me!" he screeched.

His love and hatred for Nathan couldn't have been more muddled and, at the same time, clear. But Dawn fought sympathy for Robby. All she had to do was remember Bava.

Remember what he'd done to her and Kiko without even a second thought.

As Marla wept, Nathan finally raised his head. His eyes were closed, probably because he knew the extent of Robby's mind-screwing powers. With every furious cell in her body, Dawn wished Nathan would give his son the chance to work him over.

"You're going to see," the father said, voice loud enough to carry through the window, "that I made the right decision, Rob. You're going to be a bigger star now than ever before."

What? How would this Underground manage that?

A strict glance from Breisi told Dawn that listening was their most valuable tool right now, so she'd better keep mum.

"This needs to stop, Nathan," Marla cried from the corner. "Robby's an abomination. We need to let these women help him."

Her plea might as well have been vapor.

Nathan held his hand to the window, an appeal to his son. "I've got this all planned out. The public is aching for another Robby Pennybaker—the sweet child who captured everyone's hearts and will do the same thing again. Think of how you used to feel when girls would mob you for an autograph. Think of that adoration. Do you remember how it made you feel so alive? That doesn't happen for a lot of child stars after they grow older and uglier—after they lose their baby fat. I stopped you from becoming a late-night TV punchline, Rob."

The vampire was staring at his dad's hand, his body shaking as if craving the sustenance of his old fame.

"You'll be the *new* Robby Pennybaker," Nathan added, voice slick. "Worshipped again."

Hello—did they not see that Robby was a vampire? He wouldn't fool anyone.

There was a taut pause, one in which she could feel a ripple of indecision from Robby. Wary, she concentrated on blocking him, on barring out an invader who was at her locked door, waiting to barge in.

Marla's voice came from the corner. "Haven't you punished him enough? Every time you sold him out, I'll bet you were avenging yourself because he succeeded where you'd failed—"

"*Marla.*" Nathan pushed his other hand out at her.

Dawn glanced at the woman to find that the jacket had slipped away from her face. She seemed torn between a mother's love for her son—to the extent that it existed for Marla—and her own nightmares.

As Dawn turned back to Nathan, she found that he'd raised more of his face to Robby. There was surprise widening his eyes—maybe because he now realized that Marla knew about the pimping. Had he meant to open his eyes or had shock done it?

Nathan's stare connected with Robby's. "I've been waiting a very long time for your release. I've missed you, and I'm going to look out for you. Just like old times, Rob."

The vampire raised his hand to the glass, pressed his palm against his father's, tears running down his cheeks.

The mean streaks brought back the memory of violence for Dawn, and she battled to shut out all of it—except for one thing. A vision Kiko had gotten right in this very house.

"You've killed for him," Dawn whispered.

Nathan kept lavishing a glance on Robby, their gazes meeting like a mended vein. "Never."

Bullshit. "My associate has evidence that you had blood on your hands the night Robby 'died.' Your housekeeper's blood."

A fey, absent smile wisped over Nathan's mouth as he looked at Robby.

"I was merely cleaning up after my boy," he said, his voice slurred, altered. "That simpleton Ingrid, who was supposed to be off that night, stumbled into her room just after Dr. Eternity . . . left." His face went slack. Robby cocked his head. Nathan imitated him. "Rob was still hungry, even during his pain, and he asked her for a drink. It all happened so fast . . . Since she was the woman who'd brought him milk every night before bedtime, she automatically said yes. But then she realized something was wrong with Rob. She started to run away." A strangely proud grin lit Nathan's face as he continued gazing into his son's eyes. "They say he was the strongest vampire at birth that they've ever seen; so hungry for more. The creatures won't drink from the unwilling, but he got Ingrid's permission, and he took her blood. She was his first."

Several things hit Dawn at once: the housekeeper hadn't committed suicide. And the reason Robby hadn't forcibly taken Dawn's own blood at Bava was because she'd denied him.

Too bad vampires didn't have to ask to feed on memories, too, goddamn him.

The outrage returned—shame at having her mind bared and entered. Her revolver trembled as she kept aiming it at Nathan.

On the other side of the glass, Robby began to laugh.

With a start, the dad backed away, shaking his head to clear it. "Damn you, Robby! You know what they'll do to me if I give out that kind of information!"

"They"? The Underground?

The vampire kept laughing, making it easy for Dawn to guess what had just happened. Robby had mind screwed Nathan, purposely setting his dad up for the consequences from "they."

Would Nathan be forced to stay in this Underground, allowing Robby to hold on to his dad forever this time?

There was a definite power game going on here. Revenge?

But, hey, as long as they were fighting each other, Dawn and Breisi might just get more information about the Underground—and maybe Frank—in the fallout. Then they would worry about getting Robby alone to Jonah for follow up.

It was just a matter of figuring out how to do that—what, with those red eyes still bobbing in the darkness behind Robby like flares on an ocean of night. Simple, huh?

Nathan straightened his designer shirt, averted his face from Robby again. "It's time to take you back, you ingrate."

He raised his hand to the Guards.

"Stop!" It was Marla, shooting out of her corner, jacket pooled behind her on the marble. She got in Nathan's face. "He said he doesn't want to go."

Finally. Dawn backed up a few steps, raised her revolver higher at him in agreement. Breisi was on it, too.

"She's got the idea," the other PI said. "We'll be taking Robby with us to give him peace."

"Yes, he needs peace, like she said," Marla added. "Please, Nathan."

Yet, even in the face of his dire situation, her husband laid a hand on Marla's shoulder, then pushed her away. She fell backward, sprawling on the floor in her silk pantsuit.

"First," he said, "if I lost Robby, I'd also lose the millions of dollars I've invested in this program. Second, there're a lot of . . . caveats . . . that aren't going to let you have him."

He gestured to the Guards.

Giving them permission to move on Robby.

With a burst of adrenaline, Dawn pointed her gun at the window, targeting the flicker-frizz of one creature. Breisi joined her, firing, too—the pane bursting into shards. But the pale creatures easily zagged out of the bullets' paths, their bodies beating forward as Robby charged away.

Yet the smaller vampire didn't succeed in escaping tonight—the three Guards were too close. While two flicked out their tails, coiling them around Robby and dragging him into the porch-dimmed darkness, the other stood back, its tail waving.

Then it did something Dawn had only barely noticed during the first fight with them.

Its tail barb zinged open into a bloom of long, machete-like blades. It ran one of them near Robby's throat in a slow, slashing motion. Then, instantly, the blades swallowed back into a lone metal gathering of tips. It was daring Robby to change, Dawn thought. To go into big-time vamp form with that misty body and all-powerful eyes before the Guard could decapitate him.

A challenge from one undead creature to another.

Dawn didn't understand why they just didn't zoom off with him. Were the Guards waiting for Nathan so they could take him to exact those consequences Robby had mentioned? Were they going to use the boy vampire as a lure?

Or Hell. Were the Guards after some PIs, too?

On the fringes of that thought, everything seemed to slow down, compressing all the action into one pinched second: looped time, eternally torturous.

"Mom!" the vamp screamed. His voice contained a dragged-out knowledge that he had no more father, that Marla and the PIs were his only hope now.

In the meantime, Dawn squeezed off another bullet.

Marla opened her mouth. "Robby, come in, come to Mommy!"

Then everything fell to pieces: Before the Guards' tails could snap open into blades, Robby sipped into mist and streamed out of the Guards' clutches, slamming through the window frame and into the house, his mouth yawing in a ferocious roar as he took feathery form and poised his fangs above a screeching Nathan. In a very human moment, Breisi stumbled back at the awful sight of the vampire, while Marla scuttled behind a chair. Dawn's bullet missed one Guard as all three rushed the window and halted, unable to enter. Breisi saw their hesitation, too, and while she covered Robby with her gun, Dawn raised the butt of her own revolver to hit Nathan over the head before he could invite the red-eyes in.

As he collapsed, she brought her weapon back up in a flowing arc, aiming at Robby out of pure instinctual fear and realizing only too late how futile a silver bullet might be.

Scraa—eeeee-tttccchhh!

Sensing the threat of Dawn's gun, Robby redirected his fury, raging over her now with the force of an animal clawing into the belly of felled prey.

Violated, attacked—

She bared her teeth at him and tensed, ready to shoot.

"Dawn, no!" Breisi yelled.

Robby, in her head, pawing though stinging images of Eva . . .

In a moment of clarity, she realized that she wasn't facing a child here. Robby wasn't even a poor monster that someone else had created. No, this thing above her was something that snuck into houses at night to kill, over and over again, unless it was stopped—

Dawn fired.

The silver thunked into his arm, embedding itself like a jewel in the midst of white cotton. The vampire's roar came to an abrupt stop. As Dawn avoided his eyes, he hesitated, then dropped to the floor, his body spinning back into human form.

He panted, going into the fetal position. "You didn't have to do that."

Yes, I did, she thought. For Kiko. For *me*.

Even through a filter of terror, Dawn heard sobs in back of her. Marla had come from behind the chair and . . . damn it, Nathan was holding his head where Dawn had hit him.

Unfortunately, she hadn't cracked him hard enough to knock him out, but a fine trail of blood was wiggling down his face as he stared at his son, his mouth and eyes saucered.

Maybe Nathan had just seen the *true* face of his child for the first time. He'd created this thing, and it horrified him. Good.

She heard the Guards hissing near the window, but they weren't standing in front of it. They were hiding, making themselves sneaky, tough targets.

"Blood," Robby said plaintively from his spot on the floor. "I need blood to wash the silver out."

While Breisi covered the Guards, she shouted at Dawn. "The silver is working slowly. We need to allow the boss access to him in this weakened state before the elements consume his body and destroy him."

"Daddy?" Robby crawled to Nathan, fixating on the trickle of blood. "Will you feed me?"

"Get away." Sweat poured over Nathan's face, mingling with the red. "No fangs, no fangs!"

Fear of vampires or fear of his son?

"Dawn," Breisi said, trying to get her moving.

She rolled to her good side as Robby plopped to the floor in front of his father, tilting his head.

"They're going to get you anyway, Dad." The boy vampire smiled. "You've already said too much. If it's not my fangs, it'll be theirs. You're going to be with me forever now."

"*No!* Nonononono—" Nathan's eyes were rolling back in his head. "I'll kill myself before I let them—let *you*—touch me!"

Marla resumed her place behind the chair, her gaze darting from her son to the window.

"Forever." Robby smiled. "We'll always be together."

Nathan's wide eyes locked on something to his right.

The sculpture by the door—the blob with the bladed thrust of iron coming from its center.

Robby scooted closer to his dad. "Let me feed from you."

With a long cry, Nathan darted away and ran ahead at full steam, straight at the sculpture.

Robby watched him, head cocked. "Daddy?"

"Nathan!" Marla screeched.

With a thrust of blood, the blade jabbed out of his back, making Dawn's arm lose strength as she fell to the floor in shock. He slumped against the iron, embracing the sculpture, the artistic sword holding him up.

Unintelligible words whistled out of his mouth and, for a blurred second, Dawn thought they were regrets for his son.

But then all hell broke loose as the Guards appeared in front of the window frame.

Dawn knew exactly what his last words had been.

"He invited them in!" she yelled.

Before she and Breisi could raise their guns, a baffled Robby had staggered to his feet, beginning to change back into what Dawn now thought of as "Danger Form." He flickered in his attempts, weakened as he watched his father hug the statue with more true adoration than he'd probably ever received himself.

But the Guards were already pounding forward, propelling into the room as their tails whizzed behind them. Abruptly, they reared back—from the garlic?—and clawed the air, preparing their tails to strike.

At their hesitation, Breisi's bullet found a mark, and one creature jammed back against the wall, its body shriveling into itself as if eaten by an internal vacuum.

But Dawn wasn't so lucky. With her left-handed aim, she was off, hitting the wall, plaster exploding outward. The Guard aimed a stream of spit at her, but she expected it, dodged it.

Then, out of nowhere, a blade spun out of the darkness from the third Guard's direction, chopping Robby's wounded arm off, spraying blood over Dawn's arm as she hit the deck. Instinctively, she recalled the burn from the spit and prepped herself for the pain. But she was fine. Just fi—

A roar of anguish shook the room while Robby fell to the floor, clutching his shoulder stump.

The long blade was speared into the couch, shivering.

Had that come from a Guard? And why the hell were they trying to kill Robby? Had they removed his arm as some kind of surgery to keep the silver from spreading?

In a fractured flash, her hands remembered the feel of Matt Lonigan's blade sheathed near his spine. A machete?

With one peek at the darkened window, she decided she didn't have time to sort this out. She aimed her revolver at the spitting Guard, hitting its heart this time.

Swww-uuuuck.

Two down, one to go.

In the meantime, Robby was staring at what had been his arm. Then, a little boy through and through, he began to cry.

Concurrently, as soon as Breisi had knocked off the first Guard, she'd engaged a second, ducking its tail and spit as she made her way to her saw-bow by the door. The creature had knocked her gun out of her hand with its tail and was now beating through the air toward her, wrinkling its nose and swiping at the garlic repellant.

But that's all Dawn saw, because she was facing Robby now—the boy who was starting to sputter with Danger Form. His bottled emotions were obviously fuel for the monster within.

Uninvited, memories stripped from her . . .

Uncontrollable, helpless rage had her in its thrall now, robbing her of common sense.

Ripped open, defenseless, attacked . . .

She grabbed her machete, slid it out of its sheath, swung back the blade, then leapt at the vampire.

Smack—the machete hatcheted into his neck, blood gushing over her chest, her neck and arms.

Unlike the Guards, Robby didn't spit. No, it was red matter bathing Frank's shirt as Robby fell to the floor, the blade gouged halfway into his throat.

"Dad?" he gurgled, his face wet from his tears. "Mom?"

No answer. With a glance, Dawn saw why.

The remaining Guard hadn't been going after Breisi at all—Marla had been its target. And with eye-blinking speed, it was flying out the window with the woman in tow, her mouth gaped open in a gulping scream.

Breisi rushed after them, leaving Dawn alone with Robby.

Now that he wasn't in Danger Form, she felt ill. Blood was gleaming on the marble. Red over white.

The boy sought her gaze, crimson bubbling from his lips.

Dawn wasn't sucker enough to make eye contact. "It hurt when my friend broke his back, too," she said in an effort to conjure her ire. But it was harder with this little body in front of her. A crying child.

Dawn, she told herself, don't trust him. Don't let him fool you. Don't have any mercy, because he didn't with you.

Fumbling with urgency, she cried out, yanking the machete out of his neck. Then, with feral purpose, she raised the blade over her head, swiped it at him again. *Swick*—he stopped crying.

The sound echoed as his head rolled away from his body, severed from his spine, coming to a stop near his father's impaled corpse in the foyer. Together forever.

Her heartbeat, her breathing filled the room, surrounding her in anesthetized distance from the horror of what she'd just done. But she didn't linger. No—for good measure, she calmly shot the vampire in the heart.

With a savage sucking noise, the clothing, torso, and head zipped into themselves, and Robby was obliterated. Leaving an outline of blood, like chalk lines at a crime scene.

Is this what you did for a living, Frank? Is this how it felt? Numb and inconceivable, even as you stared at the damage?

Dawn turned her head. Blocking it all out.

As a rivulet of Robby's blood ran over the marble and past her feet, she heard a sound at the window, quickly aimed at it.

Breisi, empty-handed except for her spent saw-bow.

"It got away," she said as Dawn lowered her revolver.

Now that the adrenaline had cooled, Dawn sank to her knees, holding herself up with her left hand. She wanted to throw up. And when the shakes took over, cold and throttling, she lay down, her right side pierced with agony.

What had she done? They couldn't take Robby back to The Voice now. And Marla couldn't be questioned about any lies she'd been telling.

"I didn't want him in me again," Dawn whispered between trembles.

Jonah's voice, soft and somehow understanding, came through her earpiece. "I'm sure you didn't, Dawn."

Skin spotted with blood, Breisi stood over her. But . . . why wasn't she as upset as she should've been? And why was The Voice, of all people, being so nice?

"There's one locator tuned to a Guard's body heat and one programmed to detect Frank," Breisi said. "I managed to attach them to the Guard's clothes."

Optimism somehow rose above the shakes. "We can track it?" Dawn asked.

"If it doesn't discover the bugs first."

"It's all right, Dawn," Jonah said. "This was only the beginning; a small battle in a big war. And Robby gave us some very useful ammunition." Pause. "We've just started."

Inexplicably, Dawn started to laugh—big, automatic gulps of relief, weariness, and disbelief. Crazy sounds of grief that she couldn't acknowledge because it would break her apart until she didn't exist anymore.

A war, she thought. This wasn't even close to over. God help her, not even close.

And, as the sun saturated the sky with streaks of red, Jonah drew up more battle plans, concocting a story that they'd give to the cops about Nathan Pennybaker's suicide at the news of his wife's disappearance. They would tell the authorities that the distraught man had called the PIs over and then impaled himself in their presence. The rest—burns from vampire spit, blood—they'd leave to the crime technicians to fret over.

Because skepticism about monsters and Jonah Limpet's money were powerful allies—ones they had to depend on.

Ultimately, after being questioned and released by the authorities, the women finally slouched to the 4Runner in the emerging light of day. On the way to the vehicle, Dawn took off her earring, not because she was following Kiko's advice about it getting ripped out, but because it didn't seem to fit anymore. Actually, nothing fit her now.

Except for the painful echoes of another vampire hunter's screams—her father's.

TWENTY-SEVEN

New Moon

HOURS earlier, at nightfall, a star had been reborn.

Unlike previous "deaths"—such as Jesse Shane's—this one had been made easier with the advances of technology. Certainly Dr. Eternity and his trusted group of Servants could have used Hollywood special effects to simulate Tamsin Greene's gory demise, but there hadn't been any need for it—not with the doctor's vampiric talents.

The resurrection had been deceptively simple.

As night swallowed Los Angeles, Dr. Eternity's plans had been set into motion. Using the cover of darkness and disguise to emerge Above, the doctor—or Master, as he was known to Sorin and the Elites—visited the victim's home. There, Tamsin Greene invited him over the threshold.

Greedy for forever-fame, she was eager to begin the agreed upon ritual, her makeup carefully applied, her body clothed in satin, her eyes speaking of a fear she would soon forget.

Fear of aging. Fear of losing the adoring glances bestowed upon her by millions.

Then she led him to her room, where he lay her down on the white bed, caressed her neck, encouraged the jugular vein to emerge while assuring her that he would be gentle. That her new life was going to be beautiful beyond imagination.

That she would always remain beautiful.

As her eyes glazed under his seductive words, her breath came in shallow gasps. He stroked her to calmness, his gaze a hypnotic sedative. Then, when she was primed, he carefully took her in the time-honored ritual of exchange, fangs extending as he revealed his true, terrible face.

She gasped at the shock of it, gasped at the rapid, animal pierce of broken skin at her neck. Then, after a tender and languorous feast of her blood, Dr. Eternity reared back, slit his wrist with a clawed nail, and bequeathed her his own life's water. He allowed her to drink only so much—enough to rise.

To complete the cycle, he placed his red-stained lips over hers, giving her the kiss of a Soul Taker. He drank completely again, immersing himself in her essence, feeling as revered as a one-hundred-foot god on a movie screen. Every vivid human experience: laughter, sadness, love—all the emotions he had to work so hard to possess—filled him to overflowing.

To drunken agony.

Meanwhile, Tamsin's veins constricted with the new elements in her system, her body animated by the Master's blood. Later, before the Underground welcoming ceremony, her body would fully shape itself to her new vampiric form.

But that was yet to come.

Now, she screamed at the heat of her change, straining along with her master, both of them in pain and near weeping.

Her memories consumed him: the thrill of being desired. The lovely terror of facing a thousand fans who needed you . . .

All too soon, like skin being torn from bone, Tamsin's soul screeched and separated from him, and the doctor fell to the carpet. Her essence wailed into a vial that sat on the bed, a container he had charmed with the facade of safe harbor. Her soul cowered there, not knowing any better.

To the Master, losing the soul was akin to being stranded in the darkness of forever. Alienation, isolation, the terror of not knowing what was coming next, the horror of being rejected. He reached out, scratched at the bedspread, but like eternity, there was nothing to hold on to.

Even so, he wanted more . . . *more*.

As tremors wracked his body, he capped the vial, yet one more soul to add to his collection.

An hour seemed to pass while Tamsin moaned and fumbled for him, but the Master knew that time was only stretching itself out during their agony. It tortured him with the knowledge that he was fallen and bereft, that the very people he was saving with his blood would never love him as much as he loved—or wanted to be—them.

As he held Tamsin's hand, her gaze grew wide, locked to the ceiling during a trauma she would soon rise above. Trembling, he kissed her neck, healing her bites instantly, then left her side to put her newest CD into the player. After tonight, this would always be known as Tamsin's final work, her greatest masterpiece. It would sell millions, and much of that would be in his coffers due to the payments she would always owe him.

With the first notes of a lazy love song, he slunk into the night, thus allowing Sorin to take over.

The second-in-command—*first*-in-command, as far as most of the Underground believed—strolled in by himself and waited until Tamsin's reanimated body gained enough strength to rise.

When she did, it was with the tentative wonder of an infant. She felt her body, ran her hands over her skin, staggered to her mirror.

"I look the same. Why? You promised me I'd be—"

"We have merely begun the ritual," Sorin said, never minding her tiresome Elite dramatics.

He called in the human Servants who would aid in this production. Eyes averted from Tamsin in respectful modesty, the underlings went about setting up the scene, making sure it was safe, yet convincing.

So easy compared to the ones who came before, Sorin thought.

Previous Elites had required Dr. Eternity to maim them and slow their vitals to the point where they appeared dying or dead, forcing the vampire to flee the Elite's side in a timely manner before the police arrived. But this particular presentation would be done on camera, allowing them more leeway. They had even discussed using a prosthetic throat that would gush blood, but an Internet broadcast would entail so-called "geeks" reviewing the footage ad nauseam, and they would uncover such fakery.

No matter though. Even at this stage of vampirism, Tamsin would heal, especially with Sorin's ability to mend wounds with a touch, and then the Master's astounding, final actions.

The older the vampire was, the quicker and more widespread the healing. With enough years, youngsters would ultimately gain that sort of power, as well.

After two hours, Tamsin was prepared for her biggest role yet.

Outside her mansion, Sorin waited for the broadcast to end, using an encrypted cell phone to handle Underground business: the updating of Robby Pennybaker's demise from spywork. Still doubtful of the Master's methods, Sorin's mind stayed focused on the fire that would burn in front of him; it was one of the only methods that could harm him, so caution was wise.

Predictably, the superstar performed without error.

As the flames consumed her home, the Servants, dressed in protective gear since they were stunt technicians in their Above lives, whisked Tamsin out of danger. Quickly, they substituted a body that had already been burned and stripped of identifying features. Then they carried out the necessary, routine trickery: with Robby Pennybaker, for instance, they had slowed his vitals after he had attacked his first, unlucky victim, then stolen his "corpse" from the morgue to avoid investigation; with Jesse Shane, they had wired his ambulance to explode in a remote area, leaving only body fragments behind—so mangled that the investigators would never discover that Jesse Shane's remains were not among the carnage.

And so it went with all the "deaths."

For Tamsin, they had found a suitable woman on the streets who no one would miss. No, there was not a person on earth who would care about yet another transient gone absent—not on a night when one of the world's biggest stars fell from the heavens.

In no time, Sorin and the Servants had transported Tamsin Underground without anyone Above being the wiser. Though Sorin was able to partially close Tamsin's throat wound, the cut ran deep. It would require the doctor's skills to complete her now.

While the Servants gathered with the rest of the excited Underground in the emporium where they awaited Tamsin's arrival, Sorin brought the new Elite to the Master.

He was only just slipping into the secret room himself, his aura shining. After he flipped on the radio, they heard the devastated voice of a dead-of-night DJ yelling and crying about tonight's Internet broadcast. The Master's aura brightened further, a halo surrounding an eclipsed sun.

The finest resurrection of all, Sorin thought. My master. Thank the day for this new Elite. Thank the day for his awakening at the terrible rise of the activities Above.

While the vampire they called Dr. Eternity settled his child on a bed of silk and rose petals, he spoke, profound sadness weighing his tone.

"They say my son was destroyed."

"It is for the best. In the end, Robby caused an information leak and changed the retrieval mission of him and his father into a convenient erasure. Between this rogue Elite and Lee Tomlinson, it has been made clear that betrayal will not go unpunished."

"At what price?"

"*You* were once taught to withold mercy from traitors."

"Yes." A simple acknowledgment had never sounded so sorrowful.

The Master laid a hand on Tamsin's self-inflicted wound. "One lost child is ushered out by the birth of a new one. Makes sense."

"We will grieve Robby properly. And Marla Pennybaker's mind will be wiped, leaving no trace of tonight after she is returned Above."

"No trace except for Limpet and Associates—something we weren't able to solve. I know that, Sorin. I know it very well, and we'll lock our community down until we know how to proceed, for the time being."

Relief glowed through Sorin. Perhaps the Master was planning aggressive action now. Perhaps he would soon be ready to vanquish their enemies.

The Master's aura flickered as he healed Tamsin Greene. Her skin had gone pale with the loss of blood, but her flesh was blooming back to its gorgeous, smooth, dark shade with the absorption of the Master's power. Her lips reddened.

Yet, just as she was becoming a reflection of her human self again, the Master went a step beyond, suffusing her with the true nature. The Allure she would be trained to control.

It began with her skin, which hushed a feathery mist of ghostly white—so light that her limbs seemed to float on air. Her eyes brightened open, irises mirroring a swirl of inhuman shades, hints of the afterlife, glimpses of places she would never be able to retire to now that she was without a soul.

Sorin thought of the room with the hundreds of vials—a hell on earth.

Fully turned now, Tamsin was breathtaking. Slowly, she sat up, put her hands to her face. When Sorin held up an outdated looking glass, she gazed upon herself.

Like all of the Elites, she fell in love with the new image. She drank herself in, laughing and complimenting.

From the corner, the DJ on the radio was accepting phone calls from fans in hysterical denial.

"You're a legend," the Master said to his child. "And when the world has grieved and made you more of a goddess than you ever thought possible, you'll go back to them."

"But not until after the rest of the procedure," she said.

Unlike Robby Pennybaker, Tamsin was accepting of the necessary steps because the doctor's success rate in creating new careers for the Elite was astounding.

Tonight, after returning Tamsin to her more human form, the doctor would see to her recovery. She would stay Underground for decades, long enough to make her an even bigger legend. Years of experience predicted that the public would yearn for another Tamsin Greene, would crave a remedy for their nostalgic love of a talent who had died too young.

Meanwhile, she would train to "act human" and control her new powers. Underground, she would feed off Servants and Groupies who were addicted to an Elite's angelic beauty and glamour. She would be pampered and worshipped, young and ageless, never changing until the doctor stepped in once again.

Because, before her release to a Servant Above who would maintain her career, she would undergo an alteration. Most stars had taken part in a process similar before coming Underground anyway, so it was a familiar procedure.

In the final phase before a comeback, the Elite went "under the knife," as the doctor called it. With preternatural efficiency, he would use all the skills he had been taught by a human Servant—a plastic surgeon—over fifty years ago. He would transform Tamsin's face. Give her a new identity. Work with such speed that the still-young vampire could not heal before he was finished. And, when he was done, her flesh would wrap over cheekbone and chin implants, the star bearing only an eerie resemblance to her old self. Simple cosmetic changes that did not require surgery would aid in the rest of the masquerade, completing her fresh look.

But the most important element was this: Allure shining through her eyes, convincing anyone who looked into them that she carried the essence of a dead legend—a familiar star who would have aged so tragically during the passage of years. Then, when the public noticed her eternal youth, she would return Underground to start again.

Better than Botox. And longer lasting, as well.

Although not everyone knew it, this doctor was the best career fixer in town.

Tamsin and her mirror were still enjoying an intense affair. "A legend. Just like Jim Morrison."

The Awareness between the Master and Sorin wavered, like a human chuckle.

"Your new family is waiting," the second-in-command reminded her.

The Master rested a hand on Tamsin's head, thus altering her to the quasi-human form that would house her Allure. He looked into her multi-colored eyes.

"Secrecy, my love," he said. "I don't exist for anyone except you and your siblings. Remember that."

She nodded, knowing the price of revealing the true Master. Back to mortality. Back to aging and eventually withering away. And for a professional who was so accustomed to signing non-disclosure agreements in her contracts, this step presented no difficulty.

"Yes, Master," she whispered, kissing his hand with fervent gratitude.

Then Sorin led Tamsin up from the bed, guided her out of the darkness and through the tunnels. To the emporium.

As the doors opened, the haremesque grandeur embraced them. Cut glass, rich velvets and brocades, heady incense and flesh.

Her fellow Elites—the ones who had yet to be released—stood before her, flanked by the Groupies, then a handful of Servants.

She marveled at the familiar faces: the action hero, the wild rapper, the misunderstood music idol, the gorgeous, puppy-eyed comedian—all who had died.

All old faces here to welcome their new sibling.

Old faces that had never aged during this process of becoming new faces.

Jesse Shane, whose own "death" had been designed to provoke strange, neverending speculations, raised a glass of warm blood to his little sister. "Long live the new Tamsin Greene."

The rest of the crowd repeated his words, their voices a merry chorus.

"Long live the new Tamsin Greene!"

And, years from now, after the final change when she returned Above as a different actress/singer, that's what the press would be saying, too.

Here's to the new Tamsin Greene.

Never knowing she was actually the old Tamsin Greene.

TWENTY-EIGHT

The Recovery

It was midday at the hospital, where Dawn and Breisi sat with Kiko, keeping vigil over his bed. Although they'd taken quick showers at their crash pads to clean the blood off their skin, they hadn't gotten any sleep, and it was wearing on them.

But they could always get some shut-eye in this room, Dawn kept telling herself as she forced her eyes open. She was holding Kiko's fingers in one injured hand and nursing a coffee with the other while she watched TV. On the other side of the bed, Breisi fiddled with her locator receivers, trying to goose some kind of response out of their silence. Both of them wanted to spend as much awake time with their partner as possible, because tomorrow, when Dawn and Breisi got back to tracking Frank and this Underground, Kiko would be in surgery.

Since his L1 vertebra had burst into his spinal column, he'd sustained damage to his spinal cord but hadn't severed it, thank God. In order to stabilize his back, the doctors planned to use plates and pins and, although it'd take about a year for him to make a full recovery, the professionals were telling him that he'd be walking fairly soon after the operation, with the help of a brace and rehabilitation.

All the same, Kiko kept insisting he could continue working. His brain was still good, he'd muttered in one of his more lucid moments. Didn't need surgery on *that*.

Now, he was knocked out on painkillers, his compact form swathed in hospital gear. On the TV, a Dodgers game should've been on but, much to Breisi's fan-girl impatience, the station kept interrupting the broadcast for local reaction about Tamsin Greene's suicide. The news was inescapable, the coverage wallowing in sensationalism.

It seemed like the media had totally missed Tamsin's message about exploiting her because now, more than ever, they were doing a hell of a lot of it.

A reporter was interviewing celebrities, collecting their grief in a montage of overkill. At the moment, a rising fifties-pop-inspired musician, Bradley Mistle, was wiping down his thick nerd-framed glasses that had fogged up from emotion.

A huffing Breisi muted the sound when her cell phone rang.

"What a circus," the baseball fan said as she checked the number. Her eyes were ringed with red. "Let the dead rest in peace, I say."

After last night, Dawn wasn't sure how likely that was.

After Breisi pushed a button, The Voice came on speakerphone.

"Please tell me you're getting some rest there," he said.

"Yes," both Dawn and Breisi lied. Aside from a couple of catnaps, neither of them had made much of an effort.

Breisi gave Dawn a conspiratorial nod. Dawn raised an eyebrow back.

"And how are your Friends?" the other woman asked.

"Like you, they're recovering."

In all the tragedy, Dawn had almost forgotten about how Jonah's buddies—the ghosties from the office—had lost their battle with Robby's superior powers. Earlier, The Voice had told them that his "Friends" had been drained of strength and had been summoned back to him when they realized they'd be of no more use at the Pennybakers'. Thus, their sudden disappearance.

She'd also gotten an answer about why Jonah had gone quiet on the cell phone when Nathan had shown up. In an unprecedented sharing of actual answers, The Voice had told her that, once Mr. Pennybaker had arrived with the Guards—commanding them, nonetheless—he'd suspected Nathan's intimate involvement with Robby's Underground. Since Jonah was adamant about hiding his presence from any forces that had come with the Guards, he'd protected himself by withdrawing from a possible threat, surrendering the chance to try to hypnotize either Robby *or* Nathan.

What the hell that all meant, Dawn didn't know. But she was damned well going to find out.

Along with discovering where Frank is, she thought, *I'm* going to dig into all your mysteries, Jonah: what your friends are . . . what *you* are.

The Voice continued. "It's good to hear you're all secure." Then he paused, tone softening. "Because, contrary to popular belief, I do care what happens to you."

Even though the words hadn't been aimed at Dawn, she felt her skin flushing, tingling with suggestion. And when Breisi pursed her lips, Dawn knew that she wasn't alone in thinking maybe Jonah had spoken volumes more in that one little sentence than he had in the sum of all their conversations.

Clearing her throat, Dawn glanced at the bed sheets. Suddenly, there was too much intimacy in the air.

"And how's Kiko faring?" Jonah continued brusquely, as if ignoring the previous odd moment.

Dawn patted her friend's hand. "Slumbering away."

"Sleep rebuilds the body."

"Jonah." Again, Dawn looked at the phone as if she were addressing him in the flesh. Wishful thinking. "You sound a lot more chipper than I would've ever predicted after what's happened. Our clients ended up dead or missing. We still have no idea where Frank is—"

"Ah, but we're much farther along than I'd hoped at this point. As I said, Robby leads us to the bigger picture—the main reason we summoned you."

Dawn recalled Kiko's description of his vision: Dawn, covered in the blood of a vampire, victorious. She'd been covered with red last night, all right, but she hadn't reached the victorious part. That's because she hadn't fulfilled the prediction, The Voice had told her. Not yet.

"Beginning tomorrow," The Voice added, "we shift focus in Frank's investigation. To the Underground and this Dr. Eternity we heard Nathan Pennybaker speak of."

"So it's business as usual," Dawn said, watching Kiko as he groaned in his sleep. "Almost."

"And back to secrecy," Jonah said. "We must work more quietly than ever. Surprise with these creatures is essential."

Dawn let go of Kiko and held up a hand in a mock—yet all too serious—vow. "Vampire hunter's honor."

Even if she sounded brave, a pall fell over her. How many creatures of darkness were out there? How many were hiding in the crevices of society, like Robby? Like this Underground?

And . . . just as disturbing . . . how many vamp hunters were there?

The image of Robby's arm being sliced off by that long blade shadowed her again. She couldn't help wondering where Matt had been last night while she was fighting vamps. Wondering who the hell had hired him, and why.

In her peripheral vision, Dawn noticed Breisi making a rapid swipe at her face. Crying. Damn it, what was she crying about? Kiko? Frank?

Then it hit her. *Vampire hunter's honor.*

Dawn had taken Frank's place, becoming the hunter he'd turned into. Except instead of just tracking vamps, she was tracking *him*. More than anyone, Breisi had to be aware of that.

The other woman smiled at the daughter of the man she loved. "We'll find him," she repeated. It'd become their mantra.

Before things could degenerate into an Emotion Fest, both women turned to the phone, seeking another place to look.

"I've gotta have more coffee," Dawn said.

"And *rest,*" Jonah commanded before he hung up.

Stowing the cell, Breisi turned the TV's volume back on. An old interview of Darrin Ryder, Dawn's super favorite actor, was gracing the screen as a reporter voiced-over that the star was recovering from an attack last night. A supposed mugging.

Dawn grabbed back on to Kiko and mustered a little sympathy for Ryder. Not a lot though. Karma was a sneaky bitch, and she didn't begrudge it some playtime.

A tiny squeeze tightened her fingers. She glanced down, finding Kiko half-awake, his gaze unfocused. Her heart constricted as he unlinked his fingers from hers, then reached out to touch the undershirt she'd worn after washing it.

Frank's shirt.

"Bait," Dawn thought she heard him whisper before he closed his eyes and drifted off.

Wait—had Kiko made contact with Frank again? Good news since, after some thinking, she realized that maybe Kiko got present-time clothes readings only if the subject had a conscience that still worked. It made sense, because Kik had gotten a reading from the *past* via Robby's old shirts—clothing he'd worn when he'd had a soul. Just as she hoped Frank still did.

Or was Kiko only reliving that one debilitating vision from the other night right now?

Or . . . Dawn thought of another possibility, a sad option. Maybe it was just the painkillers addling his brain.

Pain. Too damned much of it around here.

She picked up her coffee, started to down the rest of it, but found the foam cup empty.

Reacting to Dawn's frown, Breisi rose from her seat, gesturing to the cup. "I'm going out for some tea. You want more caffeine?"

"Hell, yeah. As much as my body can hold without imploding."

An image of vamp bodies sucking inward shook her.

Breisi must've been thinking much of the same thing, too, because as she left, she shot Dawn a stoic, knowing glance, then disappeared out the door.

Alone now, Dawn slumped farther into the chair, exhaustion trying to drag her down again. As she fought to keep her eyes open, the TV news continued, the name "Tamsin Greene" like a whisper deep in her brain, leading her toward sleep.

Suicide . . . Internet . . . blood . . . dead . . .

"Dawn?"

It was a whisper, too, just like all the white noise that had been fritzing through her head. The sounds of the TV floated away, becoming a part of the nothing.

Then something touched her arm.

She bolted out of her chair, blinking open her eyes as her heart pattered against her ribs. Fear and experience forced her body into a defensive stance as she tried to focus.

In the fuzz of Dawn's tired vision, Jacqueline Ashley stood, dreamlike. She was dressed in fashionably faded blue jeans, a "Drive Hybrid" T-shirt, a baseball cap that she'd shoved all her hair into, and those damned sunglasses. Carrying some white papers and a bouquet of friendly flowers, her appearance reminded Dawn that she'd invited the girl over here to see Kiko, knowing it would cheer him greatly. She also suspected Jacqueline would appreciate the company.

Relieved, Dawn found that she was actually grateful to see her. Hell, a normal chick from Pahrump, Nevada, beat a fang-wielding vampire any day of the week.

She relaxed, but her pulse still jittered her veins in the aftershock.

Jacqueline's head was tilted in obvious concern as she set the flowers on a table. "Oh, my God. You were hurt in Kiko's stunt, too?"

In Dawn's sleep-deprived world, Jacqueline's words sounded like they were being played at slow speed. Even the edges of the actress's body seemed blurred.

Dawn forced her eyes wide. Tired. Still very tired.

"Kiko and I need to be more careful with our choreography, I guess," she said, voice croaky. "He's asleep now, but he'll love waking up to the sight of his favorite up-and-coming fencer."

"Anything I can do to help. For both of you." Now that Jacqueline knew Dawn was okay, she got a big, goofy smile on her face, then started bouncing on her heels.

Dawn just gave her a curious look, still blinking the sleep away.

"So . . ." Jacqueline said. "Guess what?"

Her first instinct was to answer with a Kiko comeback that included freaky apartments and their evil residents, but she didn't have the energy right now. Subdued, she merely went along with Jacqueline's enthusiasm.

"What?" Dawn asked.

The actress made a tiny *eeek* sound and handed the papers over. Printouts from the Net. "I know you haven't had time to pay attention to gossip, but"—she hopped up and down some more—"I got the part! Can you believe it?"

"Wow." Happiness mixed with doubt. Here it went: the change of Jacqueline from nice girl to movie star, right? "Congrats, that's . . . amazing."

"Thanks." She shuffled her sneakers, looking like she was at a loss for words. "But I thought I should tell you something before you start hearing it for yourself. . . ." She began to continue, then stopped.

Dawn could hear anything at this point and not be fazed. "Just say it."

"Okay." Jacqueline blew out a breath. "Okay, here goes." She exhaled again, then offered a hesitant glance. "They're . . . well, they're calling me a throwback . . . a . . ." She shrugged helplessly.

"Jeez, this is rough. My managers want me to go with this whole thing that they dreamed up for my 'image.' So, maybe if I show you this makeover they sprung on me this morning . . . Well . . . here."

With a shy flourish, the actress took off her baseball cap.

As her bleached golden locks came tumbling down, Dawn felt the first jab of dream-addled disquiet.

But when Jacqueline slipped off her sunglasses, Dawn took an inadvertent, heart-stopping step backward, dropping the papers.

Holy . . . no. *No*.

At the fencing studio, Dawn hadn't cared to look Jacqueline in the face while she'd helped her with the jacket, and when she'd decided to finally do so, the actress had already donned her mask. And then there'd been the sunglasses . . . the ever-present dark lenses hiding her gaze.

As Dawn's vision blurred, Jacqueline anxiously waited for approval. Disapproval. *Something*.

"They say that, even though I don't look exactly like her, I remind them of your mom." The actress's eyes were shining—not so much with a color, but with a feeling.

An invitation to compare her to Eva Claremont, to think she had the same qualities that defined Dawn's mother.

Mother.

With the crash of a wall falling into a ruin of dust and vulnerability, images rushed back—images Dawn had stored and shoved into the furnace of her anguish, hoping they'd be destroyed. But now they were resurrected, called up by Jacqueline's face.

The picture. The crime-scene photo of Eva from her dad's hidden bootbox.

A woman's pale body laid against white satin sheets, her wrists tied to the bedposts, the belled sleeves of her nightgown spread like crimson wings as blood flowed down her arms from the ragged slits decorating her skin. Blond hair sunning over a pillow. Brown eyes staring at the ceiling. A peaceful smile on her lips.

Someone's fantasy angel—sweet, sacrificed, and murdered on a bed of red-soaked purity.

Eva's corpse—the catalyst of a legend born one dark night in Hollywood.

Nausea banged a furious rhythm in Dawn's temples. Blindly, she sought the wall, groping for her chair.

But Jacqueline was at her side, frantically helping her into it. "I knew this would happen. I'm so sorry, Dawn. I'm really so sorry."

"I'm okay." Goddamnit, she had to be.

But when she tried to stand back up, her body wouldn't allow it. She slumped down to the seat, unable to function.

Red on white. Blood. So much blood.

Mom.

"Here." Jacqueline dragged a chair over, then helped Dawn to relax, laying down her head on her lap, her voice soothing.

A blanket on a stormy night, Dawn thought, clinging to the fragmented hope of it, pushing it away at the same time.

"It's a shock, I know." Jacqueline stroked Dawn's hair. "Such a shock. But you know what used to make me feel better? My mom's favorite bedtime song. . . ."

And when the first tear ripped out of Dawn, Jacqueline held her even tighter, shushing her, calming her; but it didn't stop the bafflement, the anger, the bottomless questions.

Then she started to sing in a sweet voice, her hand resting on Dawn's back. On Frank's shirt.

"Hush, little baby, don't say a word . . ."

Turning her face upward, Dawn didn't even have the strength for any kind of defense. No, all she wanted to do was look into the compelling, beautiful eyes gazing down at her, the light of affection making them clearer than anything she had ever seen in her life.

"Mama's gonna buy you a mockingbird . . ."

Under the soft lyrics, Dawn's eyelids grew heavy, the slow melt of surrender. Her breathing evened out, and another tear followed the first, then another.

Blood on white sheets . . . Eva's empty eyes staring into nothing . . .

Cringing with a screaming sob that had been building for years, she held on to this woman while, at the same time, wanting to push her away in denial and rage.

Bitch, mother . . . what was she?

And why'd she come back?

Helpless in her fury and need, she buried her face against Jacqueline's . . . her mom's arm. But it didn't carry the scent of Dawn's memories; the flesh was scented with something Dawn couldn't place, slightly cold.

Abandoned, Dawn thought, mind spinning. *She left me, and now she wants to come back?*

Dawn fought the sobs, dug her nails into the woman's skin.

"Dawn!"

The cry was stamped with utter shock, punching its way through her head, pulling her out of her sorrow and into a clearer reality.

I don't want you back . . . I can't *want you back. . . .*

On a wave of anger, she pushed away from the woman, lifting a stiff arm to make sure the blonde didn't approach her again. For a baffling moment, Dawn locked eyes with her, lost in the depth of the other woman's gaze.

Mom . . . ?

A loud sound blared from the TV, making Dawn jump.

It was as if something had clicked into place, waking her up. The newscast filtered into her perception, and her vision seemed to realign, showing her the brown of the other woman's eyes, the startled confusion of a friend named Jacqueline Ashley who'd merely dyed her hair blond this morning.

Dawn's breathing evened out as she talked herself into sanity. My God, Jacqueline did look a lot like Eva, but . . .

She laughed, almost a little crazily. Dreaming. She was so tired and emotionally messed up that her brain obviously wasn't working right.

"Dawn, what's . . ." Jacqueline stood, her hand to her throat, her gaze wide. "I should've eased into this change a little better. I've shocked the tar out of you. I can tell. Should I get a nurse?"

"No."

Psycho, Dawn thought. I've gone completely nuts. Eva was dead. She had been for many years and there was no bringing her back, no matter how much Dawn might want it to happen.

"I just . . ." Dawn rubbed at her face. Her hands were shaking.

Searching for features that would distinguish Jacqueline from Eva, she glanced up again. Their chins. There, that was a difference—Jacqueline's wasn't as pointy. And Jacqueline had higher cheekbones, a slimmer nose. Uncanny, yes, but the same person?

No. Not at all.

So why did she still feel like she was sitting alone in a dark cabin while something stalked around outside? Why was there an unsettling shiver that wouldn't go away?

That something knocked at her brain.

Leave me alone. I'm not going to go crazy. . . .

Breisi walked into the room with their beverages, and Dawn stiffened. Would she see Eva, too?

When her eyes widened at the sight of the blonde, Dawn prepared herself for an escalation of emotion. How was Breisi going to react to the woman who still haunted Frank?

Or . . . not the same woman. This *wasn't* Eva.

After scrutinizing Jacqueline, Breisi paused . . . walked over to Dawn . . . gave her the coffee . . . straightened up again . . . started to lift her hand . . .

Dawn held her breath, waiting for the world to explode.

But when Breisi turned on her own smile and extended her hand to the actress for a welcoming shake, the oxygen rushed out of Dawn.

Yeah, she was losing it all right. If anyone would've had a reaction to seeing Jacqueline as Eva, it was the woman who'd taken up with Frank.

As Breisi settled next to Kiko's bedside to sip her tea, Jacqueline's cell phone rang.

"Oooo, it's my agent," she said, already heading out of the room. "Mind if I take it?"

"Not at all."

Dawn kept her gaze pasted on Jacqueline, but as soon as she was gone, she turned to Breisi.

"Did you notice it?"

The other woman slowly set down her tea. "Notice what?"

Dawn's heart did a freefall to her stomach. *Crazy.*

"Okay." Breisi's eyes locked onto the open door, and she lowered her voice. "There's a resemblance. I almost hit the roof when I walked into the room and saw her. Truthfully, I wanted to rip her face off." She got out of her seat, came toward Dawn. "But on a second glance, I realized that your friend's an imitation, just like so many other actresses around Hollywood. Madonna even had her Eva Claremont stage, remember?"

"Really? Jacqueline doesn't . . . ?"

Breisi got down on her knees on the other side of Dawn's chair and took her good hand. Her dark brown gaze was steady, doing a lot to lure Dawn out of her doubts and suspicions.

Maybe she *was* overreacting, a victim of her own imagination. That's right. That had to be it.

"You're strong enough to handle this, Dawn. Think of what you've already been through and how it's probably affecting you right now." She squeezed Dawn's hand. "And that's what I'll keep telling myself, too."

It hit Dawn at that point: Breisi was just as rattled by the close call, but she was better at containing it. She'd had more practice, and she was offering Dawn the support to accomplish the same thing.

"Time to move on from Mom, huh?" Dawn asked, swallowing back a lump of grief that had lodged in her throat. "Is that what you're going to tell me?"

"In case you haven't noticed, you've got other people you can depend on now."

They both looked at Kiko, who was still snoozing away, oblivious. But Dawn knew Breisi was right, even if part of her new team was halfway gone.

She'd spent her life trying to get back at Eva, trying to elicit a response from someone who wasn't around to react. Someone who'd never even made the choice to die.

Too much of her life had revolved around an absent mother, and that needed to stop.

As she brought Breisi's hand to her heart, Dawn closed her eyes, accepting what was offered. But, even so, there was still a heavy feeling that she would need to open her eyes soon.

At the same time, in the background, the news of Tamsin Greene's death played on.

Eternally resurrected over the airwaves.